GRAND
CENTRAL
LARGE
PRINT

ALSO BY DAVID BALDACCI

THE 6:20 MAN SERIES
The 6:20 Man
The Edge
To Die For

ALOYSIUS ARCHER SERIES
One Good Deed
A Gambling Man
Dream Town

ATLEE PINE SERIES
Long Road to Mercy
A Minute to Midnight
Daylight
Mercy

WILL ROBIE SERIES
The Innocent
The Hit
The Target
The Guilty
End Game

JOHN PULLER SERIES
Zero Day
The Forgotten
The Escape
No Man's Land

KING & MAXWELL SERIES
Split Second
Hour Game
Simple Genius
First Family
The Sixth Man
King and Maxwell

MEMORY MAN SERIES
Memory Man
The Last Mile
The Fix
The Fallen
Redemption
Walk the Wire
Long Shadows

THE CAMEL CLUB SERIES
The Camel Club
The Collectors
Stone Cold
Divine Justice
Hell's Corner

THE SHAW SERIES
The Whole Truth
Deliver Us from Evil

STANDALONES
Absolute Power
Total Control
The Winner
The Simple Truth
Saving Faith
Wish You Well
Last Man Standing
The Christmas Train
True Blue
One Summer
Simply Lies
A Calamity of Souls

SHORT STORIES
Waiting for Santa
No Time Left
Bullseye
The Mighty Johns
(A Digital Novella)

DAVID BALDACCI

TO DIE FOR

GRAND
CENTRAL

LARGE PRINT

Copyright © 2024 by Columbus Rose, Ltd.

Cover design by Tal Goretsky. Cover copyright © 2024 by Hachette Book Group, Inc.

Grand Central Publishing
Hachette Book Group
1290 Avenue of the Americas, New York, NY 10104

Grand Central Publishing is a division of Hachette Book Group, Inc. The Grand Central Publishing name and logo is a trademark of Hachette Book Group, Inc.

The publisher is not responsible for websites (or their content) that are not owned by the publisher.

ISBN: 978-1-5387-7034-4

To the memory of Guinness, the other half of
our canine dynamic duo.
You gave us nothing but love for sixteen years,
Guinn. I will never forget you.

TO DIE FOR

CHAPTER

1

TRAVIS DEVINE SAT IN THE cab staring at the note he'd just found in his coat pocket, and wondered how many more minutes he might have to live.

And here he thought he might just grab a cup of overpriced java, pick up a good book, and chill tonight after almost losing his life several times during his last mission.

And why am I still apparently in combat even though I no longer wear the uniform?

Devine had just returned from Maine, where most people ventured to fish, hike, and commune with nature. Instead, he'd run smack into people who wanted to plant him in the dirt without the benefit of a funeral service.

He read over the words again.

Nice bumping into you in the airport, former Captain Devine. We missed getting you twice before. But you know what they say, the third

time is usually the charm. At least one can hope.
See you soon. I promise.
XOXO
The Girl on the Train

The airport taxi driver, a gray-bearded Sikh wearing
a *pagri*, glanced at Devine and said helpfully, "Just put
your card or phone next to the screen, sir, and follow
the instruction. Easy-peasy."

Devine looked up at him, touched his phone to
the device mounted on the plastic shield separat-
ing the front and rear areas of the vehicle, and completed the transaction.

"See, easy-peasy," said the driver.

"Yeah, easy-peasy."

Devine got out with his bag, his Glock, and his dis-
trust of everyone and everything.

He took a few moments to perform a 360-sweep of
the area, looking for what he wasn't really sure, only
he knew it was out there. *She* was out there. First on
the train gliding like an eagle through the Swiss Alps,
then on dark back country roads in murderous and
cold-as-hell Maine, and now here within spitting distance of America's capital.

It appeared the girl on the train was getting a little
obsessive with him.

Devine walked into the hotel where he had earlier

booked a room, since he currently had no permanent residence. His occupation didn't really allow for putting down roots, and neither did his temperament. Since people were usually either trying to kill him or frame him for various felonies, he made for the world's worst tenant or neighbor. But if your thing was long-range sniper shots through kitchen glass, or a C4 stick wedged under front porch flower pots, he was your man.

Maybe I should stop paying into Social Security, because I am never making it that far.

He bypassed the front desk and kept going until he reached the rear entrance. He turned left out of the pricey building and picked up his pace. Death threats almost always required a change in plans, and he had no desire to make himself an easy target. In fact, the rulebook said you made it as hard as possible. Otherwise, some people might take advantage.

Despite what the note had said, they had actually tried to kill him *three* times before, including, initially, on the high-speed train darting between Geneva and Milan. So this would be the fourth time, which wasn't usually charming at all, not that violent death ever was. Yet if they did manage to murder him, Devine figured it would have to do more with incompetence on his part than skill on theirs.

He texted his boss, Emerson Campbell, and reported the threatening note.

Campbell immediately replied: Stay where you are, we'll come and get you.

Devine answered: No, I'll come to you. If I don't make it good luck to whoever replaces me. And in lieu of flowers make a donation to the VA.

He walked into an office building and rode the elevator to the fifteenth floor, where he looked out through the wall of windows at all the activity down below. Time and space from the battlefield allowed one to think things through, details that might be important enough later to allow you to stay alive. But when the bullets were flying and you felt like you were inside the pulsing heart of an erupting volcano, he'd take sheer luck over brains and proficiency. But the harder Devine worked, the luckier he seemed to get, so there was that equalizer in a world that otherwise didn't seem to make much sense.

Devine saw couples entering bars or restaurants; families heading to wherever families went; working folks hustling to their first, second, third, or gig jobs; and idlers idling while caressing long smokes or tutti-frutti vapes. But he saw no one who looked like they wanted to kill anyone generally, or him specifically. And from his point of view, that was a real shame and a wasted trip up to high ground in a war zone that usually revealed many answers.

He descended in the elevator while thinking of a

plan going forward. Halfway down he had come up with fragments of one. As the elevator eased to a stop on the ground floor, he had formulated a strategy that probably had a 50 percent chance of actually working. But he would take those odds right now.

He stood looking out of the elevator car and started to combat-breathe, four up, hold for four, four down, hold for four. Rinse and repeat. He wasn't expecting to kill or be killed as soon as he stepped clear of the elevator car, but his mind and nerves needed a reset, and sucking air in and letting it out in a controlled manner did that.

Devine stepped out of the elevator thinking that these people killed for a living, as he did, in certain respects. He'd just assumed he occupied higher moral ground. Yet who really knew? Dead was dead after all, with the victors left to tell the story all their own way.

He hailed a taxi but then waved it off when his warning sensors started to tingle, perhaps simply from paranoia. Better to be safe than deceased. He walked a few blocks and watched from inside another hotel lobby as the dented silver Honda pulled up across the street in response to his Uber request, the driver on his phone maybe already checking what might be next in his queue.

As he continued to observe, two men strolled into view. One on either side of the street. The humps under their jackets signaled the weapons they carried. The bumps on their rear waistbands were clear tells of the transponders powering the squiggly-lined earpieces so they could communicate hands-free.

They were trying too hard to be cool, nonchalant, and also kept their gazes dutifully averted from one another. But their guns and communication hardware and fluid synchronicity of movement were all Devine needed to conclude that they were working together with the firm goal of ending his life, unless POTUS was coming here and they were the Secret Service advance team. But they didn't look legal. They looked the opposite.

Devine got confirmation of that possibility when he noticed the bulky black Lincoln SUV with wraparound dark-tinted windows slide into view like a slimy snake bellying out from its hole looking for dinner.

They knew about the Uber. And they probably followed me here from the airport. And the SUV is here to take me to the girl on the train so she can say goodbye properly with a bullet to my brain. But that is not happening. Not right now at least. I have things to do.

He three-pointed his phone into the trash since it was now clearly compromised and thus akin to a laser sight on his skull. He didn't turn it off or take the SIM card or crush it, because they would waste time tracking it (and him, they would think) to this receptacle.

And without his facial recognition authenticator and password to access his cloud, the phone was a useless brick instead of a data treasure trove.

Devine exited the rear of the building, found an old-fashioned cabstand in front of another expensive northern Virginia hotel, and got into the lead taxi.

He gave the driver the address and said, "Ride like the wind, friend."

"I'm not looking to get a ticket," said the gent, eyeing Devine in the mirror.

Devine flashed his badge. "Don't worry, you won't. Now, just drive."

The driver noted the embossed symbol of federal authority.

"You the man?" he asked.

"I am today," replied Devine.

2

ALL DURING THE RIDE DEVINE maintained a vigilant lookout as they careened along the capital beltway with thousands of other vehicles on the hamster wheel known as the DC metro rush hour, which actually extended to more hours than any weary commuter ever dared to admit. That was one reason why Devine had never wanted a nine-to-five desk job.

As they got off the highway, he wasn't so sure.

Annandale was a bubbling brook of immigrant-owned mom-and-pop businesses, and restaurants serving dozens of international cuisines, the smells of which constantly enticed the famished. For its part, US 50 was a perpetually bottlenecked artery of weary travelers heading directly into or out of the heart of the nation's capital. There seemed to be no reason to associate Annandale's ordinary commercial and commuter activity with anything clandestine.

Which was the point and also the only reason Devine was here.

He surprised the driver by paying in actual cash,

and got out, his gaze sweeping fore and aft, threat-assessing all the way.

The outdoor strip mall looked just like thousands of other such places across America where cheap and pointless was the signature style of a nation falling into the fragments cast off from capitalistic excess. The small office located there was so bland that one would forget its existence in three or four footfalls.

That was also the intended reaction.

The front window held a sign that read BY APPOINT-MENT ONLY.

Devine had to smile at this prop of deceit, when he had little else to smile about.

This was one of the places of operation for the Office of Special Projects, a tiny, stealth sub-group under the crowded circus tent cover of DHS, the conglomerate of the government world stuffed full of acronym agencies.

Devine doubted that many at Homeland Security even knew of its existence. He worked for the little boots-on-the-ground organization that could and often did punch above its weight. However, his service was not entirely voluntary.

Devine was a closer, snooper, fixer, investigator, and sometimes he had to kill in order to keep on breathing or complete a mission. He tried not to think too much about it, just as he had when he'd worn a uniform on behalf of his country. But killing was killing, no matter the reason, noble or cruel or a combo thereof. If it didn't make you feel something, maybe you were incapable of feeling anything, becoming akin to Ted Bundy, John Wayne Gacy, or Jeffrey Dahmer, which had never been a life goal of his.

Inside, he sat across from Emerson Campbell in an office outfitted with dinged governmental hand-me-downs. His boss was a retired Army two-star whose aversion to bullshit military politics had cost him a legit shot at the third and fourth stars. He had close-cropped iron gray hair, a workingman's lead pipe fingers, and a tree trunk neck, with a low whisper that was more menacing than a drill sergeant's spit-shot baritone. He deserved lusher surroundings, but Devine also knew the man didn't give a damn about that. He had fought wars in hellscapes; impressive office furnishings and vanity photo walls like they had at the senior officer level at the Pentagon did not move Campbell's internal needle even a little bit.

He eyed Devine cautiously. "Any problems getting here?"

"Aside from the fact that they seem to know my every move, no problem at all. By the way, I need a new phone. My old one's in a trash can over in Reston. And new plastic, too. They've probably hacked that as well."

Campbell sent a text, and a minute later Devine was presented with a new phone and credit card.

Devine pocketed them and said, "Your assistant, Dawn Schuman? You thought she was the leak that I'm dealing with?"

"We haven't found her. Or her body. Yet. But it seems clear that she's the one. I still find it hard to believe that she was turned, but there's no other explanation for her disappearance."

"So she compromised my phone before she ran for it?"

"Or gave the folks she was dealing with the info they needed to crack it."

"I guess I'm lucky the girl on the train didn't stick a syringe filled with liquid fentanyl in my gut when she slid the note in my pocket."

"I *am* surprised they let that opportunity go by," noted Campbell.

"And hopefully *relieved*," added Devine coldly.

Campbell gave him the military once-over: stare, glare, but then, out of the blue, a touch of understanding, compassion even. "Look, Devine, I know you're pissed about this and you have every right to be. But we are doing all we can to resolve this as quickly as possible."

"Good, because I'm not sure I can count on them to keep sending idiots I can kill before they kill me."

"I understand your frustration, soldier. I really do."

"Then my work on that is done, sir." He drew a four-second breath to quell the fury in his chest. "What now?"

"Another assignment. West Coast."

"Why? To get me far, far away from here?"

"And to get you to a place where you're needed. To provide security for someone."

"So I'm now a glorified bodyguard?"

"And maybe a blast from the past for you."

"Okay, you have my full attention."

"Danny Glass? Name ring a bell?"

Devine nodded. "Iraq. We were thrown together during a mission. His actions helped save all our butts. I recommended him for a commendation. What's his involvement?"

"He left the Army shortly after the battle you just referred to. And his reputation is not a good one."

"I'd heard some scuttlebutt way back when about him, but feel free to elaborate."

"The government is going after him in a big criminal lawsuit out in Seattle. Buddy of mine at the Justice Department got in touch. Wanted to know if I had a good man for this mission. He mentioned Danny Glass's involvement, and I recalled that you had known Glass from your military days. It seemed like a good fit. I told my buddy that and he agreed."

"And do you trust your *buddy*?"

"Yes. We served together before he jumped to the civilian side. Saved his life once."

"In combat?" asked Devine.

"No, on the LA freeway. Road rage incident."

"Okay, what else?"

"Glass has a niece, Betsy Odom, age twelve. Her parents recently died, and Glass is her only living relative. He wants to become her guardian and eventually adopt her."

"And why does that interest DOJ?"

Campbell pulled an old-fashioned paper file out of his desk and plopped it in front of him. "To be perfectly candid, I don't know all of it, which I don't like one bit. It's not how we did things in uniform but it's something we apparently have to live with in joint ops like this. But with that said, I'm going to do all I can to get a fuller picture. And anything I find out you will know right away. I don't like sending my people into harm's way on half-ass briefings."

Devine relaxed and leaned back in his chair. He greatly respected this man who, in some ways, was an older version of himself. And Campbell's last words had hit every reassuring mark for Devine.

"Well, what else do I have, except minutes to burn and blood to shed, sir? Let's get to it."

CHAPTER

3

TWO NIGHTS LATER DEVINE WALKED reso-
lutely up a steep, slippery street in Seattle, while the
darkness, varnished with a marine layer, shrouded him
like a sheet fort laid by a child. The nearly forty-five-
degree upward angle caused his heartbeat to accelerate.
At least he wasn't carrying an eighty-pound rucksack,
only a six-ounce cup of coffee.

Behind him was a harbor filled with commercial,
military, and recreational activities all of a nautical
kind. Ahead of him the rest of the city was splayed out
on multiple hills like a modern fortress with clear views
of approaching armies. He was staying at one hotel and
now heading to another, to meet with someone. Well,
two people, actually. He knew very little, but at least
he knew that.

The flight here had been uneventful. Five hours on
a United Airlines A320. Campbell had sprung for first
class so Devine could stretch out his long legs on the
narrow-body jet. He'd also allowed himself the luxury
of a beer since it was free in that part of the plane. In

any event, it beat a vomit seat on a cram-packed Air Force C130, but then again, riding coach, or even being out on the damn wing, would've done that.

Seattle was always chilly, rainy, and foggy at this time of year. Devine had been here before and found the city interesting and consistent in certain respects. But like any large metropolis, something could jump out and bite you with little warning.

He located his destination in a part of the city that was still awaiting a full facelift. The four-story hotel was sandwiched between a vape shop and a cannabis dispensary that had fake ivy glued to its brick exterior. The combined smells reminded him of the time he'd been thrown into a Dumpster as part of an unofficial West Point meet-and-greet courtesy of a half dozen drunken upperclassmen, all of whom were now commanding armed men in uniform.

The small, shabby lobby was empty, and the single banged-up elevator was out of order. There *was* a silver coffee urn and a stack of cups set on a round table with a sign that read HOT APPLE CIDER, HELP YOURSELF.

Devine did not help himself. He threw his coffee into a trash can and headed up the stairs.

On the third floor he turned right and trudged to the end of the hall. The carpet was torn and stained; the walls needed repainting. And apparently, the fuggy cannabis smell and sickly sweet pop of the vape shop had pierced the thin exterior walls on either side of the hotel, morphing into an alchemy of intoxication for those dwelling here. Devine held his breath so he wouldn't get stoned *and* addicted simply by inhaling air.

He thought he heard the creak of a door, the slight sound of a footstep, and Devine also seemed to sense a shadow or two here and there. Yet no threat materialized, so he assumed it had to do with the curiosity of people working or staying here. He let go of the butt of his Glock and kept going.

He gave a special rap at the last door on the hall and got another one in return, which he answered with another combo of raps. He felt a bit like he was in a 1960s-era spy flick, but at least you couldn't computer-hack a secret knock. The door opened by the width of the slender burglar's chain, and a woman peered out at him.

"Travis Devine?"

"Yes, ma'am."

"ID?"

He produced it. She unchained and opened the door fully, and motioned him in. She poked her head out and glanced down the corridor before closing and locking the door.

He noted that she held a dark, matte-finished Sig nine-mill in her right hand. She was around five-five, a little lumpy in figure, and her features were drawn. Her stringy brown hair, with more than a few gray strands, bracketed her forty-something face. She looked sleep deprived and unhappy all in one dreary package.

She reholstered the sidearm and showed her credentials. "FBI Special Agent Ellen Saxby."

Devine ran his eye over the tiny room, noting the tattered carpet, the old furnishings, and the general air of neglect. Devine next spied the half-eaten meatball sandwich from Subway on a side table. An open door off this room revealed a modest bathroom that looked like it dated back to the 1970s. He also noted a closed door apparently leading into the sole bedroom. Then there was the stained couch with a pillow and blanket strewn across it that rested against one wall of the room. This was apparently Saxby's humble place to lay her weary head.

"FBI per diem gone through the shitter?" he said, eyeing the woman.

"The government has to live within a budget, too, Devine."

He thought about his flying out here first class, but that was a rare thing indeed.

"I know, but most Americans probably wouldn't think the government even has a budget. Where's Betsy Odom?"

"Napping. In the only bedroom."

"Just you here?" Devine said.

She nodded. "I've gotten about ten hours of shut-eye total over the last few days."

"How'd you get so lucky?" he asked.

"Probably because I accused my supervisor's fav boy of being a misogynistic dick. My complaint got fav boy reassigned to a cushy post at the New York Field Office and here I am, a glorified babysitter in a shithole masquerading as a hotel that smells like wolf's piss."

Devine leaned against the wall, a bit surprised by both the woman's negative attitude and her revealing such personal information to a stranger. "So tell me about what's going on."

"Your people didn't brief you?" she said, obviously caught off guard by his query.

"They said they hadn't been fully read in. So I need to get updated."

"Tell me what you *do* know and we'll go from there."

"On the other side of that bedroom door is, presumably, Betsy Odom, age twelve. Her parents recently died. The Bureau is interested in the girl because of her uncle, Danny Glass."

"Okay, do you know *who* Danny Glass is?"

"I actually knew him, briefly, when he and I were in the Army."

"Can you elaborate on that?"

"I was West Point and he was enlisted but we fought together once in Iraq. I lost track of him after that, but now I know the government is going after him for a bunch of crimes."

Saxby glanced at the bedroom door and started speaking in a low voice. "He's currently the defendant in a federal RICO prosecution that will start up soon right here in Seattle. It was originally filed in New York but a change of venue was granted, so here we are on the West Coast. Glass is out on bail because he can afford the best lawyers. But he's on a tight leash. He's got unlimited financial resources and his own jet. So they took his passport and he's wearing an electronic monitor on his ankle. One step out of line and his butt goes to jail for the duration."

"I understand he's trying to become his niece's guardian with an eye to adoption?"

"Yes. He's filed a petition for emergency minor guardianship."

"What does that mean exactly?"

"Washington state changed its laws and procedures on guardianship a few years ago. Now, it usually takes sixty days to finalize a guardianship petition. But you can circumvent that by filing an emergency petition, as Glass has done. If granted, the emergency guardianship usually lasts only sixty days. That's why at the same time Glass also filed for what's called Minor Guardianship. The family court overseeing the matter merged those two cases into one, which is customary."

"But he doesn't have custody of Betsy. The Bureau does. How did that happen?"

"DOJ went straight to court on the *same* day the Odoms died and got the court to grant the FBI temporary guardianship. But Glass's lawyers found out we were Betsy's guardian before the ink was hardly dry on our emergency application. And the next day, Betsy, since she's over twelve, was served with notice that Glass was looking to become her guardian and knock us out."

"I guess that was no surprise."

"But it was also suspicious. It was like Glass knew her parents were going to die and had everything prepared beforehand."

"Do you have proof of that?"

"I wish."

"Will he be able to become her guardian? And adopt her? I mean, the guy's a criminal."

"An *alleged* criminal. The RICO case hasn't been proven and you're innocent until that time. So technically, to the family law court, he's clean as a whistle."

"But the judge can *consider* the RICO indictment?"

"Absolutely. And we hope that's enough to keep him from becoming her guardian."

"You got guardianship on the *day* her parents died? How so fast?"

"We've been after Glass for years and knew all

about his sister and brother-in-law. We refocused on them when they came into money recently under suspicious circumstances. When they died DOJ worked their legal magic, and I was sent here to assume guardianship of a girl I'd never laid eyes on before."

"You said the Odoms came into money under suspicious circumstances?"

"We suspect Glass was the source, but have no proof. Maybe as a bribe if they knew something incriminating about him. The funds were used to purchase a home and a car."

"So exactly why is the girl important to you?"

"She could have overhead something. Seen something. If she's a danger to Glass, or he thinks she is? That's why we stepped in."

"Have you gotten anything out of her along those grounds?"

"No. She's pretty tight-lipped."

"What exactly are Glass's 'alleged' crimes?"

"The RICO suit charges drug manufacturing and distribution on a grand scale, extortion, fraud, bribery, human trafficking, and the theft and sale of historical artifacts from the Middle East and Asia, among other charges. Glass has a string of legit businesses of all shapes and sizes, and we believe the illicit proceeds are laundered through them."

"So how can a judge allow a guy like that to adopt her?"

"There are no guarantees, Devine, but we do have one potential ace in our hand."

"What?"

"Betsy has a say in all this."

"Does she *want* to go with him?"

"I don't know. Like I said, she plays her cards very close to the vest. That's why I said it was a *potential* ace."

"And I'm here to escort Betsy to a meeting with her uncle?"

"Yes. Tomorrow at the Four Seasons."

"Why do they need me? You're her guardian."

"When two eight-hundred-pound gorillas like the FBI and DHS climb into the ring with each other, Devine, who the hell knows what will happen? Now, what's so special about *you* that you got this gig?"

"I guess it's because I knew Glass from our military days back in Iraq. I suppose the powers-that-be thought that might come in handy. So how did her parents die?" he asked.

"Dwayne and Alice Odom died of drug overdoses in their car. Betsy apparently tried to revive them with Narcan. Not the first time she'd done that, I heard. Word is they ingested a heavy dose of fentanyl, so they were goners as soon as it hit their bloodstreams. Died right in front of her."

"Damn. Pretty traumatic for anyone, much less a kid."

"Their lives up till then were a bit of a shit show.

Moving constantly. Homeless off and on. Not sure how Betsy even managed to go to school on a consistent basis. We *did* learn that Glass and Dwayne Odom were not close. Glass was considerably older than his sister. Sort of a big brother protector growing up."

"So brother and sister *were* tight?"

"Apparently. But then Dwayne entered the picture when Glass was still in the Army and swept Alice right off her feet. Dwayne was also a number of years older than Alice. He'd been around in life while she was pretty cloistered and naïve. I guess Alice saw something in Dwayne that she wanted. They got married and had Betsy sometime later."

"So can I talk to her?"

A slight sound made Devine glance over at the bedroom door. It was now open. And standing there was Betsy Odom, with her curly auburn hair, freckled skin, and a round face of stone staring dead at him.

CHAPTER

4

BETSY ODOM, THIS IS AGENT Travis Devine," said Saxby.

Devine stepped forward. "You can just call me Travis, Betsy."

He ran his gaze over her. She wore baggy faded jeans with holes in the knees that looked real rather than manufactured, a pale blue Nike sweatshirt, and pink ankle socks with the right big toe showing through a tear. She was chubby in all the usual prepubescent areas, extra weight that would be used for growth spurts and to stretch out the girl's frame. Her eyes were a muted hazel, her lips set in a firm, unyielding line.

"Mr. Devine would like to talk to you," said Saxby.

"I'm hungry," said Odom, not looking at her.

"You can finish the other half of my meatball sub. I can get you a soda and chips from the vending machine down the hall."

"No. I'm not eating your shitty leftovers. I want to go out to a place to eat."

"What place?" said a startled Saxby.

"Any place."

"But Mr. Devine wants to talk to you."

"He *said* I can call him *Travis*. We can talk at the place."

"Okay, well, let me get my coat," said Saxby.

"No, not you. Just me and Travis."

"That is not—" began Saxby.

Devine interjected, "Look, it's no big deal. I passed a burger place on the next block."

"Then I need to come."

"No," said Odom. "Just Travis. You can stay here and finish *your* meatballs."

"I need to make a call," said Saxby.

"It's barely a hundred feet," noted Devine.

"I still need to make a call," Saxby reiterated.

"Then make it."

"I'll get ready," said Odom enthusiastically, seemingly sensing an advantage here.

"Betsy," began Saxby, but Odom slammed the bedroom door behind her.

Devine said, "Look, it's just the next block. Maybe you can grab a nap."

Saxby looked at the couch greedily. "That would be nice. But—"

The bedroom opened and Odom stood there wearing a faded blue ski jacket and chunky tennis shoes.

"I'm ready."

"Let's go," said Devine.

Saxby picked up her phone. "Can you just wait until I get the okay?"

Devine looked at her. "If the Bureau has a problem with this, just text me and we'll bring the food back."

Outside, the two turned right and walked to the next block.

"That lady's a wacko," said Odom as she clipped back her hair.

"No, she's just trying to keep you safe."

"From what exactly?"

Good question, thought Devine. *Maybe your uncle who wants to adopt you.*

They entered the red-and-blue-tiled burger place and stood in line.

"You an everything-on-your-burger kind of guy?" she asked.

"What other kind makes sense?" he said while performing a threat evaluation on everyone in the place. "You going for a shake and fries, too?"

"I'm already too fat."

Devine didn't really know how to respond to this. His sister had been much older than he was so he had little experience interacting with girls Odom's age. And he didn't want to in any way comment on, well, her physical appearance. But still, he felt he needed to say something because she seemed to want a response.

"Your body is just gearing up to grow like a weed and...Well, it needs the extra weight to do that," he finished awkwardly, and drew a deep breath. *Okay, that was a mess.*

"My mom was tall. I mean really tall. But my dad was just average."

"Height is usually robustly handed down in the gene pool. So don't be surprised if you land some basketball scholarships for college," Devine added jokingly.

"You're tall," she said, looking up at him.

"And so are my dad and my siblings."

"I don't have any brothers or sisters. Or parents anymore," she added glumly.

They got their food and carried it to an open table. Odom had opted for a strawberry milkshake and large fries to go with her bacon double cheeseburger with extra everything.

As they were eating, Devine glanced out the window and spotted something curious. He turned back to Odom. "I'm really sorry about your mom and dad."

She initially answered this with a scowl. "You didn't even know them. Don't say shit to try to make me like you."

"I'm just being human, Betsy. It's tragic when people die like that. And I know it must have been awful for you to be there when it happened."

She bit into her burger and drank from her shake before answering.

"It sucked. I mean, I couldn't do anything."

"You did your best. You tried to revive them with Narcan."

She gave him a puzzled look. "Nar-what?"

"Narcan. It can bring back people who have overdosed on opioids. But... but you know that, right?"

"Opioids? My parents didn't use drugs."

"I was told that they overdosed and you tried to revive them."

"That's not true!" she said heatedly, her features full of agitation.

People at other tables glanced nervously over at them.

Devine noted this and said, "Okay, okay. I believe you."

But he was thinking, *What the hell is going on?*

He watched as Odom gathered a handful of fries together and stuffed them into her mouth. She then followed that with several exaggerated slurps of her milkshake.

She glared at Devine. "Opioids! That is such bullshit."

"Can you tell me about the day it happened?"

"Why?"

"Because I'm interested. Unless you have a good reason not to tell me."

"I don't know you. I don't know why you want to know. And I don't trust you. There you go. *Three* good reasons, big guy."

"You'd make an excellent debater. Especially only being twelve."

"I'll be thirteen really soon. But that's just in calendar years."

Devine glanced out the window and saw something that once more gave him pause.

He munched on a fry and said with genuine curiosity, "Calendar years? As opposed to what?"

She took another big bite of her burger before answering. "Life-shit years, I call them. With that, I'm twenty-eight."

"How do you calculate that?"

She swallowed the mass of food. "It's *my* secret. I might sell it one day for a bunch of money. Or I might start doing dumb dance moves on TikTok or smearing *cool* lip gloss on my mouth for millions of my adoring Instagram followers for big bucks." She made a face. "People are so pathetic."

"For what it's worth, you sound more like forty-two in *life-shit* years."

"I hope I live that long actually, in calendar years, I mean."

He looked startled. Up to now he just assumed

she was playing the young smart-ass routine. But this last statement she seemed to actually believe. "Why wouldn't you?"

"I've been around for over a dozen years. That's a long time for someone like me."

"Meaning what exactly?"

"Meaning what I just said," she retorted.

He sat back. "Okay, what can you tell me about your uncle? You ever meet him?"

"Not that I remember, but my mom told me about him."

"What exactly did she say about him?"

She held up her phone. "There's this thing called *Google*. You should try it."

"Nice phone," he remarked.

Her face fell. "My dad got it for me a few months ago. It's . . . it's my first one."

Devine noted the utter sadness in her expression and wanted to say something supportive, but again, he didn't want to make an awkward remark that would set her off.

Damn, this is tougher than interrogating terrorists.

"So, I heard your parents came into some money recently. You know anything about that?"

That earned him another glare. "No, I don't! Okay?"

So much for not setting her off.

"All right. Do you want your uncle to adopt you?"

"The *Meatball* already asked me that." She added wearily, "Like a hundred times."

"You mean *Agent Saxby*. So why didn't you answer her?"

She put her burger down and stared at him for such an uncomfortably long time that he finally said, "What, do I have ketchup on my chin?"

"You look like a nice guy, clueless, but nice," she said. "So I'll answer your question and you can run back and tell Meatball, so maybe she'll get off my back."

"I'm listening." He marveled at how neatly the young girl had turned the tables on this conversation and, in effect, taken charge of it.

"Okay, here it comes, get ready...Duh, of course I want to be adopted by him."

"Why?"

"He's loaded, has a bunch of homes and his own freakin' jet." She held up her phone again. "At least according to Google."

"So wealth, that's what motivates you?"

She picked up her burger. "Who wants to be poor? Do you?"

"No. But it doesn't drive all my decisions."

"Good for you, Boy Scout. It does mine."

"Do you know how he made his money?" he said.

"How does any rich person make their money? They screw over everybody else."

"I'm not sure it's healthy to be so fixated on wealth."

"You ever been homeless? Or hungry?" she asked.

"No."

"Okay, then shut up. So I'll go see him and tell him how much I love him. And how great he is. Yada-yada, blah-blah."

"He might be going to prison."

"Then I'll get to stay at his mansions and use his jet all by myself. Even better."

"You seem to have an answer for everything."

She wiped her mouth and abruptly rose. "I need to go back and get some sleep for my fav uncle. I want to be raring to go." Odom dead-eyed him. "Just to be clear, you fuck this up, Travis, I fuck you up."

"You've got a sailor's mouth all right."

She smirked. "Actually, I'm on my best behavior because you seem so fragile."

"My job is to just escort you over and back. That's it."

"But the thing is, I think you might turn out to be Meatball Number Two. Let's go."

She strode off, making Devine leap up and hustle after her.

I just got my ass handed to me by a twelve-year-old going on forty-two.

CHAPTER

5

AS THEY WALKED BACK TO the hotel, Devine said, "Don't look now but two guys are following us. I spotted them outside the burger place, watching."

"Meatball's boys?" she said casually, without looking behind her.

"They actually look homeless."

"Are you afraid of them?"

"Should I be?"

"You don't know them, or why they're following us. So, yeah, you should be."

Back at the hotel she went immediately to her room and closed the door.

Saxby pounced. "What happened? What did you learn?"

"Well, she told me she *wants* to be adopted by her uncle because he's rich."

Saxby surprisingly said, "Well, why not go for the brass ring?"

"Even if the brass ring is a criminal kingpin?"

"She's a kid, what does she know?"

"More than you probably think," replied Devine.

He eyed the wrapper where the sub had been. Saxby had evidently had her dinner, too.

"So if Odom *is* valuable to the feds, why only one agent assigned to protect her?"

"We don't know if she *is* valuable. *Yet.*"

"How's the RICO case going?"

"It was going great until three of DOJ's witnesses were murdered."

Devine gaped. "You think Glass is behind it?"

"Probably, but we have no proof."

"Speaking of proof, contrary to what you told me, Betsy said that her parents were not drug addicts and she didn't try to revive them with Narcan. She didn't even know what it was."

"Well, here's a four-one-one, that little bitch is deceitful. And the local police report was quite clear."

"Deceitful little bitch? Losing your objectivity, Agent Saxby?"

"You try spending days on end with her. She's a piece of work."

"She's a kid who saw her parents die right in front of her," barked a visibly angered Devine.

She said contritely, "I know. Look, can you hang around here for a bit? I need a smoke."

"Sure. I think you need to clear your head, if not your lungs."

She scowled at him, grabbed her purse, and left.

Devine sat on the couch. A few moments later the bedroom door opened and Odom stood there in gray sweats and bare feet.

"I thought you wanted to get your beauty sleep?"

"I won't be beautiful when I wake up, no matter how long I sleep."

"So, when exactly did the FBI knock on your door?"

Odom sat down on the other end of the couch and rubbed at her toes. "Some cops took me to the police station. No one would tell me anything. Then people in suits came and took me away. I ended up here with the Meatball."

"That must have been really scary, Betsy. It would have been frightening for anyone."

She shrugged. "It's not like I could do anything. Adults just tell you what to do. Or they think they can," she added a little bitterly.

"So, if it wasn't drugs, I wonder what could have happened to your parents." Devine couldn't give the girl the third degree, but he had to try to get some information from her.

"I don't want to talk about it, okay? What the hell does it matter now?"

"But it's puzzling to me why the FBI is involved."

She shot him a look. "Aren't you one of them?"

"No, different agency. I'm Homeland Security."

"They just said I had to come with them."

"You nervous about meeting your uncle for the first time?" Devine asked.

"Should I be?" she countered, gazing fixedly at him.

"I don't know, Betsy, I really don't."

"You don't know much," she shot back.

You hit that nail right on the head.

Saxby came back in smelling of tobacco smoke. "I thought you were in bed, Betsy?"

Without a word Odom scooted into her room and hastily shut the bedroom door.

"So anything else you can tell me that might be helpful?"

"Need to know, Devine."

"Always hated that phrase."

"I don't make the rules," she said.

He left the woman there as Saxby gazed dejectedly down at her couch bed.

CHAPTER

6

DEVINE HAD WALKED ABOUT HALFWAY to his hotel when he sensed someone following him, and it wasn't the pair of gents from before. This pursuer was traveling solo.

Devine turned right at an intersection, picked up his pace slightly, and then turned right again at the next street.

When the man who was tailing him mimicked these movements, Devine stepped out of a niche cut into a building façade and said, "You look lost, friend."

The man gazed up at him, a smirk on his face. He was around five-five and a flabby buck fifty wearing a cheap suit and scuffed loafers. His hair was rapidly thinning, revealing patches of pale, flaky scalp. He smelled of booze and was smoking a cigarette. He looked totally unfazed by the sudden confrontation. In fact, he looked rather pleased as he flicked ash onto the pavement.

"I'm actually right where I need to be, *friend*. And maybe you are, too," he added.

"I'm listening."

"You just left Betsy Odom and her handler."

"Did I?"

A frown creased the man's face. "I'm not getting any younger so don't waste my time playing stupid or this is going nowhere."

"It's probably going nowhere anyway. What exactly do you want?"

"More to the point, what do *you* want? You're a fed. So my guess is you want information on Danny Glass, right? He wants to take ownership of the girl, right?"

"*Ownership?* Interesting choice of words."

"Glass owns people, didn't you know?"

"And why do *you* know anything about him?" asked Devine politely.

"I keep my ear to the ground. People who do that tend to know stuff, *valuable* stuff."

"You local?"

"Maybe," replied the man curtly.

"Well, Glass isn't from here. So why would you have anything on him?"

"I'm not from here, either. And they're prosecuting his ass right here in Seattle. But if you don't want to deal, I'll find somebody else who does. See you around, sucker."

He started to walk off, but Devine grabbed his thin arm, freezing the man in place.

"Let's start again. How about with your name?"

"Oh, sure, it's Fred. What's yours?"

"Okay, *Fred*, what do you know about Glass?"

"Not how it works, dum-dum. You fork over money and *then* I tell you."

"And if I don't think it's worth what I paid?" said Devine.

"You file a complaint with the Better Business Bureau. Not to worry, I'm a member in good standing."

"How much money are we talking?" asked Devine.

"A hundred grand is a nice number, don't you think? I can give you my wire transfer instructions. I don't like to carry cash. Too many criminals around here. Gut you for a gift card."

"Hundred grand? Sure, let me run to an ATM like two hundred times and see if my government debit card will actually melt."

"Take it or leave it. No skin off me."

"That kind of money comes with at least three levels of approvals and a face-to-face beat-down with a battalion of government accountants. I can have a decision by this time next year, but I don't think you'll like our counteroffer, which might actually *be* a gift card."

"Boy, I thought you had a brain—my mistake."

"So what can you tell me for, say, a hundred bucks?"

"I already told you. My name. It's Fred. So fork over the C-note."

"You are one funny man," remarked Devine.

"And you are one unfunny *loser*."

"You know anything about Betsy Odom?"

"I know Glass wants her. And maybe, just maybe, I know *why*, which I think might be valuable to you, but maybe I'm wrong." The man's look did not match his last few words.

Devine processed this provocative statement along with the man's triumphant look. "Okay, maybe I can get you some money."

"Better make it fast. I hear he's going to take ownership of the girl real soon."

"You seem wired into things you shouldn't be," noted Devine.

"Everyone has to make a living. This is how I make mine."

"Which is how exactly?"

"Providing valuable information and receiving valuable compensation in return. Hopefully from you, if you're smart enough to seize an opportunity staring you in the face."

"How can I get in touch with you?" asked Devine.

"I'll get in touch with you, if necessary. But don't wait too long."

Fred walked off and this time Devine did not stop him.

He waited until the man was nearly out of sight and then Devine took up the chase.

CHAPTER

7

THROUGH THE SOGGY STREETS OF Seattle, Devine tracked buck-fifty Fred to a part of the city where the air was briny and humid; some of the buildings dark, grim, and ready for rehab; and the traffic and pedestrian flows occurring in bursts before receding like an outgoing tide.

Fred veered off and hurried his scuffed loafers up a set of worn and stained stone steps, disappearing through a peeling red door. Devine scooted after him and eyed the sign over the door: THE SAND BAR.

Well, that's original.

He entered a large room filled with heat and humidity and clusters of bodies dancing, drinking, swaying, mingling, and some even crooning badly to the tunes piped overhead, probably from a Spotify account. The English pub-style bar was set against one wall. The parquet dance floor was in the middle; a wing to the right held the pinball, billiards, and foosball section of the offered entertainment. Boozed-up people were doing the age-old flirty ritual, while Devine was looking for

Fred, who had disappeared into the sea of drunken groovers.

Devine spotted a back hall and headed down it. He figured Fred had spied the tail and had used this place to lose him. The back door emptied into an alley. On the right was a wall with trash cans stacked in front, so Devine turned left and picked up his pace.

A minute later Devine glanced back and saw that the two men who had followed him and Odom back to the hotel were once more tracking him.

He worked his way to the alley where the Gum Wall was located. It was so named because of all the brightly colored gum stuck to one wall by passersby. Some of the gum had been stretched out and now resembled miniature and colorful stalagmites.

He had been down this alley before on a previous trip, and knew that the paving stones underneath, combined with the high walls on either side, would resoundingly echo off any footsteps fore or aft. Within a few moments he picked up the sounds of two sets still behind him.

And staggering toward him out of the misty darkness were a man and a woman wrapped around each other in an embrace, and appearing to be five mojitos on the welcome side of paradise. Yet looks could be deceiving and so Devine wondered if he had bogies at six and twelve. He eased the Glock from its holster, but kept it hidden behind his jacket. His index finger slid within the vicinity of the trigger. He tensed as the couple grew nearer, but they didn't even glance at him as they lurched by, devouring each other's lips in the process.

Devine still had the other pair on his six, which meant he still had twin problems to solve.

He trekked down another side street and then stopped and turned around.

His hand on his gun, he waited.

The men cleared the turn and continued to walk casually toward him. They stopped and stared at him. And his gun, which Devine had now made clearly visible.

"You guys lost, or just going where I'm going?" he asked.

One was Black with a bald head. He was a brick wall, thick and muscular and an inch over Devine's height. The other guy was six feet, white with massive amounts of blond hair and a soft, stocky build, with a gut that leaned over his belt. Devine immediately tagged them as Baldy and Big Hair because he somehow didn't expect them to reveal their real names.

"Been following you, dude," said Baldy, in a deep voice that matched his muscled bulk.

"Thanks for the heads-up. I never would have noticed otherwise. Care to tell me why?"

"Shit, you need that gun out?" said Big Hair, a nervous tic in his higher-pitched voice.

"I don't know, you tell me."

"We just wanna talk. We ain't here to hurt nobody, mister. I mean, damn."

"So talk," said Devine, keeping the gun right where it was.

"You watchin' Betsy Odom," said Big Hair.

"Am I?" Devine felt déjà vu all over again after his conversation with buck-fifty Fred.

"You and the federal chick," chimed in Baldy.

"What interest do you have?"

"We knew Betsy's parents. Know her, too," said Big Hair.

"How?"

Baldy said, "Went to high school with Dwayne. Then he moved away somewheres, got married, and he come back here with Alice and Betsy. That's when we hooked up again. Had some good times. Real good. Nice family."

"And now they're dead," said Devine. "Any ideas on that?"

Baldy said, "What do they say killed 'em?"

"Wasn't it in the papers?"

"We don't read no papers, dude. I mean, shit," said Big Hair, grinning. "Do we look like we get the *Wall Street Journal* or sumthin'?"

Devine hesitated but then decided it was worth it to maybe get some useful info in return. "Drug overdose."

"That's bullshit," said Baldy.

"Why?"

"They ain't use no drugs."

Just like Betsy had said.

"How do you know?"

Baldy said, "They been back here years now. Seen a lot of 'em. Ain't seen no drugs or shit like that. And if you're usin', it sure as hell gonna be at your place and on your skin, and in your eyes, and in your piss, in everythin' you got."

"And how would you know that?" said Devine.

Baldy held up one arm. "Zipper tracks down both arms." He pointed to his nose. "And I blew this middle part here right out snortin' coke. Can't smell much no more, 'cept when my chef bro' here uses too much bok choy or stinky-ass French cheese."

Big Hair nodded and said, "Meth was my devil. Popped my colon a while back. Don't recommend ever doin' that, man. Serious as shit, no pun intended."

Baldy said, "Point is we know when someone's usin' or ain't usin'. And they ain't usin'."

"Police report says otherwise. And it also says Betsy used Narcan to try to bring them back. Apparently, they'd OD'd on fentanyl."

Big Hair shook his head. "Did Betsy say she done that? Narcan, I mean?"

Once more Devine hesitated but then said, "No, she didn't. She said the opposite."

Big Hair looked triumphantly at Devine. "See? Told you."

"So what do *you* think happened to them?"

Baldy eyed Devine warily. "Don't know. But if the cops makin' shit up? Then you got your own kind doin' crap they shouldn't be doin'."

"*My* kind?" said Devine.

"You a cop, ain't you? Federal cop by the look of you."

"You have experience with cops, federal and otherwise?"

"What you think?" said Baldy defiantly. "Or do I look like I gone to Harvard with a trust fund?"

"You have records?"

Baldy laid his large brown eyes on Devine. "Hard to get a real job when you can't pass the pee test and you got you some priors. And you got to live somehow, someway. That's all I'm sayin' 'bout that."

"What about Danny Glass? The Odoms ever talk about him?"

The men looked at each other with unease. Big Hair said, "We know 'bout him. Dwayne ain't really care for the man. But Alice..."

"Alice what?"

"Alice ain't exactly share that feelin' with Dwayne."

Devine was getting more info than he'd bargained for and decided to keep going. "I heard they came into some money. To buy a place to live and a car? That come from Glass?"

Baldy shrugged his big delts. "They never say and we ain't never asked. But ain't like they got a bunch of rich friends give 'em that kind of cash."

"Where's the house?"

"Kittitas County. East a' here, out in the boonies, 'bout a two-and-a-half-hour drive or so."

"Got an address? I'd like to go see it for myself."

"Got a PO box but that ain't help you none. But we can tell you how to get there."

Big Hair gave him detailed directions, which Devine put into his phone's notes app.

"Ain't so easy to find after you get off the highway," Baldy added. "Google sure ain't gonna get you there. But you stick to what you was told and you find it."

"Thanks. You know, Glass wants to gain guardianship of Betsy?"

"Well, mister, if I was you, I would stop that shit in its tracks," said Big Hair.

"Any particular reason?"

"Why would a guy like that want a little girl 'round?"

"Well, he *is* her uncle and the only relative she has left."

"I bet lots of rich-ass criminals got them nieces.

How many want 'a have little girls live with 'em?" said Big Hair. "Seems sort 'a weird, ask me."

"You ever met Glass?"

"No sir," said Baldy. "But Dwayne tell us stuff. That Glass dude is messed up, for damn sure."

"Did he ever visit the Odoms?"

"Not that they say," replied Baldy.

"Care to tell me your names? I'd like to pass on your good wishes to Betsy."

Big Hair said, "You just look after that girl, mister. She special all right. Smart as a whip. And she got her own mind, that's for shit sure."

"Yeah, I've seen that."

"Crappy deal in life, but her parents loved her, man," said Baldy. "They just ain't never figure out how to be . . . normal, I guess. Dwayne had him a big-ass heart, but that 'bout all that boy had. Ain't never hold no job and rub two dimes together. He was always expectin' somethin' to drop in his lap and save his ass."

"A dreamer," added Big Hair.

"Well," said Devine. "He got a nightmare instead. Thanks for the info. I'll do what I can."

The two men left him, and Devine circled back toward the bar where he'd lost track of Fred.

When he heard screams, Devine started to run.

Inside the bar he saw that the music had stopped and so had the partying mood. People were gathered around something on the dance floor. One woman turned to the side and threw up probably what amounted to every ounce of drink and morsel of food she'd had tonight.

He pushed his way through the crowd and to the object of all the attention.

Fred was lying on his back, his hands cupped over his stomach like he was hiding something there. The floor under him was covered in blood and Devine could see a trail of it going off toward the back hall, as though someone had dripped red paint the whole way.

Fred's eyes opened and he saw Devine.

"Who did this to you?" said Devine, kneeling next to the man.

Fred said something garbled, and then seized Devine's arm. His next words were clearer, but still made no sense to Devine. Then Fred's eyes closed, his grip fell away, and the little man let out a long breath, which turned out to be his very last one.

8

SO THE MAN WAS OFFERING information in return for cash—was that the way it played out?" said Detective Stephen Braddock, who was with the Seattle PD.

Devine nodded as both men eyed the body of the late Perry Rollins, aka Fred, whose identity had been positively confirmed with the driver's license tucked inside his wallet. That and forty wrinkled bucks and two quarters, and one expired credit card, along with a recent receipt from a local hardware store for drywall joint compound, some paint, batteries, and a mousetrap.

Braddock was beefy and of middle height. His chin had a couple days' worth of stubble. The man possessed a pair of penetrating eyes, which lurched around in their sockets in an apparent attempt to miss nothing going on around the vicinity of their owner. He had chewed down four sticks of gum while talking to Devine.

"That's pretty much it," agreed Devine. He had stayed behind to meet with the first responders, identified his federal agent status to them, and then hung around to speak to Braddock. The CSI team was all over the premises performing their forensic dance with the available evidence. The bar goers, at least those who had not fled prior to the cops' arrival, had been shocked out of their drunkenness, and were cloistered in an upstairs room for processing and questioning.

"He have any family?" asked Devine.

"None that we know of. FYI, Rollins has crossed our path before. I believe he came out here over a decade or so ago. He did some time in the local lockups. Just petty crap. But he kept his eyes and ears attuned to stuff. He actually provided us info on a couple of cases that helped us out."

"He knew more about my situation than he should have."

"He apparently made a meager living out of knowing things he shouldn't."

"So if he was a cop snitch, maybe whoever he ratted out took their revenge?"

"Maybe," said Braddock cautiously.

"But you're thinking the timing is too coincidental?" noted Devine.

"You're tracking him after he offers to sell you something, and then, bam, he bites it?" Braddock eyed him. "Couple of witnesses said Rollins might have spoken to you before he shut his eyes for the last time?"

"He did. But I couldn't make it out. It was garbled. Guy was gushing blood, maybe delirious."

Braddock nodded. "Okay, but if the garbled becomes less garbled, let me know."

"Will do," said Devine. He'd actually made out some words, but they made no sense, and he decided not to disclose them yet.

"So he wanted to sell you info. What about exactly?"

"That would require a call to the East Coast, Detective Braddock. And at this time of night, no one would answer."

Braddock looked put off. "And here I was thinking you feds, with all those budget dollars, were a twenty-four-seven op."

"Popular myth."

"Uh-huh, sure."

Devine stared at Rollins's torn shirt. "Looks to be two knife strikes to the gut? Painful way to die. Might mean something."

"Maybe only that it's quieter than a gunshot in a crowded bar."

"Right. Well, you have my contact info."

"You make that call back East tomorrow *morning*. I'll expect to hear from you right after. And I don't care how early it is here. With my line of work, I don't really expect to sleep much anymore."

"See what I can do, Detective."

Braddock shook his head. "I don't know how you feds live with yourselves, screwing over local law enforcement."

Devine didn't know if the man was being serious or sarcastic, or somehow both.

He left Braddock hovering over the bloodied body of the late Perry Rollins. But he didn't leave the premises. Devine followed the spatter trail down the hall and to its point of origin in the men's john. The other people working away had evidently seen him talking to Braddock and thus didn't challenge his movements into the heart of their investigation.

Inside the restroom two young female techs were dusting, photographing, measuring, and scouring for microscopic detritus with the aid of sophisticated instruments and no doubt years of training and on-site experience.

"Stabbed in here, I take it?" he said. When they looked up at him suspiciously, he flashed his creds.

"I'm working with Braddock on this," he white-lied.

"Inside the last stall," said one of the women, jerking her head that way.

"Looked to be knife strikes to his gut," noted Devine.

"Fairly long blade," said the other woman. "Puncturing but not severing the aorta most likely; otherwise he never would have made it out of the bathroom. Still, the bleed out would have been relatively fast. Post will confirm."

"Anyone see anything?"

"Still processing and getting witness statements. At least those who weren't drunk."

Devine leaned out the door and eyed the camera bolted to a corner of the ceiling just down the hall.

"That security camera capture anything useful?"

"Processing," said the first tech again. She gave him a wary look, which he returned with a lopsided smile, and then, thinking he had probably overstayed his welcome, he walked out the rear door. Devine stood there breathing in the smell of the ocean and feeling light drizzle falling from the thickened clouds.

He looked down the alleyway and wondered if it was possible that Big Hair or Baldy could have done the deed before meeting with Devine. Timing-wise it would have been tight. Maybe too tight. And neither man had any blood on him. And they couldn't have done it *after* they left Devine. He'd gone straight back to the bar, while they had headed off in the opposite direction.

He walked to his hotel; luckily the rain didn't really start pounding until he had a roof over his head. He stripped off his coat and spent five minutes at the bathroom sink trying to grind Rollins's blood off his jacket sleeve, but he was only partially successful. He hung it up to dry, undressed, and slipped into bed. Sleep usually came easy for him, but not tonight. Too much had happened in too short a period of time to give his mind the time and space it needed to fully shut down.

He finally rose and went over to the window and looked out onto the damp and windswept streets. Devine checked his watch. In eight-and-a-half hours he would be picking up Betsy Odom and delivering the twelve-year-old, maybe to the devil. And that devil might have had a man with damaging information on him gutted in a men's room.

That thought did not make Devine's sleep come any easier.

CHAPTER

9

FORGOING HIS NORMAL MORNING WORK-
OUT, a weary and jet-lagged Devine slept in, rose,
showered and dressed, and snagged a coffee and bagel
from the little hotel market off the lobby.

At ten sharp he knocked on Saxby's door. The FBI
agent looked exhausted with dark rings under her eyes,
and a cup of black coffee in hand.

"How was your evening?" he asked.

"You trying to be funny? How was yours?"

"Eventful."

"Meaning?" she said sharply.

He explained about the late Perry Rollins but left out
telling her about the two men who had said they had
known the Odoms. He wasn't in a real trusting mood
right now and he wanted to see how all of this played
out before fully looping in the Bureau, if he ever did.

She exclaimed, "A guy selling dirt on Glass goes
down minutes after pitching you the business? You
think Glass had him killed?"

"I don't know."

"Well, she can't go and meet with him now," observed Saxby. "A man connected to Glass has been *murdered*."

Devine shook his head. "Like you said before, innocent until proven guilty. And if you try to put the kibosh on the meeting, your supervisor will probably transplant you permanently to a one-person office in the wilds of Alaska. I doubt you want to earn the rest of your government pension counting down the seconds of your life."

She took a gulp of coffee, ran a hand through her tangled hair, and plopped down on the couch. "I really don't need this shit."

"But for now, it's tag and I'm it. I'll take her and bring her back."

She glanced up at him. "Okay, here's the rundown. Glass has reservations at the Four Seasons hotel restaurant. They meet for two hours max. No going anywhere else. You can leave them together, but you are to maintain visual contact at all times, no matter what."

"Okay. Is Betsy ready?"

"I heard her moving around close to six, so I'd say definitely yes."

"She must be excited."

"Or nervous," Saxby shot back.

"Or both," amended Devine. "How'd you sleep?"

"That damn couch is older than I am. And I've had insomnia for two years."

"Army has a method for falling asleep. I can teach you."

"Thanks, but no thanks. Army, huh? How long were you in for?" asked Saxby.

"Little over ten."

"Then you were well on your way to a full ride and a nice pension."

"You know about such things?"

"My ex was in the Marines."

"Did he do the full ride?" asked Devine.

"Yeah, and then the asshole divorced me and married a twenty-something hair stylist, who *I* introduced him to, to work on his bald spot to make him feel better about himself, if you can believe the irony."

Again, Devine was startled by the personal information dump and didn't respond directly to it. "You have kids?"

She nodded, her mouth widening almost to a smile. "Two boys. Fourteen and sixteen."

"Who do they stay with when you're on the road?"

A frown swept the near smile away. "They split time with me and their father and his new bride. She comes from money but apparently sees herself as an *artiste* with clippers and a blow dryer. They have a place with a pool. I take it my boys just love to watch their *stepmom* prance around in her itty-bitty bikini. Makes me want to puke."

This was getting so uncomfortable now that Devine nearly cried out in relief when the bedroom door opened and Odom appeared there. She had on black slacks, lace-up green boots, and a dark blue turtleneck sweater. Her hair was freshly washed and done up in a way that had clearly taken the girl some time and effort to accomplish.

"I'm ready," she announced. "How do I look?"

"Fine," pronounced Devine.

Saxby just sipped on her coffee, looking miserable.

"Let's go," said Devine.

Odom grabbed her coat and they started out. Before the door closed behind them, Saxby clenched his arm. "Watch her like a hawk," she said in a furious whisper.

"I plan to," replied Devine evenly. "Because it's my job."

Devine ordered an Uber. The Kia SUV pulled up three minutes later and Devine scrutinized the fresh-faced young woman at the wheel who greeted them with a warm smile and an offer of hard candy. Both declined.

As they drove away, Devine looked at Odom and said, "Good sleep?"

"It was okay." She glanced furtively at him. "I had some butterflies."

"Understandable."

"I read some more online about my uncle last night. What's this RICO stuff?"

"A bunch of criminal laws the government alleged he broke."

"I knew he was kind of a bad guy."

"From your parents? Or Google?" he quipped.

She didn't answer him.

"Look, anything gets henky for you with him, just give me the high sign and I'll end the meeting."

"What kind of sign?" she said, casting him a curious glance.

Devine rubbed his hand along the seat and leaned his head to the right. "Do those two things together and I'll swoop in and it's over. Don't worry, I'll make up an excuse and take the blame," he added when Odom looked ready to protest.

Devine continued, "Those guys who were following us last night? They said they were friends of your mom and dad. Went to high school with your father." He described Big Hair and Baldy. "Sound familiar?"

She looked at him warily. It struck Devine that Odom did not trust anyone. And maybe that made perfect sense. *And not just for her, but for me, too.*

She said, "Maybe. What did they say?"

"That they agree with you that your parents were not drug users and so that could not have been the cause of their deaths."

"See," she said fiercely.

"Just because they said it does not make it true, especially when the police say otherwise."

"Then the police are lying. And *I* said my parents weren't drug users, too."

Devine caught the young driver staring at them in the rearview, a startled expression on her features from what she had overheard.

He flashed his badge and said, "Eyes on the road, ma'am. Official government business back here. And can you turn up the radio, please?"

She blushed deeply, looked quickly away, and cranked up the volume.

Over Mick Jagger's vocals coming from the radio, Devine glanced at Odom and said, "That's quite an allegation about the police."

"It's the *truth*, Travis. And you need to prove it."

"*I* do?"

"Yeah, isn't that your job? To find the truth? And you were asking all those questions yesterday."

"To which you gave almost no answers."

"That's because I don't know much. Now shut up and let me get ready for my *audition*."

"You really think you need to work for this? He clearly wants you in his life."

"In my world, you have to work for everything. And you still never get what you really want."

She sat back and stared out the window while Devine watched her.

CHAPTER

10

"Ms. ODOM?"

The man greeted them at the front door of the Four Seasons Hotel. He was in his fifties, gray-haired, and his thickened torso was sloppily housed in an off-the-rack navy blue suit with a starched cream shirt buttoned to the top and absent a tie. The loose skin on his neck flopped over the high collar and looked none too comfortable to Devine's eye.

"I'm Betsy Odom."

"I'm Dennis Hastings. I work for your uncle." He shook her hand, aimed a dismissive glance at Devine, and said, "Right this way. Your uncle is really looking forward to seeing you, young lady."

On the way, Hastings dropped back to walk next to Devine and whispered, "You armed?"

"Are you?"

"Just asking."

"Thanks. I appreciate it," said Devine.

"You have no need of a weapon."

"Does the phrase 'cold, dead hand' mean anything to you?"

Hastings moved away, muttering what sounded to Devine like "asshole."

He followed the pair to the dining room, where he could see Danny Glass sitting alone at a table with his back to a wall. His black suit stood out starkly against the brilliance of the white tablecloth. Devine noted that his shirt was also buttoned to the top with no tie in sight. Hastings had clearly copied his boss on that detail. However, Glass had no fat hanging over the collar and no bulging love handles bench-pressing his jacket. Also, the suit looked to be a custom job molded precisely to the man's lean and wiry five-feet-nine-inch frame. His shaved head revealed a perfectly shaped cranium with nary a blemish to be seen. A precisely folded white pocket square completed the picture of a successful businessman, albeit one who would have you chopped to pieces and stuck in a garbage bag if you crossed him.

Devine also noted the two large suited men hovering nearby. Their gazes and with it their focus swung around to him.

"Betsy," said Glass, rising and giving her a hug. He did not look at Devine. "I'm Uncle Danny. It's so great to finally meet you. I hope you're hungry."

They sat down and Devine stayed right where he was.

Spurred on by a meaningful glance from his boss, Hastings hurried over to Devine and said, "Hey, bud, let's give them some privacy, okay?"

Devine retreated twenty feet to a wall where his line of sight was dead-on.

Hastings again approached and said, "Come on, is that the best you can do? They're family."

Devine gave him a look as an answer. He settled himself to stand guard for the next two hours and engaged a timer on his phone.

Hastings moved off and Devine continued to watch the pair at the table. As he did so, his mind went back in time to when both he and Glass had worn the same uniform.

Near the end of his military career, Glass had been assigned to a unit in Iraq that had operated in the same sector as the then Lieutenant Devine and his platoon. The two men had shared one experience that had nearly cost them both their lives. Devine had not seen Glass since that time.

Devine had only heard dark rumors about Glass while the man had been in service. That he might have been selling drugs, or that he had stolen some artifacts from the Middle East, or that some local Iraqi women had gone missing and ended up in Asia as "companions" to wealthy men.

Army CID had dug into it, and though Glass's name had come up repeatedly, Devine had been told by some agents at the time that nothing would stick to the guy. But obviously feeling the heat, Glass had accepted a general discharge and left the military. Then, apparently, he had felt liberated to lead the sort of life he had wanted to all along. The rest, as they say, was criminal history.

Watching him, Devine could almost feel both the burn of unbridled ambition as well as the enormous chip on the man's shoulder.

Although he could be looking at life in prison, Glass didn't seem to have a care in the world, other than his niece. For that, Devine found himself with a grudging respect for the man. And they'd worn the uniform and fought and bled for their country. That also counted for something with Devine.

A couple of times the look on Odom's face appeared strained, nervous even, and once, when Glass leaned in close and was talking to her earnestly, he thought the girl might give Devine the signal to end it. He believed he could see her hand start to make the sliding motion on the table and her head start to dip to the side, but then Glass said something that made Odom laugh.

The signal would not be coming after that, Devine predicted.

And it didn't. When the meal was over, Devine's

timer had four minutes left to burn. Glass escorted his niece over to Devine and put out his hand.

"Thank you for bringing Betsy," he said, showing no recognition of Devine.

"Of course."

Glass knelt down and hugged her. "Be seeing you soon, okay?"

"Okay, Uncle Danny."

And then Glass rose and walked out, with his security team scurrying after their boss.

That's when Devine noted that Glass's pant legs were flared out at the bottoms.

To hide the electronic monitor on his ankle. Talk about a blow to the old criminal kingpin's ego.

As he and Odom left, Devine said, "So how'd it go?"

"Fine."

"Thought you were going to give me the signal for a second there."

She glanced at him, and Devine couldn't really read her look.

"Everything okay, Betsy?"

"Yeah, sure. Thanks for not screwin' things up."

"You're welcome."

During the Uber ride back she looked out the window with a pensive expression. Devine could tell something was eating away at the girl.

She finally turned to him with a curious look.

"Something on your mind?" he asked.

"I haven't cried."

"Excuse me?" Devine said.

"About my mom and dad. I haven't...you know, cried. That's...that's weird as shit, right?"

Devine chose his words carefully. "Don't judge yourself against others when it comes to grieving. Everyone handles it differently."

Her face flushed angrily. "You're just sayin' that to make me feel better."

"No, I'm just telling you *my* experience."

She glanced at him, her irritation transformed to curiosity. "What do you mean?"

"I lost friends in combat. Friends who were closer to me than my own family. And I processed it differently than others did."

"How can friends be closer than family?" she asked.

"Depends on the friends and the family, doesn't it?" he said bluntly.

"I...I guess so."

"What happened to your parents, and *you*, is hard, complicated. There're no easy answers and no right or wrong way to get through it."

"So, you...you think I will cry at some point?"

"My guess would be yes, Betsy, you will. Maybe harder than you ever thought possible," he added quietly.

She turned away from him and leaned her face

against the car window. She looked, to Devine, like the loneliest little girl in the world.

"So the guardianship is a go then, I take it?" he asked after a bit.

"Let's hope so."

"Did you talk to him about what happened to your parents?"

"I'm tired. And I need to get out of these pants and shoes. My mom bought them a while ago and I've... grown some. They're cutting off my circulation."

The rest of the drive back was made in silence. Devine didn't really know how to break through the walls he sensed had formed around the girl.

She went right to her bedroom and shut the door.

Saxby, smelling like a potent combo of menthols and Listerine, said, "Talk to me."

"She went, they ate and chatted, and that was it."

"That's it? Really?" she said, clearly disappointed.

"What did you expect? A shoot-out?"

She slumped on the couch, reached for her purse, and extracted her pack of smokes. She slipped a cigarette between her lips. "I don't know. Something, I guess."

"Do you have skin in this game, Agent Saxby?"

She shot him a withering look. "Meaning what? I'm her temporary guardian. That's it."

"And yet you seem to me to be overemotional about this whole thing."

"Don't pull the hysterical female crap with me, Devine. And I can feel for a young girl who's heading for a fall."

"But you don't know that to be the case."

"Oh, please." She pulled a slim chrome lighter from her purse and lit up.

"Can you smoke in here?"

"So I pay the fine. Who gives a shit? The whole place needs a good smoking out. Might kill some of the damn germs."

The bedroom door opened. Odom was in the gray sweats from last night, and her hair was back down around her shoulders.

"The names of the two guys who were following us last night? Nate Shore and Korey Rose. Nate is the Black guy. Built like a truck. Korey is super nice and a really great cook."

Saxby stabbed out her smoke on the table and said, "What guys following you!" She whirled on Devine. "What the hell game are you trying to play?"

"Sorry, slipped my mind." He looked at Odom. "What else can you tell me about them?"

"They had drug problems, and my parents were helping them out."

"How?" asked Devine.

"I know they gave them some money. And they stayed over at our place a lot. Before, at our apartment.

And after we got our own place. And they helped around the house. Korey would cook meals. And Nate would fix stuff. And my parents would drive them to their jobs and their rehab stuff."

"Did you talk to this *dynamic duo* last night, Devine?" barked Saxby.

"I did. And they told me that the Odoms were not drug users and anyone or anything that says they were, including police reports, is wrong."

"Same thing I told you," said Odom angrily.

"So what can we do about it?" asked Devine, looking squarely at Saxby.

"Do . . . do about what?" she said, looking tired and defeated.

Devine glanced at Odom. "Betsy, can you give us a sec here? Agent Saxby and I have some 'government' things to discuss."

"But this is stuff about me," retorted Odom. "I should be able to hear it, too."

"And you will, just not right this minute," replied Devine. "Please," he added.

She skulked off to her room and slammed the door.

Devine turned to Saxby. "Okay, we need to find out how they really died."

"That is not my jurisdiction. If *you* want to take it up with the locals, feel free."

"So the parents of someone of potential value to

the Bureau are killed and their reported cause of death may be a lie and the Bureau wants nothing to do with it?" said Devine incredulously.

"Those men could be lying," pointed out Saxby.

"But I don't think Betsy is. What would be her motive?"

Saxby glanced at the remains of her cigarette. "I don't know what to tell you."

"How about you report this up the line and request the Bureau take a look?" suggested Devine in a sharp tone.

"Two secondhand accounts from admitted drug users? I'd be laughed out of a career."

Odom burst out of the bedroom, where she had clearly been listening to this encounter. She put her hands on her hips. "Are you fuckin' deaf? *I'm* tellin' you the same thing."

"You're a child. And you watch your mouth! If you were my kid, I'd stuff a bar of soap down your damn throat."

Odom's small chest started to rise and fall fast. Before Devine could react, she had picked up an empty glass Coke bottle off a table and thrown it at Saxby. Luckily her aim was off and the bottle shattered against the wall.

The FBI agent was so astonished, she could only sit there trembling with rage. Finally, she found her voice. "How dare you, you little piece of shit!"

"Took the words right out of my mouth, you old bitch!"

Odom stormed back into the bedroom and slammed the door behind her.

Saxby looked furiously at Devine. "Can you believe that crap? That's assault against a federal agent."

"Come on. Put yourself in her twelve-year-old shoes. What would you do?"

"Someone needs to teach her some manners."

"You didn't answer my question."

"And I'm not going to. Now, you did your job, Devine. So get the hell out of here. With any luck the court will grant Glass the temporary guardianship and she'll be off my hands."

"Boy, you really did a one-eighty on your view about Glass taking control of her."

"I actually think they're meant for each other. Now go."

Devine glanced at the bedroom door, where he thought he could hear Odom crying. "Make sure nothing happens to the girl, okay?" he said.

"I'll do my job. Without any help or commentary from you."

She shoved Devine out the door.

Devine walked out into the street and phoned Emerson Campbell.

Because there is no way in hell I can leave that kid like this.

11

DEVINE WAS ON THE PHONE with Campbell all the way back to his hotel, explaining what had happened thus far, and his desire to stay in town to follow up on the situation.

"I knew this might turn out to be a lot more complicated than it was presented," opined Campbell. "There was too much unknown about it. Nice to know my instincts are still clicking."

"Yes, sir."

"This FBI agent sounds like a nutjob. What's your take on her?"

"She has her issues, for sure. But I don't have a good read yet."

"I'll find out what I can about her from some of my Bureau contacts. And Odom?"

"Mature way beyond her years in some ways. She's had a rough time of it. And I'm still not clear on why the Bureau took custody of her."

"What info on Glass could this Rollins guy have had?"

"Don't know. But the cop in charge of his murder investigation wants to know what I'm doing out here."

Campbell said, "Go easy on that for now, Devine. I need to speak with our folks before you reveal anything. The local cops could screw something up."

"And why did the Bureau even need me? Saxby could have escorted Betsy to the meeting with Glass."

"This might have started out with you escorting someone, Devine. But now this is about you hanging around until this thing is resolved, which sounds like that's what you want to do."

"She asked for help, yes. I'm prepared to give it. This thing is so messed up, I can't walk away in good conscience, sir."

"But from all accounts, Glass is one mean son of a bitch, so you need to tread carefully."

"He tries really hard not to look the part, which makes him even more dangerous. The real cowards act tough and then keel over dead when you make a fist."

"*You* have any idea why he wants the girl?"

"Not right now. If I do find out, it might even help the Bureau *and* DOJ, since they're apparently losing witnesses on the RICO case at an unsustainable clip."

"*If* you find out the truth. *And* survive."

"Right. But I'm pretty good at both."

"Tread lightly with the locals and drag things out as much as possible."

The two men spoke for another few minutes and then Devine clicked off, walked into his hotel, and rode the elevator to his room. He sat on the bed, glanced at his other jacket hanging on a peg, and saw a dead man's blood still there. He put it in a plastic bag pulled from his closet, called housekeeping, and handed it off to them to clean the stain away, if they could. Too bad they couldn't do the same to his memory of how it had come to be that way.

On the call he had also asked Campbell to dig up all he could on Dwayne and Alice Odom, and Perry Rollins. He didn't expect to get anything right away so he figured he had time to do a little investigating on his own. But first, he had another call to make.

"Hello, Detective Braddock. How goes it?"

"It'll either go well or not depending on what you're about to tell me. And I expected your call this *morning*. The East Coast feds should have been awake for a while now keeping the world safe for democracy."

"Sorry, I got tied up. You have time to meet? I don't like doing this over the phone."

"You think I'm recording this conversation?"

"Perish the thought."

"There's a coffee place I know."

"In Seattle, really?" quipped Devine.

"One hour." He gave Devine the address and ended the call.

Devine summoned an Uber, which he took to the Sand Bar. He got out and noted the yellow police tape strung across the front doors. A cop was on duty to guard the perimeter.

Devine walked up and held out his badge and creds. "I was here last night with Detective Braddock working on this case. Is he still around?"

Devine hoped not because he wanted to go over everything again, without the detective making inconvenient inquiries of him while he was doing some private sleuthing.

The young cop stared in silent reverence at the glittering DHS badge and accompanying federal credentials.

"No, he left about an hour ago. DHS, huh? Good place to work?" he asked. "I've been thinking about maybe...you know. Making the jump."

"Serving your country is always a good thing in my book."

The cop let him pass and Devine stopped to put on blue booties and nitrile gloves from twin boxes that had been set up on a table by the entrance.

He did the badge/cred waltz with another uniformed woman just inside the door, who took down his name and information for the logbook.

She said, "I remember you from yesterday. The fed?"

"The fed," conceded Devine. "But a nice fed."

She snorted. "That's a good one."

There was still plenty of activity going on with evidence techs scurrying here and there and a few bored-looking uniforms standing around sipping coffees and waiting to punch out.

The remains of Perry Rollins had been removed, but his blood still rested on the parquet dance floor, an ugly stain on a faded surface scratched by innumerable sets of drunken heels. Fairly soon, no one would remember how he died or anything else about the man.

I didn't exactly like the guy, but pretty sure he deserved better than that.

Devine spied the same tech he had seen the previous night, the young woman who had been in the men's room doing her forensic work.

He walked over and said, "I'm with DHS. I was here last night with Detective Braddock."

"I remember you," she said in a voice that Devine did not quite know how to take. "I'm Detective Beth Walker."

She smiled so wide, it lit up her face and Devine's at the same time. Now he knew exactly how to take her look.

"Travis Devine, Beth, nice to meet you."

"Same here."

She was around his age, with dirty blond hair and light blue eyes.

"So *detectives* pull this kind of duty?" he said, eyeing her scrubs.

"Makes them better detectives, at least that's the principle, and I agree."

"So were you able to dig up anything on the camera in the back hall?"

She opened an iPad and scrolled through some screens. "The camera is a piece of crap from the nineties with no bells and whistles. The video footage was grainy and glitchy as hell because they've recorded over the tape so many times. And we're not even sure the time stamp is accurate because the electrical power kept pulsing and shorting it out. You would think everybody had heard of wireless digital cameras with cloud storage by now." She looked up. "So I guess the answer is no."

"Well, thanks for trying. Any luck with witnesses from last night?"

"I just checked in with the people conducting the interviews. So far, the first anyone says they saw of Rollins is when he came staggering out from the back hall. But the people involved would have already fled, I imagine. However, someone did say that they tried to use the bathroom around that time, but the door wouldn't open."

"Any ideas on that?"

"It was a push swing door without a lock because it had urinals and separate toilet stalls inside. We found some curious marks on the floor right near the door. I think a wedge of some sort was used to keep the door closed. The killer obviously would have done that so he could be in there alone with Rollins."

"So the killer sees him go in there, waits till it clears out, and wedges the door shut. A crime of opportunity."

"Right. He stabs him, removes the wedge, and runs for it."

"But this place was packed. Someone should have seen something."

"My experience has been that people just don't want to get involved, particularly in a murder. If anyone did witness anything, they might have just run for it or tried their best to either misremember or forget what they saw. We also have some serious gang activity around here, and who wants to get sucked into that?"

"Braddock told me that he was familiar with the victim?"

"His priors are mostly petty stuff from way back. I can email you with them." She once more graced him with a smile. "I'll just need your contact info, *Travis*."

He gave it, thanked her, and she moved on to keep doing her job, while Devine headed to the men's room and eyed the space from the open doorway.

The blood trail had been marked with yellow cones. He stepped carefully around them and reached the last stall. He eased the door open and saw the yellow cone on the floor, directly in front of the toilet. The blood trail was particularly heavy at this point.

Devine glanced at the mirror hanging on the opposite wall and the sinks underneath.

Okay, he thought. *Rollins was in the stall, probably hiding from me, not knowing last night is his last one. He opens the stall door and gets stabbed. The person then knifes him again just to make sure, turns, and leaves. Rollins, bleeding profusely, staggers out, holding his belly, and makes his way down the hall, to the dance floor, where he collapses and dies.*

If the story about the wedge under the door held up, that would explain why no one saw anything inside the men's room. Devine mentally kicked himself for not checking the space last night, but he had assumed Rollins had fled out the bar's rear exit.

And the blood spatter indicated that whoever *did* stab Rollins should have had blood on him. How did people miss that? But then again, *eyewitness* accounts were the worst of all. And maybe the killer covered it up with something. And the witnesses here at the time were not exactly sober.

Devine finished looking around and nodded to Beth Walker as he was leaving. She held up her iPad. He smiled and gave her a thumbs-up. He passed by the young cop outside and walked along in the direction of where he'd be meeting Braddock in a few minutes.

He opened the email that Walker had just sent him, and reviewed the rap sheet for one Perry Rollins, deceased. Walker had been correct in saying that most of it was misdemeanors. But there was one that stood out. Years ago, in the Midwest, Rollins had been charged with being a Peeping Tom, and for attempted extortion. He had spied on a woman in her bathroom and taken pictures of her naked, and later tried to blackmail the woman into paying in return for the pictures. She knew him because he lived in the neighborhood.

What a nice guy, thought Devine. Rollins hadn't deserved to be murdered, but he was clearly a scumball. He did his jail time and then was released. He must have then moved to the West Coast because his next arrest had been in Portland, Oregon, six months later on a shoplifting charge.

Devine wondered what information Rollins had that would explain why Glass wanted to adopt his niece. Maybe he could piggyback on Braddock's investigation to find out.

Along the way to his meeting with Braddock he thought about how he could get as much help from the man as possible, while revealing as little as possible to the detective.

It would be tricky, but then pretty much everything Devine had ever done had been tricky.

But I'm still standing. At least for now.

12

BRADDOCK HAD ON THE SAME rumpled trench coat from the previous night and his face held a bit more beard stubble. He methodically sipped his coffee as he and Devine perched at a back table away from all the people staring at their phones and computers as though their lives depended on it.

"So *did* you make the call back East?" he asked. "Because if you didn't, I'm going to be one unhappy local detective and you will be an even unhappier federal agent."

"I did. But keep in mind I don't know everything."

Braddock casually looked at his watch. "Pretty early to clock the first bullshit response of the day, but go on. This might be fun. Or not. For you."

Devine met his eye. "If you really know feds, their favorite phrase is 'need to know' and yours truly is not high up in that chain. Same in the Army."

Braddock's eyebrows flickered with interest. "You were in the Army?"

"Mustered out as a captain."

"West Pointer?" asked Braddock.

"Yep."

"Like my old man."

Now Devine looked intrigued. "He still around?"

Braddock nodded, his expression turning somber. "In an assisted living facility with his memories, the few that he can recall."

"Sorry to hear that."

"My mom died a year ago, so it's better that he doesn't remember she passed. He's happy and safe. So, East Coast?" prompted Braddock.

Devine had to make a decision. And he was going to base it on his ability to read people. He was betting that Braddock was smart, tough, and a straight talker. Those were traits that Devine could get on board with, but there was something he needed to check first.

"I was sent here to escort a young girl to meet with her uncle."

"And why is that the concern of the federal government?"

"The uncle is Danny Glass. And the young girl is Betsy Odom."

Devine got the reaction he wanted to get.

"Okay, Danny Glass, the RICO man," said Braddock.

"Right. The trial is scheduled to start soon, but DOJ has three dead witnesses and counting."

"I read the papers, and our police bulletins. So I

know the score on that. And I also know that Odom's parents died from drug overdoses in the southeast corner of the state. The daughter tried to revive them, but failed."

"That's the official police version, at least."

That comment, Devine noted, definitely got the detective's attention.

"Is there another?"

Devine leaned forward and spoke in a low voice. "When I was in the Army, I had to fight lots of enemies. A few of them turned out to wear the same uniform I did. It cost me. A lot. But I thought it was the right thing to do." He leaned back. "What do you think about that?"

Braddock clutched his coffee cup though he didn't raise it to his mouth. It was as though the man just wanted to hold on to something as he thought this through.

"If you're saying what I think you are, that's a Pandora's box, Devine."

"You didn't answer my question. And without that, I don't see a way forward with you and me on this."

"What's your proof?"

"First, you tell me if you're prepared to go where the evidence takes you, even if it takes you somewhere you don't want to go."

Now Braddock drained his coffee. "Let's go for a walk."

They left the café and started down one of Seattle's main avenues as a brisk wind coming off the harbor swept across them. Braddock kept a steady pace and Devine matched him footfall for footfall.

"I'm forty-nine years old, Devine, youngest of five kids. All boys except for four sisters," he quipped. "And all of them are strong-willed and independent and thought I was, at best, an *unattractive* nuisance. But that just made me work harder. I started out in uniformed patrol, like everybody else. Pulled the First, Second, and Third Watches, like everybody else. Made sergeant right at the five-year mark, which is not all that common. Three years later I applied for and was accepted as a detective candidate; again that's on the early side but that was my ultimate goal and I worked my ass off for it. As a newbie detective I pulled duty as part of our CSI unit for a few years to get a good grounding in forensics, just like you saw those folks doing last night. Then I asked for and was transferred to MCU, the Major Crimes Unit's Investigation Bureau. I pulled that duty in Seattle's Southwest Precinct for a bunch of years. And I did well, had a ninety-four-percent clearance rate on my cases because I'm tenacious as hell with a chip on my shoulder, again probably because of my sisters and their evil ways. Then I moved to the Western Precinct, which is basically downtown Seattle and a handful of surrounding suburbs. Five years ago,

I was part of a joint op with the King County MCU. Some cartel activity and related murders for hire had crossed over from county to city and vice versa." He stopped walking and Devine did likewise.

"And we had some crooked cops on the payroll for the cartel. I found out and stood up to them. They threatened me and my family."

"What happened? Did they try to act on those threats?"

"They firebombed my home and killed my wife."

Devine had not seen that one coming. "Jesus!"

"I should have been home. And my wife shouldn't have been. She had a school thing to go to for our youngest son. But at the last minute she couldn't go and asked me to take her place. The sons of bitches that blew up my house obviously assumed I was in there and she wasn't, though I doubt they cared about her. Thank God our other son wasn't home."

"Please tell me you got the pieces of shit."

"Every last one of them, a detective and three uniforms. Life without parole. I go to see them in prison every once in a while and just stare at them. Never say a word. I just look at them. And then I smile and get up and walk out the door, something they will never be able to do the rest of their lives." He stopped and appraised Devine. "That was a long answer to your question. I go where the evidence takes me and I don't give a shit who goes down. Are we straight on that?"

"I appreciate the candidness, Detective. And I'm truly sorry that happened to you and your family."

Braddock started walking and Devine fell into step.

Devine said, "I have three people who knew the Odoms and said they never did drugs."

"What three people?"

"Two of Dwayne Odom's friends from high school, who were both drug addicts and know what telltale signs to look for."

"And the third?'

"Betsy Odom. Who also says her parents never used drugs and she swears she never tried to administer Narcan to them, despite what the official report said."

Braddock nodded and said, "If memory serves, the Odoms were found dead in the town of Ricketts, in Asotin County."

"You know the police out there?"

"Not directly. Pretty small town."

"I understand that the Odoms lived in Kittitas County. Is Ricketts far from there?"

"Over a four-and-a-half-hour drive, though a chunk of it is on the interstate. But with a lot of snow it can get treacherous going through the Cascades, even on the highway. And once you get off the highway, it's a lot of back roads, and the elevations crank back up once you get to Garfield and Asotin counties, from four to over six thousand feet."

"Any idea why the Odoms were in Ricketts?"

"No. But it wasn't my case, and the statewide bulletins we get didn't say. Did the girl know why?"

"I didn't really ask her, at least directly. And she didn't want to relive the moment."

Braddock nodded, his eyes glimmering. "If you want to see misery mixed with horror, Devine, try telling your kids that their mother's dead. So I can sympathize with that little girl." Braddock snapped back and said, "Okay, I appreciate *your* candor. So you said you came out here to escort the girl to see Glass. Has that happened?"

"It has."

"Does she want to go live with him?"

"Seems to. He's rich and she's suffered through poverty, and has no other family."

"Okay. What's DHS's interest?"

"It's not just us. The Bureau placed Betsy Odom into protective custody shortly after her parents died. She's been staying in Seattle with an FBI agent assigned to her. So Danny Glass is the obvious interest, but Odom told me she never even met the man."

"So why waste manpower and dollars on that? What can she provide the Bureau that's of value?"

"Don't know. But the Bureau could be hedging its bets in case she *does* know something."

"But if your work is done, are you out of here?"

"I made arrangements to hang around and see if I could shed any light on the case."

"And why would you want to do that?"

"I don't like things that don't make sense," replied Devine.

"Considering your age, you didn't stay in for the full retirement ride, even though you made captain. You said you stood up to those in uniform and it didn't sit well with the Army brass? Was that the reason you left the Army prematurely?"

"There's a reason for everything, and that's as good as any."

"I'll be up front, I have no jurisdiction to work the Odoms' deaths."

"But you *are* working the Rollins case. And maybe the twain shall meet one day."

"Is your theory that Rollins was killed by Glass because he was going to tell you something incriminating about him that might foul up his chances to adopt his niece?"

"It's a theory. Maybe the only one I have right now. But Perry Rollins was a low-level crook. So how does he get dirt on a global kingpin like Glass?"

"Shit happens, even to global kingpins," replied Braddock. "I think I might have to speak to Betsy Odom."

"You'll have to go through the Bureau."

"Oh, joy, joy," said Braddock, making Devine grin.

"I guess I get the FBI hedging its bets on Odom, on the off chance she has something on her uncle. But then why does Glass want to adopt her? If he had her parents killed, why not kill her, too?"

Devine thought back to Glass's manner around Odom.

"Well, from what I saw, he genuinely seems to care for the girl."

"Well, presumably he loved his sister, too, and *she's* dead."

"Maybe he knows who actually killed her and her husband, and wants to protect Betsy from them."

Braddock nodded slowly. "A guy like Glass does have a lot of enemies. But if the cops in Ricketts covered this up and wrote a bullshit report? They're working for whoever *did* kill them."

"I might have to make my way out there and look around."

"Make sure you're armed and watch your back every minute."

"But you said you didn't really know the cops in Ricketts?"

"But I know cops who do. Ricketts is isolated in a mountainous corner of the state where people do what they have to in order to get by. And from what I've been told, the longtime police chief there, Eric King, lives up to his surname. That town is *his* domain."

"Could he be bought off to falsify the circumstances of the Odoms' deaths?"

"Let me put it this way: I have good friends in WASPC, which is an organization of sheriffs and police chiefs in the state. And almost none of them are fans of Eric King."

"If his reputation is that bad, why is he still in power?"

"Police chiefs are appointed, usually by the city council. I've also been told that no one out there is brave enough to take him on. And apparently no one has been able to prove anything criminal about the man. Cops are bad about taking on other cops no matter if they deserve it."

"*You* did," Devine pointed out.

"Yeah, and look what it cost me."

"Okay, so anything on Rollins's murder?" asked Devine.

"One witness thinks he saw a man come out of the men's room shortly before Rollins staggered out bleeding. But he couldn't give a good description primarily because he was drunk. And nothing has jumped out forensically so far."

"Anything found on Rollins that might be helpful?"

"Keys to his apartment. We've been through it. If he had information to sell to you, it was either in his head only, or he kept it somewhere else. I've begun inquiries into his financial accounts, whether he had a safe-deposit box, that sort of thing."

"Mind if I have a look at his place?"

"Why?"

"Second pair of eyes, and if his death *is* connected to Glass, then the feds are going to be involved at some point. Would you rather have me, or the FBI horning in from the get-go?"

Braddock gave him the address of Rollins's apartment. "I'll alert my people that you'll be coming around. Anything occurs to you, I expect to be the first to be told. *Ahead* of the FBI."

"You have my word on that."

"Uh-huh." Braddock stopped and stared at him. "So, whatever Rollins told you before he croaked? Has it become less garbled in your head?"

Devine decided to tell Braddock, but he couldn't see how it would be helpful.

"He said what sounded like *cuckoo*, and something that sounded like *gas*."

Devine looked at the detective in some embarrassment.

Braddock said, "Okay, either a bird or he was referring to a whack job, and fuel? Hell, that breaks the whole case wide open."

CHAPTER

13

DEVINE RENTED A TOYOTA 4RUNNER. Google maps showed the Kittitas county line to be about 115 miles away, all on the interstate with passage over a section of the Cascade Mountains. Although with the directions he'd been given by Korey Rose, he would have to tack on more miles and time to get to the trailer and that would not be on an interstate. He figured he might need some extra oomph and four-wheel-drive capability once he got off the highway, especially if the weather unloaded on him.

He drove out of Seattle and headed east. The verdant wall of the Cascades ran from Northern California to British Columbia and continually filled his windshield the farther east he traveled. A herd of semis occupied all the lanes, which, during the trip, went up and down in number from four to three to two. Later, he got off I-90 and started following the directions that Rose had provided him. It was hilly, mountainous country. He became lost once but then figured out his mistake, backtracked, and pulled up to the Odoms' home about twenty minutes later after traversing a single-lane unpaved road through some dense forest. It was darker and cooler here and he was glad he had worn his heavier jacket.

The trailer was a double-wide with white aluminum siding and a black-shingled roof planted on strategically placed short columns of cinderblocks. Knotted pressure-treated plank steps led up to the front door. Nate Shore had not been kidding about the Odoms living in the boonies. Devine wondered why they had chosen this location to literally set down their first home.

He parked, got out, and looked around.

Since the Odoms' deaths had been ruled an accidental overdose, he supposed the police had not made a search here. The home was apparently just sitting empty.

He did a perimeter walk and in the rear yard saw an old blackened and dented fifty-gallon metal barrel that looked like it had been used to incinerate trash. A large propane tank was set next to the right side of the home. The back door was locked. Devine took out his lockpick gun and it made short work of this obstacle.

Devine found himself in the small kitchen, which occupied the middle of the structure. As he looked around, Devine saw that it was roomier inside than it had looked on the outside. There were three bedrooms, two baths, a kitchen with a small dining room adjacent to it, and a tiny living room as an afterthought by the front entrance. Although only about nine hundred square feet, Devine thought it must have felt like a mansion of permanence to a family that had previously endured periods of homelessness.

He did a quick search of the largest bedroom at one end, which was clearly Dwayne and Alice's space, and found nothing helpful. He also didn't find any drug paraphernalia, which bolstered Odom and her friends' claims about her parents not being users. The middle bedroom looked used, only he wasn't initially sure by whom. But when he saw some of the items in it, he had a clearer idea of the occupants.

At the other end of the trailer was obviously Betsy Odom's room. It looked like a typical preteen's room, whatever that actually meant these days, although he saw no computer or other electronic device. But Devine knew she had her phone with her. Piles of clothes and stacks of books, which he noted had been borrowed from the public library. The girl's tastes were eclectic—fantasy, sci-fi, a couple of what looked to be romances, a primer on flowers and herbs, a cookbook, three biographies on women who had pulverized glass ceilings and... He sat on the bed and looked at the last book in the stack.

Think and Grow Rich. It was a revised and updated version of the longtime bestseller.

He opened it and saw that there was a stamp on the

inside cover: BOOKCAVE SECONDHAND BOOKS. With a price tag of one dollar.

Devine flipped through the book and saw many underlined sentences and margin notes written presumably in Betsy Odom's hand. Things like, "Remember the part about believing in yourself." And "You *can* do this too." And lastly, "I *will* take care of my parents."

Okay, that qualifies as heart-wrenching.

He slipped the book into his jacket and looked around at the mess of clothes. They must not have let her come back here after her parents' deaths, or else someone had gotten Odom a few things to wear.

He then remembered her complaint about her tight clothes and shoes. He looked around, found an empty duffel bag, and piled as many clothes, shoes, books, and other things that the girl might want or need into it as he could, and zipped it closed.

He was about to head out when through a window he noted movement in the woods on the left side of the trailer. He squatted down and peered through the glass. When he saw who it was, Devine rose and walked out the rear door, the duffel hefted over his shoulder.

"What are you two doing back here?" he asked.

Korey Rose and Nate Shore, both looking startled, walked out of the woods and came over to him.

"Hey, *Korey* and *Nate*, good to see you again," said Devine.

Rose said sheepishly, "You talked to Betsy, right? She told you who we was?"

"She also said you were nice guys who helped out around here."

"They helped us mor'n we helped them, that's the dang truth," said Shore.

"She also said you were a great cook, Korey."

"I know my way 'round a stove and skillet," he replied modestly. "People got to eat, or so my old granny told me."

Shore eyed the duffel suspiciously. "Hey, you ain't takin' stuff, are you?"

"Clothes and books and other essentials for Betsy. She didn't have much with her."

"Oh, okay," said a relieved Shore. "I thought..." But he looked embarrassed and didn't finish.

"Don't tell me you have drugs stashed in the trailer somewhere?" said Devine sharply. "That would not be good."

"Ain't no drugs in there, 'cept Advil, swear to Jesus," replied Rose. "We ain't doin' that shit no more. We well on the way to the road to recovery."

"Okay," said a clearly not convinced Devine.

"I think Nate was worried 'bout his 'magazine' collection. Some classics in there all right," added a smiling Rose, giving his partner a nudge with his elbow.

Devine looked relieved as he got what Rose was referring to. "Right. FYI, I left the old *Playboy* magazines right where I found them. A vintage collection for sure. The dumbbells, too. Eighty-pounders. Impressive."

Rose laughed. "They ain't mine. I can't lift even one of 'em with my whole body. But old Nate tosses 'em 'round like cupcakes."

Shore growled, "Exercise kicks in the endorphins. Natural drug, you see. Then I don't need the other shit."

"And the *Playboys* stimulate him, too, just in another way," noted Rose. That got him a punch in the arm from his mate.

"They was my grandaddy's and he left 'em to me. I ain't throwin' 'em in the trash. They worth somethin' all right. Money in them pages. Just got to find the right buyer is all."

"Well, since you've had them things for a long time now, I ain't sure you ever gonna find the right buyer, Nate."

Devine said, "How'd you two make it to Seattle and then back here?"

"Bus," said Rose. "Dropped us off couple miles away."

"You guys had money for that?" He noted they had on the same clothes as the previous night. They also each had a rolled-up sleeping bag and blanket bound with bungies.

Shore said, "Worked the last few days at odd jobs, scrounged up some cash that way. And Dwayne give us some money from before."

"Where'd you stay in Seattle?"

Rose laughed and held up the sleeping bag. "At the Ritz, man. Leastways behind the Dumpster. They only throw away the best food there. Last night I had me prime rib and Nate had him a real nice chicken parm."

"So what are you two doing back here?"

Shore said sheepishly, "Fact is, we ain't got no place to live right now...so's..."

Rose added, "We got us a key, from Dwayne. We was hopin' to crash here a few days is all. Till we get stuff straight," he added, giving Devine a hopeful look.

Devine looked back at the trailer. "Well, I can't tell you what to do. The police clearly haven't been here, but they may come at some point."

"We see the cops comin', we get out real fast," promised Rose.

"*Real* fast," parroted Shore. "Cops and us is oil and water. We ain't criminals, but cops look at us, that's all they see."

Devine put down the duffel, reached in his wallet, and pulled out some cash. "Here, I don't know how much good it will do, but it's all I've got on me."

Both men shook their heads. Shore said, "No way, dude, we ain't takin' your last dollar. Shit, we ain't got much, but we ain't like that."

"I can always get some more. And it's the *government's*

money, not mine," he added. "And they can always print more when they need it."

Shore slowly reached out, took the cash, and gave half of it to his friend. "Thanks."

Rose said, "Wish we could print us some money."

"You can, but it's called counterfeiting when citizens do it. Now, can I drive you anywhere?"

"We ain't had nuthin' to eat today," said Rose. He held up the cash. "Nice little place a few miles from here. Know the cook, does a real good job. Pride in his food. We can spot you for a meal, on your dime." He smiled weakly.

"Come on, but it's my treat. You guys have phones?"

They shook their heads.

At the restaurant in the small town Devine drove them to, both men devoured three appetizers and an entrée each. Devine found a place to buy them a prepaid phone. Next he drove them to a grocery store and Rose carefully selected, and Devine purchased, some food for the pair. He also purchased two food gift cards for them. After that, he dropped them back off at the trailer.

"So, it's really okay if we stay here awhile?" said Shore with a little shiver and coughing into his elbow. Devine noted that his dirty coat was lightweight and the nighttime temps here would quickly fall below freezing.

"In fact, you can watch over the place. I guess now it belongs to Betsy."

"Yeah, we look after it for her," said Rose enthusiastically. "And tell her we say hello."

"Do you know how they came to live here?" asked Devine.

Rose said, "Don't know why he picked this place, but Dwayne bought a couple acres. They delivered the whole dang house on a big-ass truck. We was here when it came rollin' down the road. Barely 'nuff room to get the sucker in."

Shore added, "It come in two pieces, see, and these dudes just screwed it together." He grinned. "Like a damn dollhouse."

"They was real good," said Rose. "Did the whole thing in a few hours. Boom, boom, boom. Talked to one of the dudes. He say they got trained real good but they don't get paid shit. And no health care. I mean, what is that about? Man works hard, he should be able to go see the doc and all if he gets hurt or sick."

"All that couldn't have been cheap," noted Devine.

Rose said, "Don't know how much the land cost, but Dwayne say it cost over a hundred and thirty thousand buckaroos for the house and to set it up and all. Still way cheaper than a regular house, I guess. Don't know, ain't never had no regular house. Hell, no house."

"But what about when you were growing up?" asked Devine.

"Just lived with relatives here and there, and they

either rented or squatted, or lived in the basement of other folks' places."

"And your parents?"

"Joy juice got 'em when I was a baby."

"Joy juice?"

"Heroin and drivin' ain't too good a combo. They went right off a cliff, so's I was told."

Devine looked at Shore. "You still have family?"

"Cops and cancer got my parents. Lived some with my grandparents. Really been on my own since I was fifteen."

"I'm really sorry, guys. You said you met Dwayne in school?"

Shore said, "Yep. Went to middle and high school together. He ain't had nothin', either, same as us. We formed a little gang. Not a real one, but just for fun. I played football, and Dwayne and Kor would come cheer me on."

Rose grinned. "He was real good, call him the bull-dozer. *Dozer* for short. Put the hurtin' on you, man. Coulda got a scholarship to some football college."

"Then I wrecked a knee, came out a half step slower, and it went asses-up. Glory Days, like the Boss say."

"That's Nate's way of sayin' we fucked ourselves up real good after high school," noted Rose. "But you joined the Army, Dozer, while I was doin' my cookin' thing."

Devine focused on Shore. "Army? How long were you in?"

"Too long," said Shore curtly, while not looking at him.

"How about Dwayne?" asked Devine.

"Naw. Dwayne ain't too smart but he smart 'nuff not to do what we done," said Rose.

"Then when he was 'round twenty-five he moved away," added Shore. "When he come back, he was hitched and had Betsy. Surprised the crap out of us."

"How'd you reconnect?"

"Hell, he looked us up. Don't know for sure how he done it. But he come walkin' into the rehab place we was at one day and said, 'Hey, Kor, hey, Dozer.' Like ain't no time gone by."

Shore said, "Coulda knocked me over with a feather. Made me feel real good he 'membered us like that."

"We *was* surprised," said Rose. "But then it was like we ain't never been apart, you know? Just slid back in like it was high school again. And Alice was real nice. She and Dwayne sure loved each other. She was younger than we was. Alice really looked up to Dwayne, seemed to me."

Devine nodded at all this. "So you have no idea where he got the money for the house and car?"

Rose glanced nervously at Shore, who said, "Look, Dwayne was a real nice guy, give you the shirt off his back, but he would say shit, too."

"Like what?"

Shore shrugged. "Like he won the lottery. That how he say he got this place and the car."

"The lottery? So you didn't believe him?"

Rose chuckled. "When he say it, I was lookin' at Alice and she done this eye roll thing, man. And..."

"And what?"

"Well, she ain't look too happy is all."

"And you never asked *her* where the money really came from?"

Shore said, "Tried to, once. But, man, she ain't want to go there, so's I dropped it. Alice was real nice, but you ain't want to get on her bad side. No way, no sir."

Rose added, "She pretty much did what Dwayne wanted, but that don't mean she agreed with every-thin' Dwayne wanted neither."

"Okay, thanks for the info." Devine gave them his phone number. "If someone shows up and gives you trouble or you think of anything else helpful, or just need to get in touch for anything, call me, okay?"

The men said they would, thanked him profusely, and Devine drove away thinking: *There but for the grace of God...*

CHAPTER
14

PRU JACKSON SLOWLY MADE THE sign of the cross, just in case anyone was watching. She was actually surprised her hand had so instinctively followed the correct motions, because Jackson and God had not been on speaking or praying terms for a long time now. She picked up the dying woman's hand and looked down into a face that used to resemble her own.

Children visited their dying mothers in hospice all the time, she told herself. However, it didn't make it any easier to navigate, knowing that she had plenty of company in her personal sorrow.

There had been a definite risk in Jackson's coming here to say goodbye, but this woman was worth the risk. She had also come prepared, just in case they might still be looking for her, though they had no reason to believe she was still alive. Yet they were the sort who never stopped looking.

But I'll never stop looking for them, either.

Jackson was dressed as a woman around her mother's age. Every line, every wrinkle, every eye pouch was

exquisitely done. Jackson's feigned slow-motion manner and wobbly gait were also spot-on for an unhealthy
older woman.

The name she'd written down in the visitor's log
was Karen Crawford, who had been a neighbor of her
mother's from long ago, until Crawford had retired to
Florida to live in a modest Caribbean blue-painted cottage a half-mile walk from the beach. Crawford had
no idea that Molly Jackson's spitfire of a daughter had
assumed her identity to visit her dying mother.

Jackson had reinvented herself in a form that was
not so different than the role she had occupied on
behalf of the United States government—the shining
beacon on the hill until it came time to kill, destroy,
disrupt, displace, and generally screw over others who
stood in the way of the Stars and Stripes. She had been
very good at organizing and then executing such operations, and had been awarded plaques and promotions
for her Herculean efforts on behalf of a grateful country. And then her world had come tumbling down, and
years of her life had been spent in a hellish nightmare
that not even Orwell could have come within five hundred miles of in his deepest, darkest ruminations.

Her father, now dead, had always been a nonentity in her life, fleeing the responsibility of parenting
when Jackson was only six months old, after impreg-
nating her fortyish mother against her wishes. But her

mother had loved her only child and raised her to be a strong, independent, resilient, and tenacious person. And an adult Jackson had realized that her skill set and other personal qualities could help her become a once-in-a-generation superstar in the field of espionage.

And when she had risen to the zenith of her profession, at a relatively young age, she was sacrificed for another prize that was deemed more vital to the national interest. And at that point, when the decision had been made, nothing, not her past work, or skills, or connections, could save her. Basic human decency might have carried the day in her favor, but apparently no one she worked with had any.

Once that symbolic door closed behind her, she had survived in brutal captivity for two long years that felt like fifty, where the resolute, painful sameness of every day was eclipsed only by moments of terror and agony that she never managed to see coming. Jackson had endured things she had never meted out on those whom she had targeted, because Jackson possessed hard moral stops.

Her captors had no such issues.

It had taken another two years after her escape simply to rebuild her body. She had still not yet fully recalibrated her mind past the ordeal, but she no longer had any hard moral stops.

Her full given name was Prudence, a term with a

definite understanding. She considered herself that. But also so much more.

She bent down and kissed her mother goodbye.

Using a walker, she slowly made her way down the hall with clumsy motions of her seemingly diminished arms and legs.

There was a man in a suit hovering near the front desk when she came into the lobby. Jackson looked at him without seeming to. He stood out so much, he might as well have been flashing his government badge to everyone passing by.

So they know or more likely suspect I'm still alive?

She worked her way up to the front desk, adjusted her glasses, and smiled at the suit. She purposefully fumbled with the pen, which government man politely picked up and handed to her. She wrote her name in an old lady scrawl of cursive.

"Thank you, young man," she said in an elderly person's croak and then she headed out after surreptitiously palming the pen. Her prints were on a restricted database.

She had had the cab wait for her, and the driver loaded her walker into the trunk after helping her into the rear seat.

The cab drove off as she glanced in the side mirror. The watcher in the government suit had not even bothered to come to the doorway to see her off. Standards had surely fallen since her time there.

But there was another explanation.

They suspect it's me and are playing dumb. And they have a tail on me right now.

Well, game on.

Hours later, she had gone through several different disguises and "disruption funnels" as she termed them, which were designed to throw off any pursuers no matter how skilled.

Now safe, the old woman was gone and Pru Jackson was returned to herself, whatever that actually meant these days.

Baggy clothes hid her athletically crafted and leanly muscled body. Her captors had broken bones and they had been left to reset on their own, and had done so badly. After her liberation they had had to be rebroken with grafts and rods used to repair the damage and bring her back from painful immobility. She often rose from sleep stiff and heavy-limbed.

Passing through airport security required a doctor's note since the bells went off in the face of all the metal she now carried inside her person. That was one reason she liked to fly private, and now had the financial means with which to do so.

She took an Uber to the airport and boarded a set of wings for a ride across the country.

Seattle, Washington, was her destination. She had someone she fervently wanted to meet there.

His name was Travis Devine, formerly of the United States Army, but now just another go-along operative for the very same government that had betrayed her.

She feared and respected Travis Devine, for he had also shown himself to be a survivor.

We're perhaps more alike than not, former Captain Devine.

So it was up to her now to end the man's life, because she was done relying on anyone else to do it.

Devine could have easily killed her on that train between Geneva and Milan.

And I could have killed him at Dulles Airport, when I slipped the note in his pocket.

So they were even on that score. Now, one of them was going to die.

We just have to see which one.

CHAPTER

15

JACKSON ARRIVED AT NEARLY MIDNIGHT into the cold, drizzly maw of the Pacific Northwest. She Ubered to an Airbnb located in an upscale neighborhood she never could have afforded on Uncle Sam's payroll. In the garage was a four-door Hyundai SUV and another, smaller, vehicle, which would allow her to move stealthily around the region. She checked the latter over in the garage, and also scrutinized the other pieces of equipment she'd had delivered here along with the two vehicles. All seemed in order. She unpacked the weapons case she had carried onto the plane.

The kitchen was fully stocked with a list of special foods she had ordered. She made her dinner and chewed slowly, taking her time because she had to. Jackson's digestive system had been permanently wrecked by her years-long ordeal. Water was her only libation, and sometimes even that was difficult to get and hold down. She'd had grain alcohol repeatedly forced down her throat in a bastardized offshoot method of waterboarding and, as a result, couldn't even stomach looking at a bottle of wine, beer, or liquor. The GI guy in Belgium who'd examined her gut and intestines and treated her after she'd escaped had asked her two questions: How was she still alive? And did she want to be? After what she'd endured to survive and escape to be there seeking his help, Jackson had wanted to disembowel the medico and make the asshole eat his own intestines.

Finished with her meal, she walked into the family room, turned on the gas fireplace against the chill that had settled into her bones and metal, sat down, and opened her laptop. Jackson scrolled through the pages of intel that she had paid for from various sources and that had allowed her to set her sights on Devine. He was here, on a mission, and she needed to understand that mission better in order for her to lay a plausible trap.

She knew it would not be easy.

He knows I'm after him, and he'll do his best to get to me first. But I doubt he knows I was able to follow him here.

She knew that a man named Danny Glass was the reason for Devine's presence. She knew about some of Glass's criminal endeavors and current legal troubles with the government but had no beef with him and no skin in that game.

Every man and woman for themselves from now on, especially this woman.

Jackson went to bed and slept like the dead for six

hours, which was unusual; her sleep was still often disturbed by nightmares. She rose and went to the home's small gym, where she stretched for a half hour and then ran on the treadmill for forty-five minutes. Her limbs felt clumsy and slow and her mind wasn't much better. She hated the mornings now because that was the time during her imprisonment when she would jerk awake from a wonderful dream in which she was free and happy, only to find that she was neither.

By the afternoon, she was usually fine. She wondered if that was why Devine had managed to escape her in Geneva; she had not been at her best so early in the morning. But in truth, it was more to do with Devine. He had easily killed the two men she had brought along to murder him and they supposedly operated just fine at all hours of the day and night. They had been billed as consummate professionals at taking someone else's life. They had turned out to be no challenge for the former Army Ranger.

And I wasn't any better.

She slid her finger across her jaw where Devine had slugged her on the train. She knew from experience that his blow had been delivered with power but also control.

It was not a kill strike. He saw my knife in the train window's reflection. Bad mistake on my part. But then he committed the same mistake by letting me live.

She showered, changed, had some breakfast, and drove to downtown Seattle.

She took up surveillance across the road from his hotel, finding a space on a street perpendicular to where he was staying, with her vehicle looking dead-on at the hotel entrance.

After she'd watched the place for a while, Devine emerged from his hotel, turned right, and walked down the street. Her gaze took in all of him. How he walked, how he observed all things around him. Confident but not cocky. Prepared for anything.

Just like me. Because we have to be.

She got out of her SUV and fell in behind him, but on the other side of the road. Her appearance was bulky and matronly. She found most people would never even glance at someone who looked like that, much less feel threatened by them.

Jackson knew that her years of torture had reduced her life expectancy. The doctors had suggested this to her, and she could also feel it in innumerable ways, no matter how well she ate or how hard she worked out. Her body had been taken to places no human should be forced to go, and the damage was probably irreversible. With no time to waste and enough money saved, it was now her mission to hunt down and kill everyone in her chain of command who had betrayed her and then left her to die. And as soon as Devine was taken care of, the first name on that list was going to drop.

She followed Devine to a coffee shop, where he emerged with a cup in hand. He walked back to the hotel and was standing out front waiting for something. She deduced what that was and made her way quickly back to her SUV before his rental pulled around to the front, driven by one of the valets.

A few moments later he drove off and she hooked a right on the street and took up pursuit. They drove for a while and then Devine parked in front of the Sand Bar, which was still strung with police tape. He flashed his badge and went inside while Jackson slid into an open slot across the street.

Jackson Googled the Sand Bar and scrolled down to the recent news account that detailed one Perry Rollins having been murdered inside its premises. Her pursuit of Devine had now begun.

So let the games begin. But it wasn't really a game, was it? Not with a corpse guaranteed at the end of it.

Him or me.

CHAPTER

16

H I, BETH," DEVINE SAID TO Walker as he joined her along one wall in the Sand Bar where she was typing on her laptop. She had on her blue scrubs and her hair was pulled back into a ponytail. She wore an SPD ballcap over it.

"Hey, Travis. You back for more sleuthing?" She tacked on a grin.

"Trying. I had a good talk with Braddock yesterday before I headed out of town. He's one determined detective."

"Yes, he is." She paused, her expression turning serious. "Did he tell you about . . . ?"

"He did. I'm glad they nailed the scum."

"Steve's boys are both off to college on the East Coast now, so his work really is his life. And he's been a wonderful mentor to me and some of the other young detectives coming up."

"Speaks well of him."

"You said you went out of town?"

"Just checking into something else I'm working on.

So how are things going in the Seattle cop universe? You guys holding your own?"

"Case clearance rates have fallen across the country and Seattle is no exception to that. Some of it is lack of resources, and our rank-and-file numbers are way down, just like other departments. Lots of retirements and not many recruits who want to replace them. We're down nearly a third on our uniformed division. So everyone has to work harder and that is not good for morale, even with the bump in pay we've been seeing lately. But we bust our tails to get the job done."

"They can never pay you guys enough. Look, I was going by Rollins's apartment later to check things out. Braddock said they didn't find much, but he told me I could snoop around. You want to come along?"

"I'm just about finished here, and I *did* want to take a look as well. We've been so busy here, another tech team processed his place."

"Nothing new here?"

"Unfortunately no. Give me ten minutes and we can head out."

"Sounds good, my rental is right outside. I can bring you back here."

Rollins had lived in a decrepit apartment building in a crumbling neighborhood a few miles outside of downtown in an area that Walker told him was "transitioning." What it was transitioning to, she wasn't clear about.

"His 'business' wasn't going too well, I take it," said Devine as they walked up to the second floor, where a police officer was stationed outside Rollins's door.

They were admitted to the apartment and stood there looking around.

She said, "They found no prints other than Rollins's."

"Did he have a car?"

"We could find no registration in his name."

Devine walked to the center of the small main room, off which was a bedroom and a bathroom. The kitchen consisted of an under-the-counter fridge and a microwave. There was little food in the cabinets. A few grimy clothes were piled in the closet. An old deodorant can and a worn-down bar of soap were in the bath. There were no books, no photos, no knickknacks, nothing personal really.

"I think someone was on to Rollins before he started following me."

"You're referring to the timing of his death?" she asked.

"Right. I think they were trailing him, saw him talking to me, then followed us both to the bar. After I left, they killed him. Which means they *knew* Rollins had some information that they didn't want him to sell."

"Sounds plausible, but how does that help us?" she asked.

"Not sure. You find his cell?"

"No. He has a phone registered to him but it wasn't on his person. And there was no phone found here."

"Which means they took it after they stabbed him."

"Most likely yes."

"Can you get into the data?"

"We have a warrant request in."

"The thing is, I don't figure Rollins for a loose lips kind of guy. He made his money by finding secrets and then selling them. So how did they latch on to him in the first place?"

"Everybody makes mistakes."

"Well, he offered me dirt on Danny Glass, so maybe he offered it to others."

"Including the people who killed him?" said Walker in a skeptical tone.

Devine made a show of looking around the dingy apartment. "Well, it's not like the guy's business was all that lucrative, unless he's got millions socked away in some offshore 401(k). So he might have been that desperate."

"You don't mess with a guy like Danny Glass without having some sort of Plan B."

Devine nodded. "I think Rollins was at least smart enough to know *that*. So whatever info he had, he would have kept someplace safe, no matter what happened to him. As insurance, but it didn't seem to protect him in this case."

"So, if Glass figured that out, and let's assume he did, he would want to find it before someone else does."

"Right." The next moment Devine froze. He pulled out his phone and emailed something.

He pointed at her pants pocket, where the outline of her phone was visible. Walker read the email he'd just sent her and glanced up at him, surprised.

Devine said, "Well, I'm not ashamed to admit that it's too complicated for me. We're not going to find anything out here. Let's head on."

They left the apartment.

"The email you sent? You think they had Rollins under surveillance somehow?"

"It would make sense," said Devine.

Devine led her to the apartment that was on the other side of Rollins's place and knocked on the door. Over the noise of a TV playing inside, they also heard a thumping sound coming toward them. When it opened, the elderly woman there was sitting on a rollator with a cane in one hand. The cane's hitting the floor as she was moving along must have been the thumping sound they'd heard, Devine deduced.

"Yeah?" she said in an irritated tone. "Make it snappy. I'm binge-streaming."

"I'm sorry, ma'am." He glanced up at the number 302 on her door. "We're looking for Doug Simms. We have information that he lives in Apartment 306, but he's not answering. Do you know Doug?"

"Who's asking, fella?"

TO DIE FOR 121

Walker held out her badge. "Seattle PD. And you are?"

Scowling, she said, "Lynn Martin."

"So, 306?" asked Devine.

"This 'Doug Simms,' whoever the hell he is, doesn't live there, because nobody lives there. Been empty for weeks."

"How about Apartment 304?" asked Devine.

"You a cop, too?" asked Martin.

"He's working with us," explained Walker.

"Uh-huh. Seems fishy to me. Perry Rollins lived in 304. And he's not home because he's dead, or so says the TV news."

"You knew Mr. Rollins?" asked Walker.

"As well as anybody. Sure, he was shady, but I liked him okay. Brought some, what you call, excitement to this place. Otherwise it's just a humdrum mausoleum, so to speak, and I'm not dead, at least not yet. He helped out around my place. Repaired stuff. Leaky toilet, hole in the wall, and he repainted my kitchen. Very handy. And he didn't charge much. I mostly paid him in food. And he was always nice to Miss Persimmon."

"Who?" asked Devine.

"My cat."

"Can we come in and talk for a few minutes?" said Devine.

"No!"

"Why not?"

"I'm not wasting what little time I have left on you. And I'm streaming!"

She shut the door in their faces.

"Wouldn't want to get on her bad side," noted Walker.

"I think we just did."

They huddled in front of 306 and Devine took out his lockpick gun.

"I didn't see that," noted Walker, giving him a look.

"See what?" said Devine.

A moment later they were in the apartment. It didn't take long. Attached to the wall that adjoined Rollins's was a black device about three inches in length. Walker took a photo of it and then they left.

"Listening device," he said as Walker nodded in agreement. "Surprised they didn't come here and remove it. Any way to track where that signal is going without letting them know we found it?"

"I can try," she said. "I'll get an IT team here and see what they can do. I can stay here and meet them. They can try to capture the signal out here." She eyed him appraisingly. "We didn't have a warrant to go in there. You must do things differently at DHS."

"Yeah, we must. Be sure to fill in Braddock on all this. I told him I'd keep him in the loop."

He left her there and headed on to his next investigative stop: Betsy Odom.

17

W HAT ARE YOU DOING BACK here?" said a surprised Saxby after she'd answered the door.

Devine set down the duffel he was carrying and said, "I brought Betsy some clothes and other stuff from her trailer. And I need to talk to her."

"Why?"

"Rollins's murder."

"You didn't think it was significant enough for her not to meet with her uncle. So what's the big deal now?"

"The big deal is now we know more. So I *need* to talk to Betsy," he added sharply.

"Okay, but I'm there as well. Otherwise, you can shove off," Saxby shot back.

Devine reluctantly agreed to this, and the FBI agent got the girl from her room.

Odom looked sleepy and disheveled and still in her pajamas. Around her neck was a pair of pale green headphones.

"You okay?" he asked.

She rubbed her eyes. "Fine. Is that all you wanted to know? I was sleeping in."

He hefted the duffel. "I got you some clothes and other things from your home."

She instantly perked up and said, "Awesome. How did you even know where it was?"

"Your buds, Nate Shore and Korey Rose. They're actually there keeping watch over it."

She took the duffel from him. "Thanks, Travis. I just had the stuff I was wearing in the car, and some clothes in the trunk my mom always kept in a bag."

"Why was that?" asked Devine.

"In case we had to leave someplace...you know, fast," she replied, looking embarrassed.

"There are books in there, too." Devine glanced at Saxby. "Speaking of books, what's she doing for school?"

"My mom was homeschooling me," answered Odom.

"I didn't see any school supplies or workbooks in the house."

"She had her own way of doing things. And it worked okay for me," Odom added stiffly.

He once more looked at Saxby. "How long is she going to be kept in this place? And for what reason?"

"You *know* what the reason is."

"No, I'm not sure I do. But I'll take you both out to eat and we can discuss it."

"I'm starving," said Odom. "But does she have to go, too?"

"Yes, I do," retorted Saxby. "And for the record, *he* doesn't control my actions," she added angrily. "And neither do you."

"Get dressed, Betsy, and we'll head out," said Devine.

"Not the burger place," said Odom. "After the Four Seasons, my stomach expects better."

She went back into her bedroom.

"Great," snarled Saxby. "Now the kid's turning into a food snob."

"So what *is* the end game here, Agent Saxby?"

"Just call me Ellen," she said wearily as she collapsed onto the couch. She pulled out a cigarette but didn't light it this time. "FYI, I've communicated with my superiors about what we talked about. And they have not gotten back to me yet. Which tells me that there is some difference of opinion on how to proceed with the circumstances of the Odoms' deaths."

He sat in a chair opposite her. "What's Betsy's value to you guys? Am I missing something here?"

"Look, I'm a foot soldier like you. I just follow orders, okay?" she said, crumpling up the cigarette and tossing it into the waste can. She picked up a bottle of water and drained what remained in it. "But we can't underestimate Danny Glass," she said in a firm voice.

"The man may have an angle on this we haven't even thought of. I've worked enough cases that changed on a dime and led to an ending no one saw coming. You let your guard down even a little bit, you're screwed."

With this astute observation, Devine felt better about Saxby's abilities as an agent.

"Okay, then who out there may want to harm her?"

"Well, if her parents didn't die from a drug overdose like she claims, then whoever killed them would certainly not be a friend of hers."

"But that doesn't make any sense. Why not just kill Betsy at the same time?"

"Again, above my pay grade, Devine. So what's new on Rollins's murder?"

He filled her in, including the fact of the listening device in the apartment next to Rollins.

"Rollins apparently had dirt on Glass, maybe enough to screw up his guardianship and adoption of his niece. And someone had him under surveillance and now he's dead."

Saxby nodded. "Okay, that is definitely a motive for Glass to have him killed. And maybe he was the one to bug Rollins's place, too."

The bedroom opened, revealing Odom in some of the clothes Devine had brought.

She said eagerly, "Okay, let's go eat."

CHAPTER

18

THEY WALKED FOUR BLOCKS TO a seafood restaurant, which prominently displayed most of its elaborate offerings in the front window. Devine was hungry, and Odom looked ready to eat a car. Saxby had walked listlessly along, looking at the pavement while smoking a cigarette.

They ordered, and while they waited, Devine told Odom about Rollins, what he had approached Devine about, and then his being found dead at the Sand Bar.

"Had either of your parents ever mentioned Rollins?" he asked.

"No," said a visibly shaken Odom.

He noted this and said, "I wish I didn't have to talk to you about things like this, Betsy, but you need to know what's going on."

"But we're not going to let anyone hurt you," chimed in Saxby.

Devine glanced at her for a moment before continuing, "Rollins knew something about your uncle, Betsy. Something that he wanted to sell me."

"For how much?" asked Odom.

"A hundred thousand dollars."

Saxby exclaimed, "Damn, it must have been something really bad, then."

"Or it could be crap," countered Odom.

"It could be," said Devine. "But he had to know that if it turned out to be made up, he would be in trouble. It could be that he had *something* of value. And if so, I doubt it would just be in his head. There had to be some hard evidence backing up what he was going to tell me. And I believe he would have put that in a very safe place."

"But you have no clue where it might be?" asked Saxby.

"No." Devine eyed Odom. "If it's really bad, would you still want to go live with your uncle?"

"Depends on what you call 'really bad,'" she shot back.

Again, Devine was struck by how mature she was. At least in some respects. Then he thought of the book she had been reading and making notes in: *Think and Grow Rich*.

Devine had been raised in upper-middle-class comfort in Connecticut, provided by his father's thriving dental practice. He had never been hungry or homeless or anything approaching what Betsy Odom had endured. So he could well understand the lure of being adopted by a rich relative, no matter his morals.

Saxby said, "What will you do to find out what he knew?"

"I don't have a lot of leads."

She said, "Well, on another front, we heard from Glass's lawyers. A hearing on his emergency guardianship petition has been scheduled for Thursday."

Devine glanced at Odom to see her reaction to this.

The girl was as stone-faced as the first time Devine had met her.

"And if his guardianship is approved, then she goes to live with him where?" he asked.

"He has to remain in Seattle for the RICO case, so he can't fly off to Europe or Asia with her, if that's what you mean."

Devine noted that Odom looked alarmed that this had even been a possibility.

Saxby continued, "But I suppose he could send Betsy to one of his properties. There's no restriction on *her* travel, obviously. But he has to have the emergency guardianship granted first, and I can tell you that DOJ will fight that strenuously."

Their food came, and while they ate, Devine said, "Betsy, you mentioned your mom talked to you about her brother. What did she say about him?"

Odom kept eating her fried shrimp, dipping them liberally into the cocktail sauce.

"You can't remember anything?" said Saxby.

Odom swallowed and took a moment to wipe her mouth. "Look, she said he was rich, okay? And that he'd been in the Army. And that he had protected her growing up. I guess my grandfather was not a nice guy, or something like that."

"Did she know about any of her brother's businesses?" asked Saxby.

"You mean did she know if he was a crook? I don't think so. At least she never said that to me."

"I'm working with a Detective Braddock on Rollins's murder, but I also need to check out where your parents died," said Devine. "I know this is really painful, but anything you can tell me about that day would be helpful. If they weren't drug users, then they died another way." He added, "I want to find out the truth, like you asked me to do."

"Why am I just now hearing about her asking you to do that?" groused Saxby. "And don't say it slipped your mind again. That won't cut it, Devine."

He didn't answer her, but kept his focus on Odom. Devine had a feeling this might be a pivotal moment.

Odom swallowed a mouthful of rice, put down her fork, and played with a piece of parsley on her plate.

He said, "The town of Ricketts is in Asotin County, nearly a five-hour drive away from where you all lived. So around a ten-hour round trip for you and your parents. Why were you even there that day? Did your parents know somebody from there, Betsy?"

She stopped playing with the parsley. "They didn't tell me. We just went."

"What did you do while you were there?" asked Devine.

"We had some lunch. A place in the little downtown area."

"Do you remember the name?" asked Devine.

"No. It was just a crummy place."

Saxby said, "But do you remember anything about it? The interior? Uniforms the staff wore?"

She thought for a moment. "The waitress had on a black skirt and a white shirt."

"Pretty standard. What else?"

"There was a bar." She squinted. "And a jukebox."

Saxby said, "Do you remember if your meal had a particular name? Or did the food have a theme to it?"

Odom brightened. "Yeah, the menus."

"What about them?"

"They were shaped like a hat. A cowboy hat."

Devine glanced at Saxby. "Okay, that should be enough. So your parents never told you why they were there?"

"No. We just had lunch. Then they met some guys later while I was in the car."

Devine stiffened. "Some guys? Where did they meet them?"

"We got in the car and drove out of town a bit. My dad pulled off. There was another car parked there. Two guys got out and so did my parents. They told me to wait in the car."

"And they talked?" interjected Saxby.

"Right. For a few minutes."

"Did they just talk or did they do anything else?" asked Devine.

"One of the guys gave my dad something."

Both Devine and Saxby perked up. "What?" asked Devine.

"It was a duffel bag."

"How big?"

"About the same size as the one you just brought me with my stuff."

"Then what happened?"

"My dad set it down, opened it, and looked inside. Then he closed it and the guys left and my parents got back in the car and we drove off."

"Did they show you what was in it?"

"No, my dad put it in the trunk before he got back in the car."

"And they didn't tell you anything about the meeting? Or what was in the duffel?"

"No. I was sleepy after lunch and I was sort of dozing off when they got back in the car."

"And how much later did they start to get sick?"

"It was only a couple of minutes. Dad suddenly pulled off the road. He was having trouble breathing. I…I didn't notice right away because I guess I had started to doze off again. I asked him what was wrong and then I saw that my mom was looking bad, too. And then they…they both weren't breathing." She looked away. "I called nine-one-one and they came and…that's all I know."

"What happened to the duffel?" asked Saxby.

"I don't know. I guess it might still be in the car."

"Which is still in Ricketts?"

"The cops drove me to the police station. I don't know what happened to our car."

"Did the two guys look like any of the men with your uncle at the Four Seasons?"

"No, nothing like them."

"Did you tell the police or the FBI about your parents' meeting the men and them receiving the duffel?"

Odom glanced at Saxby. "No, they never asked."

Devine shot Saxby a look. "Okay, Betsy, thanks. This has been a big help."

"Why does DHS care about this?" asked Saxby irritably. "Is it even their jurisdiction?"

"Everything on American soil is their jurisdiction." Devine had no idea if that was true, but he had no interest in getting into a pissing contest with the Bureau right now, either.

"So what's your next move?" asked Saxby.

"I'm going to have to travel to Ricketts, where I've been told the police chief is his own little dictator."

"Exactly where is it located?" asked Saxby.

"Southeast corner of the state. Pretty remote."

"Like where we lived," said Odom. "Not many people around."

"Did your parents work?" asked Devine.

"Dad did off and on. There are some farms out there and Dad said they grow a lot of hay, stuff like that. It goes out of the country for, like, racehorses—least that's what he said. Then sometimes he'd work construction, or do some landscaping stuff. There was like a community college not too far away, where he'd go to work sometimes. Dad liked to be outdoors. My mom homeschooled me like I said, and took care of the house and all. But she would work down at the local grocery store, stocking shelves and stuff, in her spare time."

"I know it's pretty remote. But did you have any neighbors? Any friends?"

"The closest home was miles away. And there was nobody around there my age. So I just had my parents. And Nate and Kor when they would visit."

Saxby glanced at Devine. "You better be careful when you visit Ricketts; some local cops see feds as the enemy."

Maybe we are, thought Devine. He was also wondering why the FBI hadn't questioned Odom about her parents' deaths, or about any strange events on their final day of life. Did they know something Devine didn't?

After they'd finished eating and left, the older woman who had been seated a half dozen tables away and listening to something with her AirPods in watched them go, while fingering a gaudy broach pinned to her blouse.

Pru Jackson had just learned an awful lot. She was still going to kill Devine, but it had gotten a bit more complicated.

19

DEVINE LEFT SAXBY AND ODOM back at their hotel and he drove to his. As he was about to step inside, a man appeared next to him. He'd been waiting just inside the small archway that led into the hotel.

"Mr. Devine?"

He turned to see Dennis Hastings, Glass's man, standing there. Hastings was all mean-looking, and clearly not wanting to be here.

"Yeah?"

"Mr. Glass wants to meet with you."

"He'll have to make an appointment. I'm busy."

Hastings looked scandalized. "Mr. Glass wants to meet with you *now*."

"Well, like the song says, you can't always get what you want."

"That does *not* apply to Mr. Glass."

"Sure it does. And why does he want to meet with me?"

"He mentioned something about Operation Ashura? You know what he meant by that?"

This remark gave Devine pause. He said, "I do."

"So you'll come?" said Hastings politely, although his severe expression did not match his tone. Devine could tell he was hankering for a fight, which the man would lose unless he had about a half dozen other armed foot soldiers lurking around. And Hastings might, if he was smart.

"Yes, but I'll get there on my own."

"I have a vehicle right here." He pointed to a black SUV with heavily tinted windows that looked just like the one that Devine had seen sliding into view back in Virginia. But there were lots of tinted-glass black SUVs and lots of dangerous people who rode in them.

"Then enjoy your ride in it. I'll be at the hotel in twenty minutes."

A clearly frustrated Hastings walked off and climbed into the SUV, and it drove away while Devine ordered up a ride on his phone app. And he now knew that Danny Glass *had* remembered Devine from their combat days in the Middle East. That was the first and only time the two soldiers' paths had crossed.

Operation Ashura had been led by Iraqi forces along with Shia militia supported by Iran to take back the town of Jurf al-Sakhar in Iraq, which was strategically located near Baghdad. America was not supposed to have any troops on the ground in this particular conflict, but then three platoons of American soldiers had been included in the assault to make sure that it was successful. They were also tasked with coordinating U.S. air strikes on the Islamic State of Iraq and the Levant, also known as ISIL. It was hard fought on both sides, and the combat momentum had swung back and forth. However, eventually they had succeeded in retaking Jurf al-Sakhar and driven out ISIL. This also had allowed millions of Shias safe passage to undertake a pilgrimage to Karbala and Anajaf for fasting and prayers to commemorate the Day of Ashura.

Devine and Danny Glass had been components of different military elements sent in for the battle. The then Lieutenant Devine had commanded one of the platoons. He and his men had been caught in a chaotic crossfire, ultimately finding their retreat cut off by over two hundred hardened ISIL fighters who charged forward to slaughter the far smaller American force. They were also supported by RPGs, one heavy machine gun, and two light machine guns, and things were looking dicey. And Devine knew that if ISIL captured them, they would parade them on social media and broadcast to the world that American soldiers were part of the assault on Iraqi soil when they were only supposed to be there in support occupations. And then he and his surviving men would have probably been beheaded for all the world to see.

The optics would have been awful. But that day

Devine had been far more worried about the lives of his men than any political fallout.

A wounded Danny Glass had been truly heroic, saving the lives of a slew of his fellow soldiers, at great risk to himself. And it was due in large part to Glass's efforts that Devine and his men had been able to hang on until reinforcements arrived.

Devine had written a commendation letter for him, which had been awarded, so his connection to Glass was part of official Army records.

He wondered, and not for the first time, whether he had been selected for this mission because of that tie.

But why would that matter? Glass was the enemy here. Wasn't he?

He arrived at the Four Seasons and was met in the lobby by Hastings.

"Mr. Glass is in the presidential suite," said Hastings.

"Of course he is," replied Devine.

They rode the elevator up. Stationed outside the presidential suite were two scarred cartel gunner types who looked like they had never laughed in their entire lives. And both seemed like they would be delighted to bang a round into Devine's skull, no charge.

Hastings knocked and the door was opened by another man who looked just like the two at the door, only meaner. Devine and Hastings were escorted into a large living area off the foyer that had sweeping views of the bay through two walls of windows, and a large-screen TV on another wall, with a gas fireplace below. The glow of the bluish-red flames warmed the space. There Glass sat, dressed in dark slacks and a light blue cashmere sweater, looking lean, engaged, and… *happy*, thought Devine. For a man under indictment for crimes that could send him to prison for life, Glass didn't seem to have a care in the world, Devine thought for a second time. And again, he wondered why.

Glass rose from his chair and extended his hand to Devine.

"Forgive me for not acknowledging you when you brought Betsy to me. I was pretty damn sure it was you, but then I thought you were still in the Army and convinced myself it couldn't be Lieutenant Travis Devine."

"It's just *Travis* Devine now, Mr. Glass. And I mustered out as a captain."

"Make it Danny. I've never been much of a mister."

"Okay, *Danny*."

Glass indicated a chair and they sat across from one another. Devine noted that Hastings and the other side of armed beef had disappeared from view, but he doubted they had gone far.

"So, you're a federal agent now?" said Glass.

"Something like that. And you?"

Glass smiled. "I'm sure you've been thoroughly

briefed on what I've been up to. At least the government's side of things."

"So there's another side?"

"There's *always* another side, Travis. Presumed innocent and all, right?"

"Right."

"Why did you get out of the Army?"

"I had a sense my luck was running out," replied Devine.

"I can relate. Who wants to die in a foreign land for no good reason?"

"Well, we were serving our country."

"Like I said, no good reason."

Devine let this slap against the Stars and Stripes slide. "So why did you want to see me? I know you're a busy guy. Must be a reason."

"Just wanted to say hello to a fellow soldier who was with me in a tight spot."

"We all owed you. I said so in my letter to the brass."

"I'm glad you said that, Travis. The *owing* part, at least."

The tension in the room had gone from eleven all the way to doomsday.

"You understand me?" said Glass.

"I must be slow, so no, I don't."

"Betsy is a great kid. What happened to my sister and her husband? Beyond tragic."

"Yeah, it was." Devine decided to take a shot at something and also divert the direction of the conversation. "Did you know of their drug use?"

"I didn't know much of anything about them. They got married while I was overseas. I saw Alice when I was on leave, and Dwayne was off looking for work, which he almost never found. This was before they had Betsy. After she was born, they moved around a lot. Yesterday was the first time I've actually seen her in person."

"And now you want to be her guardian?"

"Our parents are long dead. And Dwayne's folks are, too. I feel obligated. I'm all she has left. Betsy is my family."

"So the owing part?" said Devine, bringing the talk full circle. "Just to be crystal clear, I have no control over what happens to her. And even if I did, I would do nothing to interfere in the process."

Glass's features went from light and upbeat to junkyard dog in a breath. "So you don't really feel like you owe me then? Your words were just bullshit?"

"You had to know I could do nothing for you, Danny. So why am I really here?"

"I remember you as a by-the-book kind of guy. But people change. Maybe you haven't."

"I haven't, at least not with respect to something like that."

"Then I have my answer and this meeting was worth it for me."

"Then let's make it worth it for *me*. You ever hear of a guy named Perry Rollins?"

"Sorry, rings no bells," Glass said so smoothly, Devine figured he was lying.

"Okay. You and Betsy seemed to hit it off at brunch."

"She reminds me a lot of Alice. And she wants to come live with me. I can provide for her."

"Even from prison?"

"My lawyers will do their thing. We'll see how it goes. I've been in tight places before and walked out alive, as you know. But regardless, Betsy will be taken care of."

"I understand the government's case has been hit with some witnesses no longer breathing?"

"If you say so," Glass said offhandedly. "I haven't been keeping track. My focus is Betsy."

"If I was looking at life in prison, I'm not sure I'd be thinking about anything else."

"Well, that's the difference between you and me, apparently," retorted Glass.

"Right. I'll guess I'll be going," said Devine, rising.

"So, what's the deal with this Rollins guy?" said Glass, who remained sitting.

"He's dead. Somebody murdered him at the Sand Bar here in Seattle."

"Why would someone want him dead?"

"Maybe he had something on somebody, something incriminating, and that person didn't want Rollins to spill."

"When was he killed?"

Devine told him.

Glass slid up his pant leg to reveal his ankle monitor. "I was here that night. And this thing will prove it."

"Why would you think I suspected you would have had a hand in his murder?"

"Because the feds keep blaming me for every little goddamned thing," Glass said coolly.

"A guy like you has other assets to do his bidding. Four of them are within calling distance right now."

"I can see you've drunk the government Kool-Aid, Mr. West Pointer. I was just a lowly grunt."

"You fought hard and bravely, Danny. I don't care if you didn't have bars on the shoulder."

"Long time ago."

"Apparently, a *lifetime* ago with how things have gone with you," said Devine. "Take care and good luck. I think you're probably going to need it."

CHAPTER

20

THE NEXT MORNING DEVINE PACKED his duffel. He had two pistols and extra mags and wondered if he could rent an RPG launcher around here somewhere for his pilgrimage to Ricketts.

As he was driving out of Seattle in the Toyota 4Runner and heading east, Emerson Campbell phoned him.

"We're still digging up background on the Odoms and Perry Rollins. It'll be emailed to you when complete."

"What can you tell me now?"

"Dwayne Odom kicked around the Pacific Northwest after high school. Then, in his mid-twenties, he headed east for a fresh start. Sometime after that, he met Alice in her hometown in Ohio. They got married and later had their daughter. Years after that, they moved back to the Seattle area. And Danny Glass was also far older than his sister. She might have been an unplanned pregnancy."

"I understand Glass was close to Alice?"

"Yes, and he protected Alice from her father. From

what we found out the man apparently was not very nurturing. A real sadist, in fact."

"But what happened when Glass joined the Army and could no longer protect her? Alice would have still been a minor living at home."

"From what we could learn, it was rough for her, although her mother apparently did what she could to shield her daughter from him. And one of the people we talked to who knew the Glasses well said that when Alice finished high school, some family friends got her a job and helped her rent a little house with a room-mate across town. She didn't see her father much after that."

"Glass said he saw Alice after she married Dwayne and he was back in town on leave. Betsy wasn't born yet, so it was early on in the marriage. Dwayne was off trying to find work."

"Well, he rarely held a job long, according to our investigation."

"I talked to his friends out here and they said the same thing. The money to buy the house and car? Any leads on that?"

"We looked at the Odoms' bank records for the time in question. They had no large deposits, cash or otherwise."

"But that makes no sense. How did they buy the trailer home and a car?"

"The money for the home purchase and related expenses, and the car, was sent directly to the sellers from a source that we have not been able to track down."

"Come on, how is that possible? There are laws and regs so as to prevent just that sort of money laundering. Or people gifting money above the annual limit without paying the requisite tax. Otherwise, people can transfer their wealth to their kids or other third parties without any monies going to the Treasury Department, thereby completely circumventing the estate tax. And a six-figure transfer is way, way over the official cutoff for a bank's fraud department to raise the red flag."

Campbell chuckled. "Almost forgot you have your MBA and worked on Wall Street. To answer your question, the laws, apparently, failed in this case. Now your turn. Report."

Devine filled him in on everything he had learned since their last talk.

"This is so muddled, Devine," noted Campbell. "We don't really even know what killed the Odoms. And the girl says the police are lying."

"And keep in mind that Nate Shore and Korey Rose back her up on that."

"So the cops out in Ricketts are being paid off? Again, the obvious suspect is—"

"—Danny Glass. He had no way of getting custody of his niece while her parents were alive."

"But *why* does he want custody? *That's* the million-dollar question."

"He strikes me as a control freak, but he couldn't control his sister. She married Dwayne, apparently behind his back, and started her family and then moved away. So maybe he wants to take charge of his niece."

"Does a guy murder two people over that, Devine? Even someone like Glass?"

"I don't know, sir."

"And what would Perry Rollins know about any of this?"

"Same answer," said Devine.

"So what do you expect to learn in Ricketts?"

"Chiefly, why the Odoms were there in the first place and who they met with. And what was in the duffel bag. If it wasn't drugs that killed them, then it seems that the Odoms might have been poisoned somehow. I can't think of anything else to account for what happened to them other than exposure to something like that."

"But how could it have been administered and no one see anything?"

"I don't think anyone was asked. It was put down right away as a drug overdose."

"Even though the girl contradicts that?" asked Campbell.

"Something tells me that her word against the police won't cut it. And like I said, there was no criminal investigation, as far as I know. So I doubt they even asked her anything or took her statement."

"Watch yourself out there. Sounds like hostile territory."

"Will do. Anything on your wayward former PA, Dawn Schuman?"

"Nothing. Any sign of the girl on the train out there?"

"No."

"Good."

Devine clicked off and kept driving. It was around six hours to the town of Ricketts, and he soon left all vestiges of urban life behind. He might as well have been on another planet, albeit one with beautiful views. He was actually relaxed.

That lasted until he entered the town of Ricketts, when a police cruiser pulled in behind him.

CHAPTER

21

DEVINE CHECKED HIS SPEED—BARELY A mile over the limit. He glanced in the rearview and noted the cop car was keeping its distance, but the two men inside seemed to be unduly focused on him.

Okay, they either got tipped off I was coming or they show everybody this level of attention. And why do I think it's the former?

Devine had a genuine respect for small towns. Not for their quaintness, but for their potential lethality. On its surface, Putnam, Maine, had looked like an idyllic few square miles on the Atlantic coast where one could spend a pleasant vacation. However, right below that ordinary plain lay a vault full of deadly secrets and people hell-bent on keeping them that way, no matter who had to go into a grave or an urn. It seemed to Devine that in smaller numbers, people tended to get a little territorial.

Once he'd reached the tiny downtown area, Devine slowed and turned right. The cruiser mimicked these movements.

Okay, they know I know they're back there. So what gives?

He pulled into a parking spot along the curb and sat in the Toyota, ostensibly checking his phone. The cops pulled across the street roughly parallel with him.

He mulled over what Odom had told him. The lunch at the cowboy hat menu place. The meeting with the two men. The duffel with something in it. The deaths of the Odoms, which might have been from some sort of poison. But if so, how had it been administered? Maybe in the food they ate or whatever they drank for lunch. But what if Betsy had shared some of it? Was she just lucky to be alive? Were all three of them supposed to be dead and the drug overdose and her Narcan revival just a story woven from the surprise outcome of Betsy emerging alive?

Or was the end game actually eliminating Dwayne and Alice Odom, leaving Betsy as an orphan?

And in steps Danny Glass?

Would you do that, Danny? Are you that much of a piece of shit? Maybe you are.

He got out of the Toyota and looked up at the business he had parked in front of.

The Cowboy Tavern. The cowboy hat menu Odom had described was displayed in the front window. He had noted that the two cops had not left their cruiser. Maybe their orders were just to observe.

Okay, keep observing.

The place was only a quarter-full this late in the afternoon. He was greeted by the hostess, a young woman in her twenties with brown hair and matching eyes. She had on tight black jeans and a long-sleeved shirt with the Cowboy Tavern name and logo stitched on it.

She escorted him to a table, where he showed his federal ID and asked her about the Odoms. She had not worked that day, the hostess told him, but went off to check to see if any of the other staff here today had. A couple minutes later a woman in her sixties walked over. She was tall and thin, her skin mottled with sun damage. With a crackly, nicotine-laden voice, she introduced herself as Wendy Roman and told Devine she had served the Odoms that day.

He held up his phone with a photo of the family on the screen. "Just to confirm."

Roman nodded. "Yeah, sure, I 'member 'em. The police already talked to me, hon."

"So the police *did* an investigation?"

"Well, I don't know 'bout that. They just asked me some questions 'bout 'em. If you call that an investigation, then I guess they done one, hon. Now, how 'bout a drink and some food? The tacos are decent and our sixteen-ounce rib eye is damn tasty. And you look like one hungry man."

"Maybe later. What can you tell me about that day?"

Her sales spiel and potential tip having failed, she seemed to wilt in front of him. "Look, not much to tell, hon. They come in for lunch. Nice family. 'Member 'em cause I didn't recognize 'em. Strangers in town. Most folks come in here are regulars, live in Ricketts. We don't get a lot of tourists, you see, 'cept those who want to commune with nature, so to speak. And they don't come when it's cold 'cause I guess they don't like nature that way." She ended that comment with a cackling laugh.

"I suppose you don't remember what they ordered?"

She smiled. "Hell, if I had that good a memory, I'd go on some dang quiz show and win a bunch'a money or go to Vegas or some such." She paused. "Do 'member the girl. Chubby little thing, like girls her age are. I was like that and now look at me. She had them headphone things on, which I thought was kind'a odd. But kids these days? Always got a phone or iPad or some kind'a electronic thingamajig in hand. Trouble is people don't talk no more. And not just the kids but their parents and their mee-maws and grandpops, too. What the hell is so important you got to be on that crap all the time? I'm old enough to 'member when you used a phone to just call somebody." She shook her head. "Not no more."

"So did they talk to anyone while they were here? Anyone come over to greet them?"

She thought about this for a few moments before shaking her head. "No. They just come in, ate, and left. Nothin' special."

"You said the police asked you questions?"

"Yeah. After them folks were found dead in their car. Drug overdose, so's I heard. They asked me if they looked juiced or anythin', like they'd taken a hit of somethin'. I told them, yeah, they did look jumpy and out of sorts." She lowered her voice. "I got experience with drugs and such and know the signs. You see it everywhere these days. Bad as it's ever been, to my mind."

"So, to be clear, you thought they were drug users?"

"Well, yeah. Felt sorry for the girl. Parents on that stuff? Not good for her."

"They might have been jumpy because they were nervous about something," suggested Devine.

"Yeah, maybe," she said skeptically.

"Did any of them say anything to you as to why they had come to Ricketts? Like you said, you don't really get tourists this time of year. Were they meeting someone?"

She drummed her fingers on the table while she thought about this. "No. I do 'member askin' where they was comin' in from, and the man said, somethin' or other place. I, uh, I don't really recall it."

"And did you see where they went after they left here?"

She shook her head. "Nope. They just paid the check and that was that. I had other tables to look after. I don't do my job, I ain't got no job, hon. Gonna work till I drop as it is. No nest egg for this gal."

"I take it you pull long hours here?"

"I work the breakfast, lunch, and early dinner crowd. Six thirty in the morning till five thirty at night. And by then I am dog-tired. But the tips ain't bad most times."

He handed her his card. "Okay, thanks. Anything else occurs to you, let me know."

She stared at the card like there was a threat written on it. Then she put it away and said, "Now, what can I get you to drink? IPAs are good and we got some Blue Moon on tap."

Devine rose and said, "I think I'll have to pass for now."

As she walked away, Devine managed to take her picture with his phone. He sent it off to Emerson Campbell with a request.

He walked out thinking her opinion on the drug use had not rung true, both because he had several accounts saying the opposite, *and* the woman looked everywhere except at him when she had said it.

It's a good thing for me that most people are terrible liars.

Hon.

CHAPTER

22

THE COPS WERE STILL IN their car. For such a small town, Devine wondered how many uniforms there were. In Putnam, Maine, there were only two officers, and that number included the police chief.

However, as he glanced through the cruiser's window, he noted that neither of them was Eric King. Devine had Googled the man and gotten his picture. His Wikipedia page looked like it had been written by the police chief himself, with multiple screens of accolades.

He looked around the rustic storefronts and saw a number of modern surveillance cameras. He wondered what the odds were of his getting to look at the feed on them from the day the Odoms had been in town.

The phrase *When hell freezes over* came to mind. But maybe there was another avenue. He texted Campbell and told him where he was and what he needed, giving specific details. Two minutes later he got a curt response.

On it.

He still didn't know where the meeting with the

two men had taken place or what was in the duffel given to the Odoms. Maybe cash? The police probably had impounded the Odoms' car, but he didn't expect much cooperation from them.

So what the hell are you doing here, Devine?

Well, when in doubt, surprise the enemy. Turn retreat into a full-on frontal assault.

He hoped it turned out more like Teddy Roosevelt and San Juan Hill than George Pickett's charge against high ground at Gettysburg.

He walked across the street to the police cruiser. The officer in the passenger seat rolled down his window.

Devine showed them his official ID.

"I'm looking into the deaths of Dwayne and Alice Odom. Any chance I can get eyes on their car?"

"Why are the feds interested in that case?" said the officer, who was in his thirties, with blond hair, a long face, and suspicious eyes. Devine glanced at his partner, who looked like a carbon copy of his fellow officer.

The officer added, "Just a drug overdose. Happens all the time 'round here."

"Has to do with an ongoing investigation," said Devine, and then he stopped and stared at the man.

"We need to check in on that request," said the officer.

"Okay," said Devine. He remained standing where he was.

The flustered officer used his radio to call in.

After some back-and-forth, the officer said, "You can follow us to HQ, sir."

As Devine tailed them in the Toyota, he very quickly found out that *HQ* was within walking distance of where he had been. Yet the building was not what Devine had been expecting for a small, rural town.

It was at least twenty thousand square feet, looked new, and was constructed of red brick and glass and rose two stories into the sky. There were twin Humvee tactical vehicles parked in a fenced-in area off to the side, along with what looked to be three armored personnel carriers, a Sat-Nav communications vehicle, and four beefed-up, tricked-out police cruisers with front-end rams. The American and state flags flapped from a long pole out front, and rippled in the gathering wind coming off the higher elevations surrounding them.

Devine got out and joined the two officers, who had exited their vehicle. They were both about his height and had seen the inside of a gym on a regular basis.

"How many officers do you have on the force here?" he asked.

The one he had spoken with before took off his reflective blue-tinted shades and said, "That's classified."

Devine thought he was joking, only, it turned out, he wasn't.

Inside the front entrance, Devine saw a marquee

with the names of prominent town officials and their office numbers.

"Mercedes King is the mayor? Any relation to Chief King?" asked Devine.

"His wife," said the other officer. "No nepotism here," he added sarcastically.

"They've been great for Ricketts," said his partner defensively.

Devine glanced at the other cop, who was now looking at his shoes, his expression tight.

Devine was led down a broad hallway with paintings and framed photos and notice boards with local information pinned to them.

They reached a double door with CHIEF marked on it in four-inch metal letters, and one of the men knocked.

"Come," said a male voice from inside.

Devine was escorted into a large corner office. There were two broad windows with high-dollar custom cabinetry set below them. On another wall was a massive TV that had a news station on with the sound muted. Behind a sleek, wide zebrawood desk sat a man in uniform with four gold stars fastened to each shoulder epaulet.

Devine felt like he'd just walked into the Pentagon to meet the Chairman of the Joint Chiefs.

"Agent Devine," said the man in a nasally voice.

"I'm Chief King. Have a seat." He waved the two officers off. They immediately retreated and closed the
door behind them.

Devine sat and looked across the width of the desk at
the police chief of Ricketts. He was in his mid-sixties,
with gray, thinning hair and a slender, even withered
frame. His features were rigid, his skin unhealthy
with dark patches on his face. From his reputation and
online bios, Devine had imagined a larger-than-life figure with a ship horn bellow for a voice and narcissism
just oozing off him.

King said, "I understand you've been making inquiries about the deaths of the Odoms?"

"Yes."

"May I ask why?"

"Alice Odom was Danny Glass's sister." Devine
stared at the man to see if the reference to the RICO
defendant sparked a reaction.

"So?" said King.

"His sister and her husband died. And Glass is seeking to adopt their daughter, Betsy."

"Does the girl have any other relatives to take her in?"

"Not that I know of."

"And why is this of interest to the federal government?"

"Danny Glass is a defendant in a federal RICO case
in Seattle."

"Okay. Anything else?" he said, his disinterest evident.

"I'd like to see the autopsy reports on the Odoms."

"Why?" asked King.

"To look at their causes of death."

"If I remember correctly, they were drug overdoses, of which we have far too many around here. Drugs of despair, they call them, and they are indeed."

"So, I can look at the autopsy reports?"

"If you really want to."

"And would it be possible for me to talk to the first responders?"

"Again, I'd like to know why," said King.

"They may have some useful information."

"About what?" asked King as he drummed his fingers on the desktop.

"I guess I'll know it when I hear it."

"I'll see if I can get you their names," replied King, sounding distracted as he glanced at some papers in front of him.

"I understand their daughter tried to revive them with Narcan," said Devine.

"If you say so."

"That was in the police report; at least I was told that," noted Devine.

"I apologize for not knowing every detail of every incident report in my department."

Devine stared at the unsmiling man, who seemed to be bored by Devine's presence. He debated whether to ask King about the duffel that Betsy Odom had mentioned, but he decided that keeping it undisclosed for now was a better option.

"Of course. Like you said, lots of drug overdoses. Now, about their car?"

"In our impound lot. I suppose you want to look over it."

"Yes, I do," said Devine.

"We were wondering what to do with it. Maybe you feds can take it off our hands."

Okay, a surprise offer, which tells me something.

"I'll definitely check into that."

"Uh-huh," said King. He picked up his phone and ordered a copy of the autopsy reports. "I can take you down to the lot. It's directly behind the building."

He surprised Devine yet again by coming around the side of his desk in a wheelchair, which Devine had not noticed, because it had not been visible from where he had been seated.

King looked up at him. "Armed robbery when I was a beat cop. Got shot. Hit the spine. Put me in this chair for life."

"I'm sorry."

"Don't be. I'm alive. Can't say the same for the other guy. *My* shot hit him in the heart. Guess we both lost, only he lost bigger."

"Guess so."

23

THERE IT IS," SAID KING, waving his hand at a dark blue Genesis four-door sedan that sat next to a wrecked Dodge pickup.

"A G70?" said Devine. "Pretty fancy."

"I wouldn't know. I only buy American. Hyundai makes that. Chinese." He said the word like it was feces on his tongue.

"Actually, Hyundai is South Korean based. One of our *allies*. I pulled duty over there."

King expertly whipped his wheelchair around and stared up at Devine. "Army?"

"Yeah. You?"

"No. My big brother. I was the youngest with three sisters in between. He fought in Vietnam. He didn't make it back."

"Sorry to hear that."

King nodded. "Key should be under the passenger wheel well. On a magnet. Help yourself."

Devine bent down, retrieved it, and unlocked the car. He glanced at King. "I'm sure you have other stuff to do. Just let me know where I can pick up the autopsy reports. Oh." He handed King a card. "And the first responders can call me directly."

King took the card. When their fingers touched, Devine felt an icy stiffness in King's. He figured that might be from the damage to the man's spine.

He watched the man roll off and then turned his attention to the car. He found the registration in the name of Dwayne and Alice Odom in the glove box. The car had been purchased new and was only a year old. He Googled the Genesis and found that a model like this would cost anywhere from mid-forties to mid-fifties, depending on the bells and whistles.

He searched the car from trunk to engine compartment and underneath as well. He'd gotten good at that overseas when supervising the checking of vehicles for explosives. He found no Narcan, no duffel, no drugs, no unmarked bills wrapped with rubber bands, no copious amounts of poison. In fact, he found nothing. Not even dirt on the floor mats.

Meaning the vehicle's been swept and stripped. That's why he let me look at it.

As he turned away from the Genesis, a door to the building opened and a woman in her forties came out holding a file. She had on a white lab coat and her glasses rode low on her nose. She briskly walked toward him.

"Agent Devine?"

"Yes?"

"Here are the autopsy reports you requested on Dwayne and Alice Odom."

She handed them over.

"Thanks. Uh, do you have whatever was found in the car?"

The woman hesitated. "It would be in the evidence room, I suppose."

"Any way I can have access to that?"

"I'll check," she said.

"Thanks."

"Will there be anything else?"

"Not for the time being, Miss…?"

"*Mrs.* Doris Chandler."

"So did you perform the posts on the Odoms?" he asked.

"Oh, heavens no. I just do the clerical work and processing for the medical examiner and other folks here. Dr. Coburn performed the autopsies."

"Is he here?"

"*She.* It's *Sara* Coburn. And no, I'm afraid she's not. She's the ME for several counties and her work keeps her on the road."

"Do you have her contact information?"

"I do but I'm afraid I can't give it out without her permission."

Devine handed her his card. "Well, here's my info. Could you ask her to contact me at her earliest convenience?"

"Is this in regard to the autopsies? They were pretty straightforward, as I'm sure you'll see when you read through the reports."

"I'm sure they are, but I'd still like to speak with her."

"I will pass along your request," said Chandler.

"And check on the evidence room?"

She turned and went back inside without answering.

Devine watched her go and thought, *How can everyone here seem so polite and helpful and not actually provide me a damn thing that's useful?*

He sat in the 4Runner and read through the postmortem results.

They *were* straightforward as far as they went. But the tox reports, which would definitely say what was in their systems at death, had not come back in yet, so there was no official cause of death. But all other forensic indications pointed to a fentanyl-induced drug overdose, or so said Dr. Coburn in clipped language that was as dry as burnt toast. She had also noted that Alice Odom had a small lump in her right breast that might have been cancerous. But, of course, it would not kill her now.

Dwayne's post didn't reveal anything out of the ordinary. He was healthy except for being dead. But what if the fentanyl had been administered to them in a larger dose without their knowledge as a way to murder them?

He walked over to the door where Doris Chandler had entered the building after giving him the report. There was a bell to ring. She came in response to his pushing it.

"Can I look at the bodies?" he asked.

"I'm afraid that's impossible," Chandler answered.

"Why?"

"They've been cremated."

Devine exclaimed, "At whose request?"

"The next of kin," replied Chandler.

"Betsy Odom is a minor, so she couldn't have authorized it."

"I wasn't referring to her."

"Then who?" said Devine.

"I believe the name was Daniel Glass."

CHAPTER

24

DEVINE WAS HEADING BACK TO his SUV when another woman approached him in the parking lot.

She was in her late thirties, five-six, blond and curvy. Her makeup was muted and she was dressed in a black jacket and matching slacks with a white blouse framed with a long pointed collar and French cuffs. Her fingers flashed with what looked to be high-priced jewelry, and her neck was encircled with a strand of small gray pearls. Her stiletto heels clicked over the pavement like exclamation points.

"Agent Devine?" she said in a raspy voice, which sounded like she was coming down with a cold.

"Yes?"

"I'm Mercedes King."

Devine's surprise was so immediate, it was impossible to disguise or hide it.

She smiled knowingly. "Eric *is* quite a bit older than I am. Not that any explanation is due," she added sweetly with a dollop of vinegar on top.

"Of course not."

"Were our people helpful?" she asked.

"Yes. Although I was hoping to look at the items found in the Odoms' car. And I was surprised that their remains had already been cremated."

"Is that a problem? I believe the autopsies had been completed. So tragic what happened to them. Drugs! The scourge of our society."

He held up the file. "I have the reports here."

"Excellent. Well, if there's anything else you need, just let us know."

"The items from the car?"

"I'll check on that."

Sure you will.

Then she proceeded to throw him a curveball. "I'd be delighted to treat you to dinner. Say eight o'clock? I've got some work to finish."

Devine wondered what that was about, but decided to accept the invitation or take the bait, whichever it was. "I'll have to stay over then. You have any recommendations?"

"The Havens on Central Street. It's next to our only movie theater. Very nice B and B. I can call and make a reservation for you."

"Thanks. I appreciate all the cooperation." He had to bite back a laugh.

"We are always delighted to work with our federal friends." She gave him the address of the restaurant.

"Is what I'm wearing okay?"

"You just bring yourself, Agent Devine. That'll be plenty."

Said the spider to the fly.

She walked off, exaggerating the swing of her hips and buttocks, he thought, but maybe she always moved that way. Some women he had met in the past did. And his encounters with all of them had ended badly.

So where will you come out, Mayor Mercedes?

He headed back to the downtown area and parked at the curb, where he texted Campbell, bringing him up to date with the latest. The cremation had ruined any chance to determine what had actually happened to the Odoms. And he was clearly not going to see what had been found in the car. He would have to attack this sucker from another angle.

He checked his rearview mirror and saw the same police cruiser that had shadowed him earlier parked on the opposite curb three car lengths back. The same two cops were inside.

He called Betsy Odom's number and she answered after two rings.

"Hello?"

"Betsy, it's Travis."

"Where are you?"

"In Ricketts, like I said. I've been, well, asking questions and seeing what I can find out about…what happened to your parents." It had just sunk in with Devine that he was speaking to a little girl about her parents' murders.

"Did you find out what happened to them?" she said anxiously. "Did somebody do it? Who?"

"Whoa, slow down. I haven't found out anything really. At least not yet."

"Did... did you see them? My mom and dad, I mean?"

Shit. Devine couldn't bring himself to tell her that their bodies had been cremated.

"No, I didn't. They were... the bodies... I mean... No, I didn't," he concluded awkwardly.

"I'm meeting with my uncle again."

A surprised Devine said, "What? When?"

"There's a court thing coming up."

"Yeah, I know, the hearing on your uncle's petition for guardianship. But why are you meeting with him?"

"He wants to see me before the hearing for some reason. Travis, can you..."

"Can I what?"

"Can you go with me to meet my uncle and then to this court thing?"

"Yeah sure, if you want me to."

"Thanks."

She didn't sound anything like the smart-ass, foul-mouthed kid from before. She sounded exactly like what she actually was: a scared, grieving, and confused twelve-year-old.

"Did you find out anything at all about my parents?"

"A little. I'll be back in Seattle tomorrow and I'll come by and see you, okay? Then we can talk about meeting with your uncle and the court hearing."

"Okay, thanks, Travis."

While he sat there killing time until dinner by going over the autopsy reports some more, the background info that Campbell had gotten for him on Rollins popped into his in-box. He scrolled through the attachments.

Perry Rollins had been born in the Midwest and then moved around some. He had been married once, no kids, his ex's whereabouts unknown. He had a sporadic employment history and his tax filings were just as random. In fact, he had an IRS garnishment on his bank account, which had only a little over a hundred bucks in it. No car was registered to him.

There wasn't much here, it seemed, but he had to go over it in detail, and so he did, reading some parts several times so the information would sink in better.

When Devine looked up a while later, he found the dark streets had totally emptied.

And that was when someone tapped on his window.

CHAPTER

25

As soon as Devine looked that way, he knew he'd let his guard down and was about to pay the price, as a second man on the other side of his truck opened the passenger door and pointed a pistol at him.

Devine checked his rearview again. The cop car was gone; indeed the whole town looked deserted in the chilly darkness.

The man climbed in while his window-tapping partner opened the driver's side passenger door and got in the backseat.

The first man said, "Drive. I'll give directions."

"If you want to carjack me, I don't have to go along for the ride," said Devine. "I actually have another appointment."

That got him a hard smack on the back of the head with the pistol held by the guy in the rear seat.

"Drive," the man said again.

His head ringing from the blow, Devine drove while the fellow fed him directions. They were quickly swallowed by the blackness of an overcast evening, with not a glimmer of natural light, or apparent hope, in the vicinity.

Devine could smell the foul breath coming from the man in the back, who hovered over him. He could also smell the stink of both men's sweat. That actually told him a lot—they were as nervous as they probably assumed he was.

Only Devine wasn't. He was the calm before, during, and after the storm. For better or worse, this was when Devine was in his element, and at his best.

"Can I ask about the agenda for our trip?" Devine asked.

"Sure, you can *ask*," said the man next to him.

Devine had cast his gaze over the fellow and his gun, and used the rearview mirror to do the same with his garlic-breathed partner in the rear seat.

In his head, Devine ran various simulations to counter his current predicament and settled on one, based solely on the men having made a single critical mistake.

Well, two if I count them taking me on in the first place.

"Turn right up ahead," said the man in the front seat as he glanced out the window.

Devine made the turn.

"Slow down," said the same man as they headed down a dirt road with thick woods on either side.

Devine eased off the gas.

"Stop up ahead."

Devine said, "I'll give you one more chance to tell me. Are you friend or foe? Because it will matter to me, which means it will matter to you."

"What are you, some kind'a comedian? Your ass is grass, maggot," said the man in the backseat. Devine saw him raise the gun again, probably to either drill a hole in his head or give him a matching bruise; it really didn't matter now.

"All I needed to know. And here's the punch line."

He slammed down the gas and the 4Runner rocketed ahead, catapulting wildly over the bumpy road; the resulting g's from the sudden acceleration threw the two men flat against their seats.

When the speedometer blew past 100, Devine used both feet to slam down on the brakes. At the same time, while holding the wheel steady, he lurched sideways because he knew what was coming. The unharnessed man in the rear seat flew over Devine and smashed headfirst into the windshield. His partner in the front had beat him to that destination by a millisecond.

Mists of blood from the man who had once been behind Devine sprayed over him. Devine rubbed the other man's corpuscles off his face and pushed him onto his buddy, who had fallen back into his seat with tiny shards of windshield sticking out of his head.

Both men were unconscious, perhaps dead. Devine didn't really care which.

He undid his harness and slid out of the truck. Devine reached back inside to check for ID on the man closest to him when a shot blew by his head. It smacked into the bark of a nearby pine, blowing wood chips off into the foggy tendrils of air.

Devine drew his Glock and burned five rounds of return fire. He then reached inside the 4Runner and pulled the man closest to him out, dumping him on the ground. As another shot exploded into the SUV, Devine hopped back into the Toyota and shut the door. He leaned over the other man, opened the passenger side door, and used his legs to propel his bloodied partner out of the vehicle.

Devine harnessed up, punched the gas, and the Toyota leapt forward, its propulsion causing the passenger door to close. He had no idea if there was a way out up ahead but he had no choice for now. Another shot caved in the back window. He ducked down as the bullet smacked into the already wrecked windshield, laying down fresh spiderwebs in the glass.

As he looked up ahead, Devine exclaimed, "Fuckin' great."

The dirt road ended in a wall of fallen trees and large rocks. He slammed on the brakes, threw the Toyota into reverse, and backed up with the tires spewing dirt like a Ditch Witch. He next tapped the brake just so, ripped the wheel to his right, slid into a J-turn, laid down on the gas again, spun the wheel straight and true, the leather skimming under his fingers, and rocketed in the opposite direction.

When Devine saw the headlights up ahead coming straight at him, he lowered his window and rested his Glock on the top of the side mirror to steady his aim. They could be two futuristic knights about to have a lethal joust.

He emptied his mag at the oncoming vehicle, shredding windshield glass and front metal grille. As Devine crouched low, they fired back at him, rounds pinging off door frames, hood, and grille and blowing out chunks of already shattered glass. But nothing pinged off him, which was what counted.

He used a finger to pop the spent mag, and dexterously inserted a fresh one using his right hand. He took both hands off the wheel for a second to rack the slide. He put the gun on the mirror once more, but before he could fire, Devine heard dozens of rounds of rapid-fire shots. He started to duck, but then realized they weren't coming at him or from the other vehicle, which had started to swerve violently. At the last possible second, Devine cut the wheel to the right and flew past what he could now see was a large Cadillac Escalade. The blown-out right rear wheel was laying down strips of burned-off rubber. The back glass was also missing and the tailgate looked like a target at a gun range.

As he looked up ahead, he saw a single taillight ahead of him.

A motorcycle speeding away from the scene? He pressed the gas to the cushioned floorboard, but the 4Runner apparently had no acceleration left to give on that end. One of the bullets must have struck something vital to the truck's performance, causing its speed to max out at sixty. He zipped by where the two wrecked and bloodied men lay in the dirt and kept going. The taillight was farther ahead and then disappeared as it hit the main road. When Devine got there, the motorcycle was gone. But whoever it was had saved his life.

He turned the heat up to blast level and still it was freezing inside because of the blown-out windows fore and aft, which also created an icy wind tunnel that made it feel like he was on top of Everest. He didn't touch the scalp and hair on his broken windshield and dashboard because his ride was now a crime scene in motion. After a mile he slowed to a moderate pace and made his way back to Ricketts to keep his dinner date with Mayor Mercedes.

Devine wondered if it would be any more exciting than what had just happened to him.

26

DEVINE PARKED ACROSS THE STREET from the steak house and felt the large, pulpy lump on the back of his head where the man had clobbered him with the butt of his gun. His fingers came away bloody. He grabbed his go-bag from the rear of the Toyota and pulled out a medical kit. He used it to clean the wound and then applied some antibiotic before smoothing down his hair. He checked that his clothes were relatively clean and mostly blood- and glass-shard-free and then crossed over to the restaurant. Whether Mercedes King was here or not might tell him a great deal. Devine figured it was all about the efficiency of the enemy lines of communication.

He walked in and was greeted by a young woman dressed all in black. He mentioned the mayor's name and she escorted him to the rear. So at least the dinner reservation *had* been made. If the mayor *was* involved in what had just happened to him, she may well be hedging her bets.

The place was quiet, with only a few patrons hovering over their meals and wine.

The woman said, "I'll show Mayor King back when she arrives."

He sat down and checked his watch. Five minutes past eight.

Okay.

He picked up the menu and his gaze flitted aimlessly down the entrées. He would have been hungry, but for almost dying a violent death and having a pounding headache from the blow to his skull.

"Agent Devine?"

He looked up to see Mercedes King hurrying over to him. She had changed clothes and now wore a black pleated skirt and a white blouse under a short lavender jacket. She seemed out of breath.

"I'm sorry I'm late. Some unexpected constituent business. I'm usually quite punctual."

"No problem," he said, studying her closely. Her refusal to look at him maybe told Devine all he needed to know. Like she was talking to a man who was supposed to be dead, and she was mightily confused and disturbed by the fact that he wasn't.

She slipped into the chair across from him and said, "So, how was the rest of your day?"

"So-so. Nice little town you have here. But once you get outside the official limits, it gets really isolated really fast. People could do anything to someone out there and no one would know it," he added.

"Really? I guess I never thought about it like that. I love it here," she added, swiping a hand through her hair as if for emphasis.

Sure you do, thought Devine. *Out here in the boonies married to a man nearly three decades older than you with the personality of a turnip.*

"Would you like some wine? I could use a glass," she added hoarsely.

"You pick, I'm not much of a connoisseur."

She held up her hand and the waitress shot over like she'd been propelled from a cannon. King ordered two glasses of red.

"So what's good on the menu?" he asked the mayor.

"The filet. Six-ounce, at least that's what I usually get. Good protein and I'm watching my figure. It's different for men. Not that you have to worry about that." She shot him a look that Devine couldn't initially decode. Flirting maybe? But clearly for her own purposes.

"How long have you been mayor?"

"This is my first term. I'm up for reelection next year."

"And you married the chief when?"

She picked up her menu and ran her gaze down it. "A while back," she replied before glancing up at him.

She set the menu down. "Can I be frank?" she asked, as though to cut off any other personal questions he might have been readying.

"Sure. *I* was planning to be."

"It's why I wanted to have a private meeting with you." She leaned forward conspiratorially, while Devine stayed pencil straight.

"What happened to the Odoms was terrible. That it occurred within the confines of Ricketts makes it my husband's responsibility, and he takes that responsibility very seriously."

"Good for him."

Her expression changed as she studied him. "You look...different."

"So do you, but you've changed clothes. What was the constituent business?"

"What?"

"The constituent business that made you late?"

"Just a gripe about something that people think a politician can control."

"You were being frank?" he prompted.

Their wines arrived and she took a sip before answering. "It is not a good look for the federal government to be in town investigating. It's making poor Eric think he did something wrong, or is not up to the job."

Devine didn't touch his wine. "*Did* he do something wrong?"

She frowned. "What exactly are you implying?"

"I'm just asking a question. It's been my experience that guilty people worry, and innocent people believe everything will work out just fine, because they have nothing to hide."

"Eric has *nothing* to hide, I can assure you," she said coldly. She flipped her luxurious hair from one shoulder to the other, as though to add physical action to her blunt words.

"Well, in answer to your statement, the federal government signs my paycheck so I go where they send me. I don't have any control over that. And when I get to a place, I'm expected to do my job."

"But what is the problem here that requires your attention? Two people died of a drug overdose. I don't see why that's a federal issue. Lots of people, unfortunately, die that way."

"But when two people who 'die that way' are tied to someone named Danny Glass, then the feds get interested."

"Danny who?"

He gave her a long stare before continuing. "Or *Daniel* Glass, as Doris Chandler told me. Glass also requested that the Odoms' remains be cremated."

"How was this Glass person able to do that?" she asked, her expression one of benign curiosity.

"He's next of kin, Alice Odom's brother."

"Oh, okay, so what's the problem?"

"Are you still holding to the position that you don't know who Danny Glass is?"

"Should I?" she replied coolly.

"Probably, but who am I to judge? He's been accused of being a world-class criminal and is currently the target of a federal RICO criminal prosecution in Seattle. It's gotten a lot of juice in the media."

She took another swallow of her wine and said, "I'm afraid I don't know much about a global criminal. I'm just the mayor of a small town and keep my full attention here."

"That government center must have cost millions to build. And all that military-grade police equipment. Another big price tag."

"Those vehicles were purchased with generous support from DHS, which is your agency, correct? They did the same thing with lots of localities after 9/11."

"The equipment I saw is nowhere near twenty-plus years old. Or even ten years old."

"We've updated, again with generous government subsidies. And Eric is highly respected in the law enforcement community, so we get those sorts of perks from the state as well."

Apparently, he's not so respected in the eyes of the other state law enforcement agencies, thought Devine as he recalled what Braddock had told him about Eric King.

"And the building?"

"Just good old-fashioned taxes."

"Didn't think the tax base here was that big."

"You know, I'm suddenly not hungry and I have unfinished business to attend to." She rose and looked down at him. "I hope you enjoy the *night* here in Ricketts, Agent Devine. And best of luck wherever it is you end up."

Like a grave, you mean? thought Devine.

She added, "I passed your car coming in here. I recognized it from earlier at the government building. The glass is shattered and there's what looks to be holes in the driver's side door."

"Just a road rage incident."

"My goodness, you must report that to the police."

"Maybe I'll take it up directly with your husband."

Devine watched as she headed off. Her hips and buttocks did not sway as before. The woman just walked like she owned the place.

And apparently she does. The whole place.

He took out his phone and snapped a picture of King's face in the reflection of the mirror she was walking toward. Devine figured it might come in handy at some point.

He next gripped the stem of her glass, poured her wine into his, carefully wrapped it in a cloth napkin, and walked out.

27

DEVINE DIDN'T BOTHER TO STAY at the bed-and-breakfast recommended by Mercedes King. He didn't think it would be good for his health. He found a hardware store still open, bought cardboard and duct tape, and did his best to fix his mess of a 4Runner for the drive back.

He got on the road and along the way he called Nate Shore on the phone he'd given the men.

"Hey, Nate, it's Travis Devine. You still at the Odoms'?"

"Yeah, man, we both are. Ain't got nowhere else to go right now."

"I'm heading your way. Be there in a few hours. You don't have to wait up. Just leave the back door unlocked. I'm going to spend the night and I need to ask you guys some things."

"Okay, sure. And we're night owls, so we'll be up. Hey, you gonna be hungry? We got some food."

"Fast food?"

"No, we went grocery shoppin' again. We run through

what you got us. Anyways, Kor made us some fish. Best thing I ever put in my belly."

"Where'd he learn to cook?"

"Taught himself. Mostly so's he wouldn't go hungry. But Kor always like cookin'. He worked at a bunch of restaurants, did caterin' on the side. Went from glorified bottle washer to line cook, grillin', fryin', sauce, seafood, and roast stations. Kor done it all. Was doin' good at a real fancy place in Seattle, cloth napkins and real silverware."

"So what happened?"

"Meth happened. Cookin' wears you down, man. Kor needed somethin' to give him a pop. And it popped him all right. Cost the dude all he had, just like my shit done to me. Been a bitch, for sure."

"Okay. See you in a few hours."

At first, Devine drove the same route he had been forced to drive with the two men. He turned down the dirt road and pulled to a stop where the two men had been lying in the dirt. They were gone, and so was the truck with the shot-up tire.

He got out and looked around, his gun at the ready and his senses on alert because bad guys sometimes did come back to the scene of their crimes. He used his flashlight to look for shell casings and found one. From where it was located, he figured it might have been fired by the person on the motorcycle. He pocketed it, looked around for a few more minutes, and then got back in the Toyota.

He drove down the road and then stopped right around the spot he had seen the motorcycle fleeing the scene. He shone his light on the slim tire track that could only have come from that sort of vehicle. He took a picture of it with his phone and got back into the 4Runner and drove off. Then something occurred to him. He hadn't *heard* the motorcycle. And those machines were usually pretty loud, particularly when they were wound up.

Okay, that tells me a lot.

The tape and cardboard mostly did their job, and he didn't freeze to death by the time he pulled in front of the Odoms' home hours later, nor did he get stopped by the police, who might have had some difficult queries about his shot-up ride. Nate Shore answered the door. He had on a white tank top that showed off impressive sets of delts, triceps, and biceps, and a pair of camouflage pants that looked like the real deal to Devine.

"Last time we talked I found out you were in the Army," said Devine as Shore closed the door. "But you got out?"

"Yeah. I joined up right outta high school. Figured I could get me some college money, or learn a skill I could use to make some bucks after I got out. Made it to sergeant, E-5. Finished my contract with the Army and then came home and hooked back up with Kor. He was doing his cookin' thing and I started workin' construction. We was doin' okay till we had our 'troubles.'"

"So you didn't re-up even though you made it to E-5? What, Army wasn't for you?"

Shore glanced away for a moment, his expression hard for Devine to interpret. "Um, I liked it okay, even qualified for Delta Force after I made sergeant. Hardest damn thing I've ever done. They beat you up, man, no lie. Didn't know I could even do some of the stuff they made us do. And I had to jump my ass outta perfectly good planes. Had some damn smart suckers in that group. Way smarter'n me. Some of them dudes were real good at foreign languages and we also had some guys who were hot shit with counterterrorism stuff. Me? My wheelhouse was weapons, hand-to-hand, and blowing shit up."

"Delta! Damn, Nate, that's an elite status," noted an impressed Devine. "Most of the Delta recruits come from the 75th Ranger Regiment, but I had some Ranger buddies who were fine soldiers who tried to qualify but couldn't cut it."

"Yeah, it was somethin' all right. Pushed me right to the wall, and then through the wall."

"So what happened? You don't make Delta and then walk away."

"*I* didn't walk away."

"I don't understand."

"Truth is some rednecks in Delta had a problem with guys who looked like me. Made my life pretty damn miserable. And the brass just looked the other way. So's I didn't re-up. I don't mind bustin' my butt to get somewhere, but I ain't spendin' my life takin' that kind'a shit from a bunch'a assholes."

"I'm truly sorry that happened, Nate."

Shore shrugged. "Ain't like I don't see that stuff on the outside, too."

Korey Rose popped his head into the room. "Hungry?"

Devine smiled. "I am, yeah. Very."

Devine's last meal had been breakfast, which seemed days ago.

"Got it all set up for you in the dinin' room. Be right in."

The "dining room" was only two strides away.

There was a place setting for one.

"We already ate," explained Shore, rubbing his six-pack belly. "You want a beer?"

"Yeah, I would. I had a glass of wine earlier, but didn't drink a drop of it."

"Bad wine?" asked Shore.

"Bad company."

Shore left and then came back with a bottle of Guinness and handed it to him. "They was havin' a sale."

"You're not drinking?"

"Drugs ain't the only thing we got problems with. The booze, too."

"So why'd you buy it?"

"For visitors. Kor likes to have things on hand to be hospitable and such. Just 'cause we got an issue, don't mean other folks can't drink a beer. But we don't never buy no liquor."

Rose came in with a tray of food in bowls along with serving utensils.

"What is it?" asked Devine.

"Cobia, nice light, flaky white fish. But with my secret ingredients it'll taste better than anythin' you've put in your mouth in the last week, guaranteed."

He plated the fish, added two scoops of seasoned couscous and some warm succotash and grilled tomatoes; a salad topped with precision-cut avocado slices and strawberries was in a separate bowl.

Devine sat, picked up his knife and fork, and dug in while the two men watched him.

"Damn," said Devine. "This is better than anything I've put in my mouth in the last *month*. And I was in Italy a month ago."

Rose and Shore high-fived each other.

"What are your secret ingredients?" asked Devine.

Rose gave him a wink. "If I told you, they wouldn't be secret no more, but to give a hint, you can work wonders with a balsamic glaze if you get the reduction just right, and sometimes I do a honey-lemon-basil pesto marinade and grill it to the point of what I call extreme *deliciousness*."

As Devine began eating again, Shore said, "You mentioned on the phone some questions?"

Devine took a swig of beer and nodded. "I've been to Ricketts, where Dwayne and Alice died. The autopsy report isn't complete yet; they're waiting on tox results. But I think they're going to stick to the drug overdose story."

"That is bullshit," exclaimed Rose.

"I know. The mayor there is married to the police chief, who's about thirty years older than she is. The town seems to live way beyond its means. You two ever been to Ricketts, or Asotin County?"

They both shook their heads.

"What do *you* think is goin' on there?" asked Shore.

"I'm not certain but something is off, maybe way off. Now, Betsy has a court hearing coming up. It has to do with Glass wanting to be her guardian."

"That man can't get Betsy," said Rose. "No tellin' what he might do to her."

"Hey, can me and Kor be her guardians?" asked Shore. "We know her. She likes us. We was real good friends with her parents. That counts, right? I mean to the judge? And we got this nice place for all of us to live in."

"You also have some problems in your past and being in and out of drug rehab will not be looked on favorably by the court," said Devine. "And you don't have regular jobs so how would you support her or yourselves?"

"Yeah," said a resigned Shore, who glanced at Rose. "Ain't the first time we hear that, right, Kor?"

Rose scratched his head and looked out the window. "Hey, what the hell happened to your truck? Your windshield's all busted up. You hit somethin'?"

"Oh, I forgot to mention that somebody tried to kill me back in Ricketts."

Shore and Rose exchanged surprised glances. Rose said, "No shit?"

"You gonna report it to the cops?" asked Shore.

"It might have been the cops who did it," replied Devine.

"Fuck me," said a stunned Rose.

Devine looked at him. "You ever think of getting back into the cooking business?"

Rose shook his head. "No way, too damn stressful. What made me do drugs in the first place. Just to keep up. But I like cookin' for friends."

"What did Betsy like to eat?"

"Burgers and fries and pizza mostly, just like all kids," said Rose with a crooked grin. "But I got her to expand her culinary horizons a little. She even tried my chicken cordon bleu. Said it didn't suck, right, Dozer?"

"Right. So what you gonna do about this court hearin' and Danny Glass?" asked Shore.

"I'm going there with her, but I don't have much leverage to make a difference."

"But if you find shit on Glass?" said Shore.

"You got any in your back pocket?"

"I wish."

After he finished his dinner, Devine went to his room and looked out the window in what had been Betsy's bedroom. All he saw was darkness, and Devine had no way to know that someone was right now watching him through a pair of superb night optics.

CHAPTER

28

PRU JACKSON LOWERED HER MONOCULAR and studied the modest home in the middle of the woods. Three men were inside. She had observed all of them through various windows. She didn't know who the other two were, but, really, only Travis Devine interested her.

She walked back to her electric and virtually silent e-motorcycle. This was the stealth piece of equipment she'd had delivered to her rental home along with the SUV. Because of its limited range, she had followed Devine to Ricketts in her SUV with the motorcycle in the back. She had deployed the vehicle when she had seen the two men take him. Later, she had tracked him to here.

She had saved his life tonight, primarily because Jackson didn't want anyone else killing him.

Yet there was another reason. The attempt on his life had felt familiar to her in a way that might turn out to be personally beneficial.

Jackson was not really speculating on this.

After shooting out the tire of the SUV in pursuit of Devine, she had fled, but once she had reached the main road, she had reentered the woods and watched as Devine's 4Runner flashed past her. Then Jackson had made her way back to where the encounter had occurred and subsequently filmed everything she had seen with a long-range camera.

The two men who had abducted Devine were placed into body bags by a group of other men and loaded onto the SUV, while the damaged tire was repaired.

Travis Devine is one helluva killing machine, she had thought.

The area was processed to remove as much evidence as possible. She had continued to watch as two men conferred on things. One of the men then made a call and talked for about a minute. Jackson wished she'd had a listening device capable of picking up the conversation at this distance. Then the vehicle had sped off and she had followed, eventually leading her to a property of cleared land about three miles away.

There, Jackson watched as a gate manned by an armed guard in a brown uniform opened and the SUV passed through. In the darkness she could make out shapes of various buildings, some of them quite sizable.

Ten minutes later a chopper appeared in the sky and landed near one of the buildings. The body-bagged men were swiftly placed in the chopper, which lifted off, but not before Jackson also took a video of it. She'd seen a bird like it before and even ridden in one. All black, even the rotors. From its shape she knew modifications had been made to the "dog house," or the nose, which contained the gear box and engines, as well as the motor's intakes and exhaust system; the latter had an infrared suppressor, designed to reduce its radar signature. She also observed it had a unique canard configuration, which would give it enhanced maneuvering capabilities and an increased top speed. Its fuselage was covered with canted flat panels, again to reduce its radar cross-section. And the main rotor was hinge-less and she was certain the tail rotor had no ball bearings, all to reduce vibration with the ultimate goal of diminishing detection.

As it soared away, its visual, radar, infrared, and acoustic signatures were substantially minimized. In a matter of seconds it vanished into the night sky.

There was really only one conclusion to all this.

My old agency, CIA, is involved somehow.

As she had sped off, Jackson's mind whirled far faster than her wheels.

The chopper she'd seen only reinforced what she already suspected. The hit put out on Devine tonight was one that she recognized because it had been done to someone close to her, an ally in the intelligence service of another country friendly to the United States. The reasons for it were political, convoluted, a cover-up of past transgressions with an unhealthy dash of ego. The blame for the murder had then been placed on a tried-and-true enemy of America.

Jackson had told her superiors about some of their own colleagues' involvement in the person's death, and she had been assured that heads would roll. And unfortunately, *hers* eventually had.

They set me up all the way.

The very next week Pru Jackson had been left behind in hostile foreign territory because she had blamed some at her agency for the murder of her ally. With that knowledge she could bring down people in high places. High enough that those very same people would probably gut their own grandmothers to save themselves. That was what power did to you. It allowed you to rationalize anything you ever did or would ever do, no matter how wrong or cruel.

As she stood here now observing the trailer, Jackson mused, *So why is CIA apparently involved in this family drama of the Odoms, with their little house in the woods on one end and big, bad Danny Glass on the other? And Travis Devine trapped smack in the middle?*

She would have to find out that connection. And Jackson also well understood that Devine was no doubt going to do his best to accomplish the same thing. And whoever got there first, without being killed, might get the grand prize.

Jackson had risked her life for a spot in the American intelligence service. If she had perished in the line of duty, she was supposed to go up on the Memorial Wall at Langley, which honored those men and women who had given their final, full measure serving their country.

And I would have been honored to be on that wall. Then they betrayed me. Well, now it's my turn.

Jackson twisted the throttle, and the bike soared silently down the lonely, cold road, with only a billion stars in a cool, vast sky as silent witnesses.

29

DEVINE STARED UP AT THE ceiling of Betsy Odom's old bedroom. There were shiny plastic stars glued there to form perhaps a universe of possibilities, maybe representing something that was as unlike the girl's life as it was conceivable to be?

While he didn't routinely wax philosophical, this mission was hitting Devine in unexpected spots, like a journeyman fighter who got in lucky punches on a better foe, and managing to do damage in sensitive places.

He pulled out his phone and went over the notes he had kept on the case. Clearly, no one from Ricketts was going to get back to him, so there would be no items from the Odoms' car for him to inspect, and no further examination possible of bodies now turned to ash. Dr. Coburn was certainly not going to contact him, and neither were the first responders to the Odoms' deaths.

He hoped that Campbell could work a miracle with the request Devine had made of him, but that was far from guaranteed. He then called the man to report in. He was simply going to leave a voicemail. Yet despite its being very late on the West Coast *and* his being three hours ahead of Devine, his boss answered promptly. Devine wondered when and if Emerson Campbell actually slept, or maybe the man had just risen to begin his day. After Devine told him about being kidnapped, he asked Campbell, "It wasn't your people who saved my butt?"

"No. You think Glass is behind them snatching you?"

"I can't think of anyone else. They might have been planning to interrogate me in the woods before they killed me. But I screwed their plans. And whoever saved me blew up those plans even more. Any luck on my request for info?"

"Still working on it. It takes time to move mountains, even for the U.S. government."

"Right."

Campbell noted, "We discussed before that perhaps Glass believes Perry Rollins told you something incriminating about him."

"But he'd have to figure I'd take whatever I knew to the cops."

"My point is, maybe you know something valuable, only you don't *know* you do. What did Rollins say to you again, right before he died?"

"It sounded like 'cuckoo' and then maybe 'gas.' I have no idea what that means, if anything. The guy was about to die, so it could be gibberish," added Devine. "Although I suppose by 'gas,' he could have been trying to say '*glass*.'"

"I think it more likely than not, but the other reference is pretty muddled. Okay, I'm going to work some angles on my end, Devine. You watch yourself."

Campbell clicked off and Devine pondered the two words again, looking for something close that made sense. *"Gas," or more likely "glass,"* meaning obviously Danny Glass. *But "cuckoo"?*

After ten minutes of trying, he stopped beating his head against a brick wall.

Then there was the matter of the men who had tried their best to kill him. And the person who had saved him? If it was an e-motorcycle the person had been riding, that spoke of premeditated stealth.

So a lot of preparation, for what end? Saving him for what reason? And what other guardian angel did he have?

He rested his eyes for a few moments. Then he sat up and looked around the space. It was small and cramped and cluttered, but it had represented a new home for Betsy Odom—perhaps her first real one. Now she was looking at living in mansions owned by an alleged international criminal. Pretty heady stuff for a twelve-year-old. Hell, for anyone, really.

Odom had mentioned her mother was homeschooling her, but he had seen nothing here that showed a serious effort was being made along those lines. But judging by the books she had, and the notes she'd made in the margins of *Think and Grow Rich*, the girl could obviously read and write, and she was clearly smart, at least street smart.

He looked down and eyed something partially sticking out from under the bed. He leaned over and snagged it. How had he missed that before?

It was a thick three-ring binder filled with pages. On the cover was written in block lettering one word.

ME

He opened it and flipped through some pages. They were a collection of photos, drawings, and text.

Going back to the beginning Devine saw that the first photos were, presumably, of Odom as a baby. He read her accounts underneath those pictures and it confirmed that what he was seeing was Betsy as an infant. He turned pages and with that saw the passage of time in the girl's life. Funny photos, and pencil and ink drawings that became more sophisticated as the girl grew older. She was quite the artist, Devine noted. The next pages revealed photos of the Odom family glued into the journal.

With a start, Devine realized that he had never before seen what Dwayne and Alice Odom looked like. There were no pictures of them displayed around their home.

In one photo Dwayne presented as pencil-thin, goofy, and laid-back with a lopsided grin and long, shaggy brown hair. The auburn-haired Alice Odom had indeed been tall. Indeed, she was at least two inches taller than her husband and it was not because of any high heels—in the photo he could see both were barefoot. And she had beautiful features and a warm and kind smile. Devine did not see a lot of her father in Betsy; daughter definitely favored Mom.

He noted some of the things Betsy had written. Dreams she had. Things she wanted to do. A drawing of a dog that she called Barney, and how much she wanted a dog for real.

Then he found it. Pages of schoolwork memorialized here: spelling lessons, multiplication tables, a short essay on making pancakes that held a few stains on the paper. When Devine lifted the paper to his nose and took a whiff, he thought he smelled maple syrup.

Three pages were devoted to the exciting purchases of the new house and car, although they revealed no source of the funds, not that Betsy would have been necessarily privy to that. There were photos of the family standing outside the mobile home. Maybe Nate or Korey had taken the pictures, he speculated.

They all looked happy, although when Devine gazed

more closely at Betsy, she actually looked...what was it? Yes, *relieved*.

There was another photo of her pretending to drive the Genesis, her smile ear to ear. It made Devine grin.

Most of the last pages of content were Betsy deciding what she wanted to be when she grew up.

There were the obvious choices in the list she had drawn up: doctor, lawyer, nurse, teacher. But when he got down near the bottom, he saw one occupation that had been underlined twice.

FBI agent?

Without meaning to stereotype, Devine still thought, *What young girl listed that as her dream job?*

When he turned to the final page, Devine jolted up from the bed.

There were only seven words:

Danny Glass, my uncle. Good or bad?

Why the hell had she written that? Danny Glass had only come into the picture as her potential guardian *after* Odom's parents had died. She couldn't have written this after that had happened. She hadn't been back here. Odom had told him so herself.

Then she *had* been thinking about her uncle. Maybe her mother had told her more about Danny Glass than she had let on to Devine, or anyone else.

Now the questions became clearer: What did she know, who had told her, and why had she withheld it? Devine thought back to that moment in the Four Seasons when Odom had looked ready to give him the high sign. What had Glass said to make her reconsider ending the meeting?

Devine closed the journal, lay back on the bed, but didn't really get a wink of sleep the whole night.

CHAPTER

30

HIS HAIR DISHEVELED, HIS SLEPT-IN clothes heavily wrinkled, and with darkened pouches under his bloodshot eyes and stubble on his chin, Devine, carrying the binder, walked into the kitchen the next morning. Well, it was actually nearly the afternoon, he thought, as he checked his watch. He was instantly flooded with the mingled smells of coffee, eggs, bacon, and toast that Rose was overseeing on the stove top.

"You sleep in too?" asked Devine.

"Yep," said Rose. "Me and Dozer are definitely night owls."

"Yeah, Nate mentioned that before."

Rose looked up, flinched, and said, "Whoa, don't take this the wrong way, but you look like shit, dude."

A moment later, Nate Shore walked in from the other doorway and said, "Yeah, like really shitty."

"Thanks, guys," said Devine. "Is the coffee ready? I think I'll just dump it on my head."

Rose set the table and ladled out the food onto three

plates while Devine poured himself a cup of coffee and Shore did likewise.

The three men sat down and commenced eating.

Rose looked Devine over. "Didn't sleep well, huh? I got somethin' to help that. Nothin' to get you hooked on," he added quickly. "I'm talkin' meditation, breathin' exercises, stuff like that. It works, no lie. It ain't heroin, but sometimes it comes close."

"Thanks, but I'm fine." Devine held up the binder. "You two ever seen this before?"

Rose said, "Yeah, Betsy put stuff in that thing all the time. She's a good drawer, too."

Shore cracked his thick neck and nodded. "And she puts photos in there. Her mom had one of them old cameras where the pictures pop out and then come to life in 'bout a minute."

"Yeah, a Polaroid," noted Devine. "You two made the cut."

He held the binder open to a particular page, where there was a picture of Betsy, and Shore and Rose.

"Damn, am I really that fat?" said Rose, peering closely at his image.

"Good cooks always fat," noted Shore with a grin. "See, they always eatin' fine. But I look pretty damn buff, if I do say so myself," he added with a chuckle.

A dejected Rose looked at his unfinished fried eggs,

buttered toast, and crispy bacon and slowly pushed his plate away.

Devine opened the binder to the last entry.

"She wrote this about her uncle. Any thoughts? Keep in mind this was *before* her parents died and before she knew Glass was going to try to adopt her."

Rose and Shore looked at the words on the page and exchanged a nervous glance, but neither man spoke.

Devine put the binder down, sat back, and gazed at them both. "Okay, guys, you say you want me to protect Betsy? Well, guess what? To do that, I need you to tell me what you know. All of it."

Shore fingered his coffee, while Rose listlessly poked at his eggs.

"Some guys come to see Dwayne and Alice last year," began Shore.

"What guys?"

"Men in suits. Dwayne and them ain't livin' here then. They was in a little apartment in a town called Roslyn. And they was about to get kicked outta there 'cause Dwayne couldn't hold a job like always and they was behind on their rent and such."

Rose chimed in, "Roslyn's where they filmed that TV show, *Northern Exposure*. Watched it when I was a kid. Good show, what you call quirky." He grinned at Shore. "Like us, Dozer, *quirky*."

Shore didn't crack a smile. "Anyway, they was livin' there and some men come by."

"Wait, you mean you two were there when they visited?" asked Devine.

Shore nodded. "We'd just finished up some drug counselin' and we had jobs, too. We slept on the floor, but it beat livin' on the street. We helped with the rent and bills and such, but we ain't makin' much and the dude that owned it wanted to sell the whole shebang. Some guy was gonna knock it all down and put up a big-ass gas station or some such. Dude like tripled the rent and no way we could pay that, even with all us workin'."

"Keep going," said Devine, as Shore paused to take a sip of coffee.

"So these two dudes in suits come by. They wanted to talk to Dwayne."

"Just Dwayne, not Alice, too?"

"I 'member they just asked for Dwayne, ain't that right, Kor?" replied Shore.

"Yep. Dwayne told us to go get us some ice cream. It was hot that day, so's we all liked that idea."

"The men didn't announce who they were or show some ID?"

"No, but Dwayne seemed to be expectin' 'em," said Shore. "I mean, least he ain't surprised when they showed up."

"But didn't Alice want to stay and see what they wanted?"

Shore nodded. "She did, but Dwayne say there was no problem. Just told us to go get some ice cream and they'd be all done by the time we got back. I pulled him aside and asked him if he was sure. I woulda stayed to help him if he needed it. Those dudes looked pretty tough, but I've kicked ass in bars all over. I can hold my own with most, no shit."

"No shit is right," agreed Rose. "I seen it. Dozer bust you up, man. But he a pussycat underneath. Gentle as a baby. Just tickle his tummy and he goes right to sleep."

"Jesus, Kor, keep that crap to yourself," growled Shore.

"Okay, go on," prompted Devine again.

Shore said, "Well, we went and got us the ice cream. I had pistachio, love me a good pistachio. Double scoop. Always get me pistachio. What'd you have, Kor?"

Rose cocked his head and thought. "Not sure. Let me see now. I think it might—"

"Hey, it was the rocky road, right?" broke in Shore. "I 'member now."

"Naw, man, I wasn't doin' rocky road then. I'm pretty sure it was—"

Devine broke in. "It's okay, guys. I don't really care about the flavors. What happened when you got back?"

Shore said sheepishly, "Oh, right, um, well, Dwayne was lookin' pretty pleased with hisself."

"What did he say had happened? And did he tell you who the men were?"

"He say they was business associates." Shore sniggered. "I mean, shit, we ain't Einsteins or nuthin' but me and Kor ain't stupid neither. If them boys was Dwayne's *business associates*, I'll run through downtown Seattle in my birthday suit singin' 'Fat Bottomed Girls' at the top of my damn lungs."

"Hope to God I don't never live to see *that*," commented Rose.

"That's all he said, 'business associates'?" asked Devine.

"Yep, but Alice pulled him into the bedroom and we heard her hollerin' at him."

"And Betsy?"

"She'd gone to her room, I think," noted Shore.

"What happened when Alice and Dwayne came out of the bedroom?"

"She looked like she'd been cryin' and Dwayne had his arm 'round her," said Rose. "They didn't say nuthin' else 'bout it. Like it ain't never happened."

Shore added, "Next thing you know, they bought that car and moved to this here place."

Devine said, "We know that the money for the car and house were paid directly to the sellers by an unknown third party. You think that was who those men were? Or who they were representing?"

"Who else could they be?" said Shore. "I mean, Dwayne had 'bout much money as we did and then he gets a car *and* a house? Some weird shit goin' on. Ain't no free lunches, right, Kor?"

"Amen to that. You get money like that, bro, you got to pay for it somehow, someway. Pay the piper, pay the damn piper. Maybe the devil."

"And you never questioned him about it later? After he got the car and this place?"

Shore said, "Tried to. But all he said was he won the lottery. Over and over."

"Over and over," agreed Rose. "Man sound like a broken record."

"And Alice?"

Rose looked at Shore before speaking. "From then on, Alice looked mighty scared sometimes, ain't you say, bro?"

"Scared shitless, I'd say."

"No free lunch, like you said, Dozer," observed Rose.

"So she thought Dwayne had done something that would come back to bite them?" asked Devine.

"Well, Alice was fuckin'-A right 'bout that, wasn't she?" said Rose, before chomping down on a thick slice of bacon.

CHAPTER

31

LATER THAT AFTERNOON, DEVINE WAS driving down the dirt road away from the Odoms' home when he observed something curious. He stopped, got out, and looked at the skinny line in the middle of the dirt road. Devine knelt down and more closely examined the tire track. He took out his phone and compared the track with the one he'd taken a picture of last night.

Perfect match on the tread. So the mysterious silent rider had come here as well. But how had the person tracked him? Devine thought for a few moments and then concluded that the person had ducked back into the woods and then taken up the tail on Devine when Devine had passed by after escaping from the kidnappers.

Yet, something seemed off about that theory; only he wasn't sure what.

He drove on and arrived back in Seattle over two hours later. But he kept a close watch behind him. He never saw an e-motorcycle or any other vehicle back there that was with him the whole ride.

He turned in his trashed rental, and was being read

the riot act by an irate agency employee until he flashed his badge and instructed no one to touch the vehicle. He called Braddock, explaining what had happened.

"I'll be there in twenty minutes with a scrub team," the detective said.

Braddock, Beth Walker, and other CSI team members showed up nineteen minutes later.

They looked in astonishment at all the blood on the seats and the cracked windshield, the blown-out rear window and all the bullet holes. Devine had told them what he'd done to turn the tables on his captors.

"Lucky thing they weren't into seat harnesses," said Braddock.

"And quick thinking on your part, Travis," said Walker admiringly.

"You fight with what you have, not what you wish you had," he noted.

"There should be enough in here for DNA analysis," opined Walker.

"Guess the rental company wasn't too happy," said Braddock.

"Don't think I'm ever going to hit their premium club status."

"So you went to Ricketts, then what?" asked Braddock.

Devine gave them a more detailed account of the attack, as well as his meeting with Eric King and his wife.

Braddock sipped on a cup of coffee and said, "So they basically stonewalled you."

"Looks to be. Oh, one more thing." He reached into the car and pulled out the wineglass from the glove box and carefully unwrapped it. "I need you to run prints on this."

"Who used that glass?" asked Braddock.

"Mayor Mercedes King. I just want to know if she is who she says she is."

Braddock said, "How did you come by it?"

"She willingly left it behind in a public place that I had access to."

Braddock stared hard at him for a few moments before nodding at Walker, who put the glass in an evidence bag and marked it.

Braddock said, "We'll run the prints, but I don't have any pull on this, Devine. My superiors will not want to get into a pissing contest with Eric King."

"It's enough that you go over the car for me and run the prints."

"You could get a warrant to access the evidence the Ricketts folks collected," suggested Walker.

"They already closed the case. And they'll say they found nothing in the car. And the bodies have been cremated. So even if I get a warrant for the remains, can you get DNA, anything really, from ashes?" he asked her.

"No. The cremation process shuts all of that down for the most part."

"And Glass authorized it?" said Braddock.

"What I was told, yeah, but not by a person I necessarily find credible. And her statement has not been corroborated."

"So you really think King had something to do with this?" Braddock said, indicating the shot-up Toyota.

"Which King, the police chief or the mayor?"

"Either or both."

"I have no proof of either one being involved, but the timing is a little coincidental. I don't think Mayor King was planning on having dinner with me, primarily because I wasn't supposed to be breathing. She showed up late with a bullshit excuse and then got all defensive and left in a huff." He gave Braddock a look. "Know anything about her?"

Braddock shook his head. "That slice of the state is just not in my purview."

"And Danny Glass?" asked Walker. "What's his connection to all this?"

"Glass asked me to meet with him. Right before I drove to Ricketts."

"What did he want?" asked Braddock.

"He intimated that I owed him because he helped out my platoon when we were both in the Army."

"And what did you tell him?" asked Walker.

"That I could and would do nothing for him when it came to Betsy Odom."

"And his response?" she asked.

"That the meeting had been worth it because he knew where he stood with me."

"And then you go to Ricketts and somebody tries to kill you," said Braddock. "I'd call that the mother of all coincidences, which means it isn't."

"But there's no proof he was involved in what happened to me," Devine pointed out.

Walker slapped on a pair of nitrile gloves. "Well, let's see if we can find some."

She headed over to the battered Toyota.

32

DEVINE WENT TO HIS HOTEL, showered, peeled off his soiled clothes, and put on fresh ones. His jacket with the bloodstain removed was back from the hotel laundry so he put that on. Then he took an Uber to Odom's hotel. He had phoned Saxby before heading over.

"Betsy's been asking about you all day," the FBI agent had told him on the phone. "What the hell is going on?"

"I'll tell you when I get there."

Saxby opened the door at his knock. Odom was waiting on the couch. She jumped up when Devine walked in.

Odom said, "I'm so glad you're here, Travis. The hearing is tomorrow, and like I said, my uncle wants to meet with me before."

He looked at Saxby. "The Bureau okay with that?"

"Yes. But I'm coming along, too. To see Glass *and* attend the court hearing."

Devine held up Odom's binder. "Stopped at your home last night and found this."

"My journal!" said Odom.

"Yeah." When she reached for it, he held it back. "One thing."

"What?" she said fearfully, as though she knew what was coming.

He opened it to the last page. "You apparently had doubts about your uncle *before* your parents died. How come?"

Saxby read off the line and then looked in confusion at Odom. "Betsy?" she said.

Odom snatched the binder and plunked herself down on the couch, crossing one leg defiantly over the other. "What!?"

"What do you have to say about that?" asked Saxby.

"About what?" she shot back.

Devine sat at the other end of the couch. "By those words, you were trying to make up your mind about your uncle. So someone must have told you something about him."

Odom fingered the binder and wouldn't look at him.

Devine finally glanced at Saxby. "When and where tomorrow?"

"We meet Glass at nine at his hotel. The court hearing is at eleven at the King County Superior Court. It's right here in downtown Seattle."

"But the Odoms resided in Kittitas County," noted Devine.

Saxby said, "Yes, but there was an agreement among the parties that the case would be transferred here. Kittitas didn't want a media circus, what with Glass being involved. And DOJ didn't want Glass traveling out there. Just all around easier to do it here."

"Okay." He looked over to catch Odom staring at him but then she quickly looked away.

"So how will the hearing run?" he asked.

Saxby said, "The judge will probably take testimony from at least Betsy and maybe Glass. The lawyers may have motions or statements to make. We'll just have to play it by ear."

"You said DOJ will contest Glass's petition for the emergency guardianship?" asked Devine.

"They absolutely will," replied Saxby.

"And I have no say?" exclaimed Odom.

"You have a lot of say, actually," noted Saxby. "But you're also only twelve and so the law says you need others to help you with this."

"No, I don't! I just want everybody to leave me the hell alone."

"Including your uncle?" asked Devine. "And have you decided if he's good or bad?"

She made an ugly face and looked away.

Devine turned to Saxby. "I went to Ricketts yesterday. I phoned Betsy from there."

"What did you find out?" said Saxby.

Devine glanced nervously at Odom but decided to say it. "I was told that Danny Glass had Dwayne and Alice's remains cremated."

"What?" barked Saxby.

Devine looked at Odom. The girl's mouth was hanging open and she didn't even look like she was breathing.

He said, "I'm sorry I didn't tell you before. It was... just awkward trying to do it over the phone."

She closed her mouth and glanced away.

"And there's something else that happened out there," said Devine. "Two men did their best to kill me."

A stunned Saxby said, "What happened?"

He gave them a short sketch of the night's events. "I think they're dead, but I can't be sure. They had backup so I had to get the hell out of there." He added, "Seattle PD is going over my car now, checking the blood and bullet holes and such." He glanced again at Odom, who looked like she might be sick.

"Were you injured?" asked Saxby.

He rubbed the back of his head. "Just where one of the guys decided to use my head and his gun to play Whac-A-Mole."

"Good God," said Saxby.

"Why... why would they want to hurt you?" asked Odom.

"Maybe because I'm trying to find out who killed your parents and someone doesn't want that."

"You really think they didn't die from an overdose?" said Saxby.

"No. Too much weird stuff going on. And the folks in Ricketts were about as unhelpful as they could be." He paused. "So, Betsy, you wanted to see me?"

She set her binder aside and composed herself. "Like I said, my uncle wants to meet with me. And I want you to be there."

"I thought you'd made up your mind that you wanted him to adopt you. So, why do I need to come with you?"

"I'd just feel better if you did," she said, not meeting his eye.

For a moment Devine thought the girl was actually going to say what was really on her mind. But then she grabbed her binder, rose, and went to her bedroom and shut the door.

In a low voice Devine said, "Has she mentioned anything to you about Glass?"

"Not specifically, no. But there's something bothering her, I just don't know what. And she's unlikely to confide in me. She seems to trust you better. So I think it's up to you to crack the code with her."

"Me? Look, *you've* got kids. I don't know how to handle this stuff."

Saxby gave him a weary smile. "Being a parent doesn't make you an expert, Devine. It just allows you to better understand your severe shortcomings on a daily basis, because your kids just relish reminding you of them in both large and small ways. As they get older, the shortcomings just get bigger until, presto, you're no longer a moron but instead transform into a genius from whom they want all sorts of advice. I'm actually anxiously waiting for that last stage to kick in. Now, Betsy seemed to want to tell you something. And what you found in her journal clearly shows that her doubts about her uncle predated her parents' deaths. We just need to find out why, but we obviously don't have much time. For all I know, the judge could rule on the emergency guardianship petition tomorrow."

"Shit, seriously?"

"Yes, seriously. It's why they call it *emergency*."

"So how do we do that?"

"You mean how do *you* do it since she can't stand me."

"But—"

"I didn't tell you everything about me, Devine. I *am* the mother of two boys, like I said. But I'm also the mother of a twelve-year-old girl."

"You're kidding me."

She took out her wallet and showed him a picture of her and a young girl. Saxby was clearly forcing a smile, and the girl looked like she wanted to strangle her mother.

"This is Dana."

"Why in the hell didn't you tell me that before?" demanded Devine.

"Because I didn't have to tell you anything to begin with, and I still confided too much as it was."

"So what do I do? How do I get through to her?" asked Devine. He felt embarrassed about pleading for help, but right now he needed it. Guns and fighting and blowing stuff up, and how to read a balance sheet and a P&L statement, he knew a lot about. Twelve-year-old females not so much.

"She's been asking to go to a bookstore. There's one close by. Take her there. Let her shop, buy her a cookie and whatever cool drink she wants, and then sit there until she decides she wants to talk."

"And you're sure she will?"

"I'm not sure of anything, Devine. She's a twelve-year-old girl. *Nobody* can figure them out."

CHAPTER

33

ODOM STROLLED AROUND THE BOOKSTORE, idly taking a book off a shelf and glancing over some pages before placing it back.

Devine paralleled her, looking around and making sure no one was taking a heightened interest in them.

"You like reading, I take it?" he said as she picked up a fantasy novel in the YA section of the store.

"Yeah. My mom told me it was important and fun. She said she wished she'd read more when she was my age. But I don't think her dad was really good about that. He didn't much care for stuff like that, I guess."

"Did she tell you anything else about your grand-father?"

She glanced up at him from the book she had been checking out. "Not too many good things. He was apparently...not too nice to her or my uncle. I never knew him, or my mom's mom. They're dead."

"And your dad? Was he a reader?"

She smiled wistfully. "Dad couldn't sit still long

enough to read a food label on the cereal box, much less a book."

"Did you know your other grandparents?"

"No. My dad's parents were in a car accident or something before I was born. He had a sister but she died in the car crash, too."

"That's really awful."

"Yeah," she said quietly. "I think... I think it made my dad feel like... helpless, you know? Like what happens, happens. So he just didn't worry much about stuff. Just thought if it was supposed to work out, it would, you know? Maybe that's why he never found something that he... you know for a job and all. But he was always there for me and stuff. We would play and talk all the time. Sometimes, it was like having an older brother, you know?"

Her tone was so poignant and her look so wistful that Devine's heart went out to her.

"Yeah, I know. Do you know how your parents met?"

Devine had learned some of this from Campbell's digging into the Odoms' histories, but he wanted to hear her perspective.

"My dad grew up around here. My mom was from the middle of the country, and my dad moved there at some point. He'd been out of school for a while by then. I guess he wanted to try something new. My mom was working at a restaurant in the place where he moved to, and my dad came in to eat lunch one day. After she got off work, he was waiting for her, with flowers. Then he took *her* to dinner. Kinda romantic. Anyway, after a while they got married, had me, and then we...well, we moved around some before coming back to where my dad grew up."

"Find something?" he asked. She had gone on looking at books while they'd been talking before pulling one out and keeping it.

"Yeah. I've read the first three in this series. They're cool. What do you like to read?"

"Besides thrillers and military histories, anything with cute bunnies."

She smiled at his quip. "Can I also get a sketch pad and some pencils?"

"Sure, I know you like to draw. Korey told me, said you were good. And I saw some of the sketches in your binder, and he's right, you *are* good."

She smiled shyly. "My mom liked to do it and she taught me."

They found a suitable sketch pad and the pencils and he bought them and the book. Then Devine suggested, "How about something to drink and a snack? I could use a coffee."

"Sure," she said excitedly. "They have scones. I saw them."

Odom got a raspberry scone to go with her iced

strawberry Frappuccino, while Devine selected a blue-berry muffin to pair with his coffee.

"Enough sugar to keep you lit for a week," noted Devine.

After they sat at a table, Odom said, "Thanks for bringing me here. It's been a while since I got a book."

"Well, you've had a lot going on."

She took a sip of her drink and broke off a bit of the scone. "Do you really think you can find out what happened to my parents?"

"I'm trying my best."

"But it's dangerous, right? Those people who tried to hurt you?"

"It's part of the job, Betsy. And it's my concern, okay? Don't add that to your worry list."

"You think it was my uncle, right? Who did it?"

"I don't know. But he's certainly on the suspect list."

"But why would he? My mom was his *sister*."

"For some people, it doesn't matter. They don't think like you and I do."

"If he wanted to be in my life, he could have been without killing anybody. So what would his motive be?"

"*Motive?* Sounds like you watch cop shows."

"I like to broaden my horizons as much as the next person," she said in such a grown-up tone that Devine had to smile.

"And I saw in your journal that you have FBI agent on your list of possible future careers."

She glanced down. "I know it sounds stupid."

"It doesn't sound stupid at all. Quite the opposite actually."

She looked up at him. "Why do you say that?"

"There are already too many guys like me doing this sort of stuff. We need a lot more women. They bring different skill sets and perspectives, and, well, it's just important. Based on my personal experience, sometimes guys' testosterone is a real problem. We escalate instead of de-escalating. And you're smart and observant. Two good traits in a federal agent."

"Thanks," she replied, looking both embarrassed and pleased.

"Nate and Korey told me about a couple of guys in suits who visited you in your old apartment. You remember them?"

"Yeah. We went out for ice cream while my dad talked to them."

"And then sometime after that you all moved to your house. And your parents bought that car, which alone cost around fifty grand by the way."

She shot him a nervous glance while she sipped on her drink. "You think they gave my dad some money, you mean?"

"No, our records show that the money was sent

directly to the vendors for the car and the land and home. Didn't you wonder where he got the funds to buy all that?"

"He said he won the lottery."

"Same thing he told Korey and Nate. You believe him?"

She said, "No. I always knew when he was lying. He had a tell."

"What sort of tell?" asked Devine.

"He giggled right after he said something that wasn't true. I don't even think he knew he was doing it. He couldn't help it. And he did it after telling me he won the lottery."

"So the men who met with your dad probably paid for the car and home. The questions are why and who did they work for. And as far as I know, the only person with money like that was your uncle."

"But he might have just wanted to help them. They *were* related. And them dying could have nothing to do with that. And he's the only family I have left so it's pretty natural that he would want to adopt me."

"Is that you talking, or him?"

"What?"

"That sounded scripted. Is that what Glass told you when you two met?"

"A little bit, I guess," she admitted.

"What else did he tell you?" asked Devine.

"I asked him about the legal stuff."

Devine tensed. "Really? And what did he say?"

"That the government had just made up their minds to go after him. But he thought it might just go away, or, be *dismissed*, that was the word he used."

"He actually said that?"

"Yeah, why? What's the big deal?"

"If it gets dismissed, it will be because the government witnesses keep on getting murdered. Three and counting so far have been killed."

She slowly put down the piece of scone she was about to bite into. "Murdered?"

"Yes. He didn't mention that?"

She shook her head.

Devine just sat there and said nothing.

"Aren't you going to ask me about what I wrote in my journal? About whether my uncle was good or bad?"

He shook his head.

"Why not?"

"I already asked. You clearly didn't want to answer. If you want to tell me, you'll tell me."

"But you'll keep trying to find out what happened to my mom and dad?"

"I will, but quite frankly I don't have a lot to go on. And after tomorrow it might be moot."

"What do you mean?" she said sharply.

"After the hearing tomorrow, your uncle may have custody of you."

"Do you mean you'll stop looking for their killer then?"

"It might be out of my hands, Betsy. I'm not my own boss. I go and do what I'm ordered to do."

She pushed the Frappuccino and scone away and sat back looking thoroughly dejected.

Devine wanted to say something, but Saxby's cautionary words came back to him and he remained quiet.

She sat there for a bit while Devine gazed around the small café component of the bookstore.

He turned back to Odom when she said, "My uncle told me that sometimes bad things happen for good reasons."

"What was he talking about?"

"You're right. I almost did give you the high sign when he said that. It made me mad. Like how could anything good come out of my parents dying?"

"So that was what he was talking about? Something good coming out of them dying?"

"Yes."

"Why didn't you finish the high sign then?"

"Because...because then he told me that I looked just like my mom when she was my age. And that she was smart and funny, just like he knew I was. And that he would have given anything to have her back. But if he couldn't, then he wanted to take care of me because that's what my mom would have wanted. In fact, he told me that she made him promise that he would in case anything happened to her or my dad."

"When did she tell him that?" asked Devine. All his senses were on high alert now because her answer could be significant.

"He said he had talked to her a while back. When . . . when my dad wasn't doing too well."

"Was this before or after he didn't win the lottery?" asked Devine.

She smiled weakly. "It was before we moved to the trailer."

"Do you think it's possible that your mother asked her brother for help?"

"I don't know. Maybe. I knew we were having money problems. My dad had lost his job again and we were going to have to leave our apartment."

"Did your mother like her brother?"

"I think she did like him, yeah."

Devine recalled what Shore and Rose had told him about Dwayne not liking Glass, but that Alice had a different opinion of her brother.

"But was it something she told you that made you write what you did in your journal about your uncle?"

She remained quiet for a few seconds and he wasn't sure she was even going to answer.

"Not my mother, no."

"Who then?"

"I...don't want to say."

"Okay, I think you already told me the answer, but do you still want to be adopted by your uncle?"

She didn't answer right away. In fact, he had to wait a couple of minutes while he watched her debate this internally. And he could tell it was not an easy process for the girl.

Finally she said, "I don't know, Travis. Part of me wants it. And part of me..." Her voice trailed away.

He gripped her hand. "This wouldn't be easy for anyone, Betsy, okay? So don't beat yourself up over it."

She nodded and he released his grip and sat back.

It was then that Devine noticed for a second time what he had glimpsed before. The woman at the far table who had glanced their way, not once, but now twice.

She looked to be in her fifties, broad hipped, pale skin, longish brown hair with lots of gray. She was dressed in jeans and a pullover sweater with hunter green boots. A white tennis visor rode on her head. She looked normal and benign and seemed to be right in her element. Perfect. Maybe too perfect.

As Odom finished her drink and scone, something occurred to Devine, and he phoned Beth Walker. She told him she was still going over the 4Runner.

"Nothing to report yet," she said. "But we might have a few things to go on."

In a low voice that could not be overhead he said, "Do me a favor—check under the chassis for a tracking device."

"A tracking device?"

"Yeah, can you do it now? It's a little time sensitive." Devine never looked at the woman at the table again, but he was keeping watch on her via her reflection in a large mirror behind the cash registers.

Two minutes later a breathless Walker said, "How did you know?"

"Thanks. I'll see you in a while."

Things are starting to make a lot more sense.

He clicked off and looked at Odom. "I'm going to call Saxby and have her meet us outside. She can take you back to the hotel."

"What? But where are *you* going?"

"I just need to check out something."

Or rather someone.

CHAPTER

34

THE CAFÉ WAS ON THE second floor so they rode down the escalator to the ground floor after Devine had phoned Saxby. She was taking a taxi over to pick up Odom.

They waited by the glass front doors. In the reflection Devine could see the same woman, who had also ridden down the escalator after them, as she browsed through a shelf of magazines. She was good, thought Devine. She never looked their way, but somehow, he knew, the woman was still watching them.

When Saxby showed up, Devine took Odom out to the car and she got in.

"I'll be by later, then we can get ready for tomorrow," he told them.

Devine returned to the bookstore and headed toward where he had seen the woman last. Only she wasn't there. And she had not come outside. The escalators were clear of customers, but there was an elevator. He noted that the doors had just closed and it was heading up to the second floor. He hurried up the escalator and was waiting by the elevator when it arrived on the second floor.

The doors opened but no one was inside it. He heard a door close somewhere close by. He saw the exit sign at the rear of the floor and Devine ran for it.

He burst through the door and heard the door on the first floor open. Devine raced down the stairs, jumping the last three steps, kicked the door open, and found himself in an alley behind the bookstore. He looked searchingly both ways but saw or heard no one.

That seemed impossible but then he saw a door on the other side of the alley that was open about a foot.

He hustled across the alley, gripped the door, and tugged it fully open. He found himself in a dusty hall with minimal lighting. He heard nothing up ahead of him, which didn't mean much if his prey was moving with stealth. He pulled his weapon, and pointing it in front of him, Devine advanced down the hall.

He quickly found that the building was being renovated. Construction materials were stacked neatly along the corridor. He could smell fresh paint and sawdust and he spied a makeshift locker room that housed work clothes, filter masks, and heavy boots. He made sure no one was lurking in there before heading down the hall once more.

He pushed open a set of makeshift double doors and found himself in the main space of the structure.

It had been gutted, but sections of wooden studs had been set up on the concrete slab, carving out where demising walls would later be. There were no workers around and Devine assumed, at this hour, they had already finished for the day.

Devine found the front door but it was securely padlocked. He ran back down the hall, then out into the alley and around to the front of the building.

Plywood had been set up over the street-front plate glass windows. Construction permits and warning signs were stapled to the wood.

So, she followed us to the bookstore, then took the time to set this place up for her escape, then returned to the bookstore and took up her surveillance. Then when she saw I had made her, she sent the elevator up without her in it. Followed me up the escalator, and while I was spinning my wheels waiting for the car to open, she commenced her escape and I gave chase.

But there was a problem with that theory, namely, where had she gone? The front doors were padlocked. If she came in the open rear door, how had she gotten out? There were no other exit doors.

Making no sense of this, another thought occurred to Devine. She might have made a mistake, based on something that Devine had noted at the bookstore.

He hurried back over there, found a manager, flashed his badge and ID, and made his demand about the woman he was seeking. He was led into a back, cluttered room where a computer monitor was set up on a metal desk piled with books.

The manager, a woman in her forties with sandy hair and an excited expression, said, "The security cameras' footage is fed into here, Agent Devine."

"I want to see the last half hour in the café and then ten minutes ago down on the first floor by the elevator in particular," said Devine.

The woman sat down and began clicking keys while Devine pulled up a chair and studied the screen.

"There," he said when the woman came up on the screen. "You can follow her on the feed."

The manager let the recorded footage run and Devine silently watched the woman, who kept her face downward and shuffled around, giving off the image of feebleness. However, Devine knew what she was really doing was avoiding looking into the cameras.

She bought a coffee and a banana from the café and he noted that she paid in cash, probably the only person to do that here all day.

She sat at the table for a while. Devine knew that was when she had been watching him and Odom at their table.

"Okay, take me to the first floor, elevator."

She did so and he watched as, just as he had predicted, she stepped into the elevator car, pushed a key, and then got off. She moved behind a shelf. The next moment Devine ran up, paused, and then hustled for the escalator. The woman emerged from hiding and followed him up the escalator.

While Devine broke for the elevator, she went to the exit door and left that way. She was now moving far more swiftly and without a hint of any physical impediment.

"I'll need a copy of what we just saw."

She downloaded one onto a USB stick and handed it to him.

"You got plastic, scissors, tape, and some paper?" he asked the woman.

"Yes."

"Go get them, please."

She brought the items back, and Devine used the plastic and tape to cover the elevator button on the first floor and the exit door handle on the second. He made signs stating that both the elevator and the door were out of order.

He then called Walker. She didn't answer. She was probably still working away on the 4Runner. He left her a message to get a print lift team over to the bookstore. He gave her the manager's name and contact info along with exactly what he wanted done. Then he told the manager to expect them.

He walked up to the second floor and taped off the

table where the woman had sat, for Walker to later process. He next questioned the employee who had rung up the purchase of the coffee and banana, getting a description of the woman that he figured was of negligible value at best, since she was clearly in disguise. But any bit of information was more than what he'd had previously.

Devine noted that she had left neither the cup nor the banana peel behind.

Okay, you've been all action up till now. Slow it down, and think it through.

He closed his eyes and went over everything that had happened in the last hour. It was like doing battlefield reenactments in the Army to see what had gone right and, more important, what had gone to hell.

Something was off. He could feel it. Now he just had to locate it.

Two minutes went by, then five, then five more.

On the next click of his mental clock, Devine opened his eyes.

The best way was usually the most direct and simplest. This held true in pretty much any task or mission, because simple meant there were fewer opportunities to screw it up. From meal recipes to building anything to running for your life.

So the woman could have simply walked out the main floor exit once she had decoyed Devine to the second-floor elevator area. Her clever plan had worked and she would have plenty of time for a leisurely stroll to anywhere she wanted.

So why waste time going up the escalator after him, and then exiting out a door, and while doing so, making enough noise for Devine to notice?

He followed her exit route once more, looking for something he might have missed before. In the alleyway he stared at the open door into the space being renovated, through which he had gone earlier, as had, presumably, the woman.

Up and down the alley he saw tradesmen entrances and several large Dumpsters. All the doors were closed, no doubt for security purposes.

So why hadn't she closed this door? It would have taken all of a second. And if she had, there would have been no way for Devine to know where she had gone. Then it struck him.

She wanted me to go in there. Which means there's something she wants me to find.

So Devine went to find it.

35

HIS GUN AT THE READY because this could be a trap, he moved slowly along the dusty interior hall, again checking everything along the way. He came out into the main front area and started going foot by foot, corner to corner.

He stopped at the second corner, halting in front of a rolling easel set against the wall, and on which were written the rules of the workplace along with tasks assigned to a list of workers. Based on the list of duties set out, Bill, Dave, Mark, and Wanda were going to be really busy tomorrow, thought Devine. Then he noticed that the easel was the sort that was two-sided and was designed to be flipped to reveal the opposite side.

He pulled it away from the wall and did so. Devine stepped back and read what had been written on the other side in block letters using a blue Sharpie.

Memo to TD: If you're reading this you're a bit cleverer than I gave you credit for, so, well done.

FYI, please erase so none of the construction workers arriving tomorrow will be unduly distressed, curious, or looking to post this on social media for their fifteen minutes of fame.

This is far bigger than DG and his problem. Or the girl and her problems. Or you and your mission. Or me and what I came here to do. The men who you met last night are ones I recognize. Not them particularly, but how they handle things. By the way, congratulations on surviving, with a big assist from yours truly. After they cleaned up the mess I followed the SUV to a remote property miles away. A bird was waiting to whisk two *bodies* away. Yes, they did not survive your counterattack. It was a pretty special bird. I've seen one before. I've even ridden in one. There are only two agencies in this country that use them. I'll leave it to you to figure out which ones. This is something more than 3D chess, so watch your back. I don't want you to die. Yet. I want to be there when that happens. You know why.

Devine looked at the name at the bottom.

The Girl on the Train
P.S. You're welcome.

Devine took a picture of the writing with his phone and then erased all of it.

He walked outside and ordered up a ride to the hotel where Saxby and Odom were staying.

On the way he phoned Campbell. When he got to the part about the girl on the train and what she'd written, he heard Campbell bark, "Son of a bitch."

Devine could understand why. "The mole is still there, sir," he said. "Dawn Schuman was a red herring."

"To let us think we'd ferreted out the real spy," said Campbell.

"Which probably means you're never going to find her body."

"And it also means she was innocent," noted Campbell.

"And someone else there is as guilty as hell."

"But, Devine, why would she have divulged all that to you? By doing that she as good as told us the mole is still around."

"Because she doesn't need the mole anymore, sir."

"So she saved your butt just so she can kill you herself? The lady must hold a grudge."

"I think it's only partly that."

"And the rest?"

"She had a mission. She failed. She's the sort who will push through every wall, run over anyone she has to, endure all the shit in the world to make it right and complete the mission."

"Reminds me of you actually."

"And she has principles. She could have let me die in those woods, and later claimed credit for it."

"A killer with a sense of honor. And her warning to you? Why?"

"I will take the woman at her word. She says this is bigger than Glass, bigger than my mission. The chopper she mentioned, ring any bells?"

"I have to make inquiries. Very, very discreet ones."

Devine quickly noted that there was suddenly a level of apprehension in the other man's voice that he had never noticed before.

"She must have gone to that building while Betsy and I were in the bookstore, and wrote out the message. Then she came back, let me make her, and then did what she did. I don't think she even went back into that building when I was chasing her. I think she hid behind one of the Dumpsters in the alley and let the open door suck me in. Then she goes on her merry way."

"Pretty good plan to execute on the fly," noted Campbell.

"She said something more than 3D chess?" noted Devine.

"There aren't many things more complex than chess, 3D or otherwise. However, the world you and I operate in is one of them."

"How can someone like Danny Glass be caught up in *geopolitics*?"

"I don't know. And we as yet can't take what she's said as true. It hasn't been corroborated."

"How do we corroborate it?" asked Devine.

"When you think of an answer, let me know, and I'll do the same. Until then, watch yourself, and let me get back to work. And you likewise."

He clicked off as Devine got out of the cab in front of the hotel.

CHAPTER

36

ODOM WAS IN THE BATHROOM taking a shower, so Devine took a few minutes to fill in Saxby on his talk with Odom at the bookstore.

"I followed your advice and it worked," he said. "Thanks for the assist."

"Any parent of a daughter could have done it. But she said Glass made her mad when he said that good things sometimes come from bad events?"

"Yeah, but he followed that up with the statement, uncorroborated, that Alice Odom wanted him to take care of Betsy in case anything happened to her or Dwayne."

"Pretty convenient for him," noted Saxby.

"My sources also tell me that Alice was really upset when two men showed up where they were living before they moved to Kittitas. I think those men, or whoever they were working for, directly paid for the Odoms' car and home."

"You think they worked for Glass and he was the one who actually paid for it?"

"I can't think of anyone else."

"So Glass gave Dwayne and Alice a car and home? They are his family."

"Dwayne didn't like Glass. I'm not sure he would have just let the man buy him that stuff. From what we found out they'd been in precarious financial circumstances for quite a long time. So why wait until recently to help them out or have Dwayne reach out?"

"Maybe Dwayne Odom had something on his brother-in-law? Like Rollins did?" suggested Saxby. "Blackmail?"

"Could be. And my same sources tell me that Alice was scared from that moment on."

"Are your sources the two drug users?"

"Look, they're actually good guys who mean well. Life just threw them some curveballs."

"As it does to us all," replied Saxby, a comment that surprised Devine.

Odom appeared wrapped in a large fluffy towel in the bathroom doorway. Her wet hair lay straight down her back.

"Travis, when did you get here?"

"Just walked in."

"Let me change and we can talk."

She rushed to her room, and five minutes later, after they heard a hair dryer running for about a minute, Odom reappeared dressed in jeans and a sweatshirt that were part of the clothes he had brought from her home.

She sat next to Devine and said, "I don't see why I have to meet with my uncle before the hearing."

Saxby said, "Just because he requested it doesn't mean you have to accept."

Odom looked conflicted. "But if I don't, he'll probably be mad."

Devine said, "That's his problem, not yours."

They all sat there in silence for a few moments until Odom spoke.

"Well, he asked me questions when we met. Now maybe I can ask him some."

"Like what?" Saxby wanted to know.

"Like where I'll live if he does adopt me. Where I'll go to school. Whether I'll get an allowance. Whether he'll set up a trust for me and put me in his will, and if so, for how much?"

Devine glanced sharply at Saxby. "Okay, you've obviously given this some thought."

Then he remembered her heavily marked up copy of *Think and Grow Rich*.

"It is *my* life, after all."

"And while you're questioning him, why don't you ask him why he had his sister and brother-in-law cremated so fast."

Saxby let out a sharp breath. "Devine, do you really want her to go there?"

"Why not? He'll know that I told her. He'll blame

me, not her. And it's a natural question. Betsy never even got to say goodbye, right?" he added, looking at the girl.

"I'll ask him," she said quietly. "Because *I* want to know the answer."

"But the real question is do you want to be adopted by him? The judge will probably ask you that. And you have to have some sort of response."

"I know," said Odom, now looking miserable and uncertain.

Saxby suddenly chimed in, "Well, since you're going to court tomorrow, you need some proper clothes."

"What?" exclaimed Odom, looking at her in surprise.

"Clothes. The ones you have are not going to cut it for court. I'll take you shopping."

"I don't have any money."

"It's on the Bureau."

"Seriously?" said Odom, while Devine was giving the FBI agent a look that asked the same question.

"Seriously."

"Well, okay, but I don't want any old lady clothes." She ran her gaze down Saxby's outfit.

"I have a daughter your age."

Odom looked stunned. "You do?"

"I know you think I'm clueless about young girls, but wait until you're a mother. The wars you'll go through? Well, what doesn't kill you makes you stronger, right? At least according to Kelly Clarkson."

"O-kay," said Odom warily.

"There's an Aeropostale store near here. There were some cute things in the window. Go get your coat. It's getting late. We don't have a lot of time."

Odom looked at Devine. "Do you want to go?"

He held up his hands and shook his head. "You're in far better hands with Agent Saxby."

Odom rushed to her room to get her coat.

Devine turned to Saxby. "Where did that come from?"

"My own daughter won't let me take her shopping because I'm not cool. And every female, regardless of age or economic bracket, deserves some nice clothes to wear that she can feel confident in."

Devine smiled. "I think I might have misjudged you, Agent Saxby."

"It's Ellen, remember? And I think I did some misjudging of my own."

"I'll be back in time to go with you to the meeting tomorrow."

"And what will you do now?"

"Places to go and people to interrogate."

"Someone wants you dead, Travis. Don't forget that."

"I never do. *Ellen.*"

CHAPTER

37

DEVINE CABBED OVER TO A rental place and got another car. It was a Subaru crossover that handled nicely. He had freaked out the rental agent by asking if the windows were bulletproof.

On the way back to his hotel he got a call from Campbell.

"Want some *good* news?" his boss asked.

"It would be different, at least."

"As you requested, we pulled video from stores along the main road in Ricketts. Everyone uses the cloud now so no more having to go in and extract a hard drive or worry about it being taped over. We didn't exactly get a warrant, but speed is of the essence. I'll send you the feed now. We used an AI filter to drill down to the pertinent time in question. Took seconds instead of days."

"Did they find anything?"

"I'll let you see for yourself. We also accessed street camera feeds for Seattle when you were at the bookstore and also ran it through the AI filter. There is no one who matches your person's description on any of them. What you got in the bookstore is all there is."

"Meaning she knew where the cameras were and worked her way around them. Any progress on finding the real mole in your group?"

"Not yet. But we *will* find the person, I promise you."

He clicked off and Devine drove the rest of the way to his hotel, went up to his room, ordered dinner, and sat there eating while he looked over the video feed he'd gotten from Campbell that showed the main road in Ricketts.

He watched as the two men approached him while he sat in his SUV, distracted.

A sitting duck. You better up your game, Devine, or you are dead next time.

He noted that the police cruiser had slid away from its place at the curb two minutes before the hit team approached.

Coincidence? I think not.

Indeed, the whole street had emptied out, so maybe the entire town of Ricketts was on somebody's payroll.

As his 4Runner rolled off with him and the two men in it, he saw the black SUV appear. He checked for the license plate. Only it didn't have one. They weren't going to get tripped up on something that simple.

He was about to turn off the feed when he saw it.

Ostensibly a woman astride what appeared to be an

e-motorcycle. She didn't look anything like a matronly purveyor of books with long stringy hair hanging in her face and bulky clothing that hid any evidence of her actual body. Here, she looked lean and lethal, just like she had on the train. The helmet covered her head, so no ID possible there.

But he closed his eyes and thought back to that train ride on Trenitalia between Geneva and Milan. The girl on the train. The college student, or at least that was the role she was playing. She'd worn shades, even that early in the morning. Should have been a tip-off, and eventually was.

The hair you could change a million different ways. The eye color, too. But the curve of the jaw, no, only he couldn't see the curve of her jaw because of the helmet and face shield. And in the bookstore the hair had been long and in her face, again by design. So no possible mental match.

But there might be one thing.

In the video she had pulled out a pair of gloves but hadn't put them on yet. He zoomed in on the five fingers on her right hand exposed in the frame.

Then he closed his eyes and remembered the hand that had held the knife on the train. Her fingers closed around the handle, waiting to plunge it into Devine's neck or heart or aorta. Only she hadn't gotten there because he'd seen the knife in the window's reflection and delivered a punishing blow to her jaw that had knocked the woman out.

Again, one of the seemingly unimportant things that blew up otherwise well-laid plans.

And kept me alive.

Devine opened his eyes and studied the image on the screen with the same intensity he had brought to every task on the battlefield.

The pinky finger visible on the feed had been broken and never reset properly, resulting in the top third skirting off slightly to the right at about a five-degree angle. He froze it there.

He brought up the mental image of the woman on the train. Her hand. That finger. Same injury. Same tilt. The girl on the train was now in the state of Washington. She had told him this already on the easel in the building being renovated. But Devine believed nothing without corroboration, and now he'd just gotten it.

So out there aligned against him he had whoever had tried to kill him in Ricketts. It wasn't the train girl, because she had saved his life. The police chief, his department, and the mayor of Ricketts seemed to be in the bank with those people, whoever the hell they were.

Which might have been the reason why Ricketts was chosen as the place for the Odoms to meet the two men, with the duffel being another payoff perhaps? Straight cash instead of a gift of a house and car?

Devine worked through this in his head. They had lured the Odoms out with the promise of something. The duffel was given to them, but then they were poisoned somehow. Next, the duffel and what was in it, which Betsy said had gone into the trunk, would have been taken back. The killers had gotten away with murder and it hadn't cost them a penny.

And Betsy had been left an orphan, and easy pickings for the uncle to step in. So was Glass the other force out there, behind the assassins? Was Ricketts Glass's town? Had he bought and paid for it? And when you bought and paid for something, you owned it. And maybe you owned everybody who lived there, too. And then gave them military-grade war machines, and a brand-new government building to boot.

A moment later a call from Walker interrupted these thoughts. She said she had been to the bookstore and checked all the areas for prints.

"They were all clean, Travis, sorry."

He thanked her and clicked off. It seemed the girl on the train also sweated the small details pretty well.

He finished his meal and was thinking about turning in when his phone buzzed again. He didn't recognize the number but answered it anyway.

"Agent Devine?"

"Yes, who is this?"

"Dr. Deborah Coburn. I performed the autopsies on the Odoms."

Devine forgot all about sleep. He had assumed he would never hear from her. But then he recalled being told that she was a circuit medical examiner. So Ricketts might not be her hometown. And maybe she wasn't on Danny Glass's payroll.

"Yes, Dr. Coburn. I *do* need to speak with you. Where are you now? I'm in downtown Seattle."

"I'm actually in the Seattle area. There's a conference here on forensic pathology starting tomorrow. I know it's late, but can you meet with me now? I'm… well, I'm scared."

"Where do you want to meet?"

She gave him the address of where she was staying.

"I'm on my way."

38

IT TOOK DEVINE ABOUT TWENTY minutes to reach the house. He drove east on Interstate 90, over Lake Washington and through Mercer Island, and then turned north toward Bellevue. The house was a fairly new two-story with a white brick front and a two-car front-load garage situated all by itself in a cul-de-sac in a wooded area. A fine mist had formed on the way over that might, at some point, turn to rain, or sleet.

There were lights on in the house, and a gray Lexus coupe with Washington plates was parked in the driveway.

He knocked on the front door and a woman's voice said fearfully, "Who is it?"

"Dr. Coburn? It's Travis Devine."

"Hold up your credentials to the door camera."

Devine glanced around, saw the door cam, and showed his badge and ID card.

The door opened, revealing Coburn, who was petite with silver hair cut short; she looked to be around fifty. She wore a cream-colored pantsuit with a navy blue blouse open at the collar. A gold chain with a crucifix was around her neck.

"Agent Devine, please come in," she said in a trembling voice.

Coburn closed the door, locking it. She led him quickly into the dining room, where a black doctor's bag perched on a chair and a sleek brown leather briefcase was open on the table. There were papers scattered next to it, along with several manila file folders.

"Nice place," said Devine.

"I don't live here. My home is in Spokane. That's the reason I'm one of the medical examiners for that part of the state. A friend who's out of town let me use her home while I'm attending the conference in Seattle. It's a forensic science smorgasbord." She smiled faintly. "But it actually feels good to catch up with colleagues and the technology is changing so fast."

"You said you were scared?" prompted Devine. "Does this have to do with the autopsies you performed?"

Coburn motioned him to a seat while she sat down across from him.

She said, "I'm still awaiting tox screens on Dwayne and Alice Odom, and those can take a while. Without that I could make no definitive cause-of-death determination. I can't quite put my finger on it, but something weird is going on."

Devine said, "Wait a minute, I don't understand.

Your reports list accidental drug overdose as the pre-liminary COD for both, and they also said you found indications of prolonged substance abuse in both their bodies."

She looked stunned. "I didn't find any signs of a drug overdose, or that the Odoms were addicted to drugs." She looked at him, dread on her features. "Do you have the reports with you?"

He slipped the pages from his jacket pocket and handed them across.

Coburn read through them carefully before hand-ing them back to him. He noted that her hands were now trembling. "Those are *not* my reports. And that is *not* my signature."

"Then who wrote them and why?"

"I don't know," she said in a near whisper.

"Maybe you should start from the beginning?" sug-gested Devine. "What struck you as weird?"

The woman looked close to losing all emotional control. He reached over and gripped Coburn's wrist. She glanced up at him.

"I'm not going to let anything happen to you, Dr. Coburn. Take a few deep belly breaths, in through the nose, out through the mouth, compose yourself, and let me hear your story." He let go of her wrist and sat back while she breathed exactly as he had told her to.

Calmed, she began, "There are nationally prescribed

procedures for MEs to conduct investigations of, and diagnose and certify deaths due to, opioid overdoses."

"Like what?"

"Examining the decedent's medical history, and checking the scene where the death occurred. Also analyzing their living space to look for evidence of substance abuse. Everything from crushed tablets to altered transdermal patches, pills not in prescription bottles, or overlapping prescriptions, cooker spoons, needles, tourniquets, and other drug paraphernalia, things like that."

"Did you do that?"

"I was given no chance to do that. That's what was weird. The Ricketts police did not hold the scene of death open for me. I wasn't even informed of its location. And I was given no opportunity to review the Odoms' medical history. And I was told their residence was unknown at the time."

"They lived in Kittitas County in a mobile home. The address was on the title to their car and I'm sure it was on their driver's licenses, so the police knew exactly where they lived."

"I was not told or given any of that. I *was* told that all indications were of an accidental drug overdose. And that Narcan was administered at the scene by the Odoms' daughter, but was unsuccessful."

"Who told you that?"

"The officers who found them."

"Their names?"

"I'd have to check my notes."

"Which are where?"

She looked hopelessly at him. "Back in Ricketts."

"Go on with your story," prompted Devine.

"Protocols also call for the collection of blood, urine, and vitreous humor as toxicology specimens. As well as stomach contents and bile of course."

"Vitreous humor?"

"Gelatinous mass in the eye between the retina and the lens. And with a suspected drug death, blood from the ilio-femoral vein is routinely considered best. It's due to the postmortem redistribution of drugs in the blood. I know this is more detail than you want, and I don't want to get too far out into the forensic weeds, but I need you to understand the situation."

"So you did all that?"

"Yes. The stomach contents showed they had just eaten lunch."

"They had at a restaurant in town. You said you ordered a tox screen?"

"Yes, but you do a tox screen for a case of suspected drug overdose *only* if certain elements are present."

"Such as?"

"Known history of substance abuse or misuse, or the same being revealed at the crime scene. Having had no access to that info, I couldn't rely on that, but just on anecdotal evidence from the first responders. Next, if the autopsy findings suggest illicit drug use, you would also order up a tox screen. There were no needle marks on the bodies. That's not conclusive because many illegal drugs are taken orally via the mouth or nose. But there was also no hepatic cirrhosis, or foreign body cells in the lungs. And no drug-induced froth in the air passages. Those elements almost always present in an overdose case."

"*Did* you find evidence of Narcan in their systems?"

"No, but my examination wouldn't necessarily reveal it. However, the tox screen would likely show traces of its presence."

"The reports say that fentanyl is the suspected drug."

"And as I said, those were *not* the reports I wrote. I would never have inserted a preliminary cause of death like that, particularly when I had found no evidence of it. Fentanyl has the ability to bypass the brain-blood barrier, which makes it ideal for pain management, but terrible for addiction. There's also a synthetic opioid coming out of Europe, two-benzyl benzimidazole. It was developed in the fifties as a painkiller but was never approved for medical use. It's up to twenty times more potent than fentanyl."

"God help us," muttered Devine.

"The point is, I've had to perform, unfortunately,

hundreds of autopsies on fentanyl overdose victims, so I know what to look for. And I did not find it with the Odoms."

"Okay, but did you find evidence of *poisoning*? Is that why you ordered the tox screen? Because you wouldn't have ordered one based solely on suspected drug overdoses, according to your findings and the protocols you just outlined. There wasn't any evidence of it."

She didn't answer right away. "You're absolutely right, Agent Devine. I actually suspected *cyanide* poisoning."

"Like in an Agatha Christie novel? What, did you smell bitter almonds?"

"No, I smelled *garlic*, Agent Devine."

39

DEVINE GAPED. "GARLIC? AM I missing something here?"

"Despite being a deadly poison, cyanide is actually naturally occurring. Found in the soil, water, air. Those types are not typically lethal, at least not in unconcentrated doses. It's also heavily used in various industries, like photography, chemical research, synthetic plastics manufacturing, and jewelry polishing."

"Okay, so it's all around us, but how does it actually kill?"

"By preventing cells from using oxygen to make energy molecules. Deprived of that, the heart and nerve cells rapidly shut down. Now, you can inhale it, be injected with it, or absorb it through your skin. Inhalation is the most lethal because it's the fastest acting. That's also why people die inhaling smoke in fires. Plastic and other industrial products are full of cyanide. Now, *ingestion* of a concentrated dose is also bad but it may give time for treatment. The Jonestown mass suicide used cyanide in the Kool-Aid. Other things being equal, poisoning via *adsorption* is probably the most survivable because it's the slowest acting."

"What are the symptoms?"

"Immediate ones are headache, dizziness, fatigue, weakness, shortness of breath. Longer exposure results in low blood pressure, convulsions, slow pulse, lung damage, respiratory failure, unconsciousness, coma, and then death, which is almost always by respiratory-cardio failure."

"What made you suspect it was cyanide?"

"There was no detectable smell of bitter almonds, as you alluded to. But the bitter almond smell is not always present, and here it might have been over-whelmed by the garlic odor I encountered."

"And where *does* the garlic come in?"

"I'm getting there. Bear with me. I noted that both the Odoms' blood and skin were pink-red, which made me think of cyanide."

"Why?"

"It shows that the blood was full of oxygen. *Too* full. That's because the cyanide was blocking it from being absorbed into the cells. Because of that, and other fac-tors, I ordered up an in-depth testing and analysis of blood and urine samples using UPLC/MS."

"You're going to have to explain that one."

"Ultra-performance liquid chromatography in tandem with mass spectrometry. It's a complicated process, but is necessary to *confirm* the presence of cyanide."

"Okay."

"Cyanide rapidly disappears from the blood and urine, so the collection of biological specimens has to be done fairly quickly. And the postmortem formation of cyanide in the body can also occur and further complicate matters. All in all, it's tricky."

"And the *garlic*? Where does that come in?"

"It was a hunch on my part. But I couldn't see how the Odoms could have *inhaled* cyanide at such a level and concentration to kill them, while their daughter was completely unaffected. And there was no corrosion of their esophagus or stomach lining, which you typically see in *ingestion* cases. But when I detected the strong smell of garlic, I thought about something called DMSO."

"Never heard of it," said Devine.

"It stands for dimethyl sulfoxide. It has a unique ability to rapidly pass through even durable membranes, like rubber gloves and human skin. Thus, it's a perfect vehicle to administer medications without the risk of injections, which can lead to infections, particularly in compromised patients. It's used with things like localized painkillers, anti-inflammatories, and antioxidants. It was once even thought to be a miracle cure for cancer, although DMSO lost some of its luster after a woman died from an allergic reaction. In 2016, the FDA approved it for medical use, for burns, cuts, bruises, clot-busting in victims of strokes, and combined with other medications, it can even reduce intercranial pressure. I didn't know all this off the top of my head. I researched it after I detected the garlic smell and thought of DMSO."

"So you smelled the garlic and . . . ?"

"If a dose of cyanide was combined with DMSO and was administered via the skin? It could kill more rapidly than you would typically find in an absorption case. Still not nearly as fast as inhalation or ingestion, but more efficiently than usual. It also might initially *look* like a drug overdose. However, neither fentanyl nor any drug that I know of gives off a garlic odor. But DMSO does."

"It couldn't have come from what they ate? You said they had lunch, which I confirmed."

"What they ate for lunch was still largely undigested. A tuna salad sandwich and a side of berries for Mr. Odom, and a waffle and scrambled eggs for Mrs. Odom," she replied. "Not usually meals that contain an abundance of garlic. And I removed and bagged the stomach contents. The garlic smell was not detectable in them outside of the body."

"And the sorts of tests you ordered would conclusively show it was or wasn't cyanide poisoning?" said Devine.

"That was my hope, yes. I very carefully collected

samples of blood and urine. And on the requisite forms I set out in great detail the tests I wanted administered."

"Did you tell anyone in Ricketts what you suspected about cyanide being present?"

"No."

"Cyanide linked with this DMSO? Pretty sophisticated?"

"Agent Devine, I would think that whoever did this is well used to killing people efficiently."

"And the reports you actually wrote? Are they on your computer hard drive?"

"No, we use a cloud."

"Can you access it remotely?"

She pulled out a laptop and did so. They looked at the pages on the screen.

"My God," she said. "It's a duplicate of what you just showed me."

"Did you do drafts of them somewhere, which would show your true work product?"

"No. But I dictate everything as I'm performing the posts. I use that to create my report."

"Where are the recordings kept? Do you have them with you?"

"No, they're at the Ricketts government building."

Devine sighed. "Okay, dollars to donuts those recordings no longer exist."

"But *I* exist," she said defiantly.

"And do you have hard copies of anything with you?"

"No. Too much to lug around and the cloud is always there. But now I guess we know the cloud can be seeded with utter drivel," she added angrily.

"The samples for the screenings? Did you send those in personally?"

"No, I left them for—" She looked up in alarm.

"Doris Chandler to send for you?" he finished.

"Yes, she handles all that." Coburn added in a hushed voice, "You think she's in on it?"

"I think pretty much everyone in Ricketts, except you, is *in* on it, Dr. Coburn, whatever *it* is. So the screens will come back with a finding of death by opioid overdose, more specifically fentanyl. And cyanide, DMSO, and garlic will appear nowhere in the tox report."

She looked up at him, the fear etched starkly in her features. "Someone else could post the bodies. That would—"

"They've been cremated."

"Cremated!"

She seemed to shrink down to nothing. "I'm in real danger, aren't I?"

"Who knows you're here in Seattle, at this house?"

Coburn looked ready to faint. "I . . ."

"Doris Chandler?"

She nodded. "So what do I do?"

"We need to get you somewhere safe. Then the FBI can take your statement and maybe we can make a dent in this case."

"Do you think we really can?"

Devine was about to reply when he heard a noise coming from the back of the house.

40

His glock out, Devine seized Coburn by the wrist and pulled her up from the table, even as he used his elbow to nudge off the light switch.

As the space fell dark, he said quietly, "What's the configuration of rooms upstairs?"

A frightened Coburn said in a strained whisper, "Three bedrooms, and three en suite baths all off one hall."

He nodded, pulled his phone, punched in 911, and told them he was a federal agent, the address of the house, and that there was an intruder. He then led Coburn out of the room, even as they now heard faint footsteps from the rear of the house.

In the front room Devine eased back the curtain. Only his vehicle and the Lexus were visible, but his instincts told him that there was someone also lurking out there.

Devine hustled Coburn up the stairs, and after making a quick scan of the room setups, Devine settled them in the far back bedroom. While Coburn stood shivering, Devine locked the door and then slid a bureau in front of it.

He looked up and said urgently, "Get away from that window."

She instantly pressed herself against the wall.

"What now?" she moaned.

"We hang on until the cops get here. Shouldn't be long now."

He had Coburn crawl under the bed and lie curled up against the bottom of the headboard, as far from the door as possible.

"Stay there and don't come out until I tell you to."

"Please don't let them kill me."

He now heard footsteps on the landing, and a few moments later they were stealthily moving down the hall. Devine took up a shooting position at an angle to the bedroom door and called out, "I'm an agent with Homeland Security. If you come any closer, I *will* open fire."

He listened. Damned if they didn't come closer.

Okay, here we go.

Devine fired three shots through the thin wood of the door. One was at eye height, the second at the gut, and the third at the shins in case they had dropped to the floor.

As soon as that last round left his gun, Devine opened fire again, discharging his weapon fast, side to side in a crisscross pattern, high to low. In the narrow confines of the hallway it would have taken a contortionist not to be struck with one of the rounds. But after his opening salvo, he doubted whoever was out there would have stayed put to be shot down. He only hoped it had bought them some precious time.

Come on, sirens.

He quickly reloaded, and keeping his breathing calm and level, he continued to listen.

A few moments later he heard something bang against the door. Not a bullet, but something hard. His mind flashed through the various possibilities. A body? A piece of furniture? A...

Shit.

He pulled the mattress down over the front of the bed as a shield and then slid under the bed, pushing himself back next to Coburn and covering the woman with his body.

"Brace yourself," he hissed. "Eyes closed and fingers in ears. Now."

Something exploded a moment later, blowing open the door and hurtling the heavy bureau against the mattress and bed frame.

"Oh my God!" screamed Coburn.

Devine did not scream. He rolled out from under the bed and immediately fired at the doorway, letting whoever was out there know that their tactic had not worked. He saw two men retreating down the hall as his shots whizzed by them.

"Stay here!" he ordered Coburn.

He leapt up and burst through the doorway, which was now twice as large as it had been. As he glanced back, Devine saw that the thick mattress was burned and shredded from the blast, but it had saved their lives.

Even though it cost him time, Devine quickly searched the house to make sure no one was waiting for him to run past before going in and finishing off Coburn. Then he hurtled to the front door. He heard sirens in the distance, which made him feel much better.

He peeked out the open front door, and then jumped back as bullets flew past him and lodged in the wall. He took another cautious look and saw the two men running away from the house. He raced outside, calling out, "Drop your weapons. Down on your knees, now, hands clasped above your head. Now, or I will shoot."

They just ran harder. He next fired a warning shot over their heads to let them know he meant business.

They still kept sprinting, running for the patch of woods across from the house. He hustled after them, aiming for the tree line into which they'd just plunged.

Why the hell were they running so hard? They outnumbered him and were armed.

Oh shit.

He stopped so fast, he almost fell over. He turned back to the house, but had taken only a single step toward it when the structure disappeared in front of him, blowing upward and outward.

Devine was thrown backward at least ten feet, landing in the dirt next to the tree line. As he lay there, concussed and bruised and fighting to catch his breath, debris hit all around him.

He heard a car start up from somewhere.

Seconds later a vehicle shot past him.

He once more heard sirens, closer this time. The cavalry was showing up, only far too late.

He rolled to his right, stood, raised his gun, and tried to fire at the car, but he couldn't manage it.

His vision was blurred, his face flushed, his lungs seized up, and his heart was racing.

A sharp pain then hit his frontal lobe.

A moment later Travis Devine toppled to the dirt.

CHAPTER

41

"DEVINE, CAN YOU HEAR ME? Devine!"

Another voice said, "Travis!"

Devine slowly opened his eyes to see Detectives Braddock and Walker staring down at him.

"Y-yeah?"

"What in the hell happened?" asked Braddock.

Devine looked around at the antiseptic walls of the hospital room and smelled chemicals and his own sweat and other odors he didn't recognize. It brought back stark and uncomfortable memories of his time in Army and civilian hospitals wondering if he was going to live or be buried at Arlington National.

Devine glanced down and saw the hospital gown, and then the IV lines jointed into his skin. He slowly gazed to the right again, and eyed Walker standing there next to Braddock. The vitals machine beeped and blinked back at him. Devine read off the numbers; based on that, he concluded he would probably make it. He'd seen far worse numbers when he'd been flat on his back on a gurney in an Army medical chopper with blood pouring out of him faster than they could put it back in him.

He tried to sit up, but Walker gently pushed him back down.

"Be still," ordered Braddock.

Devine indeed sat very still because just that slight movement had made his head feel like someone had plunged an ax right through the middle of it.

Braddock pulled up a chair and sat down. "You up for talking?"

"Why not?" said Devine, wondering when more pain meds would flow into his IV. "I've got nothing else to do at the moment."

"What happened? Start from the beginning."

And Devine did, while Walker took notes on her iPad. His wobbly tongue occasionally tripping over the words, and his brain foggy with meds, he slowly rambled through the call from Coburn and his trip to the house where she was staying. Her being scared. Her claims that the postmortem reports had been replaced with fake ones. The fact that she thought the Odoms had been poisoned with cyanide. That she had not been allowed access to the crime scene, or the Odoms' home to do a background check for substance abuse. And how someone had entered the house, prompting Devine to call 911. Then the men in the hall. The grenade landing against the bedroom door. His running outside. The men going into the woods. His realizing that he had been decoyed out. An insight that had come too late. And then. Boom. The car flashing by. And ending with his collapsing.

"Coburn?" he asked, but he really already knew the answer.

"Remains were found inside," replied Braddock quietly. "Her Lexus was damaged but not destroyed. We checked the registration. And while she was not… recognizable, we did a positive ID through fingerprints. Because of her employment, she was on the state database."

Devine stared back up at the ceiling, feeling as miserable as he ever had. Not due to the pain he was feeling, but having been suckered like that. And leaving a woman alone to die when he'd promised to protect her from harm.

No doubt sensing what he was thinking, Walker said, "I don't see what else you could have done, Travis. You couldn't have known that they had placed a bomb in the house."

"Actually, that should have been right at the top of my tactical concerns," he replied, his voice tight with the self-loathing he was feeling. "I saw that scenario played out a hundred times overseas, and it only took me once to figure it out. Here, I blew it. And it cost Coburn her life."

There was a lengthy and awkward silence until Braddock said, "So they fudged her reports and she had to die?"

Devine nodded and made fists with both hands, and though the movement hurt, it felt good.

I'm alive. And if I'm alive, I can hunt them down.

He looked at Braddock. "What do the docs say about me? Anything broken? Any permanent damage?"

"You suffered a bad concussion. You got hit by the force of the bomb blast, but no debris. Knocked you around some. Nothing permanent. You're very lucky. If you had been even twenty feet closer, my bomb guys said you probably wouldn't have made it."

"What did they use to blow the house?" asked Devine.

"They're still working on it. My guys said it was sophisticated, so the people were not amateurs."

"So when do I get out of here?"

"You're at least staying overnight for observation."

"Who says?"

"The *docs* do," replied Braddock, giving Walker an incredulous look.

"What time is it?" Devine asked.

"After midnight."

"I've got an appointment tomorrow morning with Danny Glass and Betsy Odom. Then a court hearing after that."

"News flash, you're not going to make it," said Braddock.

"The hell I'm not."

"Travis, listen to reason," said Walker. "You're lucky to be alive."

"Get the doc in here."

"Devine!" snapped Braddock. "You are not—"

"Get the fucking doctor in here. Now! I'm not letting Betsy down, too!"

The hospitalist, a woman in her thirties with dark hair and a calm expression, was summoned.

"If you leave, it will be against medical advice," she said.

"Am I going to drop dead from any of this?"

"No, but you're going to be sore as hell. Stiff as a board. Ears ringing. And you're going to have the mother of all migraines, even with the pain meds. And that's going to be for the next twenty-four to possibly forty-eight hours."

"I've got a high tolerance for pain due to my own stupidity. So just give me the meds and cut me loose. I'll sign what I have to."

"Are you quite sure?" said the doctor.

"Where are my clothes?" demanded Devine. "*And my gun?*"

CHAPTER

42

DEVINE'S RENTAL HAD LUCKILY SUFFERED no serious damage, having been mostly blocked from the bomb blast by Coburn's Lexus. That was fortunate because there probably wasn't a car leasing place left in the state of Washington that would do business with him. The police had brought it to the hospital. Escorted by a nurse and Braddock and Walker, Devine was wheeled to the exit. With his pain meds in a plastic bag, he rose unsteadily from the chair.

Braddock said, "Do you really think this is a good idea?"

"I'll get back to you on that," said Devine, wheezing a bit.

Walker gripped a wobbly Devine's arm. "This is ridiculous. I'm coming with you."

"I'm fine!"

"The hell you are! And you're on heavy pain meds. Which means you're legally impaired and not allowed to operate a motor vehicle."

"Look, Beth—"

"No, *you* look." She held up his car key. "Either I drive you, or this gets chucked into that storm drain over there. And then I'll arrest you for being an idiot."

Devine looked at her and then glanced at Braddock, who said, "Don't think she won't. She'll out-stubborn you, Devine, guaranteed."

Devine sighed. "Okay, let's go."

Braddock loaded him into the passenger side and Walker drove them off.

Devine eased back in the seat. He'd taken one of the pain meds, but it hadn't kicked in yet. He was praying it would any second.

Walker glanced worriedly over at him. "I'm sorry about Dr. Coburn. I'd actually heard her speak at a forensics conference I attended last year. She really knew her field."

"She came to me for help. And I screwed it up."

He shook his head and closed his eyes.

"Well, unless you take care of yourself, you won't have a chance to avenge her."

Devine was about to shoot some comment back but then didn't. Because she was right.

"What are you doing tomorrow?" he asked.

Visibly surprised, she said, "I actually have the day off."

"Would you like to come with me to my meeting and court hearing?"

"I would. Tell me about them."

Devine filled her in on the latest having to do with Danny Glass and his efforts to gain guardianship of Betsy Odom with an intent to formally adopt her. He also told her about his trip to Ricketts and almost being killed, though he did not go into detail about the person who had saved him.

"My God, Travis, you are one trouble magnet," noted Walker.

"I've been called worse."

"So you think Glass had his sister and brother-in-law murdered?"

"I can't think of anyone else with a motive."

"But the Ricketts folks stonewalled you. And now Coburn is dead."

"Coburn's report was altered on the official police file, so to the world it will seem that the Odoms died of a drug overdose. And now that Coburn's been murdered, there's no one to refute that."

"But she told *you*."

"That's not evidence; it's hearsay. And if she had any evidence on her, it was in a house that no longer exists." He thought of something. "How about her car?"

"Nothing was found in there related to her work. But we're having her residence in Spokane checked by the local cops. There might be something there."

"Whoever killed her probably already thought of that and searched it."

He looked out the window at the dark clouds and said, "Did you find anything in my Toyota?"

"We're running DNA samples we collected through our usual databases. There were no prints in the car."

"They were wearing gloves."

"Yes, but we recovered their weapons inside the vehicle and I was able to get a usable print off one of the bullets in the magazine."

He looked at her, impressed. "And?"

"We've also run that through the usual databases without success. Now we're expanding that search."

"Be good to know who those guys worked for. Maybe we can—" He yawned.

She said firmly, "Okay, start to dial it back. You need to get some sleep if you're going to be ready for tomorrow, which is already here actually." She paused and then said decisively, "And there's a change in plan. I'll get some things from your hotel room and then we can drive to my place."

"Beth, you don't have to—"

"I'm going to anyway," she interrupted. "It's near downtown. And I have a guest bedroom."

Feeling the meds kick in and not having the energy to argue, Devine nodded resignedly.

She took his keycard and grabbed what he needed from his hotel room. Then she drove them to her home in a quiet neighborhood in the suburbs. It was a small cottage with a broad front porch, all on one floor.

Walker helped a visibly struggling Devine down the hall to the spare bedroom.

She helped him undress and got him into bed.

"You didn't need to do that," he said.

"In for a dime," she said, smiling. "And the muscle relaxants should kick in soon."

She had obviously noted the scars from old wounds, one on each shoulder and one on his calf, because she said, "Three Purples?"

"Nope, two." He tapped one shoulder. "This one is not from combat. Civilian mission that went ass-up."

She shook her head. "Wow, okay. You need anything else?"

"No, Beth, I'm fine. And, thank you."

"I'm just glad you're okay, Travis."

"Yeah."

"I promise to wake you up in plenty of time and help you get ready. I hung a clean set of clothes in the closet. Toiletry bag's on the bathroom counter. I make a mean cup of coffee, and how about pancakes and eggs for breakfast?"

"Sounds good."

"You need anything during the night, I'm right next door."

They said their goodnights and she turned the light out and left.

In the darkness Devine stared at the ceiling. He often did that when he was thinking through difficult problems. So he watched all the mental scenes attached to his current drama march across a ceiling painted a calming seafoam green. From the note in his pocket courtesy of the girl on the train, to nearly getting blown up and everything in between.

It all somehow makes sense. I just have to figure out how.

As pain meds kicked in and he started to doze off, he thought of the dead Coburn. And Betsy Odom, whom he wanted to protect from what was coming her way. He had failed to save Coburn. He could not allow the same fate for Odom.

As he fell asleep, his last thoughts centered on the girl on the train. He knew they would probably collide at some point. But her having saved his life had muddled things. He was sure the woman had her own reasons for doing so, but her message bothered him greatly.

There were forces out there aligned against him. *And* her.

And they might be part of the same government I *serve.*

CHAPTER

43

"OKAY, I DID NOT SEE that coming."

Walker had come into the kitchen to see Devine in the sweatpants and a T-shirt he'd slept in making coffee.

He turned to her. "Slept like a bear in hibernation and then woke up feeling really good. Those muscle relaxants are something else. Haven't felt this loose since graduation night at West Point, and that required copious amounts of alcohol."

"I'm sure," she said, smiling.

Walker started prepping the meal while he poured out two cups of coffee, handed her one, and sat on a bar stool at the kitchen island. He watched her work away making the breakfast. "You from here?"

"No, Pennsylvania. I come from a family of cops. I love the outdoors, hiking, snow skiing, kayaking, and it doesn't get better than here for that. How about you?"

"I went to West Point for two reasons. I wanted to serve my country and I wanted to piss off my old man.

For him, money dictates one's self-worth, which is not my life philosophy. I made captain and then got out."

"I thought West Pointers made it their career?"

"Not always."

"Then you went to work for DHS?"

"No, after that, I got my MBA and went to work on Wall Street for a while."

"But I thought you said—"

Devine interrupted, "I hated Wall Street. It was just sort of me paying penance."

"For what?" she asked curiously.

"Old news, not worth revisiting."

"Okay, then tell me more about Betsy Odom."

He did, including the girl's past, the struggles of her parents, and her dilemma with her uncle's wanting to adopt her.

"But you said she's under the protection of the FBI. Why?"

"She's Danny Glass's only living relative. Her mom and dad might have told her stuff about him. He's the defendant in a big RICO case. They're probably hedging their bets."

"Pretty rough for the kid."

"Yeah. Someone murdered her parents, and the prime suspect wants to adopt her. And she's been poor her whole life and now she can be rich."

"I don't think I'd be able to work that one out and I'm not twelve," noted Walker.

"She's mature beyond those years, at least in some ways. In other ways, she's just a scared little kid."

"So what do you think comes out of the meeting with Glass?" asked Walker.

"He's obviously hell-bent on becoming her guardian. And he probably wants to make sure Betsy is on the same page so there are no surprises."

"But if he is this global criminal, why does he want that sort of responsibility?"

Devine said, "Glass strikes me as a transactional guy. So what value does his niece have for him?"

"Does she know something about him, like you mentioned? Or is she some sort of savant who can predict the stock market or horse races? Is she a whiz at hacking?"

"She's a smart kid. But I've seen no signs of anything like that."

"If he killed her parents to get custody of her, there *has* to be a reason."

"I've been thinking of nothing else since I got to town. Although..." began Devine.

"Although what?"

"It'll sound a little crazy, but I've seen him around her. He... well, he genuinely seems to love her, if a guy like that can love anyone. And I previously suggested to

Braddock that maybe Glass knows who killed his sister and brother-in-law, and is trying to protect Betsy."

"If he knows who murdered them, why not go to the police?"

"No clue," replied Devine.

"So does he have a shot at becoming her guardian even with the RICO prosecution?"

"He hasn't been proven guilty of anything. And three of the DOJ's witnesses against him have been murdered."

"On his orders?" she asked.

"Presumably, but it's not like there's proof of that. The guy has an ankle monitor, so he wasn't personally involved, but he has plenty of muscle to do the job."

"Anyone looking into those murders?"

"I'm sure there are," he replied.

"Can you get me the names of the witnesses?"

He looked at her in surprise. "Why?"

"I'd like to dig into it, too."

"I can," he said.

"Thanks."

After they had finished eating, Walker said, "You better shower and change, and I'll do the same. I'll drive us over in my car."

As Devine walked off, he prayed that today would go better than yesterday had.

44

WHEN THEY ARRIVED AT THE hotel, Devine made introductions with Beth Walker and Saxby and Odom. Saxby at first had seemed leery about a local police officer in the mix, but Walker's cordial manner soon put her at ease.

"What happened to your face, Devine?" asked Saxby. "It's all bruised and scratched. And you're moving a little stiff. Please don't tell me someone else tried to kill you?"

Devine glanced at Walker before saying, "Just a little blowup. No big deal."

Walker hiked her eyebrows at this comment, but then she turned to Odom. "I'm so sorry about your parents, Betsy."

"Thanks," Odom said curtly.

Devine said, "You ready to meet with your uncle?"

"Yeah, I guess."

He noted that she had on new clothes, presumably from her shopping trip with Saxby. He could tell that the pair seemed to have reached a truce of sorts; at least their manner toward each other appeared relaxed and amiable.

"And the court hearing?" asked Devine.

"Agent Saxby sort of walked me through what it will be like. I'm just going to tell the truth if I have to say anything."

"Always a good idea," observed Walker.

"And have you decided on your uncle being your guardian?" asked Devine.

She didn't answer him, but simply put on her new coat and headed to the door.

They drove over to the Four Seasons in Walker's car. They were met at the entrance by Glass's majordomo, Dennis Hastings. He was dressed in a suit, but with a tie this time.

Devine had to vouch for Walker's presence, and although Hastings didn't like the notion of a cop and an FBI agent meeting the boss, Devine made it clear that it was all or none.

Hastings phoned Glass about it, and a minute later he nodded at Devine. "Let's go."

As they were heading up in the elevator car, Devine turned to Hastings and said, "So what'd you do last night? Anything fun?"

Hastings shrugged. "Room service and a movie. You?"

"Same. What movie did you watch?"

"It was so bad, I forgot. You?"

"I forget the name, too, but I know it opened with a house blowing up."

Walker caught his eye but said nothing.

Hastings said, "Really? Sounds like something I'd watch. You know, *exciting*."

"Yeah, I bet."

"Anybody die?" asked Hastings.

"Somebody always dies," replied Devine curtly.

They were escorted down the hall and had to pass by the security team at the entrance to the presidential suite. Danny Glass was sitting in the same chair as last time. Only now he had on a dark blue suit with a striped tie for his court appearance. Hastings had, once more, taken his clothing choice from his boss, Devine observed.

Devine also noted that Odom looked around in awe at the luxurious space and the sweeping views out over the water.

Think and Grow Rich. He could almost see the wheels spinning in her head.

Glass rose, greeted and embraced Odom, and then was introduced by Devine to Saxby and Walker.

Glass smiled. "I've never felt so safe in my life with so many cops and federal agents around. Coffee, tea, water?"

They all declined.

"So what do we talk about?" began Saxby, looking directly at Glass.

"You a smoker?" he asked.

"How'd you guess? The sweet aroma on my clothes?"

"No, you just have that certain look. But this is a nonsmoking room in case you start getting itchy."

"That's okay. I don't think this meeting will take all that long."

Glass glanced at Odom. "So why does the FBI have my niece in your custody? As her guardian to be, I have the right to know. Because once I am appointed her guardian, she will be coming to live with me."

"We'll answer that question when and if the court grants your petition," said Saxby.

"I like to plan ahead for the inevitable," countered Glass.

"So do I," said Saxby. "But I hate to go spouting off willy-nilly if I don't have to."

Glass sat and motioned for them all to do the same. "Okay, I'm told that this hearing is pretty much perfunctory, with all the high-priced attorneys present and everybody represented, but that a decision on my emergency guardianship petition could be rendered today."

"Are you planning to make a statement to the court?" said Devine.

"If the judge has any questions, I'll be more than happy to answer them."

"Including questions about your RICO prosecutions for eighty-six felonies?" said Saxby.

Glass glanced sharply at Odom, apparently to see her reaction to this. The girl just sat there with her gaze on the floor. Glass looked back at Saxby. "My lawyers have told me that in this country one is innocent until proven guilty. Maybe you heard something like that in FBI school. So, right now, I'm as pure as the Pope. But I look forward to my day in court and telling my side of things."

"But a family court judge will take the charges into consideration nonetheless, because the only concern is the welfare of the child," pointed out Saxby. "Not whether you can beat the case leveled against you."

"*Qué será, será,*" Glass said dismissively. "So moving forward, I really need to know that if I am granted guardianship, the FBI will release Betsy into my custody. Otherwise, what's the point of the hearing if the judge decides in my favor? I still won't have Betsy."

"As I said, we'll cross that bridge *if* we come to it."

Glass shook his head. "No, I don't think so." Glass clicked his fingers and a dark-suited man came into the room. He was tall and cadaverous with thinning hair and a pointy chin. His eyes were light gray, his mouth shaped into a smirk. He walked over and handed a blue-backed packet of documents to Saxby. He said, "I'm one of Mr. Glass's attorneys. The FBI is hereby served." He paused and grinned. "Always wanted to say that."

Saxby didn't bother to look at the papers. "Served with what exactly? From the smell of it, maybe... horseshit?"

Odom snorted at that, and Walker raised a hand to her face to hide the smile.

The cadaver said stiffly, "It's a petition to show cause regarding the FBI holding Betsy Odom pretty much hostage. Regardless of whether Mr. Glass is appointed guardian or not, as her sole remaining blood relative, he has a vested interest in, and standing to insist, that the FBI offer clear and convincing evidence as to why Miss Odom is subject to continued physical detainment."

"I'll be sure to alert DOJ," said Saxby casually, though Devine could tell the woman had been caught off guard by this. They all had.

"Be sure you do," said the lawyer. "I doubt the Justice Department wants a default judgment entered against them. With egg on face, jobs and federal careers tumble," he added snidely.

"Well, at least on *our* side, they don't end up in the river with chains and cement blocks for screwing up," Saxby countered. "So, make sure *you* don't mess up, and give your boss a reason to *tumble* your career. And *you*."

The lawyer's smirk vanished, he gave his boss a

tremulous glance, and then he quietly removed himself from the room.

Devine looked at Glass. "So this was the reason for the meeting? To serve papers and talk tough?"

"That and I wanted to see my niece again. And to assure her and you that I have her best interests at heart. And that I will do everything in my power to keep her happy, healthy, and safe."

Odom glanced up at this and locked gazes with her uncle.

To Devine, the girl seemed supremely confused, and it was no wonder. He was, too.

"Is there anything else?" asked Saxby. "Or are we done here?"

"Unless Betsy has something to say?" said Glass.

They all looked at her.

Devine wondered if she was going to bring up her parents being cremated at Glass's instruction, and ask the other questions she had told them she had. But Odom merely shook her head and gazed down at her shoes. They left Glass sitting there.

Back in the car Saxby said, "Well, I have to hand it to the guy, that was slickly done."

"You'll need to provide the legal papers to the DOJ," said Walker.

"Really? And here I was going to use them to light my cigarettes."

An embarrassed Walker said, "Sorry. I didn't mean it like that."

Devine barely listened to this exchange. He was focusing on Odom, who sat next to him in the rear seat. He had never seen her this withdrawn.

He nudged her arm. "You okay?"

She looked over at him. "Yeah, I'm good."

"You don't seem it. And you didn't ask your uncle any of your questions."

Walker and Saxby stopped talking and glanced in the rearview mirror at them.

"I know. I just…didn't." She paused. "Do…do I really have to get up and talk in court?"

"Well, if the judge has some questions for you to answer," replied Devine.

"If I want to live with my uncle, you mean?"

Saxby said, "Betsy, the judge wants to get an understanding of you and your uncle's relationship, whether your living with him is the right thing for *you*, which is the only thing that matters."

"But what if I just say that it is? That that's what I want?"

Saxby turned around in the seat and looked at her. "Then that will carry great weight with the judge. But since you're a minor, it will not be definitive."

"What does that mean?" Odom asked sharply.

"It means the judge can consider other things."

"Like my uncle being a criminal?" she said heatedly.

"An *alleged* criminal," corrected Saxby. "But yes, she can consider that. Family court judges have great latitude in what they can take into account when placing minors with adults."

A clearly frustrated Odom blurted out, "But what if she says I *can't* live with my uncle? What happens to me then? I can't just stay in a crummy hotel with you until I'm eighteen, can I?"

"No, you can't," conceded Saxby.

"So, what then?"

"The judge can appoint another guardian."

"Who? I don't have any other relatives that I know of."

Saxby said, "Whoever they appoint might only be temporary."

"And then what?" demanded Odom, drilling her with an angry stare. "I go to somebody else? And then another stranger and then another?"

Saxby said, "I don't know. I just don't know, Betsy."

Mirroring what she had once told Devine, Odom snapped, "You don't know much."

They drove on in silence.

CHAPTER

45

THE SMALL SPARTAN COURTROOM HELD
only a few people. Glass and his attorney were seated at
one counsel table. A sullen-faced man in a light brown
suit was seated at the other. Directly behind him in the
front pew was a woman in her forties dressed in a dark
pantsuit. The pair were conversing in low voices.

Saxby went over to join them and the three started
talking in whispers. She pulled out the legal papers
Glass's attorney had served her with and the other
woman glanced over them.

Devine, Walker, and Odom were seated in the
front row.

Devine watched as Glass gazed around the room.
He looked refreshed and relaxed. And Devine couldn't
understand why, unless the man already knew what
was going to happen today.

And he might.

Saxby rejoined them, looking, Devine thought, a
bit shell-shocked. When he asked her what was wrong,
she waved him off. "Later," she said irritably.

The bailiff told them all to stand, and Judge Judith Mehan appeared from behind the bench and took her seat. She was in her fifties with graying hair cut short, and her black robe hung loosely over her. A court reporter sat off to the side, her fingers hovering over her stenographic machine.

Mehan said, "Let's get to it. I have a heavy docket today." She shuffled some papers in front of her. "Are Mr. Daniel Glass and Miss Betsy Odom in the courtroom?"

Glass's counsel and the sullen-faced man, who identified himself as the government lawyer representing Odom's interests, reported that their clients were present.

Mehan said, "I've looked over the financial records of Mr. Glass. He clearly has the resources to provide for his niece. However, I understand that there is a pending criminal case against him? I obviously would like to hear more details about that."

The woman in the dark pantsuit rose and said, "Your Honor, my name is Nancy Fine and I'm a United States Attorney. I represent both the Department of Justice and the FBI in this matter and have material knowledge of the RICO case that has been filed against Mr. Glass."

"Then let's hear from you, Ms. Fine. And I'll need to look at the relevant court filings."

Devine glanced at Glass, who did not seem bothered by this at all. Then he looked at Saxby and noted that the woman looked, well, ill.

"Your Honor, that is all now a moot point," said Fine.

"Why?" exclaimed the judge. "I consider it extremely important as to whether this court will allow Miss Odom to be placed under Mr. Glass's guardianship."

"It's a moot point because the Department of Justice has withdrawn its case against Mr. Glass."

Devine noted that Nancy Fine looked like she wanted to strangle someone as she kept her gaze rigidly on the judge.

Devine shot Glass another look. The man also seemed surprised and even upset by this development, which puzzled Devine.

Mehan said, "Are you telling me that the *entire* prosecution has been withdrawn?"

"Yes," said Fine, her teeth actually clenched.

"May I ask why?"

"We have...lost several witnesses critical to the DOJ's prosecution of this case. And our inability to prove our case by the requisite burden of proof compels us to withdraw the charges at this time."

"With prejudice?" asked Mehan, meaning that they could not be brought again.

Fine hesitated, glanced darkly at Glass, and said,

"That apparently depends on circumstances of which I have not been made aware, Your Honor. So, for now, they are withdrawn *without* prejudice."

Devine looked at Glass once more. He buttoned his coat and then ran one hand over his smooth head. Not looking happy, he leaned into his attorney and said something. The lawyer said something back, which did not seem to please his boss at all.

"Thank you, Ms. Fine," said a clearly befuddled Mehan.

Fine nodded and threw a dagger glare at Glass, who did not even acknowledge her.

Devine whispered to Saxby, "What in the hell is going on?"

She shook her head and whispered back, "Not now. After."

Mehan said, "All right. I would now like to hear from Betsy Odom."

With Saxby's prompting, Odom slowly rose, walked up to the bench, and was directed to a chair by the bailiff, where she was sworn in.

She took her seat and the judge said, "Ms. Odom, my name is Judith Mehan and I would like to ask you some questions, if that's all right?"

"Sure, okay," said Betsy in a tight voice, and squirming a bit in her seat.

"May I call you Betsy?"

"Sure, yeah."

"How long have you known your uncle, Betsy?"

Odom glanced in Glass's direction and said, "Um, we only just met the other day."

"He has not been in your life until the other day? Do you know why that is?"

Odom swiped nervously at her hair. "Um, not really. We moved around a lot, I mean, me and my mom and dad. And...and I had to keep making new friends, although I really wasn't good at that," she added. "So, um, it was really just me and my parents...you know."

She looked so uncomfortable by this admission that Devine's heart went out to her.

"Did your parents ever discuss your uncle with you? Why he was never around, or part of the extended family? And do you recall what they said?"

"Not really, no."

"No, they never mentioned him, or no, you don't recall what they said?" asked Mehan in a gentle voice.

Odom glanced over at Devine. He nodded his head and looked reassuringly at her.

"My mom liked him. But I don't think my dad liked my uncle very much, so I guess maybe that's why he wasn't, you know, around."

"Do you know why your father disliked your uncle?"

Odom hesitated and then said in a soft voice, "No, I don't."

"Were your uncle's legal issues ever mentioned by your parents?"

Odom shook her head, prompting the judge to tell her she had to verbalize her answer for the court reporter.

"No, they never talked about that stuff, at least not with me."

Mehan nodded. "All right, Betsy. Now, since this will impact you most of all, I want to hear from you about this guardianship petition sought by your uncle. Do you want Mr. Glass to be your guardian?"

"I...I don't think I have any other family."

"Granted, that is the case, but you still have the right to make your wishes known to the court." She glanced at Glass. "Like whether you desire Mr. Glass to be your guardian."

"Where will we live?" asked Odom.

"Since he is no longer subject to prosecution, at least for the time being, I would imagine he can live wherever he chooses. But where do *you* want to live?"

Odom shrugged and bit her lip. "I...don't know. I've just lived with my parents in some...places. I've never been, like, on a plane, or out of the country or stuff."

"Duly noted. So, is it your desire to have Mr. Glass become your guardian and live near here, or somewhere of his choosing?"

Glass whispered urgently into his lawyer's ear. The

man rose and said, "Your Honor, pardon the interruption, but just to be extremely transparent, my client will agree to maintain his home wherever his niece wants. Whether it's here or somewhere else. It's up to her and he will strictly abide by her wishes."

Devine stared at Glass. He did not look confident now. He just watched his niece anxiously and rubbed his thumb and forefinger together in what looked to be a sign of stress.

"All right, thank you, counsel. And this court will hold him to that," she added firmly. Mehan turned back to Odom. "Given that, Miss Odom, do you or do you not desire Mr. Glass to be your temporary guardian? For your information, if you do, and guardianship is granted to him, it is only valid for sixty days. During that time Mr. Glass is entitled to petition the court for permanent guardianship and any other available legal rights, including adoption."

Everyone stared up at Odom, while she looked only at her hands.

"Betsy? Miss Odom?" prompted the judge. "I know this is very difficult, and if you're not prepared to provide an answer now, that is perfectly—"

Odom straightened up, looked at the judge, and announced, "I want Travis Devine to be my guardian."

CHAPTER

46

DEVINE, WALKER, AND SAXBY WERE out in the hallway of the courthouse.

Saxby said, "Okay, I thought Glass's head was going to explode in there."

Devine glanced over at where Odom was sitting on a bench with her headphones on. She had not uttered a word after making her startling statement in court. She had her sketchpad out and was using a pencil to draw something.

Mehan, obviously bewildered by this development, had demanded to know who Travis Devine was, forcing Devine to make an impromptu sworn statement to the court. The flustered judge had then ordered the court adjourned, after stating that the status quo—namely Odom's being in the custody of the FBI—would remain in place while this was sorted out.

Glass and his lawyer had left the courtroom immediately. Glass had not even looked at Odom, but he had aimed a vicious glare at Devine.

Saxby said, "Nancy Fine is pissed off beyond belief. She was leading the RICO prosecution against Glass."

"Why is the case being dropped?" asked Walker.

"DOJ has lost some witnesses, to be sure, like she said. But Fine also told me that orders came from up high that the RICO matter had to go away in the interest of national security."

"I thought prosecuting a guy like Glass *was* in the interest of national security," said a stunned Devine.

"Up is down and down is up, apparently," replied Saxby.

"Well, whatever is going on," said Walker, "Betsy just threw a big wrench into the works by saying she wants Travis to be her guardian."

"But I can't be her guardian, obviously."

Saxby said immediately, "Why not?"

Devine gaped. "I'm a single guy. I have no permanent residence. I'm always traveling and my work is, well, more than a little out of the norm."

"Well, you could be her guardian temporarily, until the dust settles," suggested Walker.

"I agree," chimed in Saxby.

In a raised voice he exclaimed, "Guys, you're not listening to me. I can't be a twelve-year-old girl's guardian. It would be a disaster."

He looked over to see Odom staring at him, her

earphones still on. He didn't know if she had heard him or not.

"But the alternative could be even worse," pointed out Saxby. "The judge could still grant Glass guardianship. Or she could be placed with a stranger and that doesn't always end well. And if someone does wish her harm, she would be totally unprotected."

Devine refocused on her. "You're her guardian now. Why can't you keep on doing that until we figure this out?"

"I spoke with Nancy Fine about that, Devine. She said they won't allow the FBI to pursue an extension of its guardianship. So I'm out of the running."

"Why the hell won't she allow it?" demanded Devine.

"Well, there she is," observed Walker. "Why don't you ask her?"

Nancy Fine was storming past and on her phone when Devine and Saxby stopped her.

Saxby formally introduced Devine and Walker and said, "DHS wants to know why DOJ and the Bureau are walking away from all of this."

Fine held up a finger, and said into the phone, "I'll call you back." She clicked off and ran her gaze over Devine. "Why does the girl want you to be her guardian?" she said suspiciously.

"I guess because I treated her with kindness and listened to her."

Fine gave him a long stare before turning to Saxby. "We're *walking* away from all of this because we were ordered to. I already had this discussion with you, Ellen. I don't have time to have it again."

Devine said, "To my thinking, Danny Glass is a national security issue, so why are you letting him off scot-free?"

Fine got right in his face; he could smell coffee on the woman's breath. "For your fucking information *I'm* not letting anybody off scot-free, okay? But I have bosses, just like you. And I have to obey them or else I don't have a job. Are we clear on that?"

"I'm not saying it's your fault. I'm just trying to understand this, that's all. Wouldn't you, if the positions were reversed?"

She stepped back and her aggressive manner faded. "Look, I'm as pissed about this as you are. I was given my marching orders and specifically told to come here today and announce to the judge that the RICO prosecution against Glass is kaput. I don't know why, but I'm guessing it's so all impediments to his gaining guardianship over the kid are now gone. I don't know why he wants her that badly, but he clearly does."

"But why would the Justice Department do anything to make it easier for him to gain control over Betsy Odom?" asked Devine. "Why would they even care about that?"

"My boss works for the AG. The AG has a boss, too."

Devine glanced sharply at Saxby and said, "Are we talking at the very top of the government?"

"I'm not going to dignify that with a response," said Fine, even as she nodded.

"Why would that level of leadership give a crap about saving Danny Glass?" said Saxby.

Fine shrugged. "Glass is a big prize. But if he can help deliver a bigger one?"

Devine said quickly, "You speculating or do you know for sure?"

"It's just a theory, Devine. But it's the only one that makes sense. And we trade up all the time at Justice. Cut deals with the barracudas to snag the great white."

"Meaning the sorts of people Glass does business with, or *allegedly* does business with."

"If you have a better theory, I'd love to hear it," said Fine.

Devine said, "But the thing is, if that is the case, the great white shark has a lot of incentive to survive. And a lot of incentive to take out its revenge on Glass."

Walker added, "And maybe use Betsy Odom to do that."

Devine glanced over at the bench where Odom was sitting. Only the girl was no longer there.

47

"W HERE THE HELL DID SHE go?" exclaimed Saxby.

They all rushed over to the empty bench and looked around.

Devine eyed both ends of the hall. There were numerous people scurrying here and there, but Odom was not among them.

Devine looked at Saxby. "You go that way. Beth and I will head in the other direction. Text if you find her."

They hurried off, leaving Nancy Fine alone and confused. She sat down on the bench, pulled out her phone, and started tapping away.

Devine and Walker moved down opposite sides of the hall, opening doors and peering inside.

Walker said, "Do you think she could have been taken? Or gone off with Glass?"

"Willingly or not?" he said.

"I don't know."

"I think it's more likely she got fed up with all the crap and just wanted to get some fresh air."

"I hope you're right," said Walker.

They finished on their side of the building and Devine texted Saxby. She called him.

"No sign of her, Devine. I've got some of the marshals on the hunt for her, too. Should we bring in the police?"

"No," he said decisively.

"Why not?" demanded the FBI agent.

"Because she's walking towards me right now."

"Seriously?"

Devine told Saxby where they were and clicked off. He and Walker rushed over to Odom and Devine said, "Where did you go? We were worried."

"I was tired of listenin' to you guys bitchin'," said Odom. "I went for a walk."

"Okay, I'm sorry. It's just that today threw everyone for a loop."

Odom looked at Walker. "You're really pretty."

A surprised Walker said, "Thank you, Betsy."

"For you." She handed her a sheet from her sketchbook. On it was an excellent likeness of Walker.

"Wow, that is incredible," said Walker, showing it to Devine, who also looked impressed.

"Damn, Betsy, you are one fine artist."

Odom did not seem to be listening to him and her expression had darkened. "So you don't want to be my guardian?" she said defiantly.

"What?"

"I heard you. So you don't want to be my guardian?"

"I didn't say that."

"Yes, you did," she blurted out. "Don't lie to me!"

Devine looked flustered and out of sorts. "Look, I just said it wouldn't work out. I . . . I don't know anything about . . . It wouldn't be fair to you," he added lamely.

"Right, sure, fair to me. You just don't want the hassle, admit it."

By this time Saxby had arrived on the scene. "Damn it, Betsy, you had us scared to death."

She whirled around on the FBI agent. "Don't start on me, okay? You all act like you had the shitty day. *I* had the shitty day! You all expected me to say I wanted my uncle to be my guardian. But I didn't, did I? You think that was easy? You keep tellin' me my uncle is this bad guy. You think it was easy not pickin' him? He's pissed. I saw it. You think that was easy?" She stared up at Devine. "So I went out on a limb and I picked you. I told that judge lady. I wanted you to be my guardian. And it didn't mean shit to *you*, or any of you."

"Betsy, that is not right," countered Devine. "*I* don't think that. It meant a great deal to me."

"The hell it does. Stop lyin'!"

Devine let out a long breath. "Okay, Betsy. You're right."

"About what? What am I right about?" Odom wanted to know.

Devine could tell she was poised for a prolonged fight, so he had to choose his words carefully.

"You went out on a limb, like you said. You bucked your uncle and that is a *huge* deal. And I think you picked me because you feel like we connected. And the truth is I felt the same about you, Betsy. But you just have to understand that I've never spent much time around people your age. I will screw up. I will say the wrong thing. I will annoy the hell out of you and you'll annoy the hell out of me at times. But I will have your back, I promise you that. So I will be your guardian. I mean, if you really meant it. And *if* the court approves it. "

Odom didn't say anything for a few moments.

"Really? You're not just sayin' that?" she said in a calmer tone.

"Really. And I need your help to find out what happened to your parents. And us being together will make that easier." He turned to Saxby. "How can we make that work?"

"Let me get her lawyer involved," she said. "It might be as simple as transferring her care from one fed to another. But where will you stay? Your hotel?"

"No." He looked at Odom. "How about we go back to your place? Nate and Korey are there. We can hang with them."

"Yeah, that would be cool. I like them. A lot."

Devine looked at Saxby. "Let's do it."

"You're really sure about this?" she asked.

Devine looked at Walker, who appeared nervous but supportive. He then glanced at Odom, who had her eyes glued to him, before turning to Saxby. "I'm sure."

"Judge Mehan adjourned the hearing today so she could consider Betsy's wanting you to be her guardian. She'll be doing a deeper dive into your background. But I may be able to pull some strings in the interim and speed up the process." Saxby slipped out her phone and hurried off.

Odom said, "Hey, Travis, can I talk to you for a minute? In private?" she added, glancing at Walker.

She led him over to a corner, where she took a sealed envelope out of her pocket and handed it to him.

"What's this?" asked Devine.

"Some old lady came up to me and asked me to give it to you."

"What? What old lady?" he said sharply, looking all around.

"I don't know her. Just some lady."

"What did she look like?"

"Like a really old lady."

"How old is that?" Devine asked.

"Really, really old. Like she must've been at least fifty or somethin'."

"Okay, where did you see her?"

"When I was headin' outside."

"What did she say?"

"She knew who I was and asked me to give you this. Said it was really important," Odom added.

"Where is she now?"

"I don't know. She walked off right after she gave me the envelope."

Devine unsealed the envelope and took out the folded paper inside.

He read the contents three times through.

Meet me tonight at the Gum Wall, eleven sharp. Come alone. I see everything, so you involve the police, I will never show and you will be really sorry. I know things about your case that you need to know too. Some of it might be mutually beneficial. A win-win if you don't try to screw me. And you might get to live a little longer too. And the same goes for me.

    The Girl on the Train

"*Is* it important?" asked Odom.

Devine looked at her. "Yeah, it is."

48

SAXBY CAME BACK AND TOLD Devine that things were on a fast track for him to be named an emergency guardian for Betsy Odom. They expected Mehan to issue the order quickly, and without allowing Danny Glass a chance to respond.

"I spoke with Nancy Fine and she's helping with this. But your guardianship won't be for long," added Saxby cautiously. Odom was out of earshot sitting on a bench with an armed Walker right next to her. "And now with the RICO case gone, Glass is still the betting favorite to get Betsy in the end."

Saxby had then taken Odom back to the hotel while Walker had driven Devine back to her house and made them lunch.

"I'm sorry for taking up your day off with all this," he said as he picked at his salad.

"Are you kidding? It was fascinating. But Betsy has been through so much, the poor kid."

"Yeah, she has."

"So if you get the guardianship, you said you'd take Betsy back to her home?"

"Nate Shore and Korey Rose are good guys and Betsy really likes them. Korey can cook and Nate Shore is former Delta Force and can be a great bodyguard. And she'd be in her old place, which might be good for her," he added.

"I saw Betsy give you an envelope at the courthouse. What was it?"

Devine decided to lie. "She wrote me a note expressing her . . . thoughts about me."

"Hope it wasn't too brutal."

"It was. And she had every right to be."

"Well, she must like you. She picked you as her guardian."

"Yeah, she did," agreed Devine.

"So what now?"

"Now I head back to my hotel and check in with my boss."

"You said you'd give me the names of the three witnesses in Glass's case that were killed?" said Walker.

"Oh, right. I'll email them to you."

"Thanks."

"Did you find anything on the surveillance device next to Rollins's apartment?"

She looked nervous.

"What?" said Devine sharply.

"One of the guys in the department used to work for the feds. Not sure what he did and he won't say. But I showed him pictures of it and he said...well, he said, it was super sophisticated and..."

"And what?"

"Looked a lot like equipment he'd used in his old job."

"So *our* government was spying on Rollins?"

"I guess it's possible, yes. Or someone else with the same technology."

Devine thought back to what the girl on the train had written on that easel. The chopper. The attempted hit on him.

My government wants me dead.

"Travis, are you okay?"

He looked over at her. "Thanks for everything, Beth. I know I was a jerk at the hospital, but—"

She slid her hand over and gripped his. "If it were me, I wouldn't have even been able to articulate a coherent thought. So just forget about it, okay?"

"Okay."

She squeezed his hand and then let it go; only Devine still felt it there, warm, reassuring and...nice.

On the way back to his hotel Devine phoned Campbell and updated his boss on recent developments. He also asked for and was given the names of the three witnesses against Glass who had been killed.

Campbell said, "I heard about the RICO case being dropped."

"You have any idea why it *was* dropped? The RICO lawyer mentioned something about it being in the interest of national security."

"Yes, but I'm not going to say it over the phone."

"What then?"

"I'm coming out there."

"Is it that serious?"

"Yes, it is."

"And the chopper she mentioned?"

"If it's the bird I think she's talking about, there are only two agencies that currently deploy it, at least that I know of. DHS . . . and CIA."

"Great. The spooks at Langley are playing their stupid games again."

"Don't jump to conclusions. We don't know for sure."

"What might they have to do with Glass? Sleeping with the enemy?"

"We'll discuss when I get there. I'm coming to Seattle tonight and staying at your hotel."

Devine debated whether to tell him about the meeting with the girl on the train, but decided against it. Campbell might deploy men to follow him and that would blow up any chance of Devine getting to the bottom of this.

She did save my life. And she could have killed me at

the airport. I can't completely trust her, of course. But maybe I can listen.

"And your mole?"

"We're almost there, Devine. Almost there."

Campbell clicked off and Devine pulled over and texted the names of the dead witnesses to Beth Walker. Then he drove on to his hotel.

When he opened the door to his room Devine found that there was someone already there.

Danny Glass said, "We need to talk. Right now."

CHAPTER

49

HASTINGS, AND TWO OF GLASS'S other men, stepped out of the bathroom and surrounded Devine.

"No worries, guys," said Devine. "You can skip cleaning the room today and I won't be needing turn-down service, either."

"Shut up and sit down," barked Glass.

"And why should I do either one?"

Hastings and the men pulled their weapons and pointed them at Devine.

"Okay, I'll give you ten minutes, but only because I don't want any of you to get hurt." Devine sat on the edge of the bed.

Then Glass did something unexpected. He ordered his men out of the room.

When they were alone, Devine said, "I'm listening?"

"What did you say to Betsy to make her pick you as her guardian?"

"It was a complete surprise to me."

"Bullshit!"

"No, it's the truth," Devine replied calmly.

"You are going to tell me why, right this second."

"Do you *really* think I want to be her guardian, Danny? Or that I consider myself capable of taking care of a twelve-year-old girl? Didn't you see how shocked I was in the courtroom? I had no damn clue she was going to do that. I was certain she was going to say that she wanted *you* to be her guardian."

Glass looked as if he was going to really lose his shit, and Devine suddenly wondered if the man was armed.

Instead, Glass rose from the chair and looked out the window.

Devine glanced down at the man's pant leg and saw that the monitor was gone.

Danny Glass, a free man. For now.

Glass turned to look at him. Before he could speak, Devine said, "I was nice to her, okay? I took her out to buy a book and a Frappuccino. I listened to her. I didn't judge her. I brought her clothes and some of her other things from her home. I guess those things count with Betsy. Not all that complicated, really, if you've just lost your parents and are scared and feeling vulnerable."

Glass dropped down in the chair. He looked weak and defeated, two things Devine had never before seen in the man, in or out of uniform.

"This whole thing is so messed up, Devine, I can't see a way out."

"For who, you or me?"

"For everybody."

"I need to understand the situation. Then I might be able to find a way out. For *all* of us."

Glass snorted. "Right, like you're looking out for me all of a sudden?"

"I'm looking out for *Betsy*. I actually believe you care about her. So if helping you helps her, I'm all in."

Glass's wall of opaqueness cracked just a bit and Devine, for the first time, might have glimpsed the real man behind it.

"I do love Betsy. I always have, always will."

"But you just met her, right?"

"Not for lack of trying. Dwayne did not want me in her life. Ever since she was born, I tried to visit many times. And this was when I was still in uniform. I sent money, when I didn't have a dime to spare. When I got out of the Army and was building up my business, I offered to pay for Betsy's schooling. As the years passed, I offered to buy them a home, cars, set up a college fund for Betsy. Find Dwayne a good-paying job that would have allowed him to support his family. But he refused it all. Told me to stick my job offer where the sun doesn't shine. Wouldn't let me near Betsy. And I didn't want to force it because I didn't want Betsy—"

"—to hate you for that?"

"What can I say? She loved Dwayne, warts and all."

"Why did he dislike you so much? Because of what you do for a living?"

Glass slowly shook his head, his expression becoming bitter. "I don't think Dwayne gave a damn about how I made my money. If I'd been a cookie-cutter billionaire on Wall Street, it would have been the same result."

"Why then?"

Glass shrugged. "Who knows? The guy was never playing with a full deck."

"They were given an expensive car and a mobile home. Was that you?"

Glass shook his head. "No. I tried, believe me, like I said, but Dwayne wouldn't do it. Not with me."

"Who then?"

He spread his hands and shrugged.

"Come on, Danny, how could you not know?"

"I didn't say I didn't know, did I?"

"But you couldn't do anything about it?"

Glass made no comment.

"I really need to know who's behind this."

Glass just stared at him and said nothing.

"Okay," said a visibly frustrated Devine. "And your sister? How did she feel about you being in their lives?"

"Alice and I were always close. We communicated over the years. She actually let me send money and other things without Dwayne knowing. Not much, or else he would have caught on. But enough so they didn't starve, since Dwayne couldn't hold a damn job to save his life. But I made sure they never fell too low. I had people watching over them. I wanted to do more. A lot more. It made me sick how they were living hand to mouth because I could have given them ... so much. I loved Alice, would have done anything for her. Our old man was a real bastard to her."

"I heard that you protected her."

"Who'd you hear that from?"

"Just someone who knew Dwayne and Alice well."

Glass smiled knowingly. "Nate Shore and Korey Rose, right?"

"You know them?"

"Never met them. But my people did a deep dive on them when I learned they were close to Alice and Betsy."

"And your conclusion?"

"They've got their own personal demons, but they're both solid as rocks. And they care about Betsy. So I did nothing to persuade them to get the hell out of Dodge. In fact, unknown to them, I had people along the way who found jobs for them when they really hit rock bottom."

"Wow, Danny Glass, the man behind the curtain manipulating everyone and everything. What a big heart you have."

"Behind the curtain! That was the only role I was allowed to play with my own family," growled Glass.

"Nate and Korey are pretty intimidated by you," noted Devine.

"But you're not, Devine. Why do I think you could've taken all three of my boys out right here if I'd allowed them to push it?"

"You wouldn't be wrong," Devine said quietly. "Did you ever speak to your sister, try to reason with her? Didn't she want Betsy to have some stability, some normalcy in her life?"

"Alice was a sweet, sweet child who grew into a beautiful woman. But what Alice lacked was a backbone. If Dwayne said it, then Alice did it. It's the only thing I didn't like about her. It was all I could do to convince her to let me send her small amounts of money, and some clothes and other stuff. So, bottom line, there was no way I was going to be fully in Betsy's life."

"You mean while they were alive?"

Glass's features turned angry and the man who intimidated the hell out of most people suddenly emerged, dark and deadly.

"If you think I had any hand in what happened to them…to Alice…" His voice broke and he quickly turned away.

Devine saw the man shudder violently, and then

rub viciously at his eyes before turning back, but keeping his gaze downcast.

Had Danny Glass just shed tears? thought Devine.

"Well, if you think that, you're full of shit," finished Glass.

"But their deaths *did* open the way for you to become Betsy's guardian and then potentially adopt her. That was not possible while her parents were alive."

A wet-eyed Glass barked, "You don't think I know how this looks?"

"I think you know exactly how it looks. And I also think you had good reason to kill Dwayne. He was keeping you from what you wanted."

"I would never have done that, for two reasons."

"What?"

"Alice and Betsy. They loved the guy. I was never going to take him away from them, no matter how much I wanted to. If I had, Alice would have known. She..." He didn't finish and looked down at his loafers.

"Some men tried to kill me when I went to the town of Ricketts, to find out what happened to your sister and her husband. You know anything about that?"

"Whether I do or don't, Devine, it doesn't matter."

"Surprising admission coming from someone like you. I thought you always mattered."

"In my world, I do. But I'm not in my world right now, am I?"

"What world are you in then?"

"Your world, Devine. I'm in *your* fucking world."

"Meaning?"

"Meaning, until I can get custody of Betsy, you have to protect her, with everything you have."

"Does she have enemies?" asked Devine.

"*I* have enemies. Lots of them. Which means *she* has enemies."

"Then she's your Achilles' heel? *That's* why the FBI is guarding her?"

"Half-ass guarding her, you mean. One lousy middle-aged burned-out agent. I had six guys surrounding that hotel, followed them wherever they went. When you went to the burger place, they were there. And the bookstore."

Devine thought back to the first time he'd visited Saxby and Odom at their hotel. He thought he'd heard the creak of a door, the sound of a footfall, the presence of someone.

Danny's army protecting his niece.

"Why did the FBI go light, then, if it was so important?" he asked.

"Because apparently, you feds don't talk to each other. I don't know how the hell you get anything done. I don't know how the hell you were able to lay the RICO shit on me. You're like a bunch of snotty kindergartners running around with scissors."

"Not all of us."

Glass appraised him coolly. "You gave me all that credit for the shit that went down in Iraq. But we both know you had just as much to do with the outcome as I did. Only I was a grunt and you were an officer. You wrote me up for the commendation and the medal, and you got a pat on the back."

"I wasn't in the job for medals, Danny, and neither were you."

"Amen to that."

The two men fell silent for a bit.

Devine broke it. "Why did you have your sister's and her husband's remains cremated?"

Glass jerked up. "What the hell are you talking about?"

"Someone in Ricketts told me that you had ordered them cremated."

Glass stared dead at him. "Who told you I did?"

"Doesn't matter."

"It does matter, Devine, to me. They . . . they burned up Alice? I . . . I never got a chance to say goodbye to . . . her. To bury her properly." Glass shook his head clear. "Just one more damn thing to blow up in my face."

"Then let me give you another one. Perry Rollins said he had some dirt on you. He wanted to sell it to me. Then he got gutted in a men's bathroom at a bar."

"I already told you I knew nothing about that."

"But were you lying or telling the truth?"

"Don't push it, Devine."

"So who's after you, Danny?"

"Some people."

And Devine finally had corroboration as to why, according to Nancy Fine, the RICO suit had really been dropped.

"And these people are even more dangerous than you are? And so you cut a deal to deliver them to us, in exchange for the prosecution against you being dropped."

By not answering, Glass answered this question.

"Only they discovered you were ratting them out and now they're coming for you. And Betsy." He paused. "So that's who killed Alice and Dwayne? Your enemies?"

Glass glanced up at him. "Maybe."

"You don't know?"

"Like I said, Devine, this is not my world. I'm a little out of my depth."

"If it was your enemy, why leave Betsy alive?"

"I don't know."

"Come on, Danny. You've always been a smart guy. Always one step ahead. So how about now?"

"I have my theories. Theories that I don't want to think about right now, because they might make me do something I will regret. But I can tell you this—the feds did me no favors today."

"They withdrew the charges against you!"

"But they can bring them again if I don't toe the line. They are forcing my hand when I *don't* need my damn hand forced."

"Meaning?"

"Some folks will now believe I've agreed to cooperate. Which ups the ante all around."

"Putting you in more danger, you mean?"

"It puts *Betsy* in more danger. She's the last wild card in the whole deck."

"So what now?"

Glass rose. "*Now*, you take care of Betsy, Mr. *Guardian*. Anything happens to her, you get the same a hundred times over. And I'll fucking do it myself."

CHAPTER

50

A FEW MINUTES AFTER GLASS HAD left, someone knocked on Devine's door.

"Who is it?"

"Braddock."

He opened the door and said, "Detective Braddock,
long time no see."

"You're a fast healer."

"Lucky for me."

Devine sat on the bed and Braddock in the one chair.

"Let me guess, your men followed Glass and his
goons here and you came along to see if I was still in
one piece?"

"So what did he want with you?"

Devine explained what had happened in court.

Braddock shook his head. "So he gets off on the
RICO charges and you get stuck with the girl and
Glass is pissed?"

"There are other forces at work here," said Devine.
"Glass has heat coming his way. He's apparently in bed

with our government against a mutual adversary, and I'm not sure how this is all going to play out."

"You're DHS, so you should have *some* idea. And if that 'adversary' is here in Seattle looking to bury Glass, I need to know."

"I'm not in the loop with stuff like that, Detective, sorry."

"Then you need to *get* in the loop, Devine. For all I know, terrorists are descending on the Pacific Northwest even as we speak."

"I don't know what to tell you."

"Then *tell* me this: When will you take guardianship of Betsy Odom?"

"Tomorrow." *If I'm still alive*, he thought.

"I can provide you some protection."

"I was thinking about moving her out of Seattle. Too many people here and I won't see it coming until it's too late."

"Where are you planning to take her?"

"Need to know, Detective."

Braddock sat back, looking miffed, but clearly understanding Devine's caution.

"Okay. FYI, that print on the shell casing that Beth took?"

"Did you get a hit?"

"What we got was a notice of restricted access on a database that reeks of federal involvement."

"Translation?"

"We think one of the boys who took you was working for *your* side." Braddock cocked his head. "You don't look surprised."

"I would have been, but now that I know how the sides are lining up on this sucker, all the surprise has been drilled right out of me. Anything on Mercedes King's prints?"

"Funny you should mention that. I just got the report. Not even Beth has seen it yet."

"And?"

"Restricted database again."

"The one that reeked of federal involvement?"

"Not the same one as the shell casing print. This one, from what I was told, is even more restricted."

"So she might have been a fed at some point?" said Devine.

"Maybe. I don't even know if that's her real name or not."

"Any way to find out how Ricketts affords all that expensive police equipment, and a government building that looks like it cost more than the tax base of the entire county?"

"Full disclosure, I made those same inquiries before and got zip for my troubles."

"Why were you inquiring about that?"

"I'm part of the police force. I hear rumors. I see

what parts of the state get what, and so do my superiors. So we know all about the fancy rides they have *and* that government building. But I heard that not even the officials in Olympia know where those funds actually came from."

"And they never asked?"

"They asked, so I heard. And then they stopped asking."

"Any reason why?"

"It might be that they got shut down."

"Is Ricketts controlled by organized crime or foreign terrorists?" Devine said this in jest, but Braddock looked deadly serious.

"Or maybe it's our own government," said the detective.

CHAPTER

51

A HALF HOUR LATER DEVINE'S PHONE rang. When he answered it Walker said, "Hey, Travis."

He said, "Hi, Beth. Your boss came by and filled me in on the print on the shell casing and the interesting but inconclusive result on Mercedes King and the wineglass."

"I just saw those results, too. Puzzling to say the least."

"*You* saw them? Where are you?"

"I decided to go into work and started digging into the names of the three witnesses who were killed."

"And?"

"You up for some coffee? We can discuss it."

"Sure."

They arranged to meet at a café close to Devine's hotel.

After they were seated, Walker pulled out the file she had brought with her.

She splayed out three photos of three different men. They each looked hard, cruel, and dangerous.

"Quite the rogues' gallery," commented Devine.

"Thugs in Glass's organization. It's the standard

playbook. Grab the low-hanging fruit, give them deals, and then flip them against the real target. In this case, Danny Glass."

"How did they die?"

"Professional hits, looks to be. No evidence left behind. Quick and efficient."

"Weren't they under government protection?"

"Yes."

"So how did it happen?"

She pointed to the first man. "Todd Grainger, forty-two, one of Glass's enforcers. Up to his elbows in blood. He screws up, gets arrested, Glass's lawyers can't get him loose. He's looking at life. DOJ cuts him a deal. Testify and your ticket gets punched for WITSEC. Same deal for the other two, who were also killers to the nth degree. All standard government dealmaking."

"When did it become *nonstandard*?" asked Devine.

"All three men were being moved at the same time. This was in preparation for their traveling here to testify."

"And?"

"And they were exposed for about thirty seconds, at most. Leaving the house to get to the secure motorcade for Grainger and one of the others. The third was actually about to board a government jet to fly here when the hammer came down. And most critically, they were each taken out within seconds of the others, so there was no opportunity to send out warnings or shut down travel plans."

"How were they killed?" asked Devine.

"In each case a long-range sniper shot. And I mean *long*-range. In the case of the airport hit, about three thousand meters, they estimate."

Devine looked impressed. "There are only a handful of snipers who operate in that range. Army snipers I knew could consistently kill from a thousand meters. SEAL sniper Chris Kyle's longest confirmed kill shot was around two thousand meters, and he was one of the best in the business."

"No great loss for humanity; the three men were collectively responsible for over forty murders. So you figure Glass is behind this?"

"I'm not sure."

"Who else could it be?" asked Walker.

"Your boss was here earlier. We had a similar discussion about something related. And you know what his answer was?"

"What?" said Walker.

"That he thought maybe it was *our* government in play here."

Walker sat back. "What is going on, Travis?"

"You find it strange that Mercedes King's prints are in a super-restricted database?"

"I find it terrifying actually," replied Walker.

"And if she is tied to the feds somehow, they could be behind how a poor, rural town gets jacked-up military-grade policing equipment and a government building that you'd usually see in a much bigger city."

"So the *feds* are clandestinely funding Ricketts?" said a visibly shaken Walker. "Why?"

"That's the question at the top of my list. Oh, and Danny Glass came to visit me in my hotel room."

"Glass? What did he want?"

"He basically told me if I let anything happen to Betsy, he'll kill me personally. And that he had nothing to do with his sister's and brother-in-law's deaths."

"And you believe him?" asked Walker.

"Yeah, I think I do actually."

"Then who killed them?" she said.

"Either someone who wanted to hurt Glass. Or someone who wanted to help him."

"Help him! By killing his sister and her husband? How does that make sense?"

"There are lots of ways to help people, Beth."

"Meaning their deaths opened up the opportunity for him to adopt Betsy?"

"Yes. Dr. Coburn thought they were killed with cyanide and another compound called DMSO, allowing absorption to be quickly fatal. And they couldn't risk inhalation or ingestion of the poison because Betsy might have been killed, too. It was highly sophisticated.

Like killing three guys from thousands of meters away, because that required a lot of prep *and* inside intel."

"Wait, you think whoever did that also killed the Odoms?"

"Maybe not the exact same people, but the same organization," replied Devine.

"You mean *our* government, don't you?" she said, the dread clear in her voice.

In answer he said, "You ever watch *Stranger Things*?"

"Yeah."

"Welcome to the Upside Down. For real."

CHAPTER

52

THAT NIGHT EMERSON CAMPBELL ARRIVED, alone, at the hotel where Devine was staying. Devine met him in Campbell's room.

The burly former general hadn't even bothered to unpack his bag. He poured out a Scotch from the minibar and offered one to Devine, who accepted.

"I don't like this, soldier. Crap is going on here that I don't understand. And I can't effectively fight what I can't see or understand."

"Do you have any inkling as to what *is* going on, sir?"

Campbell collapsed into a chair. "I'm not sure it amounts to even an *inkling.*"

"Well, I just found out that the three witnesses against Danny Glass that were killed were low-level thugs of his. And they were each murdered via long-range sniper shots. One, in fact, shot from a distance that maybe only three people in the world could make."

"Yes, I heard something to that effect, too."

"They knew right where the men were and when they would be on the move. Intel and manpower like that are not cheap and even those with money will find it hard to get."

"Agreed," said Campbell.

"So tell me what you *do* know."

Campbell took a sip of his drink and gazed at Devine with a look that was difficult to interpret.

Campbell said, "Ever wonder why they tried to kill you on that train over in Europe?"

"What?" said Devine. He had not been expecting this query.

"The girl on the train and her crew? They were hired to take you out. Why?"

"I assumed it was because I had disrupted the plans of some pretty dangerous people. That was why I was sent to Switzerland in the first place. You know that."

"I assumed that, too, Devine." Campbell took another sip of his drink and then sat up straight and pointed his gaze to the floor for a moment. "But assumptions are not facts. It was an elaborate hit planned on that train. A team of three. They had details as to your itinerary, the very train car you would be on. They bought out the tickets in that car so they would have you alone."

"Because the mole in your office fed all that info to them. We thought it was Dawn Schuman, but turned out she was just being used as a red herring."

"That was also an assumption, not a fact."

"But Dawn Schuman disappeared. That *is* a fact. She's probably dead."

"Actually, the *fact* is, Dawn Schuman was found very much alive in a drunk tank in Pennsylvania, right before I was wheels up here."

"A drunk tank?"

"I told you she had financial and marital problems. Apparently they became too much for her and she just lost it. Went on a bender. Drugs, drinks, more drugs, more drinks, until the police outside Harrisburg picked her up passed out behind a bar and called us after finding her credentials."

"Okay, she wasn't a red herring. But we still don't know who the mole is."

"I don't think we *had* a mole, Devine."

"I don't understand."

"The mission we were doing in Switzerland was a *joint* op. We worked closely with another agency. The CIA, specifically."

"That's right. I had a point of contact there. He helped me a lot."

"Yeah. He did. I also think, probably under orders, that he almost helped you into an early grave."

The two men stared at each other across the width of brown commercial carpet.

"Why would a sister agency throw me under the

bus for pulling off a successful mission in which *they* were involved and desired the outcome that occurred?"

"We're not in the Army anymore, Devine. Straightforward, logical thinking will get you nowhere fast. I learned that soon after taking this job. And you're going to have to learn it, too, if you want to survive."

"Then you're going to need to spell it out because I'm not making the connections."

"The worlds of espionage and geopolitics are enormously complicated. 3D chess–complicated, like the girl on the train said. Translation for lunch-pail guys like you and me? It's screwed up beyond belief, where everyone stabs everyone else in the back and allegiances change so fast, allies can become enemies and vice versa in a single day."

"So our allies, our sister agencies, you mean?"

"One minute they like us, the next minute parts of us are expendable if another, better opportunity comes along."

"Are you telling me that components of our government will intentionally sacrifice one of their own to get an advantage elsewhere?"

"I will tell you what I believe happened after you wrapped up your mission in Geneva."

"I'm listening," said Devine, who felt his muscles knotting.

"The target was a foreign state-sponsored organization that had as one of its stated goals the hacking and destruction of some of this country's most sensitive databases. The effect would have been calamitous, across multiple fronts. You stopped that, almost single-handedly, with your being able to winnow your way into the confidence of two critical members of that organization, and get out to us vital information that allowed us to head off what they were planning. Then you were able to exit the situation with well-aimed bullets and a mindset to survive that is probably your chief asset."

"Okay, what else?" said Devine tightly.

"And then, it seems that an enemy suddenly became a friend with something of value to provide this nation. Only a 'saving face' olive branch was needed before the deal could be consummated."

"And *I* was the olive branch?" said Devine.

"Yes, apparently you were."

"And how did they know my recent itinerary?"

"We have been hacked, Devine. Hacked by our own side."

"And what are you going to do about it?"

Campbell seemed to have anticipated this question. "I've already taken this up with the highest levels of government. I laid it all out there, left nothing on the battlefield."

"And?"

"And they have not responded, nor does it seem likely that they will."

"So what now?"

"We will finish this mission, *together*. And then I am tendering my resignation. I'm done playing the bullshit games. And I'm too old and I have too much damn dignity to wrestle with pigs in the mud."

"Yes, sir."

CHAPTER

53

AT TEN MINUTES TO ELEVEN, Devine was nearing Gum Alley. It was cold, breezy, and a marine fog had settled in from the harbor, glazing Seattle into the Victorian London of Sherlock Holmes.

Devine pulled up his coat collar and kept his gaze roaming. He'd left the hotel early and performed a zigzag, in-and-out-of-buildings trek across the city to throw off anyone attempting to follow him. When he entered the alley, he glanced at the hardened gum revealed through the threads of fog and thought this was all beyond surreal, outdoing even the battles he'd fought in, where he'd seen things he could never unsee. Combat was horrible but straightforward. You tried to kill the enemy while they tried to do the same to you. Here, there were no sets of rules, no obvious goals, only puddles of darkness and shifting allegiances.

He kept walking, his fogs of breath joining the firmament of the marine layer. He glanced at his watch. It was one minute to eleven. There was no one else around because who would want to be out on such a foul night? Devine had no idea what to expect, maybe even a bullet in the back. Only he didn't have much choice in the matter. He needed help to crack this case, and ironically, the woman who had tried to kill him a trio of times seemed to be his best bet.

He made it halfway down the alley and stopped. He was armed but did not intend to draw his weapon unless it was necessary. He knew he was putting a lot of trust in the woman, and he hoped it would be rewarded.

Devine's attention turned to a shadowy figure standing along a part of the alley that was just beyond the gum on the wall.

"You want to come out where I can see you as well as you can see me?" he said.

One foot emerged and then another. Pru Jackson took three slow strides and stopped in the center of the alley facing him. She was a bit shorter than he remembered from the train and her figure was bundled under protective layers, her long coat sleeves hiding her hands. A ballcap covered her hair; dark glasses did the same with her eyes.

She looked at him but said nothing.

"I'm not in a real trusting mood, so how do I know you are who you say you are?" he asked, sensibly enough.

"The knife I was going to kill you with on the train

was a Wander Tactical Megalodon with a fixed one-hundred-millimeter blade. Black Micarta handle."

"Wander Tactical, they're more of an outdoorsy hunter's carry, aren't they?"

"Well, I wasn't outdoors on that train but I was definitely hunting. And I find that the Italians really know their knives. It cost me a packet. I don't suppose you still have it? I assumed you took it because it wasn't there when I woke up from your little love tap to my jaw."

"I must have dropped it somewhere. Thanks for confirming your identity. You working with spotters tonight or did you just trust me to come alone?"

"Intel I don't divulge," said Jackson.

"You put a tracker on my car."

"Lucky for you that I did; otherwise you wouldn't be here talking to me or anyone else."

"Okay, what's on the program for tonight?"

Jackson drew closer. "A while back you and I were on the same side."

"So you alluded to on the construction site easel. Feel free to elaborate."

"I won't tell you my name; that would be too easy. But let's just say that I have a rather large grudge against my former employer."

"Why?"

"Because of them for two years my home was in a prison in a country that is no friend of ours, and has no designs on treating their own citizens humanely, much less someone like me. If I hadn't managed to escape, that would have been the end of me."

"And why would your employer—"

"Former employer," Jackson corrected.

"—former employer do that to you?"

"Because I believe an opportunity of collaboration came along with this same *enemy*. On top of that, I had discovered that certain people at my former employer had conspired to murder an agent of one of our allies. So to save themselves, my former employer offered me up as—"

"—an olive branch?"

She studied him. "Why did that particular term occur to you? Because it's exactly the one I was going to use."

"The hit with me on the train?"

For the first time, Jackson visibly reacted to his words. "Yes?"

"Apparently your *former employer* once more got a better offer and extended *me* as an olive branch. So you were hired to do to me what had once been done to you."

Devine watched the woman closely. Cold-blooded killers were a dime a dozen. And while the woman in front of him was definitely a killer, he believed she was the rare one with principles.

Like me.

She said in a tight voice, "The client was not made known to me, nor the reason. It was a kill on demand, half the fee up front, the rest on photo confirmation."

"Would it have made a difference if you'd known?"

"I would have had no problem killing you, Devine, under most circumstances. But not under those, no."

"I appreciate the candor. You mentioned the chopper?"

"I'm sure you've investigated that," she said.

"Two agencies use it. Mine and—"

"—my former employer. As I told you before, I saw them load two bodies into it."

"Recognize anyone?" asked Devine.

"No, but I've been out of that world for some time now."

"Do you understand my current mission?"

"Danny Glass, Betsy Odom, who seems a wonderful girl full of spirit, and people who want you dead."

"And do those same people want *you* dead?" he asked.

"They think I *am* dead. So she wants you to be her guardian?"

"Betsy told you that?" asked Devine.

"No, I had other means."

"I may end up being her guardian, at least temporarily."

"Do you know who killed her parents?"

"No, but apparently, higher-ups in the government got DOJ to bag the RICO indictments," noted Devine.

"They would only do that for some platinum treasure in return."

"And I think Glass told someone he wanted to have custody of his niece. And maybe they decided to get him that, the hard way. Perhaps as a sweetener to whatever deal they wanted him to take."

"Glass strikes me as a man who doesn't depend on the largesse of others to get what he wants," said Jackson.

"I *would* think that, except I saw the man's reaction when I pretty much accused him of killing the Odoms. It was not what I was expecting."

"He could have snookered you."

Devine said, "But I doubt he can, or would, cry on demand."

"So agents of the U.S. killed two American citizens? Even in my former world that is not...usual."

"They apparently had no trouble throwing *us* to the wolves."

"True," conceded Jackson.

"You said it had to be worth platinum. Any thoughts on that?"

She drew closer. "Why would you think I would know anything?"

"Because you already know more than me," Devine

shot back, his hand slipping to his pocket. "And a smart person seeks out those smarter because they can make him look brilliant."

She studied him for a moment. "I knew about Danny Glass before all this. Just idle curiosity. His name kept popping up in certain sectors I paid attention to. I did a deeper dive on him after I came here, looking in places that are not accessible to the public, or even some government agencies. Glass lives in another world, a dark one, where there are predators and there are victims and lives get snuffed every second of every day. And those still alive just keep on rolling like nothing important happened, because, for them, nothing important has. The murders of others is just another day at the office."

"So what did you find out?" he said.

"Glass operates around the world, but he has a large footprint in the Middle East."

"So we're talking Middle Eastern terrorists?"

"No. I don't think that's it. The U.S. has intel sources all over that area. We know what shit will happen before the people doing the shit are even thinking about doing it."

"Not on 9/11 we didn't."

"Which is why the U.S. upped its game and uses laser microscopes on that space now."

"Where else, then?"

"The usual cartels are always a possibility. But why give one major drug operator a 'get out of jail free' card to catch another major drug operator? No, that doesn't work. Organized crime isn't nearly as organized as it used to be, so check that one off, too."

She took a step closer and Devine's hand closed around the grip of his Glock. He edged the muzzle forward, in her direction.

"Don't accidentally shoot yourself, or me," observed Jackson coolly.

"Just picking my way carefully through the minefield. I see you're doing likewise."

He pointed to the bulge in her wide coat sleeve that covered her hand. And something else.

"Great minds, Devine."

"You were saying?"

"Other things being equal, I would look internally."

"Meaning?" he said.

"To my mind, and in the minds of the people whose job it is to protect this country, the chief threats right now are home-grown groups that pledge allegiance like you and me. They just point that allegiance in a different direction."

"Domestic terrorists, then?"

"You could throw a rock in any direction in any part of this country and hit somebody who wants this country to look and taste vanilla and never come close to having a scoop of cherry or chocolate anywhere near the horizon of possibility. And some of these people will not stop until what we have today is replaced with something more 1930s Germany than 2020s America."

"Can you be more specific?"

"No, I can't. Because that's not my job. But if Glass knows about something big being planned like that, my former employer will move heaven and earth to stop it, and blowing up a RICO indictment and offing two citizens would just be seen as a cheap price to pay."

"I don't think I like the world you used to play in," said Devine grimly.

"Neither do I, but it's the only one I know," she retorted.

"And there's still the matter of Perry Rollins."

"The man killed at the Sand Bar? The one who approached you with dirt for sale?"

"And how did you know about that?" asked Devine.

"I'm an excellent eavesdropper. And recently I've taken it to an elevated art form augmented by the latest in surveillance technology. So any idea on what the dirt on Glass is?"

"No. But someone bought the Odoms a mobile trailer and the land around it, and an expensive car. And Betsy said when they went to Ricketts, her parents met up with two men who gave them a duffel bag maybe full of money. Minutes after that, they were dead."

"And the payer?" she said.

"I thought it was your former employer. Maybe as a conduit for Glass since he told me Dwayne Odom refused any help from him."

"But why pay and then kill them, Devine?"

"I don't know."

"And was the money found?" she asked.

"Not to my knowledge. The police chief of Ricketts is a hard-ass named Eric King. The town has military-grade vehicles, and a government building it can't afford. His wife is the mayor. She's attractive, about three decades younger than her husband, walks with a swagger, is as ruthless as they come and ambitious as hell. I'm pretty sure she knew about the attempt on my life in Ricketts. And I can still hear her weird, raspy voice— What?"

Devine had noted a discernible shift in the woman's body language.

"Describe the wife to me in greater detail."

"Her name is Mercedes King. She's around thirty-five to forty, five-five, blond, curvy, if I can use that term, confident, assertive, all the things people love in men and hate in women, for the usual stupid reasons. She can change her persona on a dime, from flirty to flinty."

"Right, but you said her voice was raspy?"

"Yeah, like a hoarseness to it. I got her prints and

had a friend run them through the usual databases. Then they hit a wall that we believe had a federal cloud behind it."

Jackson nodded at all this. "Were you able to get the prints of the men who abducted you and run them through the same databases?"

"Yes. The locals here in Seattle were handling that."

"And did they get a hit on the men?"

"Sort of. There was one database where something popped, but it was restricted. Sort of like with Mercedes King."

"I actually know that database well."

"How?"

"Because *my* prints are on it. And I'm pretty sure so are those of the woman *calling* herself Mercedes King."

CHAPTER

54

DEVINE TOOK HIS HAND FROM his pocket and drew closer to the woman, while Jackson stood her ground.

"Why are you so sure about that?" he wanted to know. "My description of King could apply to lots of women."

"Your description of her *was* mostly generic."

"But?"

"But the odd voice and the no prints available? The woman I'm thinking of suffered a serious throat injury a number of years ago and her fingerprints would definitely be on that database."

"How do you know that?" asked Devine.

"Because *I* was the one who slit her throat. They clearly repaired her vocal cords, but apparently they never came all the way back."

"And why did you do that?"

"I was trying to kill her before she could kill me."

"Care to explain?"

"We had differences of opinion on how our agency

work should be done. She pulled a knife, only I was quicker and used it against her."

"What's her real name?"

"Anne Cassidy."

"Just to make sure." He took out his phone and showed her the photo he'd taken of Mercedes King leaving the restaurant in Ricketts.

"Recognize her?" he said.

Jackson took the phone and enlarged the image. "That's her."

"You're sure?"

"She's changed her look, a lot. Colored her hair; she's actually a brunette. Had work done on her face, good work, top dollar. Her eyes are blue now; they were brown."

"So how can you be sure, then?"

"The eyes, Devine. They're the same pair of vile, cruel headlights that came at me the last time we met. She could change their color, but not the evil behind the color."

"But really how can it be the same person? She's married to a police chief and she's the mayor."

"Let me tell you something, Devine. Our government owns lots of stuff. Most of the raw land in this country, office buildings, museums, national parks, military complexes, prisons, naval bases, we all know those things. But what most don't know is that the government, particularly clandestine parts of it, owns people, and places."

"I'm not following."

"FYI, I know squat about Ricketts. But a government building it can't afford, military-grade hardware? A seemingly normal town that gives off the vibe of being anything but. Ring any bells?"

"So you're saying Ricketts is owned by—"

"Owned and run probably by my former employer, and let's just state the obvious and say *CIA*. Which may be why it was chosen as the spot to murder the Odoms. That way their deaths are 'investigated' by their own people, and the conclusion that certain folks want is reached. Case closed."

"And the odd person out, the medical examiner, blown up?"

"What?"

Devine explained what had happened to Dr. Coburn. "But what you're laying out makes perfect sense. King invited me to dinner that night. Probably just to keep me in town so they could get a shot at me. She was late getting there and was obviously surprised I was still breathing. They wanted me dead because I was throwing sand into their arrangement with Glass. Never pegged the woman for a spy, though."

"After 9/11, this country and its intel services took a good hard look at itself. The 9/11 terrorists got their pilot training in a small town with few resources. Mistakes were made that should have sounded alarm bells. So CIA, which is not supposed to operate domestically, has set up its own strategic outposts where it can gain intel, which is then fed to other agencies who do operate domestically. The stakes are high, because when I was active with the agency there were domestic groups that wanted to topple the U.S. government, and they've only grown increasingly active over time. And they could succeed." She paused and ran her gaze over him. "It's a different world, Devine, and the only thing you can be sure of is nothing and that includes people."

"So that means I can't trust you?" he said bluntly.

"Nor can I trust you."

"Then how do we work this together?"

"I want to get back at the people who betrayed me."

"Only I don't see why you need me for that. Unless it's also because you don't want to see the United States government toppled."

"Why should I give a flying fuck about that anymore?"

"And yet here you are. But since Mercedes King is probably on your to-do list, maybe you and I can achieve both goals at the same time. Although I'm not telling you anything you already haven't thought of, am I?"

"You can tell me one thing I don't know: How did you get on to us on that train?"

"A dozen little details that didn't mean much alone but, cumulatively, told me that something bad was going to happen to me. I took countermeasures, and then when the men came after me, I did what I had to, to survive."

"And me? You saw the knife in the window's reflection, right?"

"But I'd already suspected you."

"You mentioned I hadn't added to my drawing."

"That and you were trying overly hard not to look at your two *friends*."

She nodded slowly, looking thoughtful. "And why didn't you kill me, too?"

"You were no longer a threat and I don't kill people who aren't a direct threat to me and..."

"And what?"

"And I thought, however foolishly, that you might repent your evil ways."

"I'm not sure I would have done the same, had our positions been reversed."

"Nor would I expect it," he said.

"The contract on you is still open."

"And you can still earn your money."

"I'm not sure I'm that hard up, Devine."

"So do we work together, or not?"

A second later a shot zipped between them and splatted against the wall.

55

DEVINE AND JACKSON RAN DOWN the alley while gunfire chased them. They turned a corner and were, for the moment, out of the field of fire. The area they were in was deserted, as far as Devine could tell. However, the fog had thickened, the temperature had dropped, and it was hard to see more than a few feet in any direction.

Devine looked around. "Okay, let's get behind that wall over there and see if whoever was shooting at us shows themselves."

Their guns at the ready, the pair eyed the foggy area in front of them from the relative safety of the wall. When Devine slipped out his phone Jackson asked, "Who are you calling?"

"Nine-one-one."

"Don't bother. Whoever's out there will be long gone by the time they get here."

"But the sirens might scare them off."

"I'd actually rather try to find out who they are, wouldn't you?" pointed out Jackson. "And I would *really* rather not have to answer uncomfortable questions from Seattle's finest."

This gave him pause and he looked back out to the fog as he heard footsteps.

In a low voice he said, "The witnesses against Glass were taken out by snipers operating on the extreme edge of long-range shooting."

"Well, at least there are too many buildings in the way here for them to line up a shot from two miles away."

"You know about long-range killing."

Jackson eyed the foggy darkness. "The more you know, the fewer surprises life holds, Devine. And in our line of work, I don't much care for surprises. And just for the record, CIA deployed some of the best snipers in the world by poaching from the military and foreign sources. And women make extremely deadly snipers. Fine motor skills and attention to detail. It's evolutionary, from picking all those berries, taking care of babies, and sewing all those clothes, while the men were out chucking spears at mastodons."

"You always make small talk while someone's trying to kill you?" he said.

"Also evolutionary, women can *multitask*."

As soon as she said this, Jackson took aim and fired three rounds. An instant later they both heard someone scream out in pain.

Devine now saw the nearly invisible target, who had been lurking behind a trash can with his gun pointed at them. The man leapt up and staggered away, dragging his left leg behind him, and slipped into an alley.

"I didn't think CIA spent much time on weapons training," he said.

"After I escaped from my hellhole, I mapped out every skill I'd need to survive. So I spent considerable time training with one of the best shots in the world. *She* taught me a lot."

"Congrats, now stay here," instructed Devine.

"I can take care of myself," she snapped. "I *did* shoot him."

"You're my cover. Anybody else goes into that alley, shoot them, too. I'll see you back here."

Before she could answer, Devine was sprinting off into the fog line.

For a moment Devine did think about the wisdom of exposing his back to a crack shot, but after a few moments he was at the mouth of the alley and out of her line of fire. Part of him wanted to call Braddock, but he knew that the woman back there would see that as a stark betrayal when he desperately needed her help to get to the bottom of this.

He eyed the length of the dirty alley. Trash cans, Dumpsters, recycling bins. Various tradesmen entrances.

So lots of places to hide and then leap out and shoot. Even for someone wounded.

He moved forward cautiously, his old training kicking in. Devine was focused on his sense of hearing. Wounded people could not remain entirely quiet, no matter how tough or well trained. The brain did its own thing when the body was in pain. It let you know. And it let others know.

And that's when he heard it. A moan, a low one, but clearly there, along with a few choice expletives.

He slowly moved down the alley. When Devine heard the sob, he hurried forward and then stopped. Up ahead was a Dumpster.

Devine called out, "I'm with Homeland Security. Throw out your weapon and come out, hands above your head, fingers interlocked. Do it now, or I can't guarantee your safety. And I'll get medical treatment for your wound."

Devine waited, his pistol at the ready. There was no way, really, to predict how these things would turn out. You just had to be ready for all scenarios.

Three seconds later he heard a shot. It didn't come at him. It didn't ricochet off the wall.

"Shit."

He rushed forward and poked his gun and then himself around the edge of the Dumpster.

The man was lying face up on the asphalt and next to bags of trash that had overflowed from the Dumpster.

The gun was in his hand. His leg was bloody, from Jackson's shot. But that hadn't killed him. The self-administered gunshot to his right temple had.

Devine knelt down to get a closer look. He knew that man. Well, he *recognized* him.

It wasn't one of Danny Glass's men.

It was one of the police officers who had followed him around Ricketts.

When he ran back to tell Jackson all this, the woman was no longer there.

CHAPTER

56

WHAT WERE YOU DOING OUT here at this hour?" asked Braddock as he gazed down at the dead man sprawled among the trash.

Devine, who was standing next to him, said, "Running down a lead."

"And did it pan out?"

"Not sure. But I am certain the dead guy was in a police uniform in Ricketts."

"And you saw him fire at you?"

"No, but who else could it have been?"

"You winged him in the leg, then?" noted Braddock, looking down at the wound there.

Devine knew he hadn't fired his gun. And for all he knew, Jackson's slug was still in the man's leg.

"I don't know."

"You don't know if you shot him?" Braddock said incredulously.

"Things were happening fast. Bullets were flying. For all I know, he wasn't alone and one of his guys accidentally shot him. But I do know that he killed himself. I heard that shot and found him like this seconds later."

Braddock looked at him grimly. "This is going to open up a shitstorm."

"Blame the guys who were trying to kill me."

"Any idea why they *were* gunning for you?"

"Someone tried and failed to kill me back in Ricketts. I assume they followed me to Seattle and tried to complete the mission."

"The same ones who killed Dr. Coburn?"

"Probably."

"And this all has to do with Danny Glass and the town of Ricketts and the murders of the Odoms?"

"It makes the most sense, but I have no direct proof. I think Glass knows who's behind all this and why, but he's not talking."

"I mentioned it might be our own government before," noted Braddock. "And they dropped the RICO charges against Glass. And Beth told me about the three witnesses who were killed. That would take a lot of intel and planning. And inside information."

"Yes it would," agreed Devine.

"I don't like the feds doing shit like this in my backyard."

"I don't blame you. I wouldn't either."

Braddock nodded. "Okay. We're going to need your weapon for ballistics, if the round is still in the guy's leg." He knelt and peered closer at the dead man's bloody limb. "And I don't see an exit wound."

"Why do you need to run ballistics on my weapon? That shot didn't kill him."

"It's standard police procedure, Devine."

"Not for me it isn't. And I'm not walking around without a weapon. My welcome here has not been all that hospitable."

"You really want to die on *that* hill?"

"I think I'm going to have to."

"And I think I'm going to have to insist."

"Okay, but then I need to talk to my DHS superiors and they're going to need to check with agency lawyers. Until then I am not authorized to relinquish my weapon to you or anyone else for any reason."

"Where'd you get that line?"

"It's in pretty much every cop show I've ever watched. I thought everyone knew that."

"Don't mess with me, Devine."

"I'm not, Detective. But I'm not giving up my weapon. If you or your men try to take it by force, I have every right to defend myself. No threats, just for information purposes."

"Okay. I'll table that for the next couple of minutes.

FYI, I made a request to the FBI to interview Betsy Odom. I've heard nothing back."

Devine suddenly had an idea. "Let's make a deal, then."

"What sort of deal?" said Braddock warily.

"I'm about to be named Betsy's guardian." When Braddock started to speak, Devine headed him off. "So if you won't push on taking my weapon, I'll let you interview Betsy."

"I'll be able to do that anyway," retorted Braddock.

"It'll be a lot faster than going through normal channels."

"Why do I think I'm getting played?"

"If I really thought your checking my weapon for ballistics would help your case, Detective, I'd turn it over now. But it won't, guaranteed."

Braddock, seeming to sense what Devine was implying, peered out into the foggy darkness before settling his gaze back on Devine. "At some point you're going to have to tell me what really happened tonight. And *everybody* involved."

"You have my word that I will. Now, unless you need me for something else, I'd like to get a little shut-eye. Big day tomorrow."

"Really? What do you have planned?"

"Staying alive, of course."

BACK AT HIS HOTEL, HE phoned Campbell, woke the man up, and they met in the latter's room.

Devine brought him up to date on what had happened, but didn't mention Jackson.

"So a police officer from Ricketts tried to kill you?"

"Yes."

"Is that all?" said Campbell.

"Isn't that enough?"

Campbell stared at him for a long time.

"Okay, Devine. If you don't tell me right now what you've been withholding, you will be immediately terminated from DHS and I'll have them get a cell ready at Leavenworth."

Devine shot him a dark look. "So all my past missions mean nothing? I'm still a probie subject to a life sentence?"

"Yes," said Campbell. "Until I say otherwise."

Devine stood and paced before leaning against a wall and staring down at his boss.

"The girl on the train is here. I met with her tonight."

To his credit, Campbell didn't look surprised, only intrigued. "Explain, in detail."

Devine told him about the message given to him by Betsy Odom.

"So you met her and she said what?"

And Devine told him everything that he and the girl on the train had discussed.

When he was finished, Campbell rose, poured himself a glass of water, and sat back down.

"Just to be clear, the woman who tried to kill you used to work for us? Only our side sacrificed her when another opportunity came along?"

"Like you said they did to me."

"Now she's a mercenary for hire but still, understandably, holds a vendetta against those who betrayed her?"

"Yes. And she and Mercedes King, aka Anne Cassidy, had a big falling-out when King tried to kill her."

"So she sees a chance for revenge against CIA?"

"Apparently."

"She really believes that Ricketts is owned lock, stock, and barrel by CIA?"

"Yes. Have you heard of such, sir?"

"I told you before, this plane of existence is not the battlefields we're used to, Devine. And we're not the only country who plays these back-stabbing games. They all do, including our closest allies."

"She did mention domestic terrorists who may want to overthrow the government. If Glass has a way to help our government neutralize that threat, it would definitely be in their interests to work a deal with him."

"But she couldn't be more specific?"

"No. But the answer may lie in Glass's criminal enterprises. If he had valuable intel, he had to get it somewhere, and his business associates, suppliers, and clients seem the likeliest avenue."

"I'd call in reinforcements, but I'm not sure who would come and what they would do when they got here."

"Roger that."

"I know this sounds absolutely crazy, but do you trust this woman?"

Devine didn't answer right away, not because he wasn't sure, but because he wanted to give the question the thoughtfulness it deserved.

"I think she represents the best shot we have to bring this house of cards down."

"Can you get back in touch with her somehow?"

"I think so, yes."

"If we do bring all this tumbling down, our own side might be coming for us."

"I actually relish the fight, sir."

"Me too, Devine."

"And if we resign and leave the field to them, sir?

Then only the power-hungry assholes without a hint of moral conscience will be left in charge to trample all over the Constitution and the rights of every American."

"I agree. We're staying right where we are. Fuck 'em."

CHAPTER

58

WHEN DEVINE AWOKE THE NEXT morning, he had a text message on his phone.

> Ex parte meeting held with Judge Mehan. You have been installed as Betsy's temporary guardian beginning immediately. Come by as soon as you can today to be briefed and to take custody. Saxby

He rose, showered, dressed, and noticed the note under his door.

> Bookstore again, two o'clock. I'll find you. GOTT

Well, that was a nice, relaxing way to start the day, thought a still-tired Devine.

He grabbed a cup of coffee and a banana from the hotel lobby market and phoned Saxby on his way over.

"How did you manage to pull that off so fast?" he asked.

"Mehan doesn't want to put Betsy within fifty miles of her uncle. It was extraordinary relief, for sure, but this is an unusual situation and she stepped up to the plate."

"Glass already figured that she would. He was waiting for me at my hotel after the hearing. He said that if I let anything happen to Betsy, he'd give me the same a hundred times over and he'd do it personally."

"Reinforces the judge's decision, right?"

"But it also shows he wants Betsy to be safe. In fact, he told me that since the FBI only assigned you to protect Betsy, he's had six of his men watching her all the time."

"Are you serious?"

"I see no reason for him to lie."

"Who's he protecting her from?"

"Probably from whoever killed her parents," replied Devine.

"But if they wanted to harm her, why not just kill her, too, at the same time? You have any thoughts on that?"

"Yes. I'll fill you in when I get there."

Ten minutes later he hustled up to their room and knocked.

Saxby answered the door and ushered him in.

"Where's Betsy?"

"Still sleeping. She had a rough night. How about you?"

"I might have had it rougher."

"Sit down and tell me about it."

Devine gave her the blow-by-blow, from Glass in his room after the hearing to the attempt on his life last night. But he did not mention the girl on the train. Telling Campbell about her was enough. He trusted Saxby, but his instinct was to keep that on the QT. Apparently, in the world in which he operated now, few could be trusted, even fellow agents.

"I think you've used up all of your nine lives now," warned Saxby.

"Let's hope I've got a few left."

"And you're sure the man who tried to kill you was a Ricketts police officer?"

"Yes. And his body is now with the Seattle PD."

"Well, then the Ricketts police chief will have some questions to answer."

He decided to broach the elephant in the room with Saxby.

"It seems our own government is working with Danny Glass. They got him off the RICO charges."

"Maybe," said Saxby cautiously. "Nancy Fine didn't really confirm that."

"I think she did. And what if they killed Betsy's parents, too, as part of whatever deal they're doing with Glass?"

Saxby looked alarmed by his comment. "*Our* government killing two innocent people? Have you lost your mind?"

"Clears the way for Glass to adopt Betsy. Maybe that was why she was left alive."

"Look, I'm no Pollyanna, and I've seen some crazy shit in my time, and not everyone who carries the badge is a saint, but we do draw the line at the cold-blooded murder of American citizens."

"What if the survival of our country is at stake?"

Saxby slipped a smoke out of her pack and lit up. "Do I want to hear this?"

"I'm afraid you're going to have to."

He told her about Dr. Coburn's report being taken off the official record.

"She suspected cyanide poisoning combined with another compound that would make absorption nearly as quick and lethal as inhalation. I was told by the cops in Ricketts that it was a drug overdose. Coburn told me she found no evidence of that."

"Well, let's get Coburn to make an official statement to the police."

"She can't."

"Why the hell not?"

"Because she was blown up in a house on the outskirts of Seattle the night before the court hearing."

A substantial amount of blood drained from Saxby's face. "Blown up?"

"After men tried to kill her in the house."

"How the hell do you know all this?"

"Because I was there with her. I tried and failed to save her."

"That's where you got those scratches and why you were walking so stiffly?"

"Yes."

"So what are we talking, organized crime, a South American drug cartel?"

"I think we need to look closer to home."

"What does that mean?" she asked.

"I suspect Glass has some incredibly valuable information that he was willing to share with our government *if* the charges against him were dropped, and he gets his niece. Well, he got the first item on his wish list and now he wants Betsy."

"What sort of information would he have?"

"Look at the people he's done business with. Could one of them be planning something big? Maybe an attempt to overthrow the government?"

"Overthrow the United States government? Listen to yourself. For God's sake."

"If enough people believe it can never happen here, then they've pretty much assured that it will, in fact, happen on American soil."

"Okay, I need to tell somebody about this."

"No. Not yet. We need to let this play out a bit."

"But—"

"I told you all this in confidence. But there are

people in the government who know about the possible threat and are working to make sure it will be defeated."

Saxby considered all this for a bit before nodding. "Okay, I'll keep mum. But thanks for ruining my day, week, and year."

"Hey, welcome to my world."

59

AFTER ODOM GOT UP, SAXBY helped her pack her things and Devine drove them over to his hotel. He had upgraded to a two-bedroom, two-bathroom residence at the hotel on Uncle Sam's dime, and with Campbell's blessing.

He wasn't planning on staying there long, though.

Odom wandered around the spacious hotel room and then stood looking out the window.

Devine sat watching her.

"So how are you doing?" he asked.

She remained staring out the glass. "Seems like I'm always tired even when I get plenty of sleep."

"It's called puberty and stress. They both wear you out."

She sat down. "So what now? I stay in this hotel room with you until...?"

"Tomorrow, we're going to your home in Kittitas. We've already confirmed with the judge, and I let Korey and Nate know."

"It will be nice to go home, even if Mom and Dad won't be there," she said, her look one of sudden misery.

Devine decided to try to change the subject to pull Odom out of the despair that she seemed to be falling into. "So why did you want me to be your guardian?"

She turned to him. "Because I like you, and I trust you. I don't think you'll mess stuff up for me."

"Does this mean you don't want your uncle's wealthy lifestyle?"

"If he wants to give me money and things, fine. That doesn't mean I have to live with him. And why would he even want me around? It seems, I don't know, weird."

"In his defense, I think he really loves you."

"Funny way of showing it. He was never around."

"He told me your father wouldn't permit it. That he'd sent money and clothes and other things, but your father returned them and wouldn't let him visit or help you in any way."

She nodded, looking thoughtful. "Dad really didn't like him."

"Your uncle said the same thing."

"My . . . my mom liked him, though. She said he took care of her when she was young. Their father was, well, an asshole, I guess."

"I've met a lot of them in my life. I'm sure you have, too."

"Why did this RICO thing go away?"

"I'm not sure," Devine said delicately. He couldn't

tell Odom things that might get her and him in trouble. But he could sense how vulnerable she was right now. And he didn't want to lie to her, because the bond of trust he had delicately formed with her could easily be destroyed with any misstep of his.

"I think your uncle has some really good lawyers, and like I told you before, the government lost some witnesses that they really needed. So maybe they didn't have enough evidence to keep going."

"You think he had those witnesses killed, don't you? You mentioned it before."

With what he now knew, Devine wasn't so sure about that. "Betsy, I can't say one way or another, but if your uncle is guilty of the things they say he is, then, yes, he certainly could have had those people killed."

"Are you going to keep looking for who murdered my parents?" she asked.

"Yes, and I am going to find them, I promise."

"And then they'll go to prison, right? I mean, you can't kill people like that and get away with it, can you?"

"No, you can't," said Devine, even though he was thinking that, in this instance, that could happen.

"Do you . . . do you think my uncle had anything to do with it?"

Devine was on increasingly shaky ground here. Yet he answered as truthfully as he could.

"I *did* think that."

"But you don't think that anymore?" she said.

"Your uncle came to meet me after the court hearing. I asked him that very question, accused him of it really."

Odom stared at him with such intensity that Devine wanted to look away but didn't.

"And what did he say?"

"It wasn't so much what he said as how he said it. The bottom line is I believed him when he denied any involvement in their deaths. He was…shattered, I guess is the word. Like you, he loved your mother very much."

"Then who could have done it?"

"Do you remember anything else from that day? Anything at all?" Devine thought of what Dr. Coburn had told him about the cyanide combined with the DMSO. "I know this will sound weird, but did your parents touch something that you didn't? Or were they touched by people who didn't touch you?"

She stared at him in confusion. "*Touched?*"

He decided to be straight with her. "Your parents may have been poisoned, with cyanide. If inhaled, it can be deadly in less than a minute. But absorbed in the skin it takes a while to kill someone, unless it's combined with another substance that can make it quickly absorbed into the bloodstream."

"Is that what you think happened?"

"Yes. So is there anything you remember along those lines?"

She looked out the window and sighed. Then she closed her eyes and appeared to be concentrating, perhaps taking herself back to that awful moment in time. She opened her eyes. "I remember seeing that the two men who gave my parents the duffel shook hands with them."

"They did? Wait, did your parents have gloves on? Did the two men?"

She closed her eyes again, apparently trying to get a firmer mental image of that moment in time.

Odom opened her eyes. "My parents never wore gloves. But the two men had gloves on. Thick ones, I think."

Devine sat back. *That must have been it.*

"You said your dad put the duffel bag in the trunk? He didn't show you what was in there?"

"No. They got back in the car and my dad drove off and that's when he started getting sick. And then my mom."

"They couldn't breathe, you said. Were they also convulsing? Jerking around?"

She looked at him, her lips quivering. "Yes, they were. Do you...do you think the duffel was poisoned or something? Or maybe when they shook hands? The gloves the guys wore?"

"Yes, I think those two men poisoned your parents that way. Do you remember anything about them?"

"They were both tall, about your height. They had on big overcoats. One had dark hair, and the other one was blond."

"Age?"

"About your age."

"Had you ever seen them before?"

She nodded.

Devine's features tightened. "I asked you that before and you said no."

"No, you asked me if they looked like any of my uncle's guys and they didn't."

A frustrated Devine rubbed at his face. "Okay, *where* had you seen them before?"

"They were the same two guys who showed up at where we lived before. They were meeting with my dad when we went out for ice cream."

Damn, thought Devine. Contrary to what Ellen Saxby had said, CIA possibly *had* murdered two American citizens.

"Does that help you?"

He looked up at her. She appeared fragile and on edge.

"Yes, Betsy, it was a huge help. Thank you."

She said nervously, "Travis, what's going to happen to me? I mean, you've got a job and stuff, and I can't live with Kor and Nate in that trailer till I'm grown."

"I wish I had all the answers, but I do know that when someone is going through a tough time, like you are right now, it's better to take small steps. If you try to think everything through, you'll become paralyzed. But what I can promise you is that I'm going to do everything I can to help you all the way through this, okay?"

"Why? I mean, you don't even really know me."

"I know you're a good person who got dealt a crappy hand in life. No adult I know would be handling this situation as well as you are. And I like to help people who are fighters, who get back up when they get knocked down. And you are a fighter, Betsy Odom, never doubt that."

What she did next surprised Devine. She sat next to him and hugged him. And the tears finally came from the girl, until Odom was shaking with the force of her sobs.

Devine didn't really know what to do, so he just held her as tightly as he could.

CHAPTER

60

W HILE HE WENT TO HIS meeting with the girl on the train, Devine had Emerson Campbell stay with Odom. He explained to her who Campbell was, and to his credit, the older man immediately seemed at ease with the girl and she with him. When Odom had gone out of the room for a minute, Devine had asked him why he was so relaxed.

Campbell had smiled knowingly and said, "I married right after West Point and had my first of four daughters a year later, Devine. I also have eight grandchildren, six of them girls and four of them between the ages of eight and thirteen. And hell, I thought combat was tough."

Devine went to the hotel garage to get his car.

"Where's Betsy?" said a voice.

Dennis Hastings was staring at him from next to a parked car.

Devine looked at the man. "Are you authorized to know?"

"Cut the shit. The *boss* wants to know."

"And the boss always gets what he wants, like you told me before?"

"Like he got the feds to back off. Pretty impressive, wouldn't you say?"

"I guess it's all in how you look at it."

"So tell me. Now! Or it will get rough. For *you*."

Devine really didn't have time to argue, so he decided to swallow his anger and said, "She's being guarded by a combat veteran who could kill every single guy you have around this place without breaking a sweat."

Hastings drew close. "You better hope that's right, Devine. Anything happens to her—"

"Yeah, I get it a hundred times worse. I heard that song before, and your boss delivers it way better. Now get out of my face."

"You think you can talk to me that way, pissant?"

"I *think* I just did."

"You had the girl with you before, so I couldn't show you how I really feel about you. But the girl's not with you."

"Lucky me."

"I don't think so, dipshit."

Devine wheeled and ripped the metal baton out of the hand of the man who had done his best to sneak up on him. He slammed the baton into the man's gut, and when he pitched forward from the blow, Devine put his size twelve shoe up the man's nostrils. He flipped over on his back and landed hard on the pavement. Snot blew out of the man's nose and that was always a sign that your opponent was out of the fight, because the brain had pinballed inside the skull. Devine did not wait for the man to contemplate trying to be a hero and getting back up. He jacked him with two knuckled rights to the jaw. More snot, blood, loosened teeth, and then a deep sleep.

The second man leapt on Devine's back right at the moment Devine dipped his torso forward. He'd heard him coming because the idiot was breathing like a bull about to charge. The man flew ass over shoulders into a parked SUV, setting off the alarm. Devine walked over and slammed the man's head into the car door, and then did it a second time, because it was always good to trust but verify. He let go and the gent slid to the pavement with blood coming out of his nostrils and mouth.

When Devine turned, Hastings had his gun out and was pointing it shakily at Devine. So shakily that Devine doubted the man had ever shot someone, and was desperately working up the nerve to pull the trigger.

Devine rescued Hastings from this dilemma by knocking the gun out of his grip with a strike of the baton. As Hastings scrambled to pick up his weapon, Devine grabbed him by the collar, lifted him off the ground, and threw him headfirst onto the hood of the same SUV, its alarm still screaming. He next reached under Hastings's armpit and flipped the man onto his back. The battered and terrified Hastings lay splayed out, his limbs trembling as if electricity was coursing through him.

He stared up at Devine, who had pulled his gun and was pointing it in Hastings's face. "Sorry to mess up your suit. I know how you like twinning with the boss."

"Please, don't," moaned Hastings. "Please."

Devine put the muzzle against Hastings's left temple after racking the slide. "Tell your boss to back off. Tell him."

"Please don't hurt me."

"I've got a lot of shit to do and this is not helping, okay? Tell him."

"I will, I swear to God."

"Yeah, I think you will, *pissant*."

Devine slugged the man, bouncing his head off the hood. Hastings lay there out cold like a side of beef about to be sliced and diced by the butcher.

Devine holstered his weapon. When he turned around, he saw a terrified elderly couple watching him.

They backed away in fear.

Thinking quickly Devine said, "They, uh, they took my parking space."

He threw the baton in his car, climbed in, and honked at the three unconscious men as he drove off to meet a cold-blooded killer in a bookstore.

61

THE BOOKSTORE WAS FAIRLY FULL, and Devine watched as moms and dads with young kids, older people, and what looked to be college students searched through the stacks of tomes on shelves, browsed the music department, or hit the small café for sugar and caffeine.

Devine was simply trying to find the girl on the train, but had no idea what she would look like this time. As he glanced around, Devine was also wondering if Glass would send out a hit on him after Devine had cratered his security crew in a parking garage.

He finally figured if he sat at the same table he'd been at before, she would signal him, or make herself known somehow.

However, no one approached him. After ten minutes he was about to get up when two people strolled over and sat down at the table. A man in his fifties and a woman in her forties. He was in a smartly tailored blue suit with no tie and she had on dark slacks and a purple turtleneck sweater with a long black coat over them.

"Mr. Devine?" she began crisply.

He looked at them. "And you are?"

In answer, she opened her purse and pulled out a piece of paper and slid it across.

Devine unfolded it and read off what was the very same message that had been slipped under his door earlier, purportedly from the girl on the train to meet here today.

"Who are you and why do you have this?"

"We were the ones who slipped that note under your door at the hotel," said the man.

"And how did you know what to write in it?"

The man glanced around. "This is not really the place to go into all this. We have a car outside."

"I don't get into strange cars. I've found it bad for my health."

The man pulled out a small black leather case from his suit coat pocket, laid it on the table, and opened it. The woman did likewise.

Devine looked down at the credentials and then up at the pair.

"That confirms I will never get into your car," he said. "Central Intelligence is not really on my best buds list at the moment."

"We always do get the bad rap," said the man with mock jocularity. "In the movies we're looking to murder half the world. And on TV we kill the other half.

I'm Will Chambers, and my colleague is Angela Davenport, as our credentials say."

Davenport leaned forward and spoke in a low voice. "Before we get down to business on this matter, Devine, I wanted to personally thank you for clearing up the death of Jenny Silkwell in Putnam, Maine."

Devine looked at her in surprise. "You knew Jenny?"

He noted the woman's lips trembled at his query.

"She was actually my protégée. I hoped to see her take my spot in the hierarchy in due time. A wasted talent and life. You risked *your* life to clear it up. You have my gratitude and respect, sir. And that of the entire Agency."

She put out her hand, which he slowly shook.

This was all delivered with such sincerity that Devine was a bit taken aback.

Chambers leaned in. "Angie brought up the business in Maine to also illustrate another point, a connection, in fact, with where we are presently."

Davenport tapped the table with her fingernail. "The girl on the train, as you colloquially refer to her."

"And how do you know that? And how did you know what to write in the note you put under my door?"

"The word 'intelligence' *is* in our name," noted Chambers.

"And we're here to ask you about her," added Davenport.

"Why?"

"Because she used to work for us."

"I know nothing about that."

"Oh, come on, Agent Devine," said Chambers. "If you lie to us, we'll get nowhere." He glanced around again. "But can we at least stretch our legs? I know bookstores are not the usual stomping grounds for foreign spies, but I'll feel like an idiot if we're being recorded here. And I, for one, do not wish to see my thirty-year career of public service end in a professional scandal that took place across from the young adult section and a cappuccino machine."

A minute later they were walking slowly along the pavement, while Devine observed that a black Tahoe followed at a discreet distance.

"Her name is Prudence Jackson, Pru for short," said Davenport. "She was one of our best field agents." She gazed up at Devine. "Look, to be up front, I will make some statements, Mr. Devine, and share some information with you, in the hopes that you will reciprocate. I will do this knowing full well that we have no way to force you to do so."

"Waterboarding off the approved list?" said Devine.

"I tell you what," exclaimed Chambers. "Hollywood has royally fucked us over."

Davenport said, "Jackson was a first-class intelligence

officer. In the same mold as Jenny Silkwell, but with a survivalist mentality that made her the perfect choice to drop into hot spots all around the world. She served brilliantly."

"So what happened?"

"We were told that she was killed by an enemy of this country and her remains were buried in an unknown location," replied Davenport. She paused here and studied Devine once more. "I take it that whatever she may have told you does not comport with my statement?"

"How do you know she's told me anything? Or that we've ever even met? I don't even know if this Pru Jackson was the woman who tried to kill me on the train."

Davenport continued, "We have since learned that Jackson is not dead, and has been quite active. She *did* try to kill you on a train from Geneva to Milan. We have the proof."

"And she tried at least twice in Maine to put you six feet under," added Chambers.

Davenport said, "Jackson has become a mercenary. Highly placed, highly compensated."

"You know all this, but you can't find her?" said Devine skeptically.

"She is very good at what she does. And have *your* people at DHS been able to find her?" she retorted.

Got me there, thought Devine. "Okay, she's highly placed and compensated and she's good at hiding. What else?"

"Can you at least tell me something you've learned about her? It might save us a lot of time. And my instincts are telling me we are fast running out of that."

Chambers added, "We know something big is being planned, right here on American soil. Not another 9/11, thank God. But maybe, in the end, perhaps even more damaging. If you understand me."

"I've heard that from other quarters," conceded Devine.

"So, shall we join forces?" Chambers said.

"My boss, Emerson Campbell, is back at my hotel. Why don't we have a powwow of sorts and see what we can do together?"

Chambers and Davenport glanced at each other. She said, "I guess it's high time we all started cooperating. If we want to have a damn country left to serve."

CHAPTER

62

CAMPBELL ANSWERED THE DOOR AND told
Devine that Odom was in her room. Devine introduced Chambers and Davenport, and they all sat down
in the small living space off the two bedrooms.

Devine brought Campbell up to date on his conversation with the two CIA officers. Campbell said,
"I was actually wondering when someone from your
agency would arrive on the scene."

"We're not often the cavalry charging in; that's *your*
usual role," retorted Chambers.

Devine interjected, "Jackson basically told me that
she had been set up while at CIA because she knew of
a coverup of a murder of an agent of one of our allies.
A murder committed by CIA. So they threw her to the
wolves."

Davenport and Chambers exchanged looks. Davenport said, "That may be what Pru believes, but that
is *not* what happened. In fact, the people behind that
murder are currently in prison."

"What happened to her, then?" asked Chambers.

"She said she spent two years in a prison in whatever country it was." He looked at them both, but they were apparently not going to tell him a specific place, even if they did know. "From things she hinted at, I believe she was tortured during those two years."

"I see," said Davenport, her expression pained.

Campbell said, "You mentioned you thought she was dead. How did you get on to her?"

"Her mother, Molly Jackson, died in a nursing home a short while ago," explained Davenport. "We had a man posted there, just in case. An old friend showed up to say goodbye. She looked legit so our man did not challenge her. It was only afterward that we discovered the 'friend' had undergone emergency surgery and had been hospitalized during that time." Davenport added wistfully, "Pru really was so very good at disguise."

"How did you know to come to me?" asked Devine.

Before they could answer, Campbell said, "Let me just spell something out for you both." Davenport and Chambers turned to him. "I have heard rumors that your agency may have done to Devine what Jackson says was done to her. I'm talking about that hit on Devine on the Milan train."

"That was *not* authorized by us," said Chambers indignantly. "We would have had no reason to do such a thing."

Davenport looked at Devine. "Your assistance with

our joint operation prevented a very dangerous situation from escalating further. You are a valuable asset to this country, as you also proved during the Silkwell matter. The organization you helped take down is no friend of ours. We would never do business with them under any circumstances."

"I wish I could believe you," said Devine. "About me and Jackson."

Davenport and Chambers sat back and looked helplessly at one another.

She said, "We know that Jackson was behind the attempt on your life in Europe and believed that she had followed you out here. By your own words, we now know that is correct. We want to know more about that."

"She could have killed me several times," said Devine. "But she didn't."

"And why is that, do you think?"

"She sees bigger fish to fry. The people who betrayed her. I hope you recognize yourselves. And she was intrigued by the Danny Glass matter, since it seems clear that he's cut a deal with the government to walk on the RICO charges, and get his niece in the bargain."

Campbell added, "The DOJ's case was considerably weakened by the loss of three witnesses. All killed by world-class snipers with excellent inside intelligence. So excellent, it seems to have come from within the government itself. Maybe a particular *part* of the government?"

Both he and Devine stared at the two CIA people, both of whom stared right back at them.

Davenport said, "I resent that you would think we had anything to do with that. We do not murder American citizens, even those who have collectively murdered dozens of people."

"On Glass's orders," countered Devine.

"I am not going to waste a minute of my life defending Danny Glass," retorted Davenport. "He is tough and opportunistic, yes, but still scum in my book. But we often have to deal with scum to catch bigger and more dangerous scum. And while Glass *is* dangerous, in his own way, he is not dangerous, per se, to this country, as a whole. He's more of a nuisance."

"So did you have the men killed?" persisted Devine.

"No," said Chambers. "I have served my country honorably and occasionally bent the rules in so doing. But I have no interest in going to prison! Are we clear on that?"

Devine glanced at Campbell, who seemed to be appraising both of the CIA officers.

Campbell said, "Okay, we'll accept that, for now. Keep going. How did you get into bed with Glass?"

Davenport said, "Glass became valuable to us because he did considerable business with people and companies that have close ties to an organization both we and the FBI have been tracking for close on two years now."

"What organization?"

"They are known as 12/24/65."

"Christmas Eve, 1965?" asked Campbell.

"Wrong century. It's *1865*," replied Davenport.

"And the date's significance?" asked Devine.

"It's the day the Ku Klux Klan was founded by Confederate veterans in Tennessee."

"The KKK? That's what we're talking about? In 2024?" said an incredulous Devine.

Davenport said, "The more things change, the more they stay the same. Or regress, in this case. And FYI, there are now more hate groups and well-organized and -funded militia groups in this country than ever before. Some want to secede from the country. Others want to take over the country and then run it in accordance with their twisted beliefs. And 12/24 is clearly in the latter camp."

"I've never heard of them," said Campbell, as Devine nodded in agreement.

"Which is part of their plan," noted Chambers. "Stay under the radar until they're ready to strike."

"But Glass had dirt on them?"

"Far more than dirt, Agent Devine. Names, places, plans, account numbers, locations of weapons caches, and texts, emails, phone recordings. The list of members is shocking, truly. Titans of industry, political pundits you see on TV or read online. And there are quite a few who hold both state and federal government positions and who have taken up with these people." He eyed Campbell. "And there are some soldiers in there as well, high-ranking ones. But we need Glass's cooperation and testimony to back it all up."

"Are you sure he's not just leading you along?" asked Devine.

"Glass already provided some information. It was actually demanded by us and the FBI as a gesture of good faith on his part." Davenport glanced at Campbell. "And by DHS as well, General Campbell. Your own agency *is* in on this, too."

"Well, I'm clearly not in the loop on that," noted Campbell angrily.

Devine now asked the question he had been waiting to throw out.

"The Odoms? They were murdered. Know anything about that?"

"No," said Davenport decisively. "We were not involved in that."

Campbell said, "Isn't it illegal for CIA to have *any* operations within the United States?"

"It *is* illegal," replied Chambers. "Which is why we don't do it, *officially*. But we coordinate with those agencies that *can* operate domestically. But intel is intel, no matter what country it might fall in."

Devine said, "Well, somebody murdered the Odoms. And their deaths led to Glass's getting his shot at being Betsy Odom's adoptive parent, which I know was on his wish list."

"CIA had *no* involvement in that," said Davenport emphatically. "If he were convicted in the RICO case, he would be looking at several lifetimes in prison. That's plenty of leverage on our part. We didn't need any more to make him cooperate. And that's another reason we wouldn't have killed those witnesses. It would have weakened the leverage we had over Glass."

Devine said, "But it would have helped 12/24. The RICO goes away, Glass's incentive to work with the government goes away, too. That's good for the terrorists."

Campbell said, "So maybe they utilized their contacts in government to get the necessary intel to take out all three witnesses at the same time."

Devine looked at Davenport, who stared back at him. She said, "We had *nothing* to do with those men being killed."

"I guess I believe that now."

"Thank you," she said curtly. "Now, what can you tell us?"

Devine said, "After meeting with two men, the

Odoms got a house and car from an unknown source. And they met with the same two men minutes before their deaths. I think they were given money directly at that meeting. But Betsy was left alive, which makes sense if this was being done on behalf of Glass, so that he could gain custody of her." He glanced at Davenport. "Did you provide the money?"

"Why would we give these people money?" interjected Chambers.

"As a conduit for Glass. He told me he tried to give them money and other things over the years, but Dwayne Odom hated him and wouldn't accept any of it. Maybe he came to you for help."

"As I told you, the quid pro quo with Glass was the dismissal of the RICO charges, Devine," said Davenport. "Regardless of what happened to those witnesses, that was going to happen. That was the deal. His family mess has nothing to do with us. In fact, I know nothing about it."

"So why did the FBI take custody of Betsy Odom?"

She replied tersely, "That's the Bureau's business. Ask *them*."

"I did and got the runaround."

"Then I would respectfully suggest that you ask again, this time more forcefully."

Devine studied her stony features while Chambers played with a button on his suit jacket. The thing was, he believed her. And he also believed that whatever the FBI was up to with Betsy Odom, Davenport was not in agreement with. He felt perplexed and uneasy with the thought that the Bureau might be playing him, too.

"What do you want from us?" he finally asked as Campbell nodded.

"We know that you went to Ricketts, Washington," said Davenport.

Devine perked up at this. "I guess that town is well known to CIA."

"I don't know what you mean."

"Pru Jackson told me that the government owns lots of things, people, and places. And Ricketts has lots of toys it can't afford. Courtesy of Uncle Sam? Or CIA? And even though I'm sure you'll deny it, some of *your* goons kidnapped me and probably would have tortured and then killed me if Pru Jackson hadn't come to the rescue."

"And why do you think it was us?" asked Davenport curiously.

"Jackson followed the truck after it picked up the two guys I turned the tables on after they snatched me. She saw them flown out in body bags in a very special helicopter that apparently only DHS and your agency use. I'm pretty sure it wasn't DHS, so that leaves you. And SPD found a print on one of the shell casings. They ran it through the usual databases, but hit a roadblock on a special database. I'm guessing it's restricted to members of your agency."

Davenport shook her head. "Your guess would be wrong, Mr. Devine. We *were* alerted to the print search when it hit *that* database. But that database is restricted because it contains the prints of people known to associate with terrorist organizations, both foreign and domestic."

"So you're saying you deny access to forensic evidence results sought by the police when they run across really bad guys?" said Devine incredulously. "You just let them walk?"

"In no way do we let them *walk*. We monitor them to see if we can catch even bigger fish and learn about their ops and intentions. We also will go back to the police in certain instances and inform them discreetly of who they are dealing with. In this particular case, the print hit was on a man named Albert Russell. He is a known member of 12/24, at an enforcer level. We did not inform the Seattle Police of this because we did not want them to blow up our plan to bring the entire organization down in order to ID one dead bottom feeder's involvement."

"And the chopper?" said Devine.

"It was not our chopper and not our people. That sort of aircraft is also used by the other side, Devine. They are incredibly well funded. And contrary to your assertion, Ricketts is not *our* town. But it *is* owned by someone else."

"Who?" said a startled Devine.

"We believe Ricketts, Washington, to be the unofficial headquarters for 12/24/65," said Chambers.

CHAPTER

63

DAVENPORT AND CHAMBERS HAD FINISHED their talk with Devine and Campbell and left. Plans were apparently being laid by the feds. Complex and dangerous plans. Which, to Devine's mind, had little chance of actual success.

A thoroughly frustrated Campbell had eventually gone back to his room, while Devine sat in a chair staring out the window at the Seattle darkness. It was quiet and he needed the solitude to process everything. And Davenport's advice kept coming back to him: *That is the Bureau's business. Ask them.*

Twenty minutes later, certain things had crystallized in his mind. Possible answers to questions that had been troubling him clicked into place. It was like the final few pieces of an exasperating puzzle coming together.

And I made assumptions I shouldn't have. And now I have to make sure, or as sure as I can be, when everyone keeps lying to me.

He called Campbell and asked the man about some inquiries he said he was going to make.

Campbell said, "Right, Devine, sorry. With everything going on I forgot to fill you in. It will interest you greatly, I think."

After Campbell finished telling him what he'd uncovered, Devine clicked off and immediately made another call.

FBI Special Agent Ellen Saxby answered on the second ring.

"Enjoying the quiet and your cigarettes?" he asked.

"I'm actually a little lonely."

"Want some company?"

"What about Betsy...?"

"I called in reinforcements."

"All right."

"That coffee shop right down the street from your place? Twenty minutes?"

Without letting her answer, Devine clicked off, and called Campbell to once more look after Betsy. He also had one question for his boss before he met with Saxby.

"How *exactly* did my getting assigned to this mission go down?"

"Like I told you."

"In more detail, it's important."

Campbell eyed him for a moment before saying, "Well, actually, my friend at the Bureau said he'd heard of a former Ranger I'd recently brought on who'd done good work overseas. I asked him if he was referring to you and he said yes. So off you went." Campbell stopped and stared hard at Devine. "So, you're thinking...?"

"Yeah, I am."

"And where are you going now?"

"To find out the truth."

Saxby was already waiting for him. The place was half full and they sat at a booth away from the other customers. They ordered their coffees and Devine remained silent until their drinks arrived.

He took a sip and said, "I came to talk about 12/24/65. See, I figured it was time to cut to the chase. You up for it? Because I don't think it's going to be pretty."

She had been stirring sugar into her coffee and he saw her hand tremble at his words. It was subtle, but it didn't escape his notice, because he had been looking for just that sort of visceral reaction.

She put her spoon down and took a swallow of coffee.

"FYI, I'm not really into Christmas. And I wasn't even born until 1980," she added.

He stared at her for a long time before speaking, because he wanted her to understand the gravitas of the moment.

"I'll let you take another swing at that, Ellen. You answer with more bullshit, I'll take matters into my own hands and to hell with whatever the Bureau's planning. I'll blow the whole thing up. Is that what you want?"

She broke off eye contact and took a sip of her coffee. "Now, if you're referring to a certain organization that goes by that name?" she began.

"I am."

She shifted her gaze to meet his eye. "What do you want to know?"

"Everything."

"That's a big word."

"Just start with the basics then. I think I'm entitled to that."

She dropped her gaze and nodded. "Okay. Generally speaking, we've seen connections to them in large-scale marches with followers in hoods and carrying guns, and also interference in local elections. They are suspected of having ties to robust social media presences and indoctrination campaigns, and have even gained influence and a presence in myriad private school academies. And we believe that affiliates of theirs have their very own tax-exempt and so-called religious platforms that illegally funnel money to them. But again, we've never been able to run the thread directly back to any verifiable source."

"So you really can't make a case against them?"

"We have gone after those that we believe act in

concert with 12/24. But they are well financed and have first-rate lawyers, so successful prosecutions have been few and far between. Witnesses get scared or die. Or evidence goes missing because local cops are members. But no one has ever truly spilled on them."

Saxby seemed to be getting really worked up and Devine just decided to let her keep rolling. "And?" he said.

"You ever hear of the Black Hand back in the 1920s?" she asked sharply.

"No."

"Sort of the precursor to Cosa Nostra. Hundreds of murders, bombings, kidnappings, from citizens on the street to the wealthiest in the land, to top-tier politicians. Even the U.S. president back then was targeted. There was fear in all fifty states. And they damn near toppled the federal government. We would have been a banana republic or else like Nazi Germany."

"So that's the blueprint for these guys? The Black Hand?"

"They're actually more sophisticated," said Saxby. "They exhibit a mainstream, reasonable-looking façade in many quarters to draw in as many ordinary folks as possible. And then they lead them down the rabbit hole conspiracy track, mostly on social media or in their indoctrination academies to capture the youth, until they'll believe anything these people tell them. You see, even though our society is economically inequitable, the government does pass and enforce laws that try to keep some of that domination in check. And these people don't like that. They want all the wealth and power, along with a population that looks the same, prays the same, speaks the same, and where white men dominate everything. Just like the KKK."

"But now you have a shot to really take them down?"

"Yes, thanks to Danny Glass, of all people."

"So why *did* the FBI take custody of Betsy Odom?"

"Come on, Devine. We've been through this."

"No, I've asked the question and got bullshit in response, time and time again. And that needs to stop. Now."

"I don't know what to tell you."

"Well, let me tell you what I think. How about that?"

"Go right ahead but I make no commitments."

"One guard around Betsy?"

"I told you—"

"Let me finish. You presented to me like you were a washed-up, has-been agent in full midlife crisis. A sometimes bumbling, chain-smoking, fly-off-the-handle time bomb with a gun."

She took a sip of coffee and looked away.

"But my boss checked on you with some buddies of his at the Bureau and he just filled me in on what he learned. About *you*."

"Really?" said Saxby in a challenging tone. "And?"

"And you're none of those things. You're happily married, got three great kids. You didn't get assigned here because your boss dumped on you for calling out his misogynistic fav boy. You were assigned to this because you're one of the Bureau's best. Which, by the way, despite your best efforts, you allowed flashes of to show through at times."

She looked at him, her eyebrows peaked. "And what? Now you want some sort of explanation?"

"No, I doubt you're allowed to give it. So let me just keep going."

"Fine by me. I have nothing else to do today."

"Then I come into the picture. I wonder why?"

"You tell me, Devine. You're going so good now, got quite the head of steam up."

"Your people knew that Glass and I had a connection from our time in the service, which was why I was brought into this. Then I hit it off with Betsy, while you play the wicked stepmother, literally forcing her onto my side. We bond, you subtly give up more and more territory to me. Then people try to kill me in Ricketts. They try to blow me up in that house with Dr. Coburn. Now suddenly I'm Betsy's guardian."

"So now you're Betsy's guardian, so what? I had nothing to do with that. That was her decision."

"Manipulated by you! What did you tell her about

me when you went shopping? That I was a great guy who wanted the best for her? You must have been laughing your ass off when you advised me to take her to the bookstore, get her a book, buy her a drink and something to eat, and wait for her to confide in me. You manipulated and fooled me *and* Betsy. Well done, Ellen, well done."

"I have no idea—"

He broke in, "How long have you been working on this with CIA?"

"CIA? Are you nuts? The Bureau and CIA are oil and water. Everyone knows that."

"Don't think so, Ellen. They made contact. Filled us in. They said the Bureau was fully engaged in this whole op. And you just conceded that the Bureau has been after these KKK guys for a while."

"Filled *us* in?"

"Me and my boss." Devine hunkered down in his seat. "So let me get to the gist of it. One guard on Betsy. Sure, I know Glass had his goons around her, too, but it's not the same. But it is enlightening, right? Why is Glass so concerned about Betsy's safety?"

"He's afraid his enemies will hurt her to get back at him. Pretty straightforward."

"So she's an important part of all this and yet she's right here in Seattle with just you guarding her in a crappy hotel. How does that make sense?"

"I don't know what you're getting at."

"I thought that maybe CIA had killed Alice and Dwayne Odom to open the door for Glass to adopt Betsy. They denied that, vehemently, I might add. And they also denied responsibility for the murders of the three RICO witnesses. And I believe them. Now, if I was in this 12/24/65 crew, what would I be thinking about all this?"

"Tell me," said Saxby irritably.

"Kill off the RICO witnesses so the case falls apart and Glass has no incentive to cooperate with the feds. Then, as belts and suspenders, kill Betsy's parents as a warning to Glass not to cooperate, but leave Betsy alive. You kill her off, too, what leverage do they have left? Hell, if she dies, he has nothing to lose. He'll tell all, just to get back at the bastards."

Saxby cleared her throat and now appeared uncomfortable. "Look, Travis, I—"

He didn't let her finish. "You were setting Betsy up. Making her look to be an easy target. Your feigning surprise and anger at DOJ's dropping the RICO charges was bullshit. You knew all along they were going to be ordered from up high to do exactly that. And when I said I didn't want to be Betsy's guardian you jumped all over me, telling me I had to do it."

"Travis, please—"

But Devine kept right on going. "The FBI *wants*

Betsy to die so that there would be no question that Glass will cooperate. That's why you got the court to grant me guardianship. The Bureau walks away. I take Betsy to some place where not even Glass's goons can protect her. And when I suggested that was what I was going to do, I got no pushback from you or anyone else. And then what? The location gets slipped to the KKK assholes? Betsy and I end up dead, and are classified as collateral damage for the greater good, right? And Glass becomes the star witness in the federal prosecution of the century that will make all of your career highlight reels." He tapped the table and eyed Saxby. "But if they kill Glass, your plan is screwed. So how many agents do you have covering *him*, in addition to his own army? Ten? Twenty?" When she didn't respond, he struck the table so hard with his fist, it spilled both their coffees. "I deserve a *goddamn* answer, Ellen."

A few nearby onlookers glanced nervously over before turning back to their drinks and whispering furiously.

A trembling Saxby sat back, took a breath, and ran a shaky hand through her hair. "An even dozen, to answer your question about the agent coverage on Glass. They're embedded at the hotel. Whenever he travels somewhere, a silent, invisible army of agents goes with him. Strictly need to know, no leaks, no mistakes. Like you said, the trial of the century."

"How did you know I'd hang on to this case after I took Betsy to the meeting with her uncle? I could've just walked after that."

"We…we had reviewed your personnel file and current psych workup. You never walk away, Travis, not from someone in need. And…and I made sure you knew Betsy was in need by playing the role that I did."

Devine looked at her with fury. "You've *played* me for a sucker this whole damn time. I thought maybe feds would treat other feds with respect, but I guess I was wrong about that."

"I…I didn't like doing that."

"And how long were you all going to wait for Betsy to die? And if she didn't, would you shoot her yourself and blame it on the KKK assholes?"

"We don't kill children, Devine," hissed Saxby.

"Forgive me for not believing one damn word that comes out of your fucking mouth."

She started speaking in a low voice. "The plan was not to let them kill her. But *attempt* to kill her. We had other agents around her, only you never saw them. That way Glass would know that the only way forward was to fully cooperate with us to put these bastards away for good. Then he could ride off into the sunset with his niece."

"A global criminal in charge of a young girl? That's your idea of a perfect ending?'

"My mission does not require a perfect ending. Otherwise, why attempt anything if that's the bar? Would I prefer Betsy to be with someone else? Yes, of course. But that's *not* my call."

"I need to know everything because my ass is on the line along with Betsy's."

Saxby now looked truly torn. "I can't tell you anything more. And even I don't know it all."

"This stinks to high heaven."

"Are you telling me you never executed a mission you didn't agree with or had doubts about morally? Either at DHS or the Army? You really expect *me* to believe *that*?"

Devine sat back. He *had* done missions he didn't agree with, on any level. Missions that had actually used civilians as bait, or decoys. And some *had* died.

She watched him closely and seemed to read his thoughts. "It's not easy. None of this is easy. For either of us. Or Betsy."

"Ricketts, Washington, is the mother ship for 12/24/65. Did you know that?"

"Yes."

"Nice if you had mentioned that before I went out there and almost got killed."

"I'm sorry, Travis, I really am."

"If you know it's the mother ship, why not arrest the Kings and their minions?"

"There's the necessary element of proof."

"The man who tried to kill me in Seattle was one of the police officers from Ricketts. Isn't that proof?"

"And you won't be surprised to know that we've been told by Chief King that this same officer had been fired the day before the attack on you for insubordination and for theft of police property."

"In other words, they're disclaiming all responsibility for a rogue cop?"

"And let's say we swoop in and take out King and his people. But what about all the others? Devine, you have to realize that this group spans the entire nation."

"If it's so widespread, how can you possibly catch all of them?"

"We don't have to. We just have to catch enough of the *right ones* to topple the entire organization. Then the rank and file will crawl back under their rocks."

"Until the next time, you mean?"

"Yes," she conceded.

"So placing Betsy with me?"

"You're actually a much better bodyguard to her than I ever would have been. That was also figured into the plan."

"But DOJ dropped the charges. What else does Glass need?"

"The charges were dropped without prejudice, meaning DOJ can refile them."

"He told me he was pissed that you guys forced his hand. With the charges gone, 12/24 will know he's agreed to cooperate. You put a bull's-eye on him and Betsy."

"We can't wait forever, Travis. And 12/24 is certainly not going to wait much longer. We've had chatter enough to show that something big is being planned. And we needed to push Glass to fish or cut bait. We need what he knows, now!"

"Seems he's sacrificing everything for Betsy."

"Agreed."

"But why does a man who's never even met his niece until now put his entire life and empire on the line for her?"

"I don't know. I wish I did, but I don't. Truly, I don't. I swear."

Devine had other issues that were also bedeviling him.

Who was financially helping Dwayne Odom, including the day he and his wife died? And what dirt did Perry Rollins have on Glass, and who had killed him and why?

"Are you still with me?" asked Saxby.

He broke from these thoughts and said, "So I take Betsy, we go to her trailer in the woods with two of her friends, and wait to be slaughtered?"

When Saxby didn't answer right away, he said, "Jesus Christ, Ellen!"

"Not exactly, Devine."

"Not exactly, my ass."

"We *will* be there. This will not end well for 12/24/65. And good riddance."

"And if it doesn't end well? If Betsy dies?"

Saxby did not answer him.

Devine knew she didn't have to. If Betsy died, Glass would sing until the cows came home to bring down the people who killed his beloved niece. So for the FBI, it was heads they win, tails they win.

And it seems like I lose no matter what.

64

SAXBY LEFT DEVINE SITTING THERE, brooding.

As he nursed both his coffee and his professional wounds, Pru Jackson appeared and sat down opposite him.

She was dressed hipper, looking nothing like she had back at the bookstore, or even at the Gum Wall.

"I guess you had some means of hearing everything we said?" he began in a weary tone.

She laid a minuscule device on the table and took out a pair of black ear pods. "You sure walked into a shitstorm," she said.

"You haven't heard all of it yet, Ms. Jackson."

Jackson stiffened but then relaxed. "I assumed that it might come out one day. And you told the FBI agent that you talked to CIA. So tell me everything you know."

"Why?"

"It seems you're going to need all the help you can get."

"Let's get out of here. For all I know, there are a dozen people in here with the same surveillance crap you have."

They walked out into the gloom.

"So tell me what I don't know," prompted Jackson.

"Angela Davenport?"

"*She's* in the mix? *She's* your contact with CIA?"

"She told me about you and her. But I'd like to hear your take."

"Why? So you can compare it to hers?"

"Wouldn't you do the same?"

Jackson glanced around as they walked down the street. "She was my mentor at CIA. A legendary ops officer in her own right. She's on my hit list, by the way."

"What about a Will Chambers?"

"I've heard the name but never knew him. He's in town, too?"

Devine nodded. "They know you're alive. And they claim they had nothing to do with your being left behind. They were told that you were dead."

"They were in the loop, count on it."

"And you know that how?"

She gave him a stern look. "Are you really second-guessing me, Devine?"

"I just had a come-to-Jesus with the FBI. Before that I had a come-to-Jesus with CIA. Before that I had a come-to-Jesus with *you*!" He stopped and looked down at her. "You've never been wrong? Never had an instinct that turned out to be bad? You're perfect?"

"I never said that. And you know for a fact I'm not perfect. Remember, the train?"

"So tell me why you think they were in the loop. Spell it out for me. All the players and angles."

She led him over to the mouth of an alleyway and well out of earshot of anyone. Then Jackson turned and faced him.

"I was inserted into a particular region, in a country that I am not going to name. It is a hellhole of terrorist activity."

"Middle East?"

"No. It would be difficult to drop someone who looks like me into that area and be able to do anything productive. And the desert is not the only place where terrorists are present."

"Okay, fair enough."

"I infiltrated the group and communicated the intel out. Action was taken and our agency goals were achieved. On the night I was supposed to leave, I was abducted. I could hear the men speaking in a language that I'm passable in. I was betrayed, Devine. I was set up by my own people because I knew about the murder I told you about. I could take people down."

"Davenport said the people responsible for that murder are in prison and CIA was not involved."

Jackson looked shaken by this and didn't respond.

"Let's drill down into that some more. What people in particular do you think were involved in your abduction?"

"The ones I talked to about the murder, including Davenport," she said.

"How about Anne Cassidy, the woman calling herself Mercedes King, the mayor of Ricketts? The one you stabbed in the throat before she could stab you? Was she involved?"

"Cassidy was a fellow field agent. But she wasn't involved in my abduction."

"How do you know she wasn't? Maybe she was responsible for it all by herself."

"Why would Cassidy have done that on her own?"

"Why exactly was she trying to kill you? Just over professional differences like you said? I highly doubt that."

Jackson wouldn't look at him. She studied the brick wall over his shoulder.

"If we're going to help each other, Ms. Jackson, the truth would be nice."

She finally looked at him. "It's just Pru. Okay, Cassidy was a piggybacker. She let others do the work and she rode them till they died, literally. Only in my case, I wasn't going to stand for it. I finished my mission and she was trying to take all the credit. I went to her apartment. I put my foot down. She grabbed a knife and tried to take my life. I got the knife and did what I did. Two days later, I was taken."

"Two days later? Cause and effect? I mean, she had a great motive to take you out. You'd left her for dead after she tried to kill you. Maybe her revenge was years of torture in prison for you rather than a bullet to the head. Was she that kind of person?"

"Yes," conceded Jackson.

"So she delivers you up to the abductors. And then reports you as having been killed, with no body to ID. And she walks off free and clear. Why would you think it was your agency and not her that screwed you over? I mean, she had just tried to kill you!"

"Because I overheard my captors saying my agency betrayed me and—"

Devine broke in, "And she wouldn't have thought to tell them to do that? Manipulate you one last time? And cover herself on the off chance that you got away and might come after her for what she'd done? So she lays the blame on the Agency."

She gave him a hard stare. "I didn't know you ex-military were capable of such nuance."

"You mean thinking like the backstabbing, lying, let-you-die-as-an-olive-branch-to-your-worst-enemies pieces of crap that litter your old stomping grounds? Yeah, I surprised myself, actually. But I've always been a quick learner. It's why I'm still breathing."

"I guess I deserved that," she conceded.

"How much would your abductors pay Cassidy to sell you out?" asked Devine.

"A lot."

"Well, maybe Anne Cassidy walked away with a bag of money for her treachery and used that to become mayor of Ricketts. The question is why?"

"I already told you that the town is probably controlled by CIA."

"No, Mercedes King clearly no longer works for them. And the chopper and the guys you saw that night? Not CIA."

"Who then?" asked Jackson.

"As I'm sure you heard me tell Ellen Saxby just now, even though she already knew it, Ricketts is HQ for 12/24/65, the second coming of the KKK. And they're planning something really big. And killing me was apparently part of that." He studied her. "You don't look unduly surprised by this."

"Absolutely nothing surprises me anymore."

"It was suggested that they have big money backers, and people embedded at all levels of the state and federal governments, the police, the military, too."

"That would make sense."

"How so?" he asked.

"Caesar had his Brutus."

Devine shook his head. "Shooting people in a different

uniform is a lot easier. You don't have to keep looking behind you for a 'friend' holding a knife." He glanced at her. "So maybe our cooperation can start there."

"Meaning what, exactly?"

"I'm a known quantity in Ricketts now, but you could go in wearing one of your incredible disguises and snoop around without anyone the wiser, and then report back to me."

"So *Cassidy's* the one who really sold me out? Not CIA? You're certain?"

"I can't be certain of anything, but it sure as hell looks that way to me, Pru. And doesn't it make sense to find out for sure?"

"Okay, I'll do it. But now I'm really going to finish off that bitch if she did set me up."

"Well, I think you might get your chance. But that means she'll have her shot, too."

CHAPTER

65

DEVINE GOT BACK TO THE hotel, where Campbell was waiting for him. He told Devine that Odom was asleep.

Devine went through the plan as told to him by Agent Saxby.

Campbell snapped, "They're risking the life of a child on a half-ass plan like that?"

"They claim they have it under control. That she'll be protected."

"You know as well as I do that when the shit hits the fan, no one is in control. And their plan has more holes than the targets on a sniper range." He paused. "You still taking her back to her home?"

"I think it's safer than staying here. At least there I can take some precautions, put up some defenses, and see them coming. Unless the government wants to stick her in a cage surrounded by an army for the next twenty years."

"What else did you learn?"

"Pru Jackson was waiting for me after Saxby left.

She worked with Mercedes King, real name Anne Cassidy, at CIA. The two got into it, Cassidy tried to kill her, so Jackson reciprocated and left her for dead. Next thing she knows, Jackson's being tortured in a foreign prison. She had thought her agency had screwed her, like I said before, only I think it was Cassidy."

"I just got something you might find interesting. Camera feed from Ricketts on the day the Odoms died."

"You do?"

This didn't come from Devine, but from Betsy Odom, who was standing in the doorway of her bedroom.

The two men glanced at her. Devine said, "Are you up to looking at it, too, Betsy? You might be able to see something helpful."

Devine could tell by the girl's stricken features that the thought of seeing her dead parents very much alive on the screen was horrifying. But then she seemed to steel herself and nodded. "Sure, if it'll help find out what happened to them."

Campbell brought the feed up on his laptop screen and then fast-forwarded to the relevant section.

Devine watched on the screen as the Genesis pulled up to the curb in front of the restaurant. The car doors opened and the Odom family climbed out, Betsy from the backseat and her parents from the front. He shot Odom a glance and saw her lips start to quiver.

"You okay?"

She didn't look at him. "Yes."

He gripped her hand and Odom didn't pull away.

Alice Odom was dressed in jeans, boots, and a parka. Her long auburn hair splayed out over the back of the jacket. Her smile was wide and infectious.

Dwayne Odom's hair was far shorter than in the image Devine had seen of him before. He was thin with a shallow chest and no hips and glutes to speak of. A stiff wind looked like it would bring the man down. He came around the car, his smile as broad and as inviting as his wife's. It was right then that Devine could see what a happy family they had been. And it wasn't the new car or the trailer in the woods. They just truly seemed to love one another.

It was hard to fathom that in a short time two of them would be dead.

They continued to watch as the Odoms walked into the restaurant.

Devine kept his gaze on the car to see if anyone passing by paid it more than casual attention. Or whether a police cruiser was in the vicinity showing heightened interest.

Neither happened.

With one eye on the screen, Devine said, "Betsy, can you run through what happened inside the restaurant again? I mean, everything you can remember, from beginning to end."

"I don't remember much."

"Just try, please."

"How about a Coke?" said Campbell. "Lubrication for the throat might free up the mind."

"Sure, okay."

He got one from the minibar, poured the can's contents into a glass, and handed it to her. She took a sip and said, "We sat at our table. Mom and Dad were across from me. Then the waitress came over and asked us what we wanted to drink."

"Older woman, husky voice?"

"Yeah, that's right. She didn't look too...healthy. She smelled smoky, like Agent Saxby."

"Okay, drink orders?" prompted Devine.

"I had some hot chocolate and Mom and Dad had coffee. It was a chilly day."

"Did you drink from their cups?"

"No. I don't like coffee."

"What next?" said Campbell.

"The waitress brought us menus and we took a few minutes to order."

"Your dad had a tuna sandwich with a side of berries, and your mom had waffles and scrambled eggs," noted Devine.

She looked at him curiously. "Yeah, how'd you know that?"

Devine wasn't about to reveal it was from the autopsy report on their stomach contents, so he just said, "The police told me. What did you have to eat?"

"A barbeque sandwich, coleslaw, and fries."

"Did you eat off each other's plates, share any food at all?" asked Campbell.

"No, we never did that."

"Okay, and then?" said Devine.

"My dad paid the bill when it came, and we left."

"Anyone use the bathroom?" asked Campbell.

"Mom did. Dad and me didn't."

"Anybody come up other than the waitress? Shake hands with your parents? Anything like that?"

"No. I don't think they knew anyone there."

Devine sighed and sat back.

They watched the rest of the video. No one had touched the Odoms' car. They got into the vehicle exactly as they had exited it. Then they drove off, Alice and Dwayne Odom to their deaths, and Betsy to becoming an orphan.

Odom looked at him. "Did that help any?"

He forced a smile and said, "We know more now than we did before, so, yes, it was a big help."

"When are we going to my home?"

"Tomorrow. You better get some sleep."

Devine watched her head off to bed and then turned to Campbell. "The poisoning had to happen when they met the men and got the duffel bag presumably with a payoff inside."

"But how are you going to prove that *or* find the men?"

"Glass said it wasn't him. And CIA said they paid nothing to the Odoms."

"And you believe them?"

"I'm not sure I believe anybody anymore."

After Campbell had gone back to his room, Devine sat there staring at the ceiling, but the usual mental images that normally trooped across the space in neat linear sequences didn't materialize this time.

He gave up on that and thought back to what Coburn had told him. He pulled up the notes he'd taken of their conversation. Cyanide poisoning combined with DMSO, which accounted for the garlic smell she had found. Inhalation was the quickest death, ingestion the next fastest, and absorption the slowest, but sped up by the DMSO kicker.

According to his shorthand notes, she had explained: *If cyanide was combined with DMSO and was absorbed through the skin, it could kill more rapidly than typical in an absorption case.*

Now he focused on the last sentence he'd written.

But even with DMSO, still not as fast as inhalation or ingesting it.

Devine assumed that was because of the way the poison was broken down in the body and dispersed. Going into the lungs directly, or into the gut, the damage would no doubt be faster than it sneaking into the body through the skin, where it would have a long way to go to have a fatal impact.

He scrolled back to the notes he'd taken from his conversation with Betsy Odom.

She'd said that a few *minutes* after leaving the two men, her parents started showing signs of poisoning. And then soon after that they were dead.

He went online and looked up cyanide poisoning. In cases of inhalation the person could, depending on the exposure level, concentration, and environment, experience symptoms within seconds and be dead minutes later. With ingestion, symptoms could start in about three minutes, unconsciousness could result in less than six minutes, and death would be in under twenty minutes. But the article Devine was reading also said that depended on how rapidly one's gastric juices broke down the cyanide and turned it into the lethal hydrocyanic acid, commencing a body-wide organ shutdown due to lack of oxygen.

He then looked up absorption of cyanide through the skin. Time to death via that mechanism could be well over two hours depending on various factors.

However, sodium cyanide combined with DMSO was labeled "LIQUID DEATH" by a couple of websites he visited. Yet even after cutting the time to death down by 80 percent when combined with the DMSO, Devine still couldn't account for how fast the Odoms had perished, which was pretty much right in the timeline with *inhalation* of the poison. But how could they have inhaled it when meeting with the two men without Betsy seeing something? Or the men being exposed, too, if they had used some type of aerosol? And Coburn said she had seen no signs of cyanide being ingested in either of the Odoms' bodies. So that left absorption, unless Coburn had been totally wrong about that particular poison being used.

Then Devine realized he had made a critical assumption that had not been corroborated.

I'm assuming that the Odoms were exposed to the poison during the meeting with the two men. But there's no proof of that. So what if it happened earlier?

He did a timeline run-through based on what Betsy had told him, the driving distance from the restaurant to the spot where they had met the two men that had been in the autopsy reports. And then Betsy's information that her parents had fallen ill minutes after driving off.

So roughly twenty-five minutes after leaving Ricketts

and meeting with the two men, they started to experience symptoms, with death quickly following. That would be a reasonable time to death via absorption of sodium cyanide, when combined with DMSO.

Devine sat back as the truth sank in. *They were poisoned at the restaurant. Their last meal.*

CHAPTER

66

AFTER A LATE NIGHT DOING some research on several law enforcement databases, and speaking with Campbell and other folks at DHS, Devine was getting dressed early the following morning when someone knocked on the hotel room door.

It was Saxby, focused and grim.

"Betsy's still asleep," he told her.

"I actually wanted to talk to you. After how it was left yesterday," she added.

"Superiors order you here to try to repair the situation with more bullshit?"

"Can we just have a conversation, Travis? Please?"

They sat down across from each other.

He said, "I have a long to-do list so can you get on with it?"

"We have to assume that 12/24/65 knows about you taking Betsy back to her home. So we need to have a plan to counteract that as best we can."

"You mind if I call them something else? Reciting that date is getting old."

"What do you want to call them?"

"Let's call a spade a spade. How about *traitors*?"

Saxby smiled. "Works for me."

"And how do they know I'm taking Betsy to her home?"

"My father was an arborist, down in Arkansas. When I was growing up, he told me that the hardest part of his business was surprising his customers with unexpected news. That a healthy-looking tree had root rot, or blight or some other disease that would kill it. But the worst of all he told me was one thing."

"What was that?"

"Termites. Everything could look absolutely fine. A mighty oak looked as strong as solid rock, happy and healthy. But when you looked underneath the surface, it was full of holes, hollowed out, about to give way, bringing the whole thing down when it looked so pristine on the surface. He called it being eaten from the inside out."

"And that's where we are?"

"We have termites all over the place, Devine, and they are eating away at the very foundations of this country. And no secret is apparently safe from them."

"Then instead of traitors, let's just call them *termites*."

Saxby smiled again, even more broadly than before.

"You should do that more often, Ellen, it wears well on you." He hunkered down. "So what's the plan?"

"A joint ops team has already met with Nate Shore and Korey Rose, at a location away from the trailer. They seem to be solid people with Betsy's best interests at heart."

"They are."

"We can't make it obvious that we're protecting the place, although 12—I mean the *Termites*—will suspect that we'll be all over it. But we will be there, Devine. Guaranteed."

"And on the trip out to Kittitas?"

"You will be tailed, discreetly, but agents will be there."

"They'll know all this is happening, if they have people on the inside."

"Yes, but this time they won't know everything, because we have kept some things so tight, even the Termites have no access."

"With so much protection, will the Termites even make an attempt on Betsy or Glass?"

"That's the crux of the matter, Devine. They have to. When I say Glass's testimony and documentation will devastate them, I am not embellishing. We have over a hundred arrest and search warrants ready to execute when Glass goes on the record and DOJ gives the go-ahead to round these assholes up. And that's just the tip of the iceberg. And the media will have a field day, because some of the names that are going to come down? Household ones. In high places, politicians, religious leaders, media, business, police, military all working in concert to topple the government."

"Well, you know what they say, the higher they are, the more it hurts when they hit dirt. But how the hell did Glass get such valuable evidence on all those sorts of people?"

"These folks need large sums of money to fund their operations. And it can't just come from their own pockets or illegally hijacked political or religious donations. That would cause too many problems and leave a trail. So they've turned to criminal activity to get what they need: money for recruiting, equipping, and paying boots on the ground. Glass was able to facilitate all that. And then he laundered the funds on the other end through all of his legal platforms. He's got rock-solid evidence on many of the movement's leaders because of that."

"Why would they trust one guy that much?"

"Danny Glass is a world-class salesman, the king of grift. He can talk a poor man out of his last dollar and convince a rich one he's their best friend. The fact that he quit the Army and gave them the finger at the same time also didn't hurt because the Termites hate America, at least what it looks like today, as well as all institutions associated with it, particularly the military, which they see as an obstacle to their aim of overthrowing the government. And Glass is a criminal. He had every incentive to play it straight with them just so he'd stay out of prison."

"If Glass is so good at his job, how did you guys nail him?"

Now Saxby, exuberant before, seemed to withdraw. "I can't get into that with you, Devine."

Before, this would have ticked Devine off, but that was before, not now. "Okay. But you laid out a potential problem and you haven't answered it."

"What's that?"

"Betsy Odom. She's leverage against Glass. If the Termites tell Glass they won't harm her so long as he *doesn't* cooperate, where does that leave all of you?"

Again, Saxby looked troubled. "I won't lie to you, Devine, and tell you that's not a concern. Glass has been less *forthcoming* recently. And at this point we are not at all sure of his cooperation, which is absolutely vital to our national interests. That's why we had to resort to the plan with using Betsy as bait. We otherwise would never have done that. But we're pretty much desperate now. We have got to pull the trigger on this."

"So if he doesn't cooperate, what, you reinstate the RICO case?"

"I haven't asked DOJ that question. But I imagine they would."

"But then the Termites go free to rain destruction on this country?" said Devine.

"We'll have to come up with another way to get to them."

"How long will you wait to see what Glass is going to do?" asked Devine.

"Our intel is telling us that the Termites are not far off from commencing the initial phases of their coup attempt. Once that's done, Glass becomes irrelevant."

"Thanks for the info, Ellen. I mean it."

"Good luck. Day or night, call if you need anything."

She left Devine there and he was about to finish packing when someone knocked on his door again.

Jesus, it's like Grand Central this morning.

It was Braddock and Walker.

"I thought we were going to be strip-searched before they'd let us up here," said Braddock.

"Welcome to my brave new world, Detective," replied Devine.

67

"NO SAFE-DEPOSIT BOX, AND WE tore his apartment apart and found zip," said Braddock. "If Rollins hid the dirt he had on Glass, he damn sure hid it well."

"I'm sure he did," replied Devine.

"I understand that you're now officially Betsy Odom's new guardian," said Braddock.

"I'm taking her to a safe place well outside of Seattle."

"You think that's wise?" asked Braddock. "Beth told me about what happened in court. Danny Glass must be pissed that he didn't get to be his niece's guardian. He may figure if he gets rid of you..."

"I wish it were that simple."

Braddock glanced quizzically at Walker and then back at Devine.

"You mentioned telling me everything the last time we met, remember? When we were standing in an alley over a dead guy who used to work for the Ricketts Police Force?"

"But I didn't say *when* I would tell you, did I?"

"Shit, Devine, I deserve better—"

"Yes, you do," said Devine, cutting him off. "So I'll tell you this, for now. The government is not the bad guy in this, like you initially thought. Glass is cooperating with the feds and putting his life on the line to take down some very highly placed people who think a democracy is not a good way to run a country and they want a change that puts them in charge. And they want it now."

Braddock slowly took this all in, glanced at Walker again, and said, "Exactly what *country* are we talking about?"

Devine answered by pointing toward the window.

"I take it you're not gesturing toward another country across the Pacific," said Braddock.

"No, I'm not."

"Jesus Christ."

"I don't think *he's* going to help us. We sink or swim on our own."

Braddock glanced at Walker and said sharply, "Did you know about this?"

"We're finding out at the same time," she said, her features grim.

Braddock turned back to Devine. "You said I could talk to Odom? That was part of the deal with me not confiscating your weapon for ballistics."

"Yes, you can. What do you want to ask her?"

"Whether she or her parents knew Rollins."

"I don't think they did."

"Then how did he get dirt on Glass?"

"I don't know."

"I'd like to hear it from her," persisted Braddock.

Devine got Odom. She was already up and dressed and was packing her duffel.

Devine introduced her to Braddock, who said, "Ms. Odom, it's nice to meet you. I'm so sorry for everything you've had to go through."

"Thanks," said Odom in a mechanical voice.

"You heard about the death of a man named Perry Rollins?"

She nodded.

"Do you recall that name?"

"No."

Braddock nodded at Walker, who pulled out a glossy.

"This is Rollins," she said, handing it to Odom. "Do you remember ever seeing him with your parents?"

Odom studied the photo for a long enough time that Devine was thinking she might say that she *had* seen the man.

"No, I don't know him. I've never seen him before." She handed the photo back.

"This man said he had something incriminating on your uncle. Do you have any idea what that might be?" asked Braddock.

"No. I just met my uncle. And my parents never

really talked about him much." She glanced at Devine. "I did know some things about him because my dad told me. He...he didn't like my uncle very much."

"Did your dad ever say *why* he didn't like his brother-in-law?"

Odom looked troubled.

Walker gently said, "Whatever you can remember, Betsy."

"Dad told me that Uncle Danny had done some bad things, some really bad things. When he was in the Army and then after he got out."

"Did he say what bad things?" asked Walker.

"He...he said he was a liar and that he hurt people for no good reason. And then got rich off stuff like that."

"Did your mother ever talk to you about her brother?" asked Braddock.

She nodded. "She said that her dad wasn't a nice person. That he would hit her and stuff. But Uncle Danny would stand up for her. That he mostly took the beatings so she didn't have to. Or would fight back to defend her."

"So she liked him, I would imagine," said Walker.

Odom nodded. "She did, yeah."

"So it must have been hard for you to make sense of all that," noted Braddock. "Your dad saying one thing and your mom another."

Odom shrugged. "I...my dad would sometimes say stuff. Like winning money in the lottery and buying our car and house with it."

"You said you didn't believe that because he had a tell," said Devine. "He giggled."

"That's right. But my mom never, ever lied to me," said Odom firmly. "So if she said Uncle Danny was a good person, well..." She fell silent.

"Okay, Betsy, anything else you want to tell us?" said Walker gently.

"No, that's it. Look, I...I have to finish packing."

She rushed from the room.

"One confused little girl, and who can blame her," observed Walker.

Braddock said to Devine, "You're taking her outside the city somewhere? But will you all be safe there?"

"I think there are other interested parties in this that will see to it."

Braddock kept his gaze rigidly on Devine. "If you would level with me, the SPD might be able to help."

Devine had to make a tough decision here, and he went with his gut. "Ever heard of 12/24/65?"

Braddock's eyes narrowed. "Christmas Eve 1965?"

Devine glanced at Walker, who looked just as perplexed as her boss.

"It's December 24, *1865*. It's the date the KKK was founded."

"The KKK?" said Braddock dully. "White hoods and burning crosses?"

"Their current incarnation is a domestic terrorist organization with roots all over and connections in the highest places in government, military, business. And apparently the police as well. They're the ones who want to turn us into an autocratic state where the men rule and everybody looks, prays, and acts the same."

"Then how come I've never heard of it?" exclaimed Braddock.

"They keep a very low profile. The feds just recently got on to them. Glass did business with them. In that way he got potential evidence against them."

Braddock sat back. "*That's* why they dropped the RICO case. But where does the girl come in?"

"She's potential leverage against Glass. I think the Termites—"

"Excuse me, what?" said Braddock.

"Sorry, my nickname for the KKK assholes. I think the Termites killed Odom's parents, as a warning to Glass. If he cooperates, Betsy is next."

"So why don't the feds have an army around her?" said Walker.

"Maybe they do," said Devine.

"Why don't they just kill Glass?" said Walker.

"I'm sure they've thought about that. But he's under

protection. And I imagine a smart guy like Glass has an insurance policy, much like Rollins probably did."

"Evidence put away somewhere that can be used against the Termites in case he goes down?" said Walker.

"Right."

"And speaking of Rollins," said Braddock. "Where does he fit in?"

"He had dirt on Glass, so he claimed. And somebody didn't want him selling it."

"Have any idea who that might be?" asked Walker.

"I'm getting there," said Devine.

"Any idea where Rollins hid whatever he had on Glass?" added Braddock.

"Same answer," replied Devine.

CHAPTER

68

T HE MEN WERE WAITING IN the parking garage when Devine came down to get the car.

Danny Glass and four new faces. They emerged from a black Maybach and surrounded Devine.

"I don't have a lot of time so if you can make it snappy," said Devine irritably.

Glass looked at his men. "Back in the car."

Without a word the four men, who looked like they would kill Devine without hesitation if Glass so instructed, quickly returned to the Maybach.

Now it was just Devine and Glass.

Devine looked around to see if he could observe the contingent of FBI agents he now knew were following Glass's every step. To their credit, he couldn't see any of them.

"If you're here about Hastings and your boys, they started the fight. I just finished it."

"I don't give a shit about that, Devine. In fact, you have my apologies. Should never have happened."

"Okay, so what do you want?"

Glass eyed Devine's car. "Let's sit inside. Parking garages have too many ears and sight lines."

They climbed into the vehicle.

Glass said, "You know the score now, I take it?"

"Your business associates sound like a nice bunch of people. Sort of like a local Rotary Club, but only with homicidal, government-toppling intent."

Glass shook his head. "I wore the uniform. I fought so these assholes could protest and say shit all they wanted."

"So did I. And now they want to take those rights away from the rest of us."

He eyed Devine severely. "When I got wind of what these people were really up to, I read up on what the original KKK wanted to do, and did. These guys are even worse. It's not just Black folks they're going after. It's everyone who doesn't look, think, or believe like they do. It's Hitler and Stalin all rolled into one. If they ever come to power, they'll machine-gun half their supporters, only the dumbasses won't believe it until their corpses hit the ground."

"How did they let you get so close to their operation?"

"At first, it was just small nickel-and-dime stuff that I did for them. At below my usual client rates. Then as we performed at a higher level for them, it got bigger, and bigger. I eventually became an integral part of what they were doing."

"And they came to trust you?"

"They knew about my military background and how it ended. And at first they had no clue how to put something like this together, while I had a lot of experience building an operation on the other side of the law at scale and keeping it going and thriving and having free cash flow that would make a Fortune 50 jealous. They came to me all the time with problems. Problems that I always solved. So they came to rely on me. And I said the words they wanted to hear: the country was not looking like it used to, leaders were too soft and tried to be too inclusive, that if we didn't take a stand, we'd all be speaking a bunch of foreign languages, that sort of crap. They came to see me as loyal, and important to what they were doing. And I operate on the other side of the law. They had leverage over me that way. It's not like I could waltz in and tell the cops everything without exposing myself. They knew that, and were counting on it. So I got to see stuff other people didn't."

"Did you have any idea as to what you were getting into?"

"At the beginning, it was just the usual: stolen stuff, convert to money, launder the proceeds. But then, as they grew to trust me and kept asking for more and more, things got weird."

"Weird how?"

"I saw things like when I was back in the Army, scattered at secret sites all over the country. Military-grade equipment and weaponry. Training areas, ordnance sites, fleets of private planes reconfigured to drop bombs and fire bullets. Old tanks on the scrap heap being refurbished and upgraded with depleted uranium plating. Artillery the same. A boatload of fifty cals. Hundreds of millions of rounds of ammo of all kinds, hundreds of thousands of RPG launchers. Enough weaponry and supplies to equip eleven Army divisions and maybe the manpower to fill them."

Devine's jaw went slack. "The U.S. Army only has *ten* divisions currently."

"There're even old Minuteman missile sites out in Kansas that were purchased by extremely wealthy private individuals. If the feds knew what was in those right now? The Pentagon would have a collective stroke."

"Come on, how could they accumulate mountains of stuff like that and no one find out?"

"I asked myself the same thing. Here's my answer. About eighty percent of the U.S. population lives east of the Mississippi, Devine. Another twelve percent lives on the West Coast, with the majority of them in California. That leaves eight percent of the population for nearly half the land mass of this country, which means it's basically empty. Do you know how many places there are to hide shit out there? I've been to a lot of these places doing business with these folks. I mean, there's nobody there. Fucking nobody. You could drive for days and never see another human being. And they guard against being spied on from eyes in the sky. They have former military and intel people on board. They know how the sat networks are arrayed and how to circumvent that sort of surveillance. Really sophisticated operation."

"Okay, what else?"

Glass gazed at him pointedly. "The *software*. The shit that makes the hardware run."

"Such as?"

"Aside from all the brainwashed grunts on the ground carrying weapons, I'm talking congressmen, senators, governors, mayors, police captains, generals, admirals, a fleet of lawyers and accountants, Wall Street moguls, church leaders. I was at one secret meeting at a private ranch in the middle of nowhere where I saw folks you see on TV, all talking about things that would get them hanged during wartime. And then I started running into people like me, looking to score big. Mexican cartels, African crime bosses, Chinese Triad types. And some Russian mobsters, too."

"Chinese, Africans, and Mexicans? I thought the 12/24/65 people were white supremacists like the original KKK?"

"Oh, there was no love lost with the foreign folk and these assholes. But with them it was just about money. And toppling the U.S. government and becoming isolationists? Making sure we never fight another foreign war? You think the Russians and Chinese wouldn't love that? The rest of the world would be their oyster."

"Okay, and I get your point about there being huge swaths of the country that are empty, but how in the hell did they keep all this so secret for so long, with so many influential players involved? The feds only stumbled onto it recently. And probably only with your help."

"There's so much crap flying around, disinformation, people screaming fake news, AI-generated horseshit, how does anybody tell what the truth or reality is anymore, Devine? Somebody finds some dirt and they're instantly hit with a billion bots that shows they're full of lies, at least in the minds of the public, who don't have the time to deep-dive this stuff. I'm not speculating. I've seen them do just that." He looked at Devine. "So, I'm asking you, how do you prove the truth? What is it even? Is it based on how many retweets or likes or clicks you get? One million and that's reality? A billion and it's Jesus preaching the gospel?"

"But some hotshot reporter never stumbled on this trying to make a career?"

"I actually heard stories of a few who started nosing around."

"What happened to them?"

"My best guess, taken, cut up, and dumped. In places where the police were in on it. How deep do you think their investigation went? I would bet that their remains went a lot deeper."

Devine thought of Ricketts and nodded. "So why did you turn, Danny? I assume you were making money hand over fist with them."

"The RICO shit."

"Not buying it. I know what happened to the witnesses against you."

"I didn't take them out," snapped Glass.

"I know you didn't. I think 12/24 did. But the point is, you could have. Or threatened to annihilate their families. They never would have testified against you. So the RICO never happens. I think you dangled your low-level thugs as an olive branch to the government, because you wanted out and you wanted to take these traitors down. And when the feds came knocking, you negotiated a deal."

Glass looked away.

"Maybe the patriotic soldier in Danny Glass showed up?" said Devine. "And he didn't want to stand by and see his country go down the toilet?"

"Think what you want, Devine."

"But then your sister and her husband were killed by these people. And then there's Betsy."

Glass looked at him. "And then there's Betsy," he repeated. "You know and I know that they killed Alice and Dwayne as a warning to me. They let Betsy live because that's their best chance to blow up any deal I could make with the feds."

"The RICO case was a pretty big chip," Devine pointed out. "They can reinstate the charges if you don't cooperate."

"And they also know that with the witnesses they lost, they have no assurances they'll get a conviction. So that leverage is not so good. But these asshole traitors? They believe that if I think they will kill Betsy, I won't cooperate."

"And what do you believe, Danny? So long as Betsy is alive, you *won't* cooperate?"

"If I told you I'd made up my mind about that, Devine, I'd be lying."

"You must have insurance in case they get to you." He looked out the car window. "Despite the army of FBI agents out there."

"I'm not stupid, Devine. I *do* have insurance and these assholes know I do. They kill me, they go down. It's just Betsy. I..." He shrugged helplessly.

"The feds aren't going to wait forever. At some point it's do or die, Danny."

"Tell me something I don't know," snapped Glass.

"What would it take to make you cooperate?" asked Devine.

"Can you guarantee that nothing will happen to Betsy?"

"Tomorrow is guaranteed to no one, Danny."

"So we're just going in circles."

"But what if we took the fight to them?"

"How do you plan on doing that?" asked Glass.

"If I can think of a way?"

"Let me know, Devine. And then I'll let *you* know. But right now my indecision is the only thing keeping Betsy alive."

"Not the only thing. There's me."

"And you're taking her back to her home, I understand."

"Too many threats in a big city that you won't see coming. I can defend her better out there." Devine was sure that Glass knew nothing about the feds using Betsy as bait. *And I should tell him, but I won't or he might blow the whole plan up.*

Glass turned so he was staring directly at Devine.

"So why did you really come here today?" said Devine.

"I wanted to look you in the eye and ask you something, man to man."

"What?" said Devine curtly.

"If it comes to it, will you lay down your life for Betsy's?"

Devine didn't have to give it much thought. "Yes, I will."

Glass reached out a hand and Devine shook it.

CHAPTER

69

PRU JACKSON SAT IN HER SUV and did what she did best: observe.

Her target today was the picturesque town of Ricketts.

The disguised Jackson was considerably overweight, her hair short and graying. Her baggy shirt fell over stretch pants that were expanded to their absolute limit. Her shoes looked like giant waffles. She wheezed and had an oxygen line running to her nose with a small tank of it in a harness that she could wear over her shoulder. Her tinted glasses covered the one thing that could give her away: penetrating eyes.

However, she was now a nonentity. People might stare for a moment, perhaps from sympathy or even pity, but then they would look away and forget what they had seen.

Presently, she had her eyes on the government building. People had been coming and going for the last hour. Cops, admin, probably some elected officials. She had seen Eric King arriving in a specially equipped van. Jackson had continued to watch as he expertly extracted himself from the vehicle deploying a side ramp and then levering himself down using hand straps attached to the inside of the van.

His wheelchair wasn't motorized; he had to power it the old-fashioned way. And he did so with vigor, she noted.

With her long-range monocular, Jackson had also taken in the military-grade equipment housed in the fenced-in area next to the building.

Impressive. I wonder when the war is starting.

Twenty minutes later, a Porsche Cayenne painted metallic silver pulled into the slot next to King's van. Since this spot was reserved for the mayor, Jackson pointed her monocular right at the Porsche.

Mercedes King climbed out of the SUV, dragging a large purse and briefcase along with her. Jackson zoomed in on the woman. She was dressed in a tight dark dress with a short, heavy jacket over that. She had sneakers on. Jackson assumed the pumps would come out once she was in her office. She was on her phone jabbering away.

She obviously couldn't hear the woman's hoarse voice from here, but it was Anne Cassidy—she was sure of it. The unique, swaggering walk was a clear tell along with what Devine had told her.

Jackson could feel the anger and desire for revenge pulse inside her with every step the woman took. But then she dialed it back, because it was not healthy to get all worked up with nowhere to vent that rage.

Enjoy today, Anne.

She took a photo of the SUV's license plate and then hacked into the DMV. That got her the home address of both the police chief and his wife. She drove there. It was twenty minutes outside of town and secluded among a sea of dormant trees.

Jackson stripped off her disguise in less than two minutes, and, now dressed all in black, including a head covering, she wended her way through the trees to the large wood frame and stone home sprawled across a lawn that was extensively terraced and landscaped.

Jackson figured the place at about ten thousand square feet.

Clearly within the salary range of a cop and a mayor of a small town that probably had fewer residents than a Chick-fil-A parking lot at lunchtime in any metro area.

She ran her monocular over the area looking for security with heartbeats, and/or surveillance cameras. She saw none of the former and plenty of the latter, indicating that the Kings clearly relied on electronic eyes over the human kind. Smart, since humans missed a lot, even trained ones, while the mechanized version did not. *And* human eyes could blackmail you.

She looped around the house, calculating sight lines of the cameras until she found an exposed corridor on the northwest corner near the rear of the building. Jackson threaded across that narrow strip of ground and pulled a device out of her backpack.

Noting the gas line that entered the house here, she cut the dormant grass carefully back, dug out the dirt under it, set her device there, covered it up with the dirt, and placed the grass carefully back on top. There was no telltale sign that the area had been disturbed at all.

Devine had wanted her to come and snoop, which she was doing. But there was no reason she couldn't add a little personal touch to the deal, was there?

She returned to her vehicle, changed back into her large lady clothes complete with oxygen, and drove back into town.

Around lunchtime the Cayenne roared down the street all balls and brass, and parked in front of a restaurant. Mercedes King slipped out, high heels on now, and went inside.

Jackson, who had followed the Porsche, parked on the other side of the street, struggled out of her car, and, using a walker, she slowly moved into the restaurant.

A young woman escorted her back to a table, a table that Jackson needed to ask to be changed because it was not in a sight line with Mayor King. She looked around and saw a possible solution without causing suspicion.

"I'm sorry, dear," she said in her old woman drawl. "But I need to be near a bathroom at all times. My plumbing ain't what it used to be, sweetie."

The young woman's eyes swelled in alarm. "Oh, okay. Um... the restrooms are right over there, so you just pick where you want to sit, ma'am."

Jackson chose a booth near the bathroom, but which also held a commanding view of King, and the tall, suited man who was just now sitting down to join her.

Jackson put on a pair of AirPods and positioned a device she drew from her pocket onto the front of her clothing. It was the same gaudy broach she had worn when electronically eavesdropping on Devine at the restaurant he'd been at with Odom and Saxby. Embedded in it was a sophisticated listening device.

Jackson ordered a pot of hot tea and saw that King and the man—who over her AirPods she had heard King call Nick—had ordered glasses of red wine.

The man did much of the talking and it was an interesting conversation. However, when Jackson had first heard the woman's hoarse voice, a product of damaged vocal cords that had never truly healed, her fingers had involuntarily turned to fists.

And some of the man's words were particularly galling to Jackson.

King had said to him, "Based on what you told me, when you come to power, you're going to do things that will anger your supporters. They may have buyer's remorse. But the thing is, you don't want widespread turmoil on your hands. I speak from experience. I dealt with many of those situations in other countries that were transitioning to new regimes."

He had replied, with a slick smile and in a confident tone, "Remember, sweetie, right now I *do* need supporters. But as anyone who has read any history can tell you, when you're actually in charge, with all the guns behind you, all you need are *followers*. And they will have no choice in the matter except to follow, if they want to stay out of prison or continue breathing. And that includes my *supporters*."

Sure it does, you son of a bitch, thought Jackson.

Then the two started discussing something that might provide an opening both to Devine and Jackson. The focus of the conversation was a certain someone at the government center, and what they were doing there.

Once, King looked over at her. Jackson was staring down at her food and pretending to have trouble with her fork. From the corner of her eye, she could see King's gaze boring into her. She waited for any sign of recognition on the other woman's features, but then King looked away and continued her conversation.

An hour later Nick paid the bill and left King sitting there. King ordered another glass of wine. After it was brought, the woman thumbed through her phone, perhaps sending texts, emails, or death threats, mused Jackson.

After finishing her wine, King rose to leave.

A few moments later, Jackson sensed a presence next to her table.

King said, "Are you visiting our fair city?"

Jackson peered up at her, trying to discern if the woman had recognized her and was just playing coy.

In her old lady voice, with pauses to snort on the O_2 line, Jackson said, "Just passing through. I'm on my way to visit my daughter in Idaho. Little place right across the state line. Need to see my new grandbaby."

"Well, I'm the mayor here, so if there's anything I can do to make your stay better, you just let me know."

She slipped a card from her pocket and passed it across to Jackson.

"Honey, I sure appreciate that," replied Jackson, putting the card away. "And what a cute town you got here."

"Thank you."

She watched King flounce out of the place.

Yes, flounce *is the right word*, thought Jackson.

God help you, Anne, when I'm done with you. But then again not even God will be able to put you back together again.

CHAPTER

70

"Looks like it might storm," said Devine as he drove along. They were about twenty minutes away from the Odoms' home in Kittitas.

Odom had her headphones on and didn't respond. He had seen earlier that she was watching a movie on her phone.

He had alerted Shore and Rose and given them an ETA. Rose promised that a delicious meal would be awaiting them.

Devine had continually checked the traffic behind him and seen nothing unusual. But that told him that there was probably an army of agents tailing them. He was also sure that Danny Glass would have some of his minions around Kittitas, since the man clearly did not trust the feds to do a proper job.

He glanced at Odom and thought about the promise he'd made to her uncle. That he would sacrifice his life to save hers. Devine had done that very thing in combat, taken an oath and exhibited a willingness to sacrifice his life for his country so that his fellow citizens could live free and in peace.

He had shaken Glass's hand on it, perhaps an old-fashioned touch, but it had meant something to Glass obviously. And it had meant something to Devine as well.

However, this really had nothing to do with Glass. This had to do with a twelve-year-old girl named Betsy Odom to whom life had dealt an unfair hand and who really had no one else to protect her now, other than Devine.

So if it came to it, he would lay down his life for hers, even though he'd known her only a few days.

Even though it feels like years.

Later, they came to a stop in front of the trailer. The door opened and there stood a smiling Nate Shore. He helped with the bags after hugging Odom and shaking Devine's hand.

Devine whispered to him, "We need to talk about . . . stuff."

"Damn right we do," said Shore, the smile gone.

"Hey, Bets," exclaimed Rose, who came out of the kitchen wearing a full-length white chef's apron.

"Hey, Kor," said a grinning Odom as they exchanged a hug.

"Hope you're hungry 'cause I made your fav," said Rose.

"Cheeseburgers and fries?" she cried out.

"Okay, *second* fav."

"Pepperoni pizza with extra mozzarella?"

He high-fived her.

Standing in the doorway watching the pair, Shore said in a low voice to Devine, "Some serious federal dudes come to see me and Kor. They told us 'bout stuff with Betsy and her uncle and all, but I want to hear it from you."

"You want to hear it before or after the pepperoni pizza with extra mozzarella?" asked Devine.

"How bad is it, really, dude?"

"How active is your imagination?"

Shore grimaced. "Let's chow down first then. Might be our last time."

The storm hit right as they were finishing the last slices of pizza, with raindrops pinging off the roof.

"Damn, Korey, that is the best pizza I ever had," proclaimed Devine.

"He makes his own crust," said Shore. "Got up early this mornin' to do it and the sauce, too. For all I know, dude raised hogs and cows, slaughtered 'em, and made his own pepperoni all in eight hours."

"It's all in the balance between the pork and beef," said Rose knowledgably. "And the trick to a great sauce is never to open a bottle or can. Just fresh ingredients and a hand-crank grinder."

"And elbow grease, and time," added Shore.

After the meal and some more catching up between Odom, and Shore and Rose, Odom went to her room to unpack.

Devine used this opportunity to fill in Shore and Rose. He didn't give them all the background on 12/24/65, but said that the "Termites" were dangerous as hell and probably coming for Betsy Odom. He explained that there was protection around them. But he didn't tell them that the FBI was counting on an attempt on Odom's life to push Glass over the goal line on his cooperation. That would just further complicate an already convoluted situation.

Devine took out his backup Glock and two extra mags and handed them to Shore. The man expertly checked the ammo, racked the slide, pocketed the spare mags, and put the gun in his rear waistband.

"They go through us to get to her," he said firmly.

Devine glanced at Rose. "You cool with that, Kor?"

Rose reached over to the kitchen counter and lifted up a long narrow box with a clasp. He opened it and took out a knife nearly a foot in length with a serrated blade four inches wide.

"I don't really shoot all that good. But I can julienne with the best of 'em."

"Ain't no lie," said Shore. "Dude's hands move so fast, you can't even see 'em."

Later, Devine glanced at the window in the living room, where the light was starting to dim, along with maybe all hope. Despite the reinforcements out there, all Devine could reliably count on was himself and two men he'd just recently met.

Let's hope we're enough.

71

THAT NIGHT DEVINE CHECKED HIS weapons: the Glock, with extra mags, a K-bar knife from his Ranger days, the metal baton he'd kept from Hastings and company's attempted beatdown of him, and a backup pistol Campbell had given him, a compact Glock 42 that weighed less than a pound with a full mag.

Guns obviously had been an important and integral part of Devine's long military career. They made things less and more complicated. Perhaps more of the latter than the former, at least in the long run. But no problem was ever solved in the long run with a pull of a trigger. It merely tended to create new dilemmas; yet it wasn't bad for short-term challenges.

He sat on the bed that the Odoms had shared. The room was uncluttered and scrupulously clean and contained little touches of femininity and playfulness, no doubt courtesy of Alice Odom. As Devine looked around the spare quarters, he thought back to the photo of the Odoms he had seen. A family, all together in love with no idea what the future held.

He stood and checked the front area of the trailer through the gap in the blinds. The darkness held nothing but silhouettes of trees. He couldn't even see any telltale clouds of chilled breath from the clusters of armed personnel he assumed were out there in the cold. He then ventured around the small room, opening drawers and examining things. He stopped when he saw the old-fashioned photo album stored in one drawer. He was surprised that people from the Odoms' generation would even have one.

When Devine pulled it out and opened the album, he understood that he was both right and wrong.

The pictures were of a younger Alice Odom, and her mother and father and her brother, Danny Glass.

Glass Sr. was a short, burly, red-faced man with features full of bitterness. His wife was petite with a countenance of extreme unhappiness wedged under her fake smile.

Danny and Alice were next to each other and looking into the camera with what seemed to be genuine happiness. The teenage Danny was holding little Alice's hand.

Devine wasn't sure when the photo was taken, but "little" Alice was nearly as tall as her mother. Danny Glass had a full head of dark hair that mirrored his father and mother. Alice's auburn hair was a trait that her daughter had inherited.

Now they were all dead, except for Danny Glass. That was probably why he was clinging so hard to Betsy, the only link he had to his beloved sister.

Continuing his impromptu search, Devine next found in a cabinet a manila file marked HEALTH. He found in the pages, to his surprise, not the usual routine medical checkup reports he had expected, but rather material on IVF treatments from well over a decade ago. Apparently the Odoms had had difficulty getting pregnant. There were also some wellness checkup forms from when Alice had been pregnant with Betsy, and vaccination records that showed Betsy had been inoculated against the usual childhood diseases.

The last piece of paper puzzled Devine. It was the only one in the file having to do with Dwayne Odom. Devine read over the test results.

How could that possibly be?

The next moment his phone buzzed, and he looked at the message he'd just gotten from Emerson Campbell. It was in response to a photo that Devine had sent him previously. The info filled in a lot of holes for Devine and also gave him an idea. He set down the medical file and focused on the details Campbell had just provided.

A minute later his phone buzzed once more and he read the text.

It gave a place and a time and was signed *PJ.*

He went to check on Odom. She was asleep.

He looked in on Shore and Rose and asked them to keep watch while he was gone. Shore pulled the Glock and Rose his knife.

"We got her," said Shore. He was looking Delta Force serious.

Devine nodded, stepped outside the front door, and climbed into his car.

As he headed down the road he felt the presence of people there, watching.

Let's hope they're all on our side.

Since they had clearly seen just him and not Odom get in the Subaru, no one had followed him, which was a relief.

When Devine arrived at his destination, he saw a wink of light coming from about a hundred yards away.

His hand slipped to his waistband and the big Glock came out.

Devine maneuvered his way from tree to tree until he was within ten feet of the light.

"I was wondering when you were going to show up," he said.

Jackson stepped out into the open. She was dressed all in black, and until she removed her face covering, she was nearly invisible.

"I saw Anne Cassidy today. She even spoke to me.

If I hadn't been working so hard to keep from gutting her, I would have been laughing my ass off."

"But she didn't know it was you?" said Devine.

"I almost wished she did recognize me. Then I *could* have just ended her right then and there."

"We all have regrets."

"The hardware I saw in that town was impressive. You'd think someone was going to start something big," she added with a knowing expression.

"Yeah, you would," agreed Devine. "Is that all you came to tell me?"

"The Kings have a large home outside of town. I visited it."

"And?"

"And I visited it," she said curtly. "I saw the two guys with you. Capable?"

"One is former Army. The other is a great chef."

Jackson hiked her eyebrows. "Well, let's hope he gets an opportunity to flambé somebody, but it's not exactly the way I would have played it."

"You play the hand you have," replied Devine. "And you fight with the army you have."

She said, "Speaking of chefs, there seem to be too many cooks in the kitchen on this one. It was a fundamental problem in my life as a fed."

"I can't disagree with you there, based on my recent experience."

"My advice to you is throw out the official manual and go with your gut when the shit hits. And it will."

"Thanks for the input."

"Okay, to business. Anne was meeting with a guy named Nick. I happened to overhear the conversation."

"You get a good look at him?"

"Better than that, I took his picture." She texted it to him.

Devine looked down at the handsome man with a cruel expression. "Any idea who he is?"

"Nicholas Dawkins."

"How do you know that?"

"He paid the check. After the bitch left, I went over and had a gander at the bill. You should have your people do a deep dive on him. The man's interests are... interesting."

Devine glanced up. "What were they talking about?"

"Well, first of all, they're planning on taking power in this country. And then doing stuff that will piss off even their own supporters. But as Nick said, once he's in power, they will have no choice but to toe the line, if they want to remain free and breathing."

"Spoken like every other wannabe dictator in history."

"They've also apparently caught a rat in their midst. They're holding him prisoner in the government center."

This news stunned Devine. "What! Who is it?"

"No names were mentioned."

"Who did the person rat out?"

"It seems that intel has been leaking to a third party and they tracked it down to this person. They're probably beating details out of him before they kill him."

"Okay," said Devine, processing this. "Any idea who the third party is?"

"Take a wild guess."

"Danny Glass."

"Smart boy gets a gold star. I hacked the construction records of the government building. Seems there's a holding cell on the basement level. I can text you details if your people might be interested."

"We are," said Devine.

"Any idea yet who snuffed Odom's parents?"

"Tomorrow I plan on testing a theory in Ricketts. And I can check out your info, too."

An expression of surprise lined her face. "Into the lion's den? I thought you were persona non grata there."

"Sometimes the best retreat is an offensive."

"Did they really teach that at West Point?"

"The classroom can't really show you what it's like when the guns are firing for real. Like you just advised me, throw out the manual and go with your gut."

"Every time we meet, I see how we're more and

more alike. Want some backup when you venture into the lion's den?"

He eyed her steadily. "In for a dime?"

"Something like that," replied Jackson.

"Then yeah, I do."

CHAPTER
72

AFTER HE RETURNED TO THE trailer, Devine slept well. When he went into the kitchen the next morning, it was clear that Shore and Rose had not.

"You *both* look like shit," he said, grinning at the irony from the pair's having previously told him the same thing.

They glanced up at him bleary-eyed from the small kitchen table, coffee mugs in hand.

"You try stayin' up all night," grumbled Shore.

"Yeah, never done that," replied Devine as he poured a cup of coffee. "I peeked in on Betsy. Sleeping well." He sat down across from them. "I'm going to Ricketts today."

"Have you lost your damn mind?" said Shore. "Thought you said that was a bad place?"

"There's something there I have to find out about. Which means you two will have primary guard duty on Betsy. You up to it?" He looked at them both.

Shore nodded. "They go through us to get to her."

"But you got other folks around, right?" said Rose nervously.

"Yes," said Devine. "But you're the last line of defense."

"If they was gonna kill her, why not do it when they killed Dwayne and Alice?" asked Shore.

"Leverage over her uncle," said Devine. "They kill Betsy, they lose any chance that they can stop him from helping the feds."

"*Helpin'* the feds?" said a stunned Shore. "I thought they was suin' his ass."

"It's a long story, but to be brief, Glass has the dirt on some really bad folks who want to turn this country upside down. He can help bring them to justice. In return, they let him walk on the other stuff."

"But when does that leverage go away? When the dude testifies?" asked Shore.

"Or when they kill him, too?" added Rose.

"For now, just watch her like it's your last minute on earth."

Devine was waiting outside her door when Odom woke up and came out of her room.

"You hungry? Korey made pancakes."

Still in her sleepwear, shorts and a long-sleeved T-shirt and long pink socks, she rubbed her eyes, squinting at the morning sunlight streaming into the trailer.

"Yeah, I could use some food." She eyed him. "Why do you have your coat on?"

"I have a few errands to run."

"Where?"

"Need to know." He finished that statement with a smile.

"Can I go with you?"

"You need to stay here, with Korey and Nate, for now."

"They want to hurt me, right? Like my mom and dad."

"It's a little more complicated than that, Betsy."

"The government needs my uncle to help them and he wants to. Only he's afraid if he does, the people who killed my parents will hurt me, right?"

"Yes," admitted Devine.

"And if he decides to help you?"

"Then I imagine you both will be put into witness protection. New identities, new lives."

"So I won't be me anymore?"

"You will always be you, Betsy, just under another name."

"When does he have to decide?"

"Soon," said Devine.

"Well, I better go have those pancakes then. While I still can."

She trudged off, looking, to Devine, like the loneliest person in the world.

And it absolutely broke his heart, when Devine didn't think anything ever could again.

Later, as he cleared the forest and hit the main road, he called Emerson Campbell. He had previously told his boss about King's meeting with Nicholas Dawkins.

"On the way," he said.

"Good luck."

"All plans go as the conditions on the ground go, sir."

"What kept me alive in Vietnam and you in the Middle East. DOJ and the Bureau think they have this sucker all figured out. Let's show them how the Army does things."

"Roger that."

"You need any backup?" Campbell asked.

"I've got all I need."

Devine clicked off and kept driving straight toward the Termites' mother ship.

73

DEVINE'S FIRST STOP WAS THE restaurant where the Odoms had eaten. He looked through the window until he saw the waitress who had served the family that day. She was carrying a lunch tray to a table. He ducked back so she wouldn't see him.

Devine next drove to the government building and asked to meet with Eric King.

The man was in his office, but not behind his desk. He was seated at a table near one of the broad windows going over what looked to be reports. A foldaway desktop had been grafted onto the arms of his wheelchair.

"What brings you back to town?" asked King, not even looking up from his paperwork.

"I wanted to ask you about the man found dead in Seattle who tried to kill me."

King grimaced. "How we came to employ a person who would do something like that is beyond me." He shook his head.

"I understand he was fired from his post here that same day. Can I ask why?"

He laid his papers aside and looked up at Devine. "Insubordination. He refused a direct command from a superior officer. And then we did an audit and found items missing from the evidence room. Two of them were found on his person. I fired him myself. And good riddance. I don't mean I'm glad the man is dead, but only that I'm thrilled he no longer works here as a sworn police officer."

"I was wondering if you had any idea why he would take a shot at me?"

"I can't begin to imagine what was going on in that man's head. You think you know someone? Well, it's shaken my faith in human nature, I can tell you that."

"So how is law and order going in Ricketts?"

"We have the same challenges as other small towns. But we're holding our own."

"At least you're better equipped than other towns your size."

King leaned back in his wheelchair and said, "If I've learned anything in my career, it's that the squeaky wheel gets the most attention. I know that some of my brethren around the state don't like that I get more budget dollars than they do, or resent the fact that I have a good working relationship with federal agencies, including your folks at DHS. But resources are in limited supply. And if I can, through my efforts, get more of them for the benefit of the law-abiding citizens of my town? Well, I have done so and will continue to do so."

"You should take that stump speech and run for office," commented Devine.

"That thought has crossed my mind."

Or maybe just cut to the chase and help overthrow the government instead, like you're doing.

"But maybe you don't want to compete with your wife?"

King gave him a contemptuous look. "Is there anything else?"

"I was wondering if I can get the remains of the Odoms? My last trip here I was told they had been cremated. I want to bring their ashes to their daughter."

"That's fine." King looked down at the papers on the table and then said offhandedly, "Damn shame about Dr. Coburn. Gas line, I heard. Folks up in Seattle need to be more careful."

"Yes, it was a terrible loss."

"Do you know where to find Doris Chandler?"

"Yes, I do."

"Then goodbye, Devine."

"Have a good day, Chief."

While you still can.

CHAPTER

74

J UST SIGN HERE AND HERE," said Chandler.

Devine was sitting across from her in the woman's small office. Devine had passed a door marked MORGUE on the way. He had tried the door; it was locked.

Devine signed where she had indicated and handed the papers back.

Chandler provided him with a receipt and then pulled out two gray boxes. Devine saw that they were both identified with Post-it notes—one was labeled DWAYNE ODOM, and the other was marked ALICE ODOM.

"So I guess you heard about what happened to Dr. Coburn?" Devine asked.

"Oh, yes," said Chandler as she filed the paperwork Devine had signed. "What a tragedy. I heard it was a gas leak? At least she didn't suffer."

"Yeah, I'm sure she didn't. So, is the tox report back yet? On the Odoms?"

"Oh, heavens no," she said, chuckling. "The TV shows have those reports coming back right after the commercial break, but in reality they can take weeks, or months, depending on the backlog."

"I see."

"But it was a drug overdose. Dr. Coburn is, *was*, very good. And that's what her preliminary report clearly said."

"I guess I'm just dotting *i*'s and crossing *t*'s."

"Is there anything else?"

"Is the mayor around?"

"I thought I saw her come in a few minutes ago. Her office is at the end of the main hall."

"Thanks."

"We take our obligations to be good neighbors with our *federal* friends very seriously."

And your "federal friends" take all of you very seriously as well, thought Devine as he walked out and over to the mayor's office. He knocked on the door and was told to enter.

"Mr. Devine, what a pleasure to see you again," said Mercedes King brightly as she rose from behind her desk, came around to greet him, and extended a hand.

Her dress was navy blue and her heels the same color. Her blond hair was swept back into a ponytail, and her smile was beaming. He could only imagine the woman had been ordered to play nice with him. Apparently, the Termites were getting nervous with Devine running around their little hamlet.

Good, because nervous people make mistakes.

He held both boxes of ashes in one hand and shook her hand with the other, then took a seat opposite her by a coffee table near the window and placed the boxes on the table.

"So what brings you back here?" she asked.

He tapped one of the boxes. "I was just retrieving the Odoms' remains for their daughter."

She made a mock pouty face. "Oh, how sad. And how is...what was her name again?"

"Betsy Odom."

"I've never had children, but I imagine this has been very hard on her."

"It has," he said. "I was sorry to hear about Dr. Coburn," he added.

She glanced at him for maybe a beat too long. "Yes, it was awful. Gas main explosion or something like that, I heard. How tragic."

Well, they all seem to have their stories straight on that, thought Devine.

"And the former lawman employed here that tried to kill me?"

"Eric was so upset. Goes to show that one can never be too careful in vetting people." She stared at him, as though daring him to suggest culpability on her or her husband's part.

"Otherwise, you get some real bad apples," replied Devine. "I'm sorry for how our last meeting ended."

She waved this off. "Long day that left me in a bad temper. Oh, I did read about this Danny Glass person in the papers."

"Really? And?"

"It seems the government has dropped its case against him. I wonder why."

"Well, some of the witnesses against him died. And the burden of proof is pretty high." Thinking quickly, Devine added, "But from what I understand, they can reinstate the charges any time against him. And may well do so."

"I wonder what will be the basis for their decision-making?"

Devine let this very odd question hang out there for a moment.

"Well, it might come down to them getting some more witnesses against him. If that strengthens their case, they can go after him again. I know for a fact that they want to take him down really badly."

"Is that so?" said King, who did not seem convinced of this.

"He *is* an alleged global criminal," retorted Devine. "I would imagine your husband would like to see him behind bars, too, as any good lawman would."

King's face changed color and she said, "Yes, of course. You're right." She gave a mock shiver. "Too many homicidal maniacs out there as it is."

Yes there are, thought Devine. *And I'm probably in the presence of several of them in this building, including you.*

He left the mayor there and drove out of town far enough that no one from Ricketts had eyes on him any longer. He arrived at a spot where an e-motorcycle was waiting for him, courtesy of Pru Jackson. He hunkered down until dark and then returned to town.

Now Devine needed to be spot-on perfect. Otherwise, everything was going to blow up in his face.

75

DEVINE WAS HIDING IN AN alley adjacent to the Cowboy Tavern's rear parking lot. He watched as the waitress who had served the Odoms lunch, and whom Devine had spoken with earlier, came out of the restaurant around quarter to six. She had previously told Devine her work hours, which was why he had expected her to leave the place around this time.

She got into a dented and ancient Honda hatchback, took a moment to light a cigarette, and then put the car in gear and drove off.

Devine headed after her on the e-motorcycle with his headlights turned off as he followed the taillights in front of him.

Three miles later she pulled down a tree-lined dirt road and stopped in front of a ramshackle cottage a very few nails from falling down.

She got out, fumbled with her bag, pulled out the keys, lit another cigarette, and unlocked the door. She went inside and dumped her bag on top of a mountain of clutter by the front door. In the kitchen she grabbed a beer from the fridge, took off her shoes, rubbed her feet, and sat in a recliner by a woodstove that gave off a red glow from behind the safety glass, the occasional ember from the pellets inside firing off like a shooting star.

She took a swallow of the alcohol, leaned back, and closed her eyes, a deep, contented sigh leaving her lips.

"Long day?"

Her eyes shot open and she sat up so fast and agitated that she clenched the can of beer too hard and some of the liquid shot out like a geyser.

Devine was sitting across from her.

"Who in the hell are you?" she said fearfully.

He flashed his badge. "Travis Devine, Homeland Security. We spoke before, remember? And you're Madeline Trumbull."

"No, I'm Wendy Roman."

"No, you're not. You have quite the criminal record."

"I told you I did some drugs."

"I'm not talking about drugs."

She sputtered, "Look, you scared the shit out of me. And...and you can't just barge in here like this. I got rights."

"I was just in the neighborhood and thought we could follow up our chat. And if you don't want surprise visitors, you should lock your back door."

"Follow up our chat?"

"The Odoms' death?"

"I told you all I know 'bout that, mister."

"You didn't tell me one thing."

"What?"

"*How* you killed them."

She stared across at him, unblinking. For a moment Devine thought she was going to hurl the beer can at him.

"I don't know what the hell you're talkin' 'bout."

"With the super-absorbent additive DMSO, it would be sucked right into their bloodstreams. Then the clock started ticking. Then they drove out of town, and died."

She shook her head. "You better just get yourself outta here, mister, before I call the cops on your ass." She pulled out her phone.

Devine took out his phone and pulled up a screen. "I took your picture the first time we met. I sent it to DC. They ran AI facial recognition on it and got a hit. You're Dr. Madeline Trumbull. Board certified in endocrinology, with a PhD in chemistry from Johns Hopkins. You were on the faculty at Emory University and then Vanderbilt. And then you fell off the grid about five years ago. You resurfaced briefly in an investigation regarding a mass poisoning attempt involving a municipal water treatment plant near Akron, Ohio. Your name has also popped up in connection with two

militia groups who have been named as terrorist organizations by both the FBI and DHS. But you vanished
after a series of poisonings killed a federal prosecutor, a
government witness, and a rabbi from Georgia. So you
can stop with the hillbilly routine, Doc."

She looked at him coolly. "You obviously know what
happened to poor Dr. Coburn, since you were there
and were very nearly blown into fragments yourself.
Pity you weren't. One less federal jackboot is always a
sublime result."

"Federal jackboot?" he said. "I can see you've drunk
the Kool-Aid."

"No, I've embraced the *truth*." She paused and took
a swallow of beer. "You know what you're up against?"

"Care to elaborate?"

"You should join us," she said.

"In what exactly?"

"Taking our country back."

"I wasn't aware it had gone anywhere."

She smiled, but it never reached her eyes. "Then
you're not paying attention."

"Is this where you run me down a conspiracy rabbit
hole filled with bullshit?"

Her features turned to stone. "Judgment Day is
swiftly approaching."

"For *you*, it is."

"You have nothing on me," snapped Trumbull.

"Well, I actually have *four* outstanding federal arrest warrants. I hope you agree to come quietly." He took out his gun.

She stiffened and then wilted so quickly, it looked like she might be having a stroke.

"You can't be serious. You'll never get out of here alive."

Devine said, "You tell me how you killed the Odoms and we might be able to work something out for our mutual benefit."

She smiled at him. "This is so much bigger than you imagine. You don't have a chance."

Devine looked at her simpering, smirking face and he felt his temper swell. "I served my country in a lot of places where everyone told us we didn't have a chance. In fact, since the Revolutionary War, people like you, meaning *enemies* of this country, have been telling us we don't have a chance. And yet we're still standing."

When her smile deepened and she started to say something, he aimed and fired a round so close to her head that it blew off one of her dangling earrings.

She gasped, clapped her hand to her ear, and cried out, "You could have killed me."

"If I wanted to kill you, you'd be dead. But the night's still young."

He rose and placed the muzzle of his gun against the center of her forehead and slid his finger to the trigger. "Like this, Trumbull."

"You won't pull the trigger," she said shakily. "You're with the law."

"I don't remember telling you I was with the law."

"You're Homeland Security," she sputtered.

"And our mission is to protect the homeland against all threats, foreign and, like you, domestic. And I have the authority to use deadly force when threatened."

"I'm *not* threatening you," she moaned.

"You told me I didn't stand a chance, and that I'd never get out of here alive. That is a direct and immediate threat to my personal safety, so extreme measures are justified. And you won't be around to dispute it, will you?"

His finger edged to the trigger.

"Please, please don't," she whimpered.

"I can't go away empty-handed, Trumbull. I came all this way. So either you talk, or at least I can tell my boss I removed one traitor from the mix. And you sure fit that bill." When she said nothing, he pushed the muzzle deeper into her flesh and said, "Okay, bye-bye, Doc."

She cried out, "W-wait. W-what do you want to know?"

He withdrew the pistol from her forehead.

"Tell me about 12/24/65. Eric and Mercedes King. Danny Glass. And how the Odoms died."

"But—"

He held up his weapon. "Start talking or I will end

you, right here, right now. You're a traitor, and you and your kind have declared war on this country, and they execute traitors during wartime. And I have no problem being the executioner."

And she started talking, laying everything out, as Devine asked pointed, detailed questions.

When she finished, he looked down at her.

"What happened to you?" asked Devine. "To make you follow this madness?"

"Go to hell."

"We can still cut you a deal," said Devine.

"You can't prove anything I just told you."

"We already have. You were just the cherry on top. And now you'll need to come with me. There's transport waiting to take you out of here and then to a federal facility."

This seemed to strike Trumbull especially hard. "What sort of deal?"

"You testify, you go into WITSEC, no prison time. Otherwise, you'll never see the sun rise or set again."

She considered this. "I can't stay here. And I'll need to get some clothes."

He followed her to her bedroom. "I'll just be a minute," she said as she pulled out some clothes. She reached inside the pocket of one and quickly clapped a hand to her mouth. Devine was a split second too late to stop her. She swallowed and looked triumphantly at him. "My own concoction. Even more lethal and fast acting than *cyanide*."

She started convulsing, her breathing erratic, her pupils flipping out of sight. Trumbull dropped to the floor and started gyrating on the carpet, while Devine could only watch helplessly. Then she stopped moving.

And seconds later she stopped breathing.

Her pupils had rotated back into place. But they now stared unseeing up at him.

Devine looked over his shoulder. "Did you get it?"

Pru Jackson came out of the darkness holding her phone. "Eleven minutes and five seconds of crystal clear video. I did *not* film you threatening her with the gun or her offing herself," she added.

"Good call."

76

DEVINE CARRIED TRUMBULL TO HER bed where Jackson undressed her and put the dead woman under the covers. Devine had found in a cabinet the bullet he'd fired and dug it out and then smoothed over the damaged wood. Their hope was that whoever discovered her would conclude that Trumbull had died of natural causes.

After finishing with Jackson, Devine drove back to the trailer in Kittitas County and found Odom, Shore, and Rose eating a late-night dinner.

"Glad your butt got back here alive," whispered Shore.

"Yeah."

After the meal, Devine led Odom into the living room and showed her the boxes with her parents' remains.

"I know this is so hard, Betsy," he said as she ran her fingers along the tops of the boxes. "But I thought you'd want to have them."

"Thanks, I...I do."

He took a breath and said, "I found out what happened to your parents."

"You know who killed them?" she said, her features strained.

"The waitress at the restaurant where you ate?"

"The old lady who smelled like smoke?"

"She used to be a doctor and a chemistry professor. She got caught up with some very bad people."

Floppy tears gathered in the girl's eyes, "How... how did it happen?"

In answer, Devine took out something from his pocket and held it up. "Look familiar?"

It was a pack of bacterial wipes.

Odom gaped. "Oh my gosh, the waitress brought us each one of those. She said they were asking everyone to use them because the town had had an outbreak of the flu. I...forgot. I'm sorry."

"It's okay."

"But I used one, too."

"Yes, only the one she gave you had no poison on it. Just your parents'."

"And I remember the waitress came and collected them with tongs."

"I'm sure she did. The poison would have been rapidly absorbed into their skin. The woman told me that within sixty seconds you could have shaken hands with your mom and been fine. But it was still risky, for you."

"Where is this bitch? Did you arrest her?"

"No. But she won't be hurting anyone anymore."

Odom started to protest, but then realization spread across her features. "She's...?"

"Yes. She took her own life."

She wiped at her tears and said, "When will all this stop? When will they stop hurting people?"

"They're not going to hurt you, Betsy. Now it's their turn to hurt."

"Happy Birthday!" Shore and Rose said together as they trooped into the room. The latter was carrying a birthday cake with thirteen candles.

Devine looked from them to the teary-eyed Odom, who made a valiant effort to smile.

"This is so awesome, guys," she said, quickly rubbing her eyes.

"Look at her, Dozer, girl's so happy, she got all teared up," gushed Rose.

Shore had paper plates, napkins, and plastic silverware.

"Today is your birthday?" said a stunned Devine.

"I told you it was coming up when we first met," she reminded him.

"And look, Betsy, thirteen candles, like the movie," said Rose.

"That's *sixteen*, dumbass. *Sixteen Candles*," said Shore, nudging him with his elbow.

"Oh, well, I'll make you one with *sixteen* in three

years. And it's chocolate, strawberry, and vanilla on the inside. And that's no crappy powdered sugar frosting. That is buttercream, sweetie, just like you like it."

She gave them both hugs and blew out the candles. They cut the cake and had two slices each.

"What did you wish for?" asked Devine quietly, after Shore and Rose had gone back to their room.

"What does it matter?" she said, glancing at the boxes containing her parents' ashes.

"Happy Birthday, Betsy," he said, because he could think of nothing else to say. The words sounded lame as soon as they left his mouth.

Devine went to his room and called Campbell. He had earlier sent to him the video of Trumbull's confession that Jackson had taken, along with details about Trumbull's killing herself.

Campbell said, "That was good work, Devine. I've forwarded the video to the appropriate parties. They're analyzing it now."

"She didn't directly implicate the Kings unfortunately, or anyone else for that matter."

"It's still usable. So while you were interrogating her, who was taking the video?"

"I think you probably know," replied Devine.

"Prudence Jackson is dangerous, Devine. To you."

"Right now, she's far more dangerous to someone else."

"You know, we would like to take Mercedes King alive if possible."

"I will keep that as a top priority, sir, but I can't guarantee it."

Campbell sighed but didn't respond.

Devine said, "So what'd you find on Nicholas Dawkins, the power-mad guy King was meeting with?"

"Nicholas Dawkins is a thirty-four-year-old heir to an industrial fortune that was built up by several generations of Dawkinses. Nick didn't have the same business bug as his ancestors. He's whittled down his inheritance to finance a number of militias and anti-government groups and also runs a social media platform that would make most white supremacists blush. He also reportedly has the largest collection of Nazi memorabilia in the world."

"So just another nice rich guy."

"With connections to 12/24." He paused. "Did you tell Betsy what happened to her parents?"

"Yes, and she now has her parents' ashes."

"That little girl has been through hell and back."

"Several times," said Devine.

He clicked off and looked around the room. He picked up the photo album again and was paging through it when he noted the back cover had come partially loose. He examined it to see if it could be repaired when he noticed something that had been slipped into the revealed crevice. With a bit of manipulation, he managed to free it.

It was an official document.

When Devine ran his gaze over it, his lips parted in astonishment.

It was a certificate whereby Daniel Glass Sr. and his wife had adopted one Julia Bennett, just six months old, and renamed her Alice Glass. He took a picture of it with his phone along with the picture of the Glass family and the other document he had found previously.

Before he could even begin to process this, a light flashed in the window of the bedroom. Devine rushed over and looked out.

Something appeared to be coming at them and coming fast.

Shit.

Devine raced through the trailer, grabbing a stunned Odom from her room and yelling for Shore and Rose, who were in the middle bedroom.

"Go, go, go," he shouted. "Out the back, now!"

Shore and Rose emerged from their room and raced to the back door, which Shore slammed open.

"Run, run!" shouted Devine once they were all outside.

They hurtled through the dark woods. When Odom stumbled and fell, Rose scooped the girl up and carried her.

"What the fuck's goin' on?" shouted Shore.

Before Devine could answer, the trailer exploded and the concussive force of the blast hit them like a wave, lifting them into the air and sending all four of them tumbling through the woods.

Devine landed hard and was propelled across the ground, tasting dirt. When he stopped rolling, he looked up at the dark sky as a second explosion made day from night.

He sat up thinking, *That was the propane tank.*

"Betsy!" someone screamed out.

Devine leapt to his feet and saw Rose and a man struggling up ahead, while a second fellow had hold of the girl, who was fighting back. Rose was swiftly slashing at the man with his knife. The man collapsed under his attack.

Devine raced past a stunned Shore, who was trying to sit up.

Before Devine could reach Rose and Odom, the second man pulled a gun and shot Rose twice in the chest.

"Kor!" screamed Shore, who had seen this and gotten to his feet.

Devine raced past the fallen Rose and after the man, who was now sprinting away with Odom.

Devine pulled his gun but couldn't fire because he might hit the girl.

The man cleared the tree line and Devine heard a vehicle start up.

He redoubled his efforts, but got to the road only in time to see taillights disappearing.

Devine turned and sprinted back into the woods. He called Campbell on the way, telling him what had happened. He saw Shore kneeling in the dirt and ran up to him.

Shore gazed at him, the tears streaming down his face. "He's dead. Kor's dead."

A horrified Devine looked down at the body.

"I'm gonna kill those mutherfuckers. Kill 'em!" screamed Shore.

He turned back to look down at his dead friend, while Devine stared up ahead at what was left of the trailer. And then he looked behind him, where Betsy Odom had just vanished.

77

EARLY THE NEXT MORNING DEVINE sat in Campbell's hotel room in Seattle with Campbell, Nate Shore, Ellen Saxby, and Detectives Braddock and Walker.

Shore had not said a word all the way into Seattle. He was now sitting in a chair and staring at the carpet, his body so tensed, it looked like he had been frozen.

"We had alerts out everywhere from the minute you called me," said Braddock. "So far there's been no sighting of Odom."

A morose-looking Saxby said, "They have a lot of resources. She could be far away by now."

Campbell said, "We're attempting to ID the other dead man. Your friend pretty well sliced him up." He paused and said to Devine, "How did you get out of there alive?"

"Saw what looked to be a drone directly coming our way. Didn't figure it would be on our side. And it obviously had a bomb attached."

"I don't see how it ran the circle of security we had put up," noted Saxby.

"To hell with the fuckin' 'circle of security,'" bellowed Shore. "We need to find Betsy and get the sonofabitch who killed Kor."

Devine put a calming hand on the man's thick shoulder. Shore looked like he wanted to punch right through the wall he was staring at.

"And we will, Nate, I promise."

"How? How we gonna do that sittin' 'round here talkin'?"

"Us running around with no purpose or plan is not going to help Betsy or catch the people who killed Korey," said Devine.

Shore hung his head and didn't respond.

Campbell said, "They did kill two of the perimeter guards on the rear flank, which opened up a hole. And that old logging road they escaped on didn't show up on any map we had."

"Someone knew the area well," Braddock said.

Devine said, "I think the drone came on hot and heavy so I could spot it."

"Making you flee out the back, you mean?" said Saxby.

"They funneled us, and then they exploited it."

Campbell said, "And there's only one reason for them to take her."

"As leverage over Glass," said Devine. "And now all bets are off for his cooperation." He looked at Saxby, whose lips were set in a grim line.

"Which means the bad guys win," said Walker glumly.

Devine looked at her. "Not by a long shot."

"What are you going to do?" asked Braddock with a puzzled expression.

Campbell began, "When the enemy takes the high ground—"

"You take it back," finished Devine.

Braddock looked at the two men nervously. "Okay, but this isn't a war, and the state of Washington, the last time I checked, was not a battlefield."

"Looks like one to me," countered Devine.

"We *do* have laws here, Devine," said Braddock.

Campbell interjected, "And we will abide by them, to the extent we can."

"That is not making me feel any better," noted an anxious Braddock.

"You remember you told me you'd go wherever the evidence led you?" Devine reminded the lawman.

"And that has not changed. But I also haven't seen any evidence, nothing concrete at least. Until then—"

"Then we'll just have to get you some," broke in Devine.

"I'd *like* to be kept in the loop on this," exclaimed Braddock.

Campbell said, "We will to the extent we can."

"I'm getting tired of that phraseology," retorted Braddock.

"Not as tired as I am having to say it," Campbell shot back.

Devine eyed Saxby. "I need to talk to Glass. Now."

"Why?"

"It's personal."

CHAPTER

78

DEVINE WASN'T SURE WHAT WOULD await him when he met up with Glass. With Betsy missing, the man might actually try to murder him.

And maybe I deserve it.

He got off the elevator and ran the gauntlet of guards, all of whom looked like they wanted to punch Devine's ticket permanently. Word no doubt had gotten around that Devine had lost the boss's niece.

But did I lose the boss's niece?

Glass was standing by the window. His clothes were rumpled, and if he'd had hair, Devine supposed that would have been in disarray, too. As he turned to Devine, the man looked like he'd aged a decade.

"Sit," he said curtly.

Devine did so.

Glass took his time coming around to take a seat opposite him. "Tell me why I shouldn't put a bullet in your brain right now, Devine."

In response, Devine took out his phone, opened his

photos, and tossed it across. "Take a trip down memory lane, Danny. Swipe from the right, last three pictures."

Glass nimbly caught the phone, but didn't seem inclined to look at the screen.

"The sooner we get this squared away, the sooner I can get Betsy back."

"How are you going to do that?" barked Glass.

Devine flicked his gaze at the phone.

Glass looked down at the first photo on the screen.

Devine said, "The Glass family. Short mom, short dad, you at medium height, and your 'sister' an Amazon. And a redhead when all of you are dark. Swipe."

Glass did so.

"Official certificate. Your parents adopted Alice when she was an infant. She's not your sister by blood, but by adoption. Swipe."

Glass's shaky finger moved the screen to the last photo.

"Dwayne's health record." Devine paused. "He was incapable of fathering children. And yet there's Betsy."

Glass tossed back the phone, his eyes glistening.

Devine said, "I also found out that your family and Perry Rollins hail from the same town in Ohio. When Rollins first approached me, he told me that he wasn't always from the Seattle area."

"Stop, Devine."

"In fact, he was living in the same neighborhood where Alice had moved to. This was *after* Alice married Dwayne, and they were living in the house she had been renting with a roommate. Dwayne was off looking for work when you came home on leave and visited her."

"I said, stop."

"That test on Dwayne was done over a year before Betsy was born. They'd obviously tried to conceive, even looked at IVF, but then they found out Dwayne was firing blanks."

"Don't go there," Glass said grimly.

Devine sat back. "Rollins had already been arrested for being a Peeping Tom in that neighborhood. Took pictures of a woman in her bathroom naked."

Glass looked up at him. "You *don't* want to go there."

Devine sat forward. "I don't give a damn what happened between you and Alice, Danny. But if you'd been straight with me from the beginning, I wouldn't have been spinning my damn wheels over Rollins's murder. Did you have him taken out because he was trying to blackmail you?"

Glass didn't answer. He just looked away, the crushing stress the man was under heavily stamped into every feature.

"Or did you have him killed because he was trying to sell your secret to someone else?"

Glass now looked up at him. He seemed drained of all fight, of all energy.

"I didn't need to kill him, Devine, because someone already knew about my secret."

"Who?"

"Dwayne Odom."

A surprised Devine sat back. "You're going to need to explain that."

Glass glanced out the window. "Alice was *technically* my sister, but I was so much older and we weren't related by blood." He turned to Devine. "So it was just different."

"Different how?" asked Devine sharply.

"I never did anything like what you're probably thinking, Devine. I never, ever molested Alice. Never thought about it. But when I came back on leave years later, she wasn't ten anymore. She was a woman. A beautiful one. That was one reason my mother and some friends got her out of the house. My father... Well, let's just say he had no problem thinking of Alice as... not his daughter."

"And?"

"And she married Dwayne while I was in the Army. They wanted to have a baby but..."

"...but Dwayne couldn't. So why not adopt?"

"It wasn't so easy at the time, I guess. And Alice... Alice wanted to carry the child. It was important to her."

"You could have been a sperm donor," suggested Devine.

"That was very expensive. And I didn't have any money to help them with that." He slowly shook his head. "Anyway, Alice wrote and asked me if I would... help... with her getting pregnant. She said it would mean a lot to her."

"Okay," Devine said awkwardly.

Glass glared at him and barked, "I know it all sounds weird as shit. But I would have done anything for her."

"So...?"

"So I got leave and flew home. Dwayne was out of town looking for work. We... It was... well... not what I thought it would be. We were both... uncomfortable. But the important thing was she got pregnant."

"And Perry Rollins got evidence of this? How?"

"I don't know, Devine. I'd never heard of the guy until you mentioned him. Maybe he took pictures of us like he did to the lady in the bathroom. But I don't know if he even knew who we were. Pics of two adults in bed? Not sure how valuable that would be. But you're wrong about one thing—he never came around trying to blackmail me."

"He *did* find out about you two at some point, and when you became who you are, he figured the pictures could be valuable."

"How do you know for sure he found out about us?"

"Because he said some seemingly crazy words to me right before he died that now make sense."

"What words?"

"Cuckoo and *gas*."

Glass shook his head. "Not following?"

"Try *cuckolded* and *Glass*."

The man sat back, realization spreading over his features.

"Rollins clearly knew that Alice and Dwayne were married and living together. He didn't know who you were but caught you in bed with Mrs. Odom. Before he could do anything with it, I think he was arrested for taking photos of the woman and went to prison for a while. When he got out the Odoms had long since moved."

"Whatever," Glass said dismissively, clearly losing interest in this subject.

"You said Dwayne knew about what had happened with you and Alice? How?"

"Alice told him. He knew he wasn't the father, obviously, but I don't think he ever imagined that I would be the one. And he wasn't happy about it when he found out. Probably the reason why he hated my guts. But... the dumbass made a big mistake."

Devine sat forward again, something dawning on him. "The people who bought them the car and trailer home. He sold your secret to *them*?"

Glass nodded.

"Who were they?"

"The same ones you're after. They were looking for extra dirt to keep me in line and found a willing source in old Dwayne."

It all seemed to click in Devine's brain. "So 12/24/65 paid off Dwayne to get your secret. But how would they even have known he knew something like that about you?"

"I think Dwayne actually went out and shopped what he knew. These people, who were on the lookout for anything having to do with me, for obvious reasons, found out. And paid him off."

Devine thought this through. "Okay, then later they found out Rollins was trying to sell the same secret and they took him out. Otherwise their hold over you would be diluted."

"*That's* another reason why I haven't committed to cooperating with the feds, even with them dropping the RICO case."

Devine said, "You don't want Betsy to know that you're her father?"

Glass looked up at him, tears now sliding down his cheeks. "She loved Dwayne. He was her real father, not me. And if she finds out that 'Uncle Danny' slept with her mom, my *sister*, even if she was adopted? She'll hate my guts. I can survive a lot, Devine. And I have." He shook his head. "But I can't survive that."

"But why would they kill Dwayne and Alice if they had already paid them off?"

"Dwayne, like I said, made a big mistake."

"Which was?"

"He told me he was going to go public with the truth of my fathering Betsy. To make sure she and I would never have a relationship. These people found out and offered him a shitload of money to lure him to Ricketts. Then they killed him. And Alice. I'm not sure how it was done, though."

"They were poisoned by a chemist turned waitress at the restaurant where they had lunch. She was part of 12/24. But how could they know they would stop there to eat?"

"They were told to eat there by someone before the meeting with the two men. They said they would leave a message at the restaurant telling Dwayne where to meet the men with the money."

"If you knew all this, why didn't you stop it?" demanded Devine.

Glass retorted, "Because I didn't know before! I only found out *after*."

"From whom?"

"I got somebody on the inside with these people. She told me."

"*She?* Let me guess—Mercedes King?"

Glass looked surprised. "How'd you know?"

"She's ex-CIA and is obviously hedging her bets by playing both sides. I've been told that Ricketts is the mother ship for 12/24/65, but I'd like some corroboration on that."

Glass gave him a sideways glance that showed more than a glint of dread. "There are actually about a half dozen 'mother ships' around the country that I know of, and Ricketts is one of them."

"Right now I'm only concerned with the one in Ricketts."

"Why?"

"Because I think they have Betsy there."

"Are you sure?" Glass said sharply.

"I'm not sure of anything, Danny. But it makes the most sense. They control that town. They take her somewhere else, even by private plane, or another country, it gives someone who's not on their payroll an opportunity to see something and say something."

Glass stood. "Then we need to go and get her."

"No, *I* need to go and get her. It was my job to protect her. It's my job to get her back. And they have every incentive to kill you, Danny. So you need to stay on the sidelines behind a wall of federal lawmen."

Glass bellowed, "Why should I trust you, Devine? You let them take Betsy."

"Think back to that battlefield outside Baghdad. You got the commendation. And you earned it. But you *saw* what I did there. You *know* what I'm capable of, don't you?"

The men did a stare-down for a long moment before Glass plopped back in the chair.

"And we have to make sure you're around to testify and save the country."

Glass eyed him. "What, you think it's my penance? To save the good old U.S. of A.?" he said scornfully.

"Everybody has a penance that needs to be paid, Danny."

"Even you?"

"Even me."

"Is that why you got out of the Army early? Was that your penance?"

"Let's just agree that it was," said Devine. "But if you're keeping score, and I know you are, saving the good old U.S. of A. isn't a bad way to go out."

CHAPTER

79

ALL THE FED'S HORSES AND all the fed's men weren't going to be able to get this done, thought Devine.

It's going to be me. And a little unofficial help.

He was armored and gunned up and was presently looking through next-gen optics at the Ricketts government building. He eyed the security car parked in front. Devine felt like he was back in the Army getting ready to hit a target, hard.

And I guess that's exactly what I'm doing.

After Jackson had told him about the person who had ratted the Termites out to the feds and who might be imprisoned in the holding cell in the basement of the government building, Devine reasoned that they might be keeping Odom there, too.

In his earpiece, Emerson Campbell's clipped, authoritative voice came through.

"Okay, Devine. Let's do a last run-through. The cell is in the basement. Down the stairs and turn left. Two hundred feet and on the right. If they're holding her in that building, it will be there."

There was one armed guard who made rounds every half hour. Devine had watched him go past twice now, and the man was clearly not into his mission. He had continually looked at his phone, and wandered this way and that at times, once even leaning against the building and taking a smoke break. He had now just gone into the building through the glass front door.

"Roger that. Security seems a little lax here."

"They don't think anyone can hit them on their home turf."

"A cardinal error that many a successful attack has exploited."

"And hopefully we can add this one to the list. Rules of engagement are deployment of equal force. It's a bit tricky obviously since we're going into a government building, but we'll figure that out on the other end. And if they're holding her in there, no court will rule against us. Okay, I've confirmed that your *partner* is locked and loaded. Let's roll. Good luck."

Next moment Devine was on the move.

He hustled to the front of the building and out of the sight lines of the nearest cameras. He secreted himself into the shadows near the front door and waited.

A moment later a figure crept out of the darkness and slid up near the security car. Then the person raced forward and collided with the vehicle so hard, it rocked on its wheels. The next moment the intruder vanished as the car's lights and alarm came on, breaking both the darkness and the silence.

Twenty seconds later the front door burst open and there was the guard, his pistol in one hand, a phone in the other.

He looked around and then focused on the flashing car. He let go of the door and ran forward, reaching the vehicle in seconds. He looked around and then pulled his keys from his pocket, hit the button, and the lights went off and the alarm ceased.

He glanced around once more and then retreated, walking backward, into the building, until he had to turn to use his key card to open the secured door.

The guard pulled it closed behind him and made a call as he disappeared down the hall.

Devine came out from behind another door inside the building. Hiding in the shadows, he had slipped in through the front door when the guard had burst out of the building. He had made sure no one had followed him in, but the idiot hadn't taken the same precaution when exiting the building.

A masked and gloved Devine made his way down the stairs to the basement level and threaded his way carefully along the corridor. As Campbell had said, the holding cell area was on the right.

As Devine reached it, he heard groaning coming from behind the door.

He pulled a pick gun from his belt, studied the lock, fixed a specific bit in the gun, and inserted it in the lock. It took only ten seconds to defeat the obstacle.

His Glock out, Devine slowly pushed open the door. The holding cell held a sole occupant.

Unfortunately, it wasn't Betsy Odom.

CHAPTER

80

THE POLICE OFFICER WHO HAD made the nepotism crack about Mayor Mercedes King on Devine's first trip to Ricketts was lying on a cot behind a set of bars as Devine walked in. He didn't appear to have noticed Devine's presence.

His face was bloodied and covered in purplish welts. His knees were drawn up and he showed every sign of being in considerable pain. His moans were pronounced and steady.

Devine drew near the bars. "Who did this to you?"

The man flinched and turned his head to look at Devine.

"Please, please don't hurt me anymore. I...I didn't do nothing. I swear. I never told nobody nothing."

This was the man accused of ratting out the Termites. As Jackson predicted, it seemed clear he had been beaten to try to make him talk.

"I'm not here to hurt you. I can help you."

The man just shook his head. "Please, I didn't talk to nobody. I swear."

He moaned louder and gripped his belly.

"I want to help you," Devine said in a louder voice. "I'm not part of the people who hurt you."

The man stopped moaning and looked at him, maybe seeing him for the first time.

"Who...who are you?"

"I was sent here to rescue you."

"W-why?"

"I know you didn't rat anybody out. You were set up."

"I...I was," he gasped. "H-hey, don't I know you? Wait, hell, you were that...fed. A fed!" He looked terrified.

Devine thought quickly. "I *am* that fed. But I'm here to help you. Because I know that Mayor King set you up."

The man's fright slowly faded. He nodded and said angrily, "That b-bitch. She done it. She lied. Set me up."

"You think she was the mole but framed you to take the heat off her?"

Devine knew the answer but wanted to keep the man focused and engaged.

The man sobbed, "God, I hurt so bad."

"I can help you. But you need to help me."

"H-how?"

"Betsy Odom. Where are they holding her?"

From somewhere Devine heard a noise.

Over his earpiece Campbell said, "Eric King and his wife have just entered the building. They may be coming your way."

Devine turned back to the man and said urgently, "Betsy Odom. Where did they take her? If you tell me, I can get you out of here."

"It hurts so bad. They...they beat me bad."

"I can get you help with that. You just need to tell me where they have her."

Devine heard a door open and close.

"Come on, tell me. Now. And the pain goes away."

"Can...can you get me out of here first..."

Devine pulled out his pick gun to defeat the door lock and was figuring the logistics of getting the man out of there when he looked up.

The prisoner's arm was dangling over the side of the cot; his eyes were staring fixedly up at the ceiling.

"Hey," hissed Devine. "Hey, you still with me?"

It was clear that the man was no longer with anyone, not even himself.

Shit.

Devine eased to the outer door, listened, and heard the hum of an elevator. He closed the door and made sure it was secure.

He headed down the hall but then slipped behind another door when he heard a raspy voice.

He opened the door a sliver and peered out. Mercedes

and Eric King and the security guard on duty rounded the corner and headed over to the outer door of the holding cell.

Devine pointed his phone at them and hit the button to start the video.

The guard opened the door and they all went in. A minute later they all came out.

Eric King looked up at his wife from his wheelchair. "I told you not to go so hard on him."

"And exactly how is him being dead a problem?" she retorted. "He was a spy. Spies deserve to die during wartime, which is what we're in. A war!"

"But now we have a damn body to get rid of, Mercedes," said the police chief.

His wife swung around and gazed at the guard. "Well, isn't that what we pay people like him for?"

When the guard said nothing, she barked, "Isn't it?"

The guard, realizing she was talking to him, snapped to attention and said, "Yes, ma'am."

"Then take care of the body. Now."

The man ran back into the room.

Mercedes turned to look at her husband. Eric King said, "And the girl?"

"Betsy Odom is worth three times her weight in platinum right now. If Glass does the right thing, he'll get her back in one piece, but with a warning."

"And if he doesn't?" asked her husband.

"He gets her back in *pieces*. I'm leaving here to go and have a talk with her. Then she can contact her uncle and tell him, in her own terrified words, that we are not screwing around."

"I don't like this," said Eric King. "It's getting out of control. I'm a lawman, for God's sake, and here we are kidnapping and killing people."

"No, dear Eric, you are a soldier in a greater cause. To make this country what it's supposed to be."

He stared up at her. "Do you really believe that crap? I thought we were in this for the money?"

"I can multitask, Eric, even if you can't."

"I heard you met with Nick Dawkins."

"He envisions an expanded role in the organiza-tion suitable for my talents. He's actually meeting me tonight so we can talk to Odom together."

Eric King bristled. "And if I say no? I *am* your hus-band. And that man only wants one thing from you, trust me."

She bent down. "Our marriage is only a little itty-bitty piece of paper, Eric. And another piece of paper can end it. But either way, it won't be your call. And I know exactly how to handle little old Nick. *Trust* me."

"I'm sleeping in my room here," he snapped.

"Oh, what a pity. I was thinking of how much fun we could have later."

She blew him a kiss and waltzed off, leaving her husband staring dejectedly after her.

From his hiding place in the room across the hall, Devine hit the stop button on the filming, and used his phone to send off several texts. Then he spoke into his mic and told Campbell what had happened.

"Follow King. She can lead us right to Betsy," ordered Campbell.

"On it."

After Eric King rolled off, Devine emerged from his hiding place and reached the front door in time to see Mercedes King climb into her Porsche. A few moments later she sped off.

Devine sprinted down the road until he saw a pair of headlights pop on.

He jumped into the passenger seat and looked at Nate Shore, who earlier had rammed into the guard's car to force him to come outside and allow Devine to get inside.

"The Porsche, follow it," barked Devine.

Shore spun the van around and took up the chase.

81

"THE LADY WE'RE FOLLOWING IS going to where they have Betsy," said Devine as they drove along.

"Whoever's got her is sure as shit gonna feel some pain from me."

Devine didn't say anything for a few moments. "Delta Force?"

"What about it?" said Shore, shooting him a glance.

"You didn't just let some redneck assholes run you off like you told me before."

Shore looked uncomfortable. "What you talkin' 'bout?"

Devine's gaze bored into the man. "The Army is one big file cabinet, Nate, and they never throw one scrap of paper away. And I wasn't about to let you in on this op without drilling down on what you told me. You put two of those rednecks in the hospital and the Army thought it best if you didn't re-up, while the two assholes got to stay in. I would be pissed if I were you."

"I *was* pissed. But you think that was the first time that shit happened to people who look like me? If you do, you're so fuckin' stupid, you gonna get us *both* killed tonight."

"The point is, I need you to bring your Delta Force skills, which is the only reason I let you come tonight. But you have to channel them with precision, just like you were trained to do. I know what happened to Korey makes you mad as hell. I get that. But if you're going to avenge him, you need to do it smart, not testosterone stupid. There are no do-overs possible. Once someone's dead, they are dead and that includes us and Betsy. Are we clear on that?"

All the tension seemed to ease out of Shore. He nodded. "I got this, Travis."

"I believe you so don't let me or Betsy down. Now, another man is meeting her there, a Nick Dawkins."

"Who's he?"

"To sum it up, he's a rich guy who's a maniacal mix of George Wallace and Joseph Goebbels, with the largest known collection of Nazi memorabilia in the world."

"Gee, sounds like my kind'a dude. Wonder what beer he drinks. We can shoot the shit before I deep-six his ass."

They drove on until the Porsche slowed and turned down what looked to be a private road. Devine told Shore to stop near the turn-off. Devine got out and ran down the lane. He was back in under a minute.

"Pull the van off the road behind those bushes, and we'll go the rest of the way on foot."

Devine contacted Campbell and briefed him on the latest.

"Same rules of engagement, Devine, but with the proviso that you are to do whatever is necessary to bring Odom out of this safely. I have authorizations at the very highest level that will cover any action you take. But you are to let King and Dawkins leave before taking any action. Repeat, they must be allowed to leave before you take any action."

"Roger that," said Devine. He understood the basis for the command, but he didn't have to like it.

"And I have backup twenty minutes out from your position."

He acknowledged this, and he and Shore made the trek down the lane, flitting from one cover spot to the next until the large, three-story house came into sight. The Porsche and a burgundy Range Rover were parked in front.

Devine noted the two perimeter sentries patrolling their respective grids with vigor and attention. And it would all be for naught as Devine and Shore split up to do what needed to be done here tonight.

The first sentry had just checked in on his comm when the knife was leveled against his neck. One swipe, a gush of blood from severed arteries, and he fell dead at Devine's feet.

Quick, clean, no fuss. And mission-focused Devine felt nothing except one small step in the rescue plan accomplished as he dragged the man off to some underbrush after taking his comm pack. He listened to the chatter coming over it and gained some valuable intel.

He edged closer to the house and crouched down behind a clump of evergreen bushes. He gazed up at the house. Lights burned in one upstairs room. That must be where they were keeping Odom, Devine concluded. He contacted Shore and told him where to rendezvous.

A minute later he saw movement to his right and waited as Shore crept up and squatted next to him. He noted that there was what looked to be a knife slash and blood over the front of his armor.

"Problems?" asked Devine.

"Only for the other guy," replied Shore curtly.

Devine held up the comm pack. "According to the chatter we have eight more guards between her and us."

"I don't mind those odds," said Shore. "But those muthers shouldn't like them."

"We have armed backup on the way. But we need to wait for King and Dawkins to leave before engaging."

"What the fuck? Why not just nail them all right now?"

"Because that's not all of them."

"But what if something happens to Betsy?"

"Nothing is going to happen to Betsy, because they need her to leverage Glass. And they're going to have Betsy call her uncle tonight and reinforce the message that if he cooperates, she dies. They probably already had her do it."

"So Glass won't cooperate and these assholes win? Well, at some point they ain't gonna need Betsy no more."

"That's *their* plan, Nate, but it's not ours. All we have to get tonight is Betsy. Focus on that."

They sank lower behind their cover when King and Dawkins came out of the house and paused on the porch. Then the two exchanged a kiss and a lingering hug while Devine filmed it with his phone.

"Ain't she married?" whispered Shore.

"Yep."

"Guess she don't love her husband."

"I think the only person that woman loves is herself."

As the Porsche and Range Rover both pulled away, Devine looked at Shore. "Ready to do this?"

"Delta ready," replied Shore.

82

THEY REACHED THE REAR OF the house without incident. The door there had a deadbolt, but there was also a sidelight. Devine cut out a pane of glass, put his hand through, drew back the bolt, unlocked the door, and they slipped in. There was no sentry posted here. Devine figured the folks inside the house had no doubt counted on their perimeter security to alert them if anyone was approaching.

The men glided down the hallway, Devine watching the front and Shore covering their rear flank. Devine had turned down the volume on the comm pack he'd taken because he could hear it from another device obviously on the person of someone just up ahead.

They rounded the corner and glimpsed the man standing there at the bottom of the stairs. He was speaking softly into his walkie-talkie. He slipped it back into the holder on his belt and looked to his left.

Devine nodded at Shore, who readied himself to launch. Devine took aim and fired. His weapon had an integrated suppressor, and a subsonic round fired off with a minimum of noise, sounding more like a hard slap. It struck the man in the neck. As he fell dead, Shore caught him and slid him off to the side.

They went up the stairs side by side, with Shore again watching their rear.

On the next landing another man was posted. Shore slipped the knife from his belt, took aim, and flicked it. The blade bit into the man's neck, lodging there. He gagged and tried to cry out but the blade had severed his vocal cords.

Before his tumbling down the stairs could alert the others, Devine snagged him and set the dead man on the floor. Devine pulled Shore's knife free, wiped off the blood, and handed the blade back to him.

"Haven't lost your Delta touch," noted Devine.

"That shit ain't somethin' you ever lose till you dead."

They kept climbing.

When they reached the top landing, Devine peered down the long hall that ran to his left. He nodded at Shore and they put in their earplugs. Devine pulled the flash bang, engaged it, and tossed it down the hall.

Seconds after it went off, he and Shore charged down the hall to find five disoriented men curled into fetal positions amid the smoke, their ears burning and their eyes temporarily blinded by the flash. Devine took the baton out of his pack and struck each of the men in the head with it, rendering them unconscious.

"There's one more guard," said Devine.

The next moment they heard Odom scream from inside the room, "Help!"

Shore plowed into the door, ripping it right off its hinges. He sprawled on top of it inside the room. Devine followed him in and saw the eighth and final guard at the open window. He was trying to pull Odom through it. Devine also saw that one end of a flex escape ladder had been placed over the windowsill.

Devine pointed his gun at the man. "Get away from her, now."

The man pulled a knife from his belt. Before he could do anything to Odom with it, Devine fired a round into his head.

Odom screamed as the man fell back and slipped through the open window, falling three stories to the dirt.

Shore rushed forward and hugged Odom. She had blood on her from the man.

"You okay, Bets?" said Shore anxiously. "You ain't hurt?"

Sobbing, she shook her head and sank to her knees. "Is...is he..."

Devine holstered his weapon and knelt down in front of her. "It's okay, Betsy. You're okay. And now we're getting you out of here." When she tried to stand, her legs failed her. Shore picked her up and said, "I got you."

Outside the room Devine quickly zip-tied the still-unconscious men.

Before they reached the landing where the first dead man was, Devine said, "Close your eyes, Betsy. And keep them closed until I tell you it's okay."

She didn't ask why; she just shut them.

When they got outside, Devine told her she could open her eyes, and he radioed Campbell that they had Odom safe and sound.

"Okay, backup is on-site and will secure and clean the area," Campbell replied.

Devine clicked off and Odom said, "Where is Kor? I know he was fightin' with the men who took me." She gazed anxiously from one to the other.

Devine glanced at Shore, who dropped his gaze. Devine said, "He didn't make it, Betsy."

Her eyes immediately filled with tears. "He's... Kor's dead?"

"Yeah," muttered Shore.

"He lost his life helpin' me," said Odom, as though it were a crime. "He didn't have to do that."

"He *wanted* to do it, Bets," said Shore. "Dude loved you."

Her eyes brimmed with even more tears. "I... I wasn't worth... that."

"He thought you were," said Devine. "And that's what counts. Now we need to go."

They passed the backup team as they headed to their van and Devine took a minute to fill them in.

As Shore drove them off, he looked back at Odom, who was curled up into a little ball in the backseat, quietly crying.

Hours later, as they were nearing Seattle, Campbell's voice came over Devine's mic.

"We've got a problem, Devine."

"What?"

"Danny Glass has gone missing."

CHAPTER

83

THE NEXT DAY DENNIS HASTINGS, his face still puffy from the beating he'd absorbed from Devine, sat sullenly in Danny Glass's hotel suite and faced off with Devine, Campbell, Saxby, Braddock, and Walker. Nate Shore was back at the hotel with Odom and a half dozen federal agents.

"What in the hell happened?" barked Saxby.

Hastings gave her a menacing look. "The boss wanted to go out to eat. We got the team together. We went to a place that stays open real late. He had to use the john. I sent a guy with him. When he didn't come back within a couple minutes, I went looking for him. I found Joe, one of my guys, out cold and Mr. Glass was gone."

"Did you do a search?" asked Saxby.

"No, I just sat on my ass and ordered another drink. Of course we searched!"

"And?" persisted Saxby.

"And he was gone. Vanished. Nobody saw anything.

And your people couldn't find him, either, so get the fuck off my case."

"What did *Joe* have to say?" asked Devine.

"Somebody cold-cocked him."

"He didn't see anything, hear anything?"

Hastings shook his head. "It was lights out until I dumped a pitcher of water on him."

Devine glanced at Braddock. "Have your guys checked cameras, questioned everybody?"

"We processed the scene once, but we're doing it again in case we missed something. There was CCTV but it had been disabled."

"So this was planned?" said Saxby.

"Apparently so."

"It has to be the same people," noted Walker. "They took him to stop him from testifying."

"The problem with that theory," said Devine, "is that they already had Betsy to stop him from testifying. They had no way to know that we'd freed her when they abducted Glass."

"So why snatch him?" asked Saxby.

Campbell said, "They didn't. He orchestrated his own escape. Only way this makes any sense."

Hastings looked offended by this suggestion. "Why in the hell would Mr. Glass do that?"

"Because he's a control freak and one seriously

impatient man," interjected Devine sharply. "And he might have just ruined everything."

"What the hell does that mean? And why would he orchestrate his own disappearance?" asked Saxby.

Devine said, "He cut himself loose so *he* could negotiate for Betsy's release. He was not going to count on me or anyone else to do that for him. So Danny decided to take charge."

Saxby looked dumbstruck. "Do you mean to say that he's gone to these crazy-ass bastards to exchange himself for her?"

Braddock interjected, "But how would he manage that? How do you do the exchange if it's only him involved? They're not going to release her until they have him. And if there's no one for them to give her up to? It just doesn't work."

"There's no way the boss would do that," protested Hastings. "He's way too smart for a rookie move like that."

"Yeah, but love sometimes makes you do stupid things," pointed out Devine.

"Okay," said Saxby. "Assuming you're right, what do we do? We have to get him back."

"Your people have all the obvious points of exit covered? Airports, train stations?" asked Devine.

"Yes, by the playbook."

"This is *not* going to go by the playbook, Ellen."

He shot Hastings a glance. "Take me to the restaurant where it happened."

"Why?" snapped Hastings.

"Because I want to see it for myself."

"He's long gone, Devine," barked the man. "You'd just be wasting time and we don't have any to waste."

Devine studied Hastings, easily reading everything going through the other man's mind.

"Nobody likes getting their ass kicked," Devine said. "And nobody likes losing the boss on their watch."

Hastings winced at these blunt but accurate words.

"But I'm trying to save Danny's life. So will you take me to the place, or not?"

Hastings rose. "Come on, I'll drive you myself."

84

CAMPBELL, SAXBY, BRADDOCK, AND WALKER rode with Devine and Hastings in his SUV. They pulled up in front of the restaurant.

Devine glanced at Hastings. "Did he pick this place?"

"Yeah. He came in and told me he wanted to go out to eat. We had to scramble. The feds and everything."

"Didn't he have dinner?" said Campbell. "Was there a reason he needed to eat that late?"

Hastings shrugged. "Half the time I have to remind him to eat. It's not a priority."

Campbell said, "Then he was meeting someone here. And *they* picked the spot."

"Agreed, sir," replied Devine.

They all went inside and flashed their badges at the woman who came out to greet them. The restaurant wasn't open yet and would not open again until the crime scene processing had been complete.

Hastings led them through the dining room to the table where they had been eating. Hastings pointed out the locations where his men and the feds had been stationed.

"Okay, when it was noticed that he was missing, what happened?" Devine asked Hastings.

"All the security, us and the feds, converged on the bathroom. Then we spread out and covered all the bases."

They followed Devine down a hall to the rear of the building. There was a door off the kitchen. He opened it to reveal a storage closet. A short walk down the hall led to the rear exit. Devine opened the door into a wide alleyway behind the building lined with Dumpsters. It could be entered off the street to the east and led to the next block over.

"Plenty wide enough to drive through," noted Braddock.

"Where all the delivery trucks come probably," noted Saxby.

"Did the sentries stationed here also converge on the bathroom?" asked Devine.

"Yes, it was an all-hands-on-deck call," replied Hastings.

"How long between everyone leaving their posts and the wall being put up around this place?"

Hastings thought for a moment. "Maybe a minute."

Campbell opined, "So if I'm Glass, I knock out his own guy, go hide in that storage closet. The alarm sounds and he hears everyone rushing past. He steps out, exits out the rear door, and..."

"And what?" said Hastings. "Hoofs it on foot? We would've seen him."

Devine walked into the kitchen. They all followed him.

He asked the same woman who had greeted them where the staff took their breaks.

"In the alley," she replied. "Smokes and water."

"I know they've been held here for questioning, and I need to talk to all of them."

A minute later with the personnel lined up in front of him, Devine asked who had been out in the alley at the time in question. One young man, he was a busboy he told them, had been taking his smoke break. He was in his early twenties, with a small goatee, a thin frame, and he looked exhausted.

Devine held up his phone with a picture of Glass on the screen. "Did you see this man come out?"

"No, sir."

"Did you see anything unusual?"

"What do you mean by unusual?"

"Something you'd never seen before in that alley," replied Devine.

"Oh, well, yeah, I did."

"What was that?" Devine said patiently.

"Most all the vehicles you see back there are delivery trucks. Food, wine, that kind of stuff."

"And last night?" said Devine.

"Well, there was a real fancy ride that pulled in while I was smoking a cigarette."

"Can you describe it?"

"It was a Tesla."

"Did you see the person driving?"

The busboy nodded.

Devine held out his phone again with a different image on it. "Her?"

The man looked at the photo of Mercedes King. "Yep."

"Then what happened?"

"Some dude came out wearing a hoodie. Never saw his face."

"Where did he go?"

"He got in the car and it tore out of here."

Devine looked at Braddock. "Didn't anybody ask these questions before?"

"Yeah, they did," said a befuddled-looking Braddock, while Hastings nodded in agreement.

Walker said to the busboy, "I was here doing some of the interviews, but I don't remember seeing you here."

Devine looked back at the busboy. "Care to explain?"

"I went off duty right after I saw the car. Finished my smoke and went home. Just came back here when one of my buddies told me what happened. So I wasn't here last night to answer any questions."

Devine took a moment to ponder all of this.

Mercedes King aka Anne Cassidy has Danny Glass. But she was in Ricketts last night. So how could…

"*Exactly* when did your boss go missing?"

Hastings told him.

Devine did the math in his head and then turned to Campbell. "I'm assuming Nick Dawkins has a private jet?"

"He does. Dassault Falcon. Why?"

"I need you to check to see if it filed a flight plan last night. Ricketts to Seattle."

"Who is Nick Dawkins, Devine?" asked Braddock.

"One of the money men behind the Termites aka 12/24."

Campbell made the call and two minutes later he had an answer.

"His jet touched down in Seattle two hours before Glass went missing."

Devine said, "I overheard Mercedes King saying that they were going to have Betsy call her uncle last night. She was in no condition for me to ask if she had, but I'm assuming Betsy made her plea for her uncle to do what her kidnappers wanted. Then King probably called Glass on the flight here, made the arrangements, and executed the plan," said Devine.

"What plan?" said an exasperated Hastings.

"*Her* plan, as opposed to the Termites' plan."

"Why would Mercedes King have Glass's contact info?" asked Saxby.

"Because she's been feeding Glass inside intel. For her benefit, not his." Devine turned to the others. "I need your help. And we don't have much time."

"Do *you* have a plan?" asked Saxby.

"I do."

"Do you know where they've got Glass?" said Saxby.

"I think so, yeah. But I need to make sure."

"How do you do that?" asked Braddock.

"I need to talk to someone."

85

THE SUV PULLED UP TO the curb and Devine
hopped in.

As Pru Jackson sped off, she said, "You got the girl?"

"Yeah, but your *friend* got Danny Glass."

"You told me on the phone that Anne had been
leaking intel to Glass."

"I talked with Betsy. King had her call Glass and
plead for him to do what the kidnappers wanted. Betsy
said she saw no woman there so King never revealed
herself to Betsy, which makes sense. No way for Betsy
to ID her later if things went to hell. She could have
had someone else put the screws to Betsy and oversee
her calling her uncle. Then I think King called Danny
shortly thereafter, probably with an offer to help free
Betsy. Neither of them knew at the time that Betsy had
already been freed. Her henchmen at the house where
Betsy was taken have already made statements and
implicated King. And when she communicated with
them early this morning to check on the status of their
'prisoner,' we had them pretend everything was fine."

"So why would she snatch Glass?"

"She suckered him in, and has probably delivered his ass back to 12/24 for some big payoff. So they must be at the place where you saw the chopper leave from."

Jackson shook her head. "I don't think she brought Glass back to 12/24 for a payoff."

Devine looked startled. "Why not?"

"You need to understand Anne Cassidy. She was already working with the KKK people, so why expect them to pay her any extra? And when I overheard her and Nick Dawkins talking at the restaurant, she never once mentioned that she had opened a secret communications channel with Glass. She's playing this op like she played all ops at CIA, strictly close to the vest and for her personal benefit. And that tells us something vital."

"What?"

"What does Danny Glass have that Anne Cassidy may want?"

Devine thought for a moment. "For starters, a criminal empire worth billions."

"I don't think she wants to run an empire."

"Then cash. A ton of it."

"And if she could get her hands on that by making Glass think she could get Betsy back for him? Or maybe she sells Glass to any number of his other enemies who bid the highest? Then she takes the treasure and disappears and leaves this mess for everybody else to clean up."

He thought this through and then glanced at her. "You must have been one hell of an operative at CIA."

"I did my job. You have a team put together?"

"I can put one together pretty fast. You want to be in on it?"

"Why should I?"

"Because Anne Cassidy will be part of the bag."

"So she gets arrested and probably kicks the charges with the lawyers she can afford. Why should I risk my life for that?"

"Pull over."

"What?"

"Just pull over!"

She slid to the curb and put the vehicle in park. "What?"

"The only person I care about is Danny Glass. I get him, I'm out of there. What happens to anyone else is not my concern."

They stared at each other for a few seconds.

"Wait, are you saying what I think you're saying?"

He answered, "You in or not?"

"I'm in," she said. "So how are you going to pull the bitch into this?"

"We're going to ask her."

"You're going to ask her?" parroted back an incredulous Jackson.

"In a way that she can't refuse."

"And what about finding out where Glass is being held?"

"Based on what you just told me, I think it's one of two places."

"How will you know which one?"

"I'll let someone else do that for me."

CHAPTER

86

THE NEXT DAY, IN RICKETTS, Mercedes King walked to her Cayenne where it was parked at the government building.

Before she could get in, Detectives Braddock and Walker appeared and confronted her. Braddock said, "Police. You're under arrest and you need to come with me. Now."

She whirled around and barked, "Police? From where?"

Braddock flashed his badge. "SPD."

"This is not your jurisdiction. So you can't make me go anywhere."

A voice called out, "Actually, we can."

Ellen Saxby walked over and held up a piece of paper along with her credentials. "Special Agent Ellen Saxby, FBI. I have a federal arrest warrant for one Mercedes King. My state colleagues here are assisting."

"Based on what!" exclaimed King.

Saxby held up her phone and touched the screen. A video of Mercedes and Eric King started playing and showed them talking about the death of the man being held in the government building, and also the kidnapping of Betsy Odom. A minute later another video showed King and Nick Dawkins coming out of the house where Odom had been taken.

"In addition, we have five of your people in custody who were at the house where Odom was being held prisoner. They have sung long and hard. So legally, you're screwed. Your husband has already been arrested and so will your boyfriend, Nick Dawkins, as soon as we catch up to him. But Odom is safe and sound."

"But I—"

"But you got reports from your men that everything was A-OK?" said Saxby. "Yeah, we told them exactly what to say in their communications to you. Which is another piece of evidence against you since that conversation was recorded."

King looked at Saxby and then glanced around at the others. Something seemed to occur to her. "Where is Travis Devine?"

Saxby said, "He helped to rescue Betsy Odom. And unfortunately, he was killed during the mission. And we intend to charge you as being an accessory to his murder."

King took a step back. "Look, I have no idea what you have on that phone, but anything can be created digitally. And these five people? I don't know them."

Another voice said, "Well, another charge is aiding in the murder of a federal agent."

King slowly turned to stare at Will Chambers and Angela Davenport as they joined the party.

Davenport continued, "Then there's the espionage and treason counts. You're looking at life in prison, Anne, or do you prefer Mercedes? You always did have expensive tastes."

For the first time, the woman looked worried. "How did you—"

"CIA *is* an intelligence agency," proclaimed Chambers.

"What federal agent did I help kill?"

"Prudence Jackson," said Davenport. "Because of you, she was taken prisoner by enemies of this country, was tortured, and died."

King looked around and, gaining back some of her cockiness, said, "Five people to arrest little old me? And we wonder why the national debt is so high."

Saxby said, "Actually, we came to make you an offer. One you probably can't refuse, unless you're really, really stupid."

"What offer?" King said quickly.

"You help us, you get a deal," replied Saxby.

"What sort of deal?" King said sharply.

"New identity, new life."

"No prison time?"

"If you're a really, really good girl," said Saxby. "We

want 12/24. You're just a pain in the ass. You deliver them, you essentially get to walk."

As Saxby stared at the woman, she could almost see the wheels turning in King's brain.

"What do I need to do?" King said a few moments later.

"My, how I've always admired your loyalty," noted Davenport.

Saxby said, "We need Danny Glass back safe and sound."

"Glass? I don't know anything—" She stopped when Saxby held up her hand.

"You lie, they'll just fit you for a lifetime prison wardrobe and throw away the key. But if Glass is dead already, you have nothing to negotiate with."

"He's not...dead...yet," said King.

"So 12/24 is still *debriefing* him?" asked Chambers.

King hesitated and then nodded.

"So we need to get there ASAP," said Saxby. "And you're going to be our way in."

King said urgently, "He's heavily guarded. And these people are fanatics. They made me work with them. They threatened me."

"You always did have the nicest *playmates*, Anne," commented Davenport.

"That's part of the deal," said Saxby. "You get us in, or no deal."

King looked unsure for a few moments, but then a cagey expression graced her features.

"I'll call and tell them to keep Glass alive until I get there. And I need to pick up some things I'll need from a building behind the government center. But then I have a way to get you in."

"I knew you would," said Saxby.

87

MERCEDES KING STEERED THE CAYENNE slowly down the road and then made the turn onto the property where Pru Jackson had seen the chopper lift off into the darkness bearing two dead bodies courtesy of Travis Devine. Two uniformed sentries held up their hands for her to stop. In addition to the main house, there were several large outbuildings, including a massive barn. Parked behind the barn were rows of military-style vehicles, in addition to a half dozen four-wheelers.

One of the sentries searched the interior while the other ran a wheeled probe under the Porsche's chassis looking for anything that should not be there.

"All clear, Ms. King," said the first sentry politely. "As I knew it would be."

She smiled. "Thank you, Earl."

She drove off and parked by the barn. She got out and put her keys in her purse.

She used a security badge to access the barn door. It

slid open, its hydraulic power making a slight hissing sound.

King walked in and looked around. The main area was set up as office cubicles where dozens of people were working away on computers while several others were conversing in front of smart boards where graphs and maps were displayed. But, interestingly, the large space also held a combat ring, where a half dozen bare-chested men were engaged in training exercises. On the walls were racks of weapons. Boxes of ammo were organized behind padlocked wire mesh doors.

King said hello and nodded to a number of people as she passed by them. She reached a double door and knocked. It was opened by Nick Dawkins wearing a tailored, brown military uniform with stars on the shoulders.

"Mercedes, welcome. I didn't expect to see you here. I thought you'd still be in Seattle."

"Thanks for letting me take your jet there. My business is all finished. And I hope you like surprises."

"When you're one of them, I do."

He closed the door behind her, and she settled into a chair while he sat down behind a large desk.

He said, "Now look, I'm actually glad you're here. We really need to get to Danny Glass. We can't just hold his niece in perpetuity. You said you were going to be working on that?"

"After the call his niece made to him, I'll have him hook, line, and sinker shortly."

"That's my girl."

"That's right," said King. "I am." Her hand went to her jacket pocket, where there was a small device inside. She pushed the button.

An explosion from outside rocked the barn as the bomb in the Porsche's engine compartment detonated.

"What in the hell!" shouted a panicked Dawkins as he jumped up and glanced wildly around.

He looked at King as she slipped a gun from her bag.

"What is going on, Mercedes?" exclaimed a clearly terrified Dawkins.

"It's called cutting my losses, dear, sweet Nick. And if you wear the uniform, try to walk the walk and not act so fucking scared. It's a real turnoff."

She pointed the pistol at him.

He took a step back. "What the hell are you doing?"

"Just call me one of your supporters who don't want to be made into a follower against their will."

She shot him in the head and Dawkins fell to the floor dead, with blood running down his face and fouling his uniform.

King opened the door and rushed out into the main room. Amid the chaos, people were hurtling around and screaming as they grabbed guns from off the walls and ammo from behind the mesh doors. In addition to more explosions, small arms fire could be heard just outside.

King used the confusion to her advantage, and snuck out a back door. She slipped off her pumps and replaced them with a pair of ballet flats taken from her coat pocket. From every direction she heard sirens and the roars of powerful engines. She assumed that the full weight of the state of Washington's constabulary, along with the FBI, was descending on the compound. Luckily she had planned for such an eventuality. And she now intended to execute that plan.

She climbed aboard a four-wheeler and headed down a dirt road at the rear of the property. After about a half mile she turned onto another road, which wound past a small pond. She rode up to a security fence, shot the lock off, and drove through. She stopped and glanced back to see plumes of smoke rising into the air from back at the compound. She heard gunfire and small explosions echoing across the distance.

Total chaos, and she loved it.

King smiled, hit the throttle, and roared away.

CHAPTER

88

HAVING ALLOWED MERCEDES KING TO choose for him, Devine and Nate Shore were crouched outside of the woman's home.

Shore said, "She went to those assholes' HQ, which told you that was *not* where they were holding Glass?"

Devine nodded as he scanned the rear of the house. "That, and someone who knew her well told me that King was running her own op, so she never would have shared Glass with those guys. She wanted a personal payoff, and playing Glass for a fool was the only way to get it. I don't think she ever believed the crap Dawkins and his kind were spewing. She was always playing her own game. She's at their HQ right now probably blowing the place up and killing who she needs to kill to save her own ass. And Danny Glass represents her golden goose."

"Shit always comes down to money," said Shore in disgust.

"We got the plans for the house. They have a panic room behind a wall on the top floor. And they pulled a sat with see-through capability for us." Devine spoke into his mic. "Ready to execute."

Campbell came on the line. "The satellite is in place and we're just now getting images. Best route for entry is the exterior door on the south-facing side. We have incapacitated the alarm system and frozen the security cameras. You are invisible that way, but they could have eyes at windows so take precautions. Turn on your camera and I will see what you see."

"Roger that."

Devine turned on his head cam and confirmed that Campbell had visuals.

Devine turned to Shore. "Let's hit it."

They threaded their way through the woods until they reached the back door at the rear of the house.

Devine used his lockpick gun to defeat the door and they slipped inside.

It was quiet, too quiet for Devine. He glanced at Shore and could read the same thought crossing his mind as well.

They made their way through the kitchen and living areas on the main floor.

Campbell came back on over Devine's ear mic. "Two flights up we have received thermal images of five armed guards clustered outside the panic room, which is at the end of the hall. Steel door built into the wall on invisible hinges. We have another image of one person inside the panic room. It must be Glass. There is no one else in the house. Use extreme caution. They might have booby traps set."

"Roger that," replied Devine.

They reached the stairs and peered upward. Two flights away was their goal. And five heavily armed men were standing between them and Danny Glass.

Devine placed his foot on the first riser and then froze. He had looked down in time to see hovering a millimeter in front of him a slight disruption of dust molecules. If the bottom of his pant leg moved at all, it would hit it.

Shore noted this, too, and looked urgently at Devine. "Trip laser?"

Devine nodded and said quietly, "Move to my left, kneel down, and pull my pant leg back. Slowly."

Shore did so and Devine eased off the first riser and studied the challenge.

"Okay, follow me," he finally said.

He climbed on top of the stair rail, which was attached to the wall. Keeping one hand against the wall he made his way up the rail till he had cleared about a half dozen risers. Shore was right behind him. Devine slipped an infrared light from his belt and shone it on the steps below. The first three risers all had trip lasers. The rest of the staircase was clear. He made his way quietly back onto the stairs, and Shore just as silently followed. Both men looked at each other and let out relieved breaths.

They reached the first landing, made the turn, and headed up again, after checking the risers ahead of them for more traps.

When they neared the top landing, Devine put up a hand and they both halted.

Devine whispered into his mic. "At top landing. Update."

Campbell came back on. "Five men still outside the panic room door. They are crowded together in the center of the hall."

Devine passed this info along to Shore. Then he said into his mic, "Engage the diversion in five."

"Roger that," said Campbell.

Devine counted to five. When the sirens coming from outside shattered the quiet, they heard footsteps above them and the chatter of suddenly excited men.

Using this noise as cover, Devine and Shore raced up the steps in parallel, turned the corner, and pointed their weapons at the men scrambling around in front of them at the end of the hall.

"Federal agents, put down your weapons," roared Devine.

The men made the mistake of not putting down their weapons, and instead fired wildly.

Both Devine's and Shore's guns barked and their

aims were precise. The five men dropped to the floor dead or dying.

Devine called out, "Danny? Danny Glass? It's Travis Devine."

They heard a muffled voice that seemed to be coming from behind the wall.

Devine and Shore quickly searched the dead men. Shore held up a small key fob he'd found in one of their pockets.

"Try it," said Devine.

Shore hit the button and a part of the wall swung outward. Revealed in the doorway was Danny Glass.

"Betsy?" he said anxiously.

"Safe."

"Thank God. And thank you, Devine."

"You dudes save the happy talk for later, and let's get the fuck outta here," exclaimed Shore.

They piled the dead men inside the panic room and Shore pressed the button on the remote to close the door.

"That's going to be a hell of a cleanup on aisle four," noted Glass as they ran down the stairs, avoiding the ones with the laser trips by jumping over them to the landing below.

"Not our problem," said Devine.

"And what about Mercedes King? She set me up."

"Taken care of," replied Devine as they left the house.

89

MERCEDES KING PULLED THE 4-WHEELER to a stop in front of her home and leapt off. She didn't have much time to get this done. Her Porsche was destroyed, but there was still a Lexus sedan in the garage that would do for now. She had made prior arrangements, and the call she had made on the way here had initiated those arrangements. All she had to do was get to a certain place at a certain time with a certain someone named Danny Glass in tow. From there she would be in a chopper that would take them to a private airstrip, where a private jet was waiting to take them out of the country. And then all her dreams of riches would hopefully come true once she sold Glass to whichever of his enemies bid the highest amount, and who would then take over his criminal empire. She had decided to start the bidding at half a billion dollars and see where it went from there.

She unlocked the front door and called out to the men she had stationed here. They were not part of

12/24. They were loyal only to her. But when they didn't answer, she did not take that as a good sign.

King pulled out her gun and her phone. She called them. Nothing. She tried again. Same result.

She hurried up the stairs after using a phone app to turn off the trip lasers.

She reached the top landing and saw the blood on the floor and along the walls. She used her own key fob to access the panic room. When the door swung open and King saw the bodies piled inside, the woman wheeled around and ran to her bedroom. She grabbed her go-bag and flew back down the stairs.

And then her phone buzzed. It wasn't a call; it was a FaceTime.

What the hell?

She answered it and found herself looking at a woman wearing sunglasses though it was now growing dark outside.

King tried to process all of this, was unable to do so, and finally exclaimed, "Who are you? And how did you get my number?"

The woman took off the sunglasses.

"Hello, Anne," said Pru Jackson. "I didn't think I was ever going to have the chance to come back and face you, but that goes to show what one can achieve if one never gives up hope."

King's expression was one of confusion, and then that was replaced with dread.

"Pru?"

"Here in the flesh."

"I'm...I'm so glad. I was worried something had happened to you when you vanished years ago."

"Your caring about me is so very appreciated, Anne." She pointed to her neck. "No hard feelings, right? For what it's worth, I think you sound very sexy with damaged cords."

King looked upward and then back at the phone. "You've been in my house. You took something that belonged to me. Something I really needed. And I want it back. Maybe we can do a deal. It'll be lucrative, I can tell you that."

"I have never been *in* your house."

"We can still work together on this. Like old times. I really can make this worth your while."

"I'm always interested in worthwhile things."

"Great, but I don't have a lot of time to haggle. I need to get going and—"

Jackson cut in. "And just so you know, the one thing that kept me *going* all this time was the dream that one day I would be in this exact situation talking to you. And now that dream has finally come true."

"I don't know what happened to you, but I can assure you that I had nothing to do with it."

"You had everything to do with it, Anne. Everything."

"Look, I don't have time to deal with this right now. Where are you?"

"Far closer than you think. And I spent a long time with a world-class sniper, Anne. I can literally shoot the wings off a fly at five hundred meters."

King quickly moved away from a window. "Well, unless you can fire through walls, Pru, I don't think it matters, dream or no dream. So if you don't want a deal, we have nothing to discuss."

"No, we do. You see, I want you to admit that you were the one to betray me."

"I don't have time for this shit."

"It'll only take seconds."

"Fine. Yes, I fucked you over. Satisfied? You slit my throat and left me for dead. And the only thing I'm sorry about is that you're not still in that prison being tortured every minute of every day. So, why don't you go eat shit and die, okay?"

"But I wanted my shot at revenge. I've dreamed about it, actually."

"You will never get a shot at me, Pru. You're not up to it."

"You misunderstand. I already took my shot, Anne, when I was at your home the last time."

"You said you were never in my house."

"That's true. I was just on the *outside* of it."

Jackson held up a small black box with a single red button. "And just so you know, Anne, the reality is actually about to become far better than even the dream."

King's eyes widened slightly. "Oh shit." She threw down the phone and started to run.

Pru Jackson waited a second and then pressed the button on the device.

The explosive she had earlier buried right under the gas line going into the house detonated. Combined with the natural gas, the resulting blast blew all ten thousand square feet of Mercedes King's beautiful home into small pieces, and did the same to the woman right along with it.

From nearly a mile away, Jackson watched the fire and smoke rise above the tree line in the distance. She stood there for a few more seconds taking it all in, every last moment of it. She drew a deep, cleansing breath of the crisp mountain air.

Thank you, former captain Travis Devine. You are an officer and a gentleman.

She slid her glasses back on, climbed into her car, and drove slowly away.

CHAPTER

90

DEVINE KNOCKED ON THE DOOR of Lynn Martin's apartment; she was Perry Rollins's elderly neighbor. Devine had with him a man dressed in faded overalls and holding a satchel of tools.

Martin answered the door and Devine said, "Remember me?"

"No."

She was about to close the door when Devine put a hand on it.

"Hey!" she snapped.

"Streaming again?" asked Devine.

"So what if I am, asshole?"

Devine slipped a piece of paper out of his pocket. "This is a check from the federal government for five thousand dollars made out to you. Interested?"

"What's it for?" she asked suspiciously. "Tax refund?"

Devine glanced at the man next to him. "We need to check something in your wall. My friend here will do the honors and then fix everything. And you get the money."

"My wall?"

"Specifically, the spot where Perry Rollins patched it. Remember, you told me about that?" He held up the check enticingly. "Streaming or cold, hard cash?"

"Federal check?" she said.

"Yes."

"Will it bounce?" she said derisively.

"I don't think you have to worry about that."

"Right, they'll just print more money," she said in disgust.

Martin let them in and showed them the spot where Rollins had fixed her wall.

As Martin and Devine watched, he said, "I found a receipt for drywall joint compound in Rollins's wallet. Thought it was curious that a guy like that would patch your wall, or do other repairs for you. He just never struck me as the altruistic type."

Something seemed to click in Martin's head. "Wait, you think he hid something there?"

"I really hope so."

The man used his tools to cut out the section and stepped back.

Devine used a light to check the opening. Taped to one of the studs was a USB stick.

"What is that thing?" asked Martin, as Devine pulled it out.

"Something worth a lot more than five grand to a certain acquaintance of mine." He handed her the check. "Happy streaming."

After leaving Martin's building, Devine drove over to the local police precinct and met with Braddock and Walker, who had come there to meet him.

Braddock said, "Two of the men taken into custody at the place where they were holding Betsy Odom confessed to Perry Rollins's murder."

"I'm sure there will be lots of confessions coming from that group."

"Oh, and they were also the ones to bug Rollins's apartment because he had been sniffing around. That way they learned of his plan to peddle what he knew about Danny Glass. And they took him out before he could do that."

"Makes sense."

"And exactly what information was so damaging about Glass?" asked Braddock.

"I wish I knew."

Braddock nodded, but clearly didn't believe this. "Your methods are unorthodox, Devine, but you get results, I'll give you that."

"And I appreciate your following the evidence where it led you."

"As you know, along with the Bureau, we raided the

compound of the 'Termites,'" said Walker. "Nicholas Dawkins was found dead. He'd been shot."

"My money would be on Mercedes King's having done that."

"She escaped from there, not sure how," said Braddock. "But we got everybody else. And with Glass back on board, DOJ is salivating at the prosecutions that are going to be coming out of it. Lots of heads in high places are going to roll, so I heard. Guess all of them are lawyering up and hiring big-time PR firms. You know they're guilty if they do that."

Walker added, "The Kings' house blew up. Remains were found inside. Looks to be several men and at least one woman. We're waiting on positive IDs, if we can get any. You know anything about that?"

She and Braddock stared at Devine.

"House was still standing when we got Glass out of there. Probably a gas main explosion."

Braddock said his goodbyes, and Beth Walker escorted Devine out.

"Think you'll make it back here at some point?" she added hopefully.

"If I do, you'll be the first to know."

"You know what happened to Mercedes King, don't you?" she said.

He looked at her, his expression turning serious. "If

I had to speculate, I would say that a terrible wrong might have finally been set right. And justice was done. That's the business both of us are in, right? Justice?"

"Yes, it is," said a taken-aback Walker.

"Then let's just leave it at that, Beth."

CHAPTER

91

AT THE SEATTLE AIRPORT, DEVINE and Campbell met in a private, secure room with Glass, Saxby, and Betsy Odom. Nate Shore was also there, dressed in a sleek suit that rode well on his chiseled physique.

Shore had earlier informed Devine that Glass had hired him to accompany them in their new life, a move that Odom had heartily approved of.

Odom hugged Devine fiercely. "Thank you, Travis."

"I'm glad I could help," said Devine, hugging her back.

"Uncle Danny said we're going to another country for a while until things settle down. I might have to learn another language." She sounded excited by the prospect.

"Well, that sounds like quite an adventure. And life should be full of them."

"Do you think you can come and visit me?"

Devine glanced up first at Saxby, who nodded, and then Glass, who actually managed a smile and nodded as well.

"That's a deal."

"Oh, and there's this," she said, handing him a piece of paper.

On it was quite a good drawing of Devine holding hands with...Odom.

"I thought you could use it to remember me," she said.

"Thank you for this, but I will never forget you, thirteen going on forty-two Betsy Odom."

She laughed and gave him another hug.

"Hey, if you're serious about being an FBI agent when you grow up, look me up when you graduate from college. I can help."

"Deal," she said.

Devine shook hands with Shore and wished him the best.

In a low voice Shore said, "You think I'm doin' the right thing, man?"

"I think for Betsy and you, it's the *perfect* thing. And as part of the deal, Glass has had to give up all of his businesses. The assholes he employed are all gone. He still has tons of money to live on, but I think you might find him a reformed man. But anything starts looking weird, call me."

"Hold you to it, Devine."

Devine next pulled Glass aside.

"Having a kid is a big responsibility, Danny," said Devine.

The man nodded, looking a bit shell-shocked. "Running my old business was a breeze by comparison."

"Good move bringing Nate along."

"Betsy's going to have enough change as it is. I thought a familiar face would be good for her. And that's my only goal: what's good for Betsy."

"Never, ever lose sight of that," Devine said firmly.

When Glass shot him a look, Devine held out his hand for the man to shake.

Glass came away with the USB stick. He looked up in confusion at Devine.

"Doubt there's anything important on there, but I thought you could see for yourself."

Glass pocketed the stick and said in a low voice, "I know I made a big deal about you owing me for Iraq. But the fact is, I owe you more than I can ever repay. I mean that."

"You can repay me, Danny, by devoting yourself to your daughter. Help guide her to be an amazing adult that we can all be proud of."

"I promise you that I will do my best."

Devine next gave Saxby a hug. "Hope you can check in with your family soon."

"I'll see them tonight."

"Good luck, Ellen."

He and Campbell left them there and headed to their gate.

Campbell sat in a chair and opened his laptop.

"Still on the clock?" asked Devine.

Campbell looked at him incredulously. "Devine, I have *six* Danny Glass–level shitstorms I'm dealing with, every day, all day."

"But everybody needs a little downtime."

"I can do that when I'm dead. So can you."

"Well, right now, while I'm still alive, I'm going for coffee."

"Get me one. And a muffin, blueberry. And make sure you charge Uncle Sam."

Devine returned with the coffees and muffin, and set one coffee and the muffin next to Campbell, who was still working away on his laptop.

His phone buzzed, and Devine pulled it out and read the text that had just dropped.

I just wanted to say that I've had many regrets in my life but running into you was not one of them. You are a good man who has to work in a terrible slice of the world, and you do it with honor and sacrifice and principles. But you are also not above bending the rules when the cause is just, which I most admire about you. I am planning to travel, and then settle down in a little village somewhere and just do nothing. I don't know how long that will last, but I just want to see how it feels.

I hope your life is long and fulfilling, and that you accomplish all you want.

But if you ever need me, I'm just a call away, former Captain Devine.

XOXO for real this time. The Girl on the Train

Devine smiled broadly and put the phone back in his pocket.

Campbell noted this and glanced at him.

"Everything good, Devine?"

"Everything's just fine, sir."

ACKNOWLEDGMENTS

———————

To Michelle, your suggestion that we take a trip to Washington inspired a new venue for Travis Devine to work his magic.

To David Shelley, a hearty welcome, and here's to many years of continued success.

To Ben Sevier, Kirsiah Depp, Jonathan Valuckas, Matthew Ballast, Beth de Guzman, Ana Maria Allessi, Rena Kornbluh, Karen Kosztolnyik, Albert Tang, Andy Dodds, Joseph Benincase, Alexis Gilbert, Andrew Duncan, Alana Spendley, Tiffany Porcelli, Lauren Sum, Bob Castillo, Rebecca Holland, Mark Steven Long, Marie Mundaca, Nita Basu, Lauren Monaco, Chrissy Heleine, Melanie Freedman, Elizabeth Blue Guess, Rachel Hairston, Tishana Knight, Jennifer Kosek, Derek Meehan, Donna Nopper, Rob

Philpott, Barbara Slavin, Rich Tullis, Mary Urban, Avi Molder, Fantasia Brown, Julie Hernandez, Laura Shepherd, Dominic Stones, Leah Collins Lipsett, Jeff Shay, Carla Stockalper, Ky'ron Fitzgerald, and everyone at Grand Central Publishing. Thank you all for the hard work and dedication.

To Aaron and Arleen Priest, Lucy Childs, Lisa Erbach Vance, Frances Jalet-Miller, Kristen Pini, and Natalie Rosselli. The thrill of working with you all never goes away.

To Mitch Hoffman, for always telling me what I *need* to hear.

To Joanna Prior, Lucy Hale, Francesca Pathak, Stuart Dwyer, Leanne Williams, Raphaella Demetris, Sara Lloyd, Claire Evans, Jamie Forrest, Laura Sherlock, Jonathan Atkins, Christine Jones, Andy Joannou, Charlotte Williams, Rebecca Kellaway, Charlotte Cross, Lucy Grainger, Holly Martin, Becky Lloyd, and Neil Lang at Pan Macmillan, for continuing to excel at every level.

To Praveen Naidoo and the wonderful team at Pan Macmillan in Australia. Can't wait to see you all in person.

To Caspian Dennis and Sandy Violette, whom I adore.

To the charity auction winners, Betsy Odom (Amelia Island Book Festival) and Nate Shore (Share Our

Strength/No Kid Hungry), I hope I did you proud. And to the friends and families of the late Korey Rose (Camp Korey) and the late Stephen Braddock (Amelia Island Book Festival), I hope you enjoyed the characters based on your loved ones.

And to Kristen White and Michelle Butler, who do everything to perfection, day in and day out.

ABOUT THE AUTHOR

DAVID BALDACCI is a global #1 bestselling author, and one of the world's favorite storytellers. His books are published in over 45 languages and in more than 80 countries, with 150 million copies sold worldwide. His works have been adapted for both feature film and television. David Baldacci is also the cofounder, along with his wife, of the Wish You Well Foundation, a nonprofit organization dedicated to supporting literacy efforts across America. Still a resident of his native Virginia, he invites you to visit him at DavidBaldacci.com and his foundation at WishYouWellFoundation.org.